1636

THE DEVIL'S
OPERA

1636
THE DEVIL'S
OPERA

ERIC FLINT
DAVID CARRICO

1636: The Devil's Opera

Copyright © 2013 by Eric Flint & David Carrico

A Baen Books Original

Baen Publishing Enterprises
P.O. Box 1403
Riverdale, NY 10471
www.baen.com

ISBN: 978-1-4516-3928-5

Cover art by Tom Kidd
Maps by Gorg Huff

First printing, October 2013

Distributed by Simon & Schuster
1230 Avenue of the Americas
New York, NY 10020

Library of Congress Cataloging-in-Publication Data

Flint, Eric.
    1636 : the devil's opera / Eric Flint, David Carrico.
        pages cm. — (The ring of fire series)
    ISBN 978-1-4516-3928-5 (hardback)
1. Thirty Years' War, 1618–1648—Fiction. 2. Revolutions—Fiction. 3. Americans—Europe—Fiction. 4. Time travel—Fiction. 5. Europe—History—17th century—Fiction. 6. West Virginia—Fiction. I. Carrico, David. II. Title. III. Title: Sixteen, thirty-six. IV. Title: Sixteen hundred, thirty-six. V. Title: Devil's opera.
    PS3556.L548A61866 2013
    813'.54—dc23

                                                    2013023217

10 9 8 7 6 5 4 3 2 1

Pages by Joy Freeman (www.pagesbyjoy.com)
Printed in the United States of America

To the memory of
Karen Bergstralh
and John Zeek

Contents

United States of Europe

N

Pomerania

Poland

Luebeck

Mecklenburg

Hamburg

Brandenburg

Saxony

Brunswick

Magdeburg

Netherlands

Westphalia

Dresden

Essen

Hesse-Kassel

★

Bohemia

Prague

Province of the Main

State of Thuringia-Franconia

Frankfurt

Nuremberg

Oberpfalz (Upper Palatinate)

Upper Rhine

Bavaria

Augsburg

Munich

Austria

Swabia*

Ulm

Strassburg

Swiss Confederation

*Swabia is still under direct imperial administation and not yet a self-governing province as of March 1635

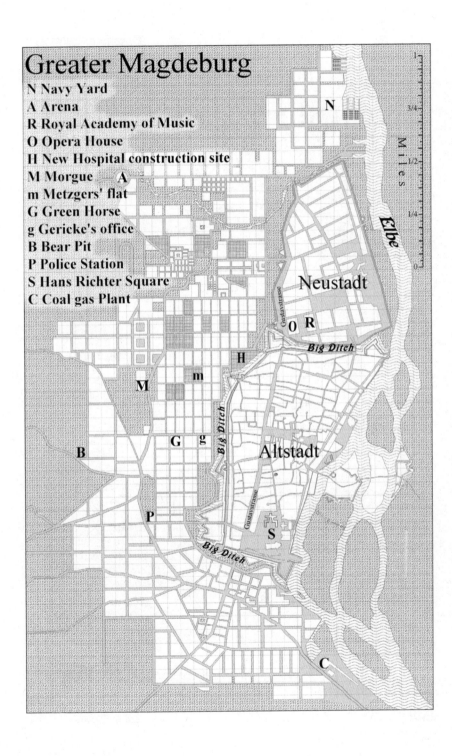

Greater Magdeburg

N Navy Yard
A Arena
R Royal Academy of Music
O Opera House
H New Hospital construction site
M Morgue
m Metzgers' flat
G Green Horse
g Gericke's office
B Bear Pit
P Police Station
S Hans Richter Square
C Coal gas Plant

N

Miles

3/4

1/2

1/4

0

Elbe

Neustadt

O R

Big Ditch

H

Big Ditch

Altstadt

M

m

G g

B

P

S

Big Ditch

C

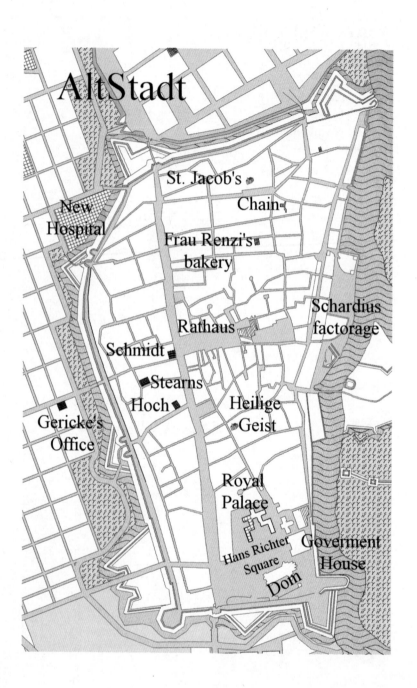

AltStadt

St. Jacob's

Chain

New
Hospital

Frau Renzi's
bakery

Schardius
factorage

Rathaus

Schmidt

Stearns

Hoch

Heilige
Geist

Gericke's
Office

Royal
Palace

Hans Richter
Square

Goverment
House

Dom

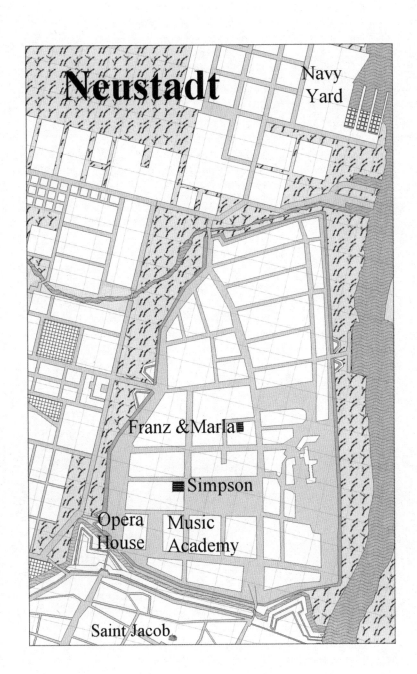

Part One

December 1635

Music directly imitates the passions or states of the soul...
when one listens to music that imitates a certain passion,
he becomes imbued with the same passion...
—Aristotle

Chapter 1

Simon came out to the river at least once a week, usually in the predawn light, and walked the bank of the Elbe looking for anything he might scavenge and use or sell. Today the sun was just barely visible over the eastern bank of the river, and the dawn light had not yet dropped down to the shadowed eddy under the willow tree. There was something large floating in the water.

He stared down at the floating corpse. It wasn't the first one he'd ever seen in his young life. It wasn't even the first one he'd seen in the river. But it was the first one he'd seen that he might be able to get something from, if he could only get to it. He edged down to where the water lapped on the bank where he stood, and for a moment crouched as if he was going to reach out and draw the body ashore. That moment passed, though, for as the light brightened he saw that there was no way he could reach the corpse without wading out into the water, which he was loath to do since he couldn't swim.

The boy glanced around. There were no stout sticks nearby, so he had nothing at hand that he could maybe use to draw the body closer. He frowned. There might not be much in the man's pockets, but anything would be more than he had.

His head jerked up at the sound of other voices coming nearer. No help for it now. He'd have to hope the men coming this way would give him something.

"Hey! This way. There's a deader in the water by the tree."

A moment later two of the local fisherman came bustling up. "Och, so there is," the older of the two said. "Third one this year. Well, in you go, Fritz."

"Me?" the younger man replied. "Make him do it." He pointed at Simon, then ducked as the older man made to cuff his ear.

"And a right fool I'd be to send a lad with only one working arm out into even still water."

The young man whined, "Why is it always me that has to go in the water after the deaders?"

"For I am your father, and I say so," the older man replied. "Now get in there afore I knock you in."

The younger man muttered, but he kicked off his shoes and stepped into the water, hissing as the chill moved up his legs. The boy shivered in sympathy as he watched, glad it wasn't him getting wet in the winter breeze. Three strides had the corpse within reach, and Fritz drew it to the bank by one arm.

"Fresh one, this," the older man grunted as he rifled the dead man's pockets with practiced hands. "Ah, here's something." He lifted up something and showed his son. "One of them new clasp knives like Old Barnabas bought." The boy watched with envy as the blade was folded out and then back again. It disappeared into the older man's coat. "Help me turn him over, Fritz."

They flipped the corpse onto its back. The dawn light fell on the face of the corpse, and men and boy stepped back at the sight of the bruises and cuts. "*Scheisse,*" the old fisherman said. "This one's no drowning." He shook himself and returned to rifling the clothing, feeling for pockets. "No money, not even a Halle pfennig. His coat's worn worse than yours. His shoes... aye, they might do. Off with them now, and run them to your ma and tell her to set them near the fire to dry."

Simon almost laughed to see the younger man struggling with the corpse to get the shoes off. "Ach, you worthless toad," the older man shoved the young one out of the way and had the shoes off in a moment. "Now get with you, and I'd best not beat you back to the boat."

He turned back to the boy. "Now, you, lad." He looked at him with narrowed eyes. "Seen you about before, I have. Simon, isn't it? Go find a watchman, one of these newfangled *Polizei*, and tell him that Johann the fisher has found a deader in the river. Say nothing to him about the knife and shoes, and tonight there will be a bowl of fish soup for you, and maybe a bit of bread to go with it. Fair enough?"

Simon didn't think it was fair, but he gave a nod anyway, knowing that it was the best he would get. The older man returned the nod, and Simon turned to scramble back up the bank to find a city watchman.

Chapter 2

Otto Gericke looked out the small diamond-shaped panes in his office window at the sprawl of the exurb of Magdeburg, what some had taken to calling Greater Magdeburg. When Gustavus Adolphus had chosen Magdeburg to become the capital of his new continental realm, what had been a city of perhaps half a square mile within its fortified walls had quickly mushroomed into a metropolis that, if it wasn't in the same league as Paris or London as far as size, bid fair to grow into that league in the not-too-distant-future. And as the up-timers put it, it was Otto's baby...or his headache, depending on which up-timer you talked to. He was mayor of Greater Magdeburg, appointed so by Gustavus Adolphus, who had then scurried off to war without giving him much more instruction than "Clean up this mess, and build me a capital to be proud of." Certainly there was no provision for a city council for Greater Magdeburg to share the work, or for an election of a replacement. Which meant that everything of any consequence, and most items of little consequence, ended up on Otto's desk. He had started mentally labeling days as "baby" or "headache," and when he had shared that thought with up-timers like Jere Haygood, all they had done was laugh.

Looking at his clock, Otto decided that he'd best get back to work. He had just settled back into his chair when the door to his office opened and an elderly man was ushered in by his secretary.

"Thank you, Albrecht," Otto said. "See to it that we are not disturbed, if you would." The secretary nodded and closed the door as he stepped out.

Otto stepped around his desk and embraced the man in turn. "Jacob, it is good to see you." He smiled. "Even if you did catch me somewhat *deshabille*." He indicated his jacket on the coat tree and his rolled-up shirt sleeves.

Jacob Lentke, a family friend of both Otto's late father and his late father-in-law, stumped over to a chair obviously prepared for him, sat down and lifted his foot onto the waiting stool. He leaned back with a sigh, holding his cane with loose fingers.

"I see the gout still troubles you," Otto commented as he walked to a sideboard and busied himself with a wine decanter. "Have you not read what the Grantville doctors are saying about gout?"

"I have, and what is worse, my wife has. And I am, with reluctance, willing to moderate my eating, but I will not give up my daily regimen of wine. After all, it was Saint Paul who said, 'Take a little wine for thy stomach's sake,' and who am I to disregard the instruction of an apostle and saint?"

Otto returned to offer a glass of wine to the older man. "With all due respect, Jacob, I somehow doubt that the good saint had in mind the quantities of wine that you drink."

Lentke chuckled, then took a sip of the wine. His eyebrows climbed his forehead, and he looked at the glass with respect. "Where did you get Hungarian wine around here?"

The destruction of the war so far had caused devastation in much of the farmlands of the central Germanies. The wineries in particular had been hit hard. Not much had been produced for several years, and the quality of what had been bottled was noticeably lacking.

"Wallenstein, actually," Otto responded, settling into his chair behind the desk. He grinned at the frown that crossed Lentke's face. "He felt he owed Michael Stearns somewhat, so as a favor he shipped a small portion of the Bohemian royal wine cellars to Michael. Rebecca Abrabanel was kind enough to provide a small share of that to me. A small share of a small portion, to be sure, but I understand that the Bohemian wine cellars were, umm, significant, so there were more than a few bottles." He chuckled as he swirled the wine in his own glass.

"Indeed," Lentke said, lifting his glass again. "Small recompense for the damage Wallenstein's dog Pappenheim did to Magdeburg, but I suppose we should be thankful for small blessings, no matter the source."

Otto thought that was a remarkably temperate statement from one who had been in Magdeburg before the sack and resulting destruction done by Pappenheim's troops several years before when he served under Tilly. Most survivors' comments concerning the erstwhile Austrian army field commander began with the scatological and descended quickly to the infernal and blasphemous. The fact that Pappenheim was now firmly ensconced in Wallenstein's court, and Wallenstein was now at least nominally allied with the USE and Gustavus Adolphus, had little effect on the depth of rancor that the survivors of the sack of Magdeburg had for him.

"Enough of unpleasant topics," Lentke declared. "Why did you ask to meet with me, Otto?"

"Jacob, you are still a member of the *Schöffenstuhl*, correct?"

Gericke was referring to the senior jurisprudence body for the *Magdeburger Recht* association, the group of cities in central Europe which had been granted laws and rights by their sovereigns that were drawn from the laws and charter of Magdeburg itself. It had been located in Magdeburg, and until the sack had functioned as what the Grantvillers would have called an appellate court for cases that their own courts could not address or whose decisions needed ratification.

"Yah, you know that I am, but that means nothing now, Otto." Lentke shook his head. "All of our files, all of our books, all of our documents were destroyed in the sack, except for a handful that I managed to snatch up in the face of the flames. Centuries of work, centuries of civilization, centuries of wisdom, now nothing but ash at Pappenheim's hand." From his expression, he would convert the soldier to a like condition if it were in his power. His mouth worked as if he desired to spit, but he refrained.

"But you and some of your fellow jurists still live." Otto leaned forward, his expression very intense. "Your names still carry weight. People still respect your wisdom, especially people in this part of the USE. Maybe not so much over in the west or by the Rhineland, but definitely in Saxony, Brandenburg, Thuringia-Franconia, and even into Bohemia, Poland, and the Ukraine."

"And if that is so?" Lentke shook his head again. "It is a dying reputation, Otto. What use is it to talk of it?"

"Ah, Jacob. Perhaps the wine has affected more than your foot,"

Otto said with a small smile. "Your position and authority as jurists has never been recalled or revoked. And Magdeburg the city needs you. I need you."

"Say on," Lentke replied.

"You want work to do. I can give you that work."

Otto watched Lentke rock back in his chair with a bit of a stunned look. He rallied quickly, however. "Oh, come now, Otto. We are in no position of authority."

"You may not now be, perhaps," Otto conceded, "but you do occupy a position of undoubted moral authority. And I can give you proper legal standing."

"How will you accomplish that?" Lentke looked at Otto in some surprise.

"Magdeburg is an imperial city in the USE, you know that. We are independent of the province of Magdeburg, yes?" Otto spoke incisively. "That means we should have an independent magistracy and judiciary as well. I've been making do, but we need the *Schöffenstuhl* to resume, to serve as the senior judiciary for the city, including as what the up-timers call an appellate court. Some of the matters that are coming before me and the other magistrates," he shook his own head, "should be coming to you. So take on this work as the reconvened *Schöffenstuhl*, and I will then empanel you as part of the city governance. You will have good work to do, and it will take a fair amount of work off my shoulders."

"And paper out of your office, no doubt," Lentke retorted, looking at the files stacked on various tables and cabinets.

"A side benefit." Otto waved a hand airily.

"And you have this authority?"

Lentke was sounding interested, Otto thought to himself. That was a good sign. He chuckled, then held up a hand as Jacob frowned at him.

"I think you will find, Jacob, that within the boundaries of Magdeburg, Imperial Province and Free City of the United States of Europe, my authority is limited only by the will of the emperor himself. He never got around to giving the new city a charter or giving me much of a job description before his injury, and until he or his heir or Parliament does..." Otto shrugged.

Before Lentke could respond to that thought, there came an interruption. Albrecht opened the door from the outer office and stuck his head in.

"Excuse me, Herr Gericke, but your stepfather is here and wishes to see you."

"By all means, let him in, Albrecht." Otto stood hurriedly and moved out from behind his desk just in time to embrace the man who almost charged past the secretary. "Papa Christoff, it is good to see you!"

"And you as well, son."

Christoff Schultze was a lean man who was active beyond his years, as the thump he gave to Otto's shoulder bore witness. He had married Otto's mother after the death of her second husband, and had never treated Otto with anything other than care and consideration. Love may not have come into play between them, but certainly affection had, and it showed in their greetings.

"Please, be seated."

Otto gestured to the other chair in front of his desk, and returned to the sideboard to quickly pour another glass of wine for his stepfather.

"Aah," Schultze sighed after taking his first sip. "I do like a glass of good wine. I only wish I had time to properly savor this one."

"Then I take it you are here on some official matter?" Otto asked.

"Indeed," Schultze replied. "Ludwig sent me."

That would be *Fürst* Ludwig von Anhalt-Cöthen, Otto thought to himself, Gustav Adolf's appointed administrator for the archbishopric's properties, owned by the *Erzstift* of Magdeburg, which in turn was now owned by Gustavus Adolphus.

"And how is *Fürst* Ludwig these days?" Otto asked, wondering just what errand could have forced the good *Fürst* to send his chief lieutenant.

Schultze's response was very sober. "Concerned. Very concerned."

"And who isn't?" Lentke responded dryly. "The news from Berlin is not good, and Chancellor Oxenstierna's actions do little to inspire one to confidence." Otto nodded in agreement.

A darker tone entered Schultze's voice. "Indeed. You know of Gustav Adolf's condition." Schultze was not asking a question—it was well known that the emperor's head injury received in battle with the Poles and the resulting wandering wits that Dr. Nichols called "aphasia" had for all intents and purposes rendered him *non compos mentis*. "I assume you also know of what Oxenstierna is attempting."

Both Otto and Lentke started to reply. Otto waved his hand at Lentke, who nodded and said, "Every child above the age of three in Magdeburg understands what the Swedish chancellor is attempting. He desires to roll back, make null, the many changes that Gustavus has made in the governance of the USE, or at least the ones that changed the social order and the religious tolerance—or should I say, lack of tolerance?"

The older man looked over to Otto, who picked up the thread. "He and his allies have some kind of hold on Prime Minister Wettin, and between that and Oxenstierna's position as chancellor of Sweden, they look to control the government of the USE. I believe they have misread the tenor of the times, but I am deathly afraid that we will all pay for their mistakes before they go down."

Schultze nodded. "Your judgment, Otto, is much the same as *Fürst* Ludwig's. And his situation as administrator of the property formerly owned by the Archbishopric of Magdeburg is a bit complicated. On the one hand," Schultze held out his left hand, "his authority comes from Gustav Adolf; he gave an oath to the king of Sweden before he became emperor, and therefore he might be considered to be under the chancellor's authority as he acts as regent for Princess Kristina during her father's incapacitation. On the other hand," he held out his right hand, "he detests Oxenstierna, so he would dearly love to tell him to, ah, 'take a flying leap,' as one of the Grantvillers described it. Even for a Swede, the chancellor is overbearingly arrogant. On yet another hand..." Otto smiled as he saw his stepfather struggle for a moment over which hand to hold up again, only to drop them both back into his lap, "Wilhelm Wettin, the prime minister, is his nephew. And although he loves his nephew and would ordinarily support him just on that cause, he is very much concerned that Wettin has made some ill-advised decisions in recent months. So he has a great desire to be very cautious as to what he does."

"I can see that," murmured Otto, who nonetheless wished that the *Fürst* would be more direct. And his earlier feeling was proven correct—this was going to be a headache day. He propped his head on his hands, massaging his temples.

"So, he is delaying responding to demands from the chancellor and his nephew, while he sent me hurrying from Halle to meet with you here. I had planned to ask Otto to bring you here,

Jacob," Schultze focused his gaze on Lentke, "so the coincidence of finding you here at the moment simply speeds my errand. Jacob, I need you to reconvene the *Schöffenstuhl*."

Otto burst out laughing as Lentke's jaw dropped. A moment later Lentke pointed a long finger in Otto's direction.

"You put him up to this, didn't you? Confess it!"

Still laughing, Otto raised both hands to the level of his shoulders. He finally choked back the hilarity enough to speak.

"Before the throne of heaven and all its angels, Jacob, I did no such thing. I had no idea that Papa Christoff would even be here today."

He turned to his confused stepfather.

"You see, I just told Jacob I need him to bring the *Schöffen-stuhl* back into being in the service of the city of Magdeburg."

Both of them started chuckling as Lentke directed a dark look first at one of them, then the other.

"Oh, leave off, Jacob," Schultze finally said, waving his empty hand in the air. "There is no collusion here."

"Well enough," Lentke said, shifting his foot on its stool. "And if that be so, then what brings you here seeking the *Schöffenstuhl*?"

"What the *Fürst* would ask of the *Schöffenstuhl* is an opinion, a judgment, as to whether under USE law, custom, and practice, the chancellor of Sweden can serve as regent for Gustav's heir for the USE in the absence of a specific appointment by Gustav."

For the second time in less than an hour, Otto saw Lentke taken aback. He could see the objection in Lentke's eyes, and spoke up before the older man could.

"Authority," Otto said. The eyes of both the other men shifted to him. "As we discussed, Jacob; you already possess the moral authority, and I will give you the legal standing and authority."

He could see the words really sink in this time. Lentke responded with a slow nod.

"Such a judgment could have great effect, you know," Schultze observed in a quiet tone.

"And what if we were to rule in favor of the chancellor?" Lentke demanded.

Schultze shrugged. "Ludwig is willing to take that chance. And in truth, if you ruled that way, it would allow him to support family, which for a man of his lineage is always an important consideration." He paused for a moment. "But I do not think that is the ruling he truly wants. As much as he finds many of the recent changes distasteful, Ludwig is fearful of what will result from Oxenstierna's machinations."

"And why do you not send this request to the *Reichskammerg-ericht*, or rather, the USE Supreme Court, as it is called now?"

"Time, Jacob," Schultze responded. "We need an opinion soon, and if we send our request to Wetzlar, who knows how long it will take those 'learned men' to respond?" It was evident from the sarcasm in his voice that he did not have a high opinion of the Supreme Court.

Otto thought about the matter for a moment, then looked to Lentke. "Jacob, do it. You know you want to."

Lentke snorted, then turned to Schultze. "Have it your way, Christoff. Let *Fürst* Ludwig have the petition and brief drawn up and sent to us. I will convene my fellows, and we will deliberate; perhaps even consult with someone like Master Thomas Price Riddle from Grantville, or Doctor Grotius at Jena. I will even endeavor to conduct the deliberations at a pace somewhat faster than deliberate." He smiled at his little joke.

"And you, Otto," Lentke looked back to Gericke, "if you would have us do this, then find us space. The rebuilt *Rathaus* in Old Magdeburg will not contain us. And it is most likely that those members serving on this year's council will not allow us to use it anyway, once they hear of what we are doing, Brandenburg sympathizers that they mostly are."

There was a tinge of distaste in the way he said "Old Magdeburg." The term was commonly used to refer to the half-a-square-mile within the fortifications that was the original city. Despite its near-total destruction in the course of the sack of Magdeburg by Tilly's army, the still-official status of Old Magdeburg enabled its authorities to maintain a legal façade for their behavior. Obstreperous behavior, so far as both Lentke and Otto were concerned.

Schultze pulled a folded document from an inside pocket of his coat. Otto began chuckling as the document was unfolded and seals dangled from the bottom of it. "Here," Schultze said, "one petition and attached brief, duly executed and sealed by the petitioner."

"The *Fürst* anticipated me, I see," Lentke said with a wry grin.

All three men sobered quickly. "Yes, he did," Schultze replied.

"And his last words to me were 'Tell them to hurry. The time when I will need this is fast approaching.' Ludwig is not one to jump at shadows, you know. If he feels fear, then should we all."

With that thought Otto had to agree.

Chapter 3

Gotthilf Hoch, detective sergeant in the Magdeburg *Polizei*, walked out the front door of his family's home in the *Altstadt*, the oldest part of Magdeburg. The early morning air was cold, even for December. He remembered hearing that the up-timers from Grantville sometimes said this was the "Little Ice Age." On days like today, when his breath fogged in front of him and the hairs in his nose tingled when he breathed in, he could believe it. The old pagan stories about Fimbulwinter were easy to accept right now.

He pulled his hat down over his ears and pushed his gloved hands into his coat pockets, then started off down the street. Just his luck, when he wanted a cab, there wasn't one to be seen.

When he reached the Gustavstrasse, he turned right and headed for Hans Richter Square, where he turned right again and headed for the nearest bridge across *Der Grosse Graben*, the moat that encircled the *Altstadt*, which was usually called the Big Ditch. He passed through the gate in the rebuilt city wall, which triggered his usual musing about the fact that the walls had been rebuilt. He'd never seen much sense in all that time and effort being spent on that task, but the city council of Old Magdeburg had insisted on it, saying that the contracts they had signed years ago to allow people to seek protection in times of war and siege required it. From what Gotthilf could see, all it did was emphasize a boundary between the old city and the new. Which, come to think of it, may have been what the city council was intending all along.

Gotthilf looked over the railing of the bridge at the water moving sluggishly through the moat. Dark water; it looked very cold. He shivered and moved on, feet crunching in the gravel after he stepped off the bridge.

Only the busiest streets in the exurb of Greater Magdeburg were graveled. Most of them were bare dirt. One thing that Gotthilf did appreciate from the cold was that the ground was frozen most of the time, reducing mud to solid. He still had to watch his step, because an ankle turned in a frozen rut could hurt like crazy, but at least he didn't have to scrape the muck and mire off his boots like he did in the spring and fall.

There were more people on the streets now, as the sun rose higher in the eastern sky behind him. The bakers had been up for hours, of course, and he swung by one to grab a fresh roll for breakfast, since he hadn't felt up to facing his mother across a table that morning. He munched on that as he walked, watching everyone walking by.

Construction workers of every stripe were moving briskly about; carpenters, masons, and general laborers were in demand for the new hospital expansion, as well as several other projects in the city, not to mention the navy yard. Several women were out selling broadsheets and newspapers, including the shrill-voiced, hawk-faced young woman who handed out Committee of Correspondence broadsheets in that part of town.

But still no cabs. He shook his head. Never a cab when you wanted one.

A hand landed on Gotthilf's shoulder, startling him. He looked up to see his partner, Byron Chieske, settling into place alongside him.

Gotthilf had to look up at Byron. In truth, he had to look up at most adults. He wasn't very tall; not that he was a dwarf, or anything like that. Nor was he thin or spindly. He was a solid chunk of young man; he just wasn't very tall.

Byron, on the other hand, was tall, even for an up-timer. He stood a bit over six feet, was well-muscled, and had large square hands. His clean-shaven face was a bit craggy in feature, but not of a nature that would be called ugly.

"Yo, Gotthilf," Byron said. "Ready for the meeting with the

captain this morning?" The captain would be Bill Reilly, another up-timer. Byron was a lieutenant. The two of them had been seconded in early 1635 to the Magdeburg city watch to lead in transforming that organization from what amounted to a group of gossips, busybodies, and bullies to an actual police force on the model of an up-time city police group. They had both been involved in police and security work up-time; they both had at least some education and training in the work; and they had both been in an MP detachment from the State of Thuringia-Franconia army that was stationed in Magdeburg at the time, so they had been available.

"As ready as I'm going to be," Gotthilf muttered, "considering we have nothing of worth to report."

"Yeah, Bill may chew on us a bit," Byron conceded as they walked down the street toward the station building. "But he knows we can't make bricks without straw. No information, no leads, no results."

Gotthilf snorted. Byron looked at him with his trademark raised eyebrow, and the down-timer snorted again, before saying, "You know, for someone who professes to not darken the door of a church, you certainly know your way around Biblical allusions."

Byron chuckled. "Oh, I spent a lot of my childhood in Sunday school, Gotthilf. I may have drifted away from it some as an adult, but a lot of it stuck." He shoved his hands in his coat pockets, and grinned down at his partner.

Gotthilf grinned back at Byron, who seemed to be in a garrulous mood this morning—by the up-timer's standards, anyway. Byron was ordinarily one who wouldn't say two words where one would do, and wouldn't say one where a gesture or facial expression would serve instead. So to get five sentences out of him in as many minutes bordered on being voluble.

As they stepped on down the street, Gotthilf's mind recalled their first meeting, ten months ago. He had trouble now even remembering why he had joined the watch; something to do with wanting to do something to prove to his father he was more than just a routine clerk, if he recalled rightly. He had been smarting from another comparison to his brother Nikolaus, studying law at Jena. Not that his father was impressed with the city watch, either, as it turned out.

On the day that he met Byron, Gotthilf was the youngest

member of the city watch, the newest, and possibly the angriest. He hadn't really wanted to be paired with the lieutenant, and he wasn't of a mind that the over-tall up-timer had anything to teach him or anything to bring to the city watch. But their first case—one involving the murder of a young girl and a young blind lad involved in petty thievery—had opened his eyes to what the *Polizei* could do.

So now, even at his young age of twenty-three, Gotthilf was an ardent supporter of the captain and the lieutenant, having quit his clerking position and thrown himself into the job. He was now one of three detective sergeants on the force, partnered with Byron, and still one of the youngest men in the *Polizei*.

And that and a pfennig will get me a cup of coffee at Walcha's Coffee House, he gibed at himself.

The two men walked into the station house, hung their coats on pegs in the hallway, and headed for their desks. They flipped through the papers and folders lying there, then looked at each other.

"See the captain?" Gotthilf asked.

"Yep," Byron responded.

They headed for Reilly's office on the second floor. Byron took the lead.

"Chieske, Hoch." The captain set down his pencil, folded his hands on top of the document he was reading, and nodded toward a couple of chairs a bit to the side of his desk. "Have a seat. Any progress on that floater case?"

"The one the riverfront watch pulled out of the water a few days ago who looked like he'd been run through a meat tenderizer before he got dumped in the river?"

"That's the one. The floating corpse who was identified as..." Reilly picked up a different document from his desk. "...one Joseph Delt, common laborer." His eyebrows arched.

"Officially, nothing to say," Gotthilf began.

Reilly nodded. "And unofficially?"

"Nothing," Byron responded with a shrug before Gotthilf could speak.

The captain steepled his hands in front of his face. "Why? Or why not?"

"No leads, Captain," Chieske responded.

"Make some. Start flipping over rocks and talking to bugs and snakes if you have to, but get me some results, and soon. You know as well as I do what's going on here, Byron. It's not as if American history wasn't full of it."

Seeing Sergeant Hoch's quizzical expression, the police chief elaborated. "Magdeburg's a boom town full of immigrants, with more coming in every day. We had a lot of cities like that in America back up-time. It went on for centuries. Certain things always came with the phenomenon, and one of them was the rise of criminal gangs. I'll bet you any sum you want—don't take me up on it, I'll clean you out—that what we're seeing here is one or more crime bosses trying to establish themselves in the city. These men being killed are the ones who were too stubborn, too stupid—or just couldn't learn—to keep their mouths shut."

He leaned back in his seat. "There's no way to completely stop it from happening, but we need to at least keep it under control. Because if we don't and it gets out of hand, sooner or later the city's Committee of Correspondence will decide it has to crack down on the criminals. I don't want that, Mayor Gericke doesn't want that, you don't want that—hell, the Fourth of July Party and even the CoC itself doesn't want it. But it'll happen, sure as hell."

Gotthilf made a face. The leader of Magdeburg's Committee of Correspondence was a man named Gunther Achterhof. Like most people in today's Magdeburg, he was an immigrant. He'd arrived from Brandenburg with his younger sister, the two of them being the only survivors of a family ravaged by the mercenary armies that had passed through the region.

Gunther had also arrived with a sack full of the ears and noses of stray mercenary soldiers he'd killed along the way. He was an honest man, but one whose concept of justice was as razor sharp as the knife he'd used to kill and mutilate those soldiers. If he unleashed the CoC's armed squads on the city's criminal element, they'd certainly bring order to the streets—but they'd also shred any semblance of due process and reasonable legality in the doing.

As it stood, there was already a fair amount of tension between the CoC and the city's fledgling police force. If these kinds of killings continued with no one apprehended, the CoC's existing skepticism concerning the value of a duly appointed police force would just be confirmed.

"You got it, Captain," Byron said.

"Go on," Reilly waved a hand. "Go encourage the good citizens of Magdeburg to be good citizens."

Gotthilf followed Byron up the hall, down the stairs, and out the main entrance of the building, grabbing their coats on the way. He caught up with his partner outside, waving for their driver to bring up the light horse-drawn cart they used for transportation.

"So what are we going to do?" Gotthilf asked as the cart pulled up.

"Dig some more," Byron replied tersely. Gotthilf followed his partner onto the cart, and they left to begin digging.

The city of Magdeburg in the year 1635 was unique throughout Europe—throughout the world, actually. There was no place like it.

On the one hand, it was old. The city name originally meant "Mighty Fortress," and historical records indicated that it was founded in the year 805 by none other than the Emperor Charlemagne. Histories of the Germanies, whether contemporary or from the up-time library in Grantville, mentioned the city often. It had many connections with Holy Roman Emperors over the years. It became the See of the Archbishop of Magdeburg in 968, and its first patent and charter was given in 1035. It was even one of the easternmost members of the Hanseatic League. And Martin Luther had spent time there, beginning in 1524, which perhaps explained the subsequent dogged Protestantism of the city.

On the other hand, Magdeburg was new. The city had been besieged by the army of the Holy Roman Empire from November 1630 until May 20, 1631. The siege culminated in the Sack of Magdeburg, in which over 20,000 residents were massacred. Over ninety percent of the city was destroyed by fire, and what little wasn't burned was ransacked, looted, plundered, and pillaged. Magdeburg was devastated; prostrate.

Then came the Ring of Fire, with the arrival of Grantville, West Virginia, from the future. And everything changed.

Gustavus Adolphus, king of Sweden and champion of the Protestant cause, connected with the up-timers from Grantville, and set in motion a train of events that gave birth—or rebirth, if you prefer—to the modern Magdeburg of 1635.

Pre-Ring of Fire Magdeburg was small, by up-timer standards. The area within the city walls was about half a square mile. It was shaped something like a right triangle, with the long side of the triangle running parallel to the river Elbe, and the hypotenuse side running from northeast to southwest. The normal population of the city had been about 25,000 people. That boosted to nearly 35,000 during the siege, as everyone from the surrounding regions who had a contracted right for shelter and sanctuary moved into the city when the HRE army approached.

Magdeburg in 1635 was a very different creature. Instigated by the up-timers, north of the city were the naval yards, where the ironclad and timberclad ships of the USE Navy had been constructed. There wouldn't be any more ironclads in the foreseeable future, and the timberclad construction had slowed down considerably. But the yard was still working and its work force was still fully employed. The navy yard's machine tools and facilities were being turned into the USE's major weapons manufacturing center and were now working around the clock. In theory, that was to provide the army fighting the Poles with the weapons they needed. But nobody was oblivious to the fact that those same weapons could easily be used to defend Magdeburg itself, in the event the current crisis turned into an all-out civil war.

South of the city was the coal gas plant, surrounded by a constellation of factories that were powered by the plant's output. All of these operations drew hungry unemployed and underemployed men from all over the Germanies. So, since early 1634, the city had become home to a horde of navy men, factory workers, and skilled craftsmen. Inevitably, construction workers had followed to provide homes for the work force and facilities for the employers. All this gave Magdeburg a certain flavor, a "blue-collar" spirit, as some of the Grantvillers called it, which was certainly fostered by the Committees of Correspondence. It also made for interesting times.

But workers, and their families, need places to sleep, and food to eat, so rooming houses and bakeries and such began to grow up to the west of the old city. And it turned out that the big businesses along the river side needed smaller businesses to make things for them, so various workshops began to appear in the western districts.

By late 1635, Greater Magdeburg occupied several square miles along the riverside and to the west. No one had a good estimate as to how many people lived in the new city because of the constant influx of new residents, but the Committees of Correspondence had recently told the mayor that they thought it was approaching one hundred thousand. Germans, Swedes, Dutch,

Poles, Hungarians, Bohemians, even the odd Austrian, Bavarian, or Romanian could be found in the city streets or swinging a hammer at the Navy yard.

A population of that size would naturally have a leavening of rough-edged men. Hard men, one might call them, who would be more inclined to follow the ways of Cain than of Abel. Mayor Gericke realized in late 1634 that the city watch of the old city was not able to deal with the influx of these men, so in early 1635 he requisitioned a couple of Grantvillers with police experience from the up-timer units contributed to the USE army to try to mold the city watch into something that could provide up-time style civic protection and police services to the whole city.

The city watch had never been held in high esteem, so there was a certain reservation on the part of many of the citizens and residents to take issues to them. The well-to-do patricians and burghers of Old Magdeburg could afford to utilize the courts. The workers of Greater Magdeburg couldn't afford a lawyer, most times, so their recourses were three: take it to the Committees of Correspondence, if the matter was one that the CoC was interested in; handle it themselves or with the aid of their friends; or take it to the newly formed *Polizei*.

Such was Greater Magdeburg in December 1635: newly born, vibrant, alive, with a spirit like no other city in the world, and sometimes an edge to it that could leave you bleeding.

Such was the city Gotthilf thought of as his own. Such was the city that he and his partner watched over.

Chapter 4

Mary Simpson stood as her guests entered the room.

"Good morning, Representative Abrabanel, President Piazza."

When Rebecca Abrabanel had asked to visit, Mary had suspected that the resulting conversations would involve politics to some extent. After all, given that Rebecca was a member of the USE parliament from Magdeburg, that her husband was the former (and first) prime minister of the USE, and that she was one of the leaders of the Fourth of July political party, it would be difficult to find something to discuss with her that *didn't* involve politics in some manner. And seeing Rebecca accompanied by Ed Piazza, President of Thuringia-Franconia, up-timer, and also a leader of the Fourth of July party, simply confirmed her suspicions.

"Mary," Ed said, holding out his hand. She grasped it, glad that he was a seasoned enough politician to know the difference between a firm grip and a crushing one, even—or especially—for someone as small as she was.

Ed released her hand, and she turned to Rebecca, who offered her hand in turn. "Ed, Rebecca, it's good to see you," Mary said as she shook hands with the other woman. "You know Lady Beth, of course." Lady Beth Haygood, the up-timer who was head of the Duchess Elizabeth Sofie Secondary School for Girls in Magdeburg and also happened to be one of Mary's lieuten-ants, stepped forward from where she stood before her chair for another round of handshakes.

"Please, be seated," Mary said, motioning to the nearby chairs. They settled in as Mary motioned to Hilde, who was hovering nearby, to present the coffee tray. Mary poured the cups and handed them around, then settled back with her own, grateful that it was strong and hot enough to fight the chill from the outside weather. Like many people who were both short and slight, she seemed to suffer more from cold than larger folks. Thinking back to winters in Pittsburgh, she shivered a bit, and took another sip.

"One of the reasons I like to come to your parlor," Ed said with a smile. "You do serve a good cup of coffee."

Lady Beth nodded in agreement.

"Thank you," Mary said. "Don Francisco finally made connections for us with a supplier of the best beans, and Hilde has learned the best ways to roast and grind them, so I'll admit to enjoying my own coffee."

"Walcha's Coffee House isn't bad," Lady Beth observed. "A lot of the teachers go there."

The conversation continued on that line for a couple of minutes, until Mary brought it to a close after there was a brief lull. "To see both of the leading lights of the Fourth of July Party sitting in my parlor puts me in mind of the days when the Pittsburgh politicos would come around looking for a favor." She smiled at them over her cup.

Rebecca set her cup down on a side table, and leaned forward a bit in her chair, expression becoming more intent.

"Mary, I want to thank you and Lady Beth for agreeing to meet with us on such short notice. And you are correct; we do have something important to ask of you."

Mary took another sip of coffee to feel the warmth slide down her throat. She had had some contact with the senator in the past, of course. How could she not? Rebecca Abrabanel was not only a government figure in Magdeburg, but was also the wife of Michael Stearns, who'd been the prime minister of the USE during the time when Mary had become the leading social light of Magdeburg. They weren't close friends, not by any standard, but there was a solid respect between the two women.

"Rebecca, if you and Ed need to bring something up with us, then, given the times, we'd best be available to you. So what's up?"

Mary almost expected Ed Piazza to take the lead, since he

was an up-timer and would be perfectly comfortable speaking to another up-timer. Her estimation of the senator went up when she continued as she had begun.

"We need your help," the other woman began. "With everything that's going on with Gustavus Adolphus and Oxenstierna, it's pretty obvious that the chancellor is trying to draw what Ed calls the center of gravity from Magdeburg to Berlin."

Ed continued, "It's like this, Mary. If Oxenstierna gets everyone to start thinking that Berlin is the center of power and all things governmental..."

"Then he's gone a long way toward becoming the *de facto* government," Mary completed the thought, "regardless of the legalities involved."

"Right." Both Rebecca and Ed sat back in their seats.

"I'm neither a politician nor a political theorist," Mary said, "so I'm not much help in the political arena." Ed Piazza snorted at that, but Mary ignored him. "You must want something from me, though, or we wouldn't be having this little chat."

Rebecca resumed with, "Mike told me that you once said you wanted Magdeburg to glitter. Well, right now we want, or rather, we need you to make Magdeburg glitter like it never has before. We want every newspaper in the empire and all the surrounding countries to be filled with news about Magdeburg. We want Magdeburg to be so present and so prominent that Berlin seems like a country village beside it."

Mary set her cup aside and steepled her fingers beneath her nose. After a moment, she looked up. "Unofficial propaganda, huh? By downplaying Berlin, you downplay the chancellor and his cronies."

"Exactly!" Ed barked with a grin.

Mary frowned. "I can see that. But you realize I can't be overtly political in this—in anything. I *am* the Admiral's wife, after all." They all heard the capital letter as she pronounced her husband's title.

Admiral Simpson's stand of neutrality in the chaos swirling in northern Germany was widely known. Everyone over the age of twelve had their opinions as to whether or not it was a wise or prudent position for him to have taken, but no one doubted that he meant what he said.

"Caesar's wife," Lady Beth inserted in support of her leader.

"Who must be without reproach, yes," Rebecca said. "We are not asking for coordination and collusion. Simply that you do those things you would ordinarily do, but as prominently and loudly and, ah, 'splashily' as you can, if there is such a word."

"There is now," Mary replied with a smile. She sipped her coffee while she thought on everything that had been said, and much that hadn't.

Naturally, she was tempted to ask for some funding. The arts *always* needed more money, and squeezing the powers-that-be for it was something Mary Simpson had done for so long—first in Pittsburgh, in another universe; now here in Magdeburg—that it was almost second nature to her.

But it would be a bad idea, in the long run. As much as she'd love to add an additional revenue stream to the Arts Council, she needed to maintain a public image of political neutrality. She could afford to let that image get strained, but not get broken outright.

No, this was something that would just have to be done for its own sake. When her cup was empty, she set it down on its saucer on the table before her and looked to her guests.

"No cooperation, no collusion, no conspiring. We will do what we think is best, and you will find out about it through normal channels."

Rebecca looked at Ed. He nodded.

"Agreed."

"Then I think we have an understanding," Mary said. "Keep an eye on the papers."

When her guests left, Mary accompanied them to the door. Just before the door closed behind them, she heard Ed Piazza exclaim, "Not political, hah!"

She was still smiling when she returned to Lady Beth in the parlor. Mary looked over at her friend and lieutenant as she refreshed their coffee. "What do you think?"

Lady Beth had a notepad open and was already reviewing notes. "Salons, concerts, recitals, parades, feast celebrations, we can do lots of things. There are at least a couple of news reporter types in town that we can probably work with for articles, maybe more."

Mary nodded. "We need to commission some musical works from the local composers, but at least one of them needs to be based on King Arthur. The theme of the wounded king who would return to his people in their time of trouble would just absolutely resonate with most of the folks."

Lady Beth frowned. "It might be better to use Barbarossa as the subject, since he was a German emperor and his legend has many of the same elements—especially the theme of the sleeping ruler who will someday return to save his nation."

"It's a possibility," Mary said, "but... The problem is that I can't see the legend serving well as the story for an opera. So Emperor Barbarossa is sleeping with his knights somewhere under—what mountain was it?"

"There are variations. Some say Kyffhäuser, in Thuringia; others say it's Mount Untersberg in Bavaria."

Mary shook her head. "How do you do an opera based on a bunch of sleeping men? And what's probably still worse from a dramatic standpoint is that there would be no suitable female roles in such an opera. Well, I suppose..."

She made a face. Lady Beth laughed. "Yes, a bit difficult! The only woman anywhere in the Barbarossa legend is his wife Beatrice, who was insulted by the Milanese. And the emperor took his revenge by forcing the authorities of the city to eat figs coming out of the hind end of a donkey. How in the world would you stage *that*?—much less put it to song!"

Both women chuckled. Then Mary said: "No, best we stick with the Arthur legend."

"Great idea," Lady Beth said enthusiastically. She rubbed her hands together. "Get a couple of memorable songs out of it to put on the radio and send out the sheet music, and it could weld people together like nothing else. Only make it better than *Camelot*. I never could stand that show," she muttered. "Julie Andrews—*pfaugh!*"

"And I know just the people to pull it off," Mary said. "How soon can we get Amber Higham and Heinrich Schütz over here? What's the use of having a theater director and a great composer among your friends if you don't put them to use?"

Chapter 5

Magdeburg Times-Journal
December 4, 1635

There was a formal groundbreaking last week for the construction of the new surgical wing of the Magdeburg Memorial Hospital in Greater Magdeburg. Participating were Mayor Otto Gericke, Dr. James Nichols, Dr. Balthazar Abrabanel and Dr. Paul Schlegel. Also present were Georg Kühlewein and Johann Westvol, members of the City Council of Old Magdeburg, respectively Altbürgermeister and Bürgermeister of that august body. Masters Kühlewein and Johann Westvol are among the leaders of the syndicate that won the contract to design and build the new wing. It is to be hoped that the new wing will be completed with all dispatch, as our growing city needs to be able to offer the best medical care available.

Stephan Burckardt, private secretary to Master Georg Schmidt, merchant, leading member of Magdeburg society, and member of the Council—the *Rat*—of Old Magdeburg tapped on the open door.

"Yes?" Herr Schmidt didn't look up from the contract he was reading. "What is it, Stephan?"

"The newspaper has arrived, master."

Now the merchant lifted his gaze from the paper he was scanning and held out his hand. "Let me see it."

Stephan steeled himself—the boss would not be happy about this—advanced far enough to hand Schmidt the paper, then retreated through the doorway as quickly as he could.

From his chair at his desk out of sight of the merchant, Stephan licked his lips and wiped his forehead. The air seemed to be getting thicker, much like a sultry afternoon right before a thunderstorm. Except that this was colder.

Stephan picked up his pen, put it down, and shuffled some papers, unable to focus. The quiet in the other room was ominous. He knew from experience that nothing good could come from this. It was times like this he wished he was back with the men in the room across the hall, simply making entries in ledger books all day long; not subject to Master Schmidt's direct gaze all day, nor privy to so many of the master's secrets.

"Stephan."

"Master?"

"Come take dictation."

Maybe, Stephan thought to himself, the master wasn't taking it so badly after all. He clung to that thought until he rounded the door frame into the office, whereupon the thought expired as if it were a mouse trod upon by an ox.

The master's hands were clasped in front of him, and his head was bowed. Stephan stopped as he saw Schmidt's fingers were twisted almost to the point of breaking, and they were clasped so tightly, the flesh of his hands was nearly corpse white. Tension radiated from the master's shoulders, and Burckardt really wished he could be someplace else at just that moment.

Schmidt raised his head. Stephan swallowed at the fury boiling in the man's eyes. His employer was by nature an angry man. God above knew that the master had shown a plenitude of evidence of it in the past. But this was beyond anything Stephan had ever seen before.

At least the master was not looking at him. Stephan edged away from the path of his gaze, as if out of the line of sight of a weapon.

"One would think," Schmidt said, his normal rich baritone almost a whisper and sounding as if it were being forced through a sieve, "that one could count on his relations. I needed—my partners and I needed—that contract. And all my august brother-in-law, the oh-so-magnificent Otto Gericke, who gazes at the world from the heights of Magdeburg's Parnassus and whose chamber pot does not stink like other men's—all he had to do was hint to the hospital committee that they should favor our contract proposal." His voice started to rise, his words coming more quickly. "But apparently that was beyond him! It was too much to ask him to help the husband of his sister. Or rather, his half-sister. His older half-sister. Let us by all means be precise. Never mind that Sophie—"

Schmidt broke off that thought. Presumably, some things he would not say, even in front of Stephan—who, for all practical purposes, had the position of a slave.

Stephan knew that losing that contract had hurt the master's pride. But even more important to the pragmatic Schmidt, it had hurt him in the strongbox. Stephan was aware just how badly the master had needed that contract, since he also served as Schmidt's accountant. Funds were tight since the Sack of Magdeburg back in 1631. To make things worse, his wife Sophie was not the most frugal of women. And he had been forced by his associates to put up a sizeable share of the funds to pay the architect and prepare the offer. He had *needed* that contract, but Kühlewein and Westvol had gotten it instead.

"It is bad enough," the master resumed after a moment, speaking again in that strained whisper, "that he allowed those bastards Kühlewein and Westvol to win out over us. But now he *celebrates* with them?"

Schmidt exploded into motion, sweeping his arm across the desk to send a thin-walled Venetian rose-colored glass wine decanter and matching glasses flying to crash against the wall and shatter into tiny slivers. Then he picked up the pages of the newspaper and slowly and carefully tore the paper in half, making sure that the picture of the grinning Kühlewein and Westvol was sundered in the process. He tossed the shreds of paper onto the spreading pool of wine, then spat on the mess for good measure.

Stephan found himself backed against the wall by the door, wishing that he could escape.

Schmidt spun and stared out the window for some time, his back to Stephan, obviously still seething.

Eventually, the master squared his shoulders. "Very well, then. We'll start a new game." He seemed to be talking to himself. Then he half-turned his head and said: "Take a letter, Stephan."

He barely gave Stephan enough time to sit down and pull out a notebook. "Address it to *Signor* Nicolas Benavidez, Venice, Italy."

"To *Signor* Nicolas Benavidez, Venice, Italy."

Stephan's ability to read and write Italian was a major reason why Schmidt had hired him years ago. He tried not to think of why he was still working for the merchant. A temptation to... adjust... Schmidt's accounts and pocket the difference had not gone undetected, with the result that he was now bound to Schmidt with chains he saw no way of breaking.

"Look up the address, add the usual greetings and pleasantries," Schmidt said. "Here's what I need to say: Esteemed Sir, I find that I am in need of that favor that you promised to me some years ago. It would be a great help to me if you would send me two of your best men to assist me in a matter. These need to be men that know how to handle difficult situations."

Stephan noted all that down. He looked up to see the master staring at him.

"Got all that?"

Stephan nodded.

"Good. Close it with the usual. Make it even more flowery than you usually do. Have it ready for me to sign when I get back. No copy for our files."

Schmidt spat again on the now-soggy newspaper, picked up his hat and started to leave. He paused in the doorway long enough to add, "And clean up that mess."

After the outer door slammed behind Schmidt, Stephan laid his notebook down on his own little desk in the outer room, found a scrap of towel and a box, and walked back into the master's office. He knelt to gather the sodden newspaper scraps and place them in the box, then gingerly picked out as much of the broken glass as he could find. Finally he mopped up the spilled wine as best he could.

After disposing of the box and its contents, Stephan straightened the chair behind the desk, neatened the contract pages where they were still open on the desktop, and generally made sure the rest of the room was in order. Then, returning to his own desk, he pulled out cheap paper to draft the letter on and a much better grade for the final copy. Every movement was precise, subdued, exact. As you'd expect from a lowly clerk who'd once made the mistake of thinking he might soar into the heights of embezzlement.

The analogy with Icarus didn't occur to Burckardt himself. He was a clerk born into a very modest family, not a figure from myth. Icarus had plunged to his death in the sea. Burckardt has gotten his wages lowered, his hours lengthened, his person demeaned. His prospects ruined also, of course—but they'd never been good anyway.

Chapter 6

"No!"

Franz Sylwester winced as Pastor Jonas Nicolai jerked back in surprise at the vehemence in Marla Linder's voice. For all that his wife normally shone with a pleasant temperament, she had a temper that, when stirred, rivaled the tempests on the seas. Unfortunately for the pastor, he had just invoked the tempest. And, judging from his expression, the poor man had no idea what had gone wrong, but he had just enough perception to realize that something had.

Pastor Nicolai from the *Heilige Geist* (Holy Ghost) church had asked if he could call on them. Franz remembered that he and Marla had looked at each other quizzically when they received the note. Neither of them knew the man, since they did not attend any of the Lutheran churches in Magdeburg, but they decided they would do the polite thing and allow the call.

In the flesh, Pastor Nicolai proved to be somewhat urbane, and his tone had a supercilious air to it. Within five minutes of conversation Franz was wishing the man would say what he had to say and leave. Within the second five minutes it became clear that the pastor was hoping to recruit them as musicians for his church, and Franz became heartily sick of the man. Within five more, as the pastor revealed that his specific purpose was to make a pastoral and consoling visit to the bereaved family that he hoped to pull into his parish, Franz was sick to his soul and desperately seeking ways to cut the visit short.

The stillbirth of their first child in October had put Marla on the edge of a mental precipice. It had only been a couple of weeks ago that she had been turned away from it through the help of some of their musician friends. She wouldn't talk about it now. From conversations with Mary Simpson and Lady Beth Haygood, Franz knew that she might never talk about it. But he knew in his heart that she had spent those weeks staring into the abyss of Hell, unable to even grieve properly for their stillborn daughter Alison. And he knew that although she no longer did so directly, and although her face was alive again and her smile could be seen from time to time, she was still subject to times and days of darkness.

And now, out of a misguided desire to comfort the bereaved parents—at least, Franz hoped it was misguided and not an intentional trespass—this idiot of a pastor had opened his mouth and spilled out the one religious doctrine common to all the reformers that he had hoped to keep from Marla until she had regained her balance.

"Frau Linder..." Pastor Nicolai began in a worried tone. "I'm afraid it is true, Frau Linder. Holy Scripture is quite clear that children who are miscarried or stillborn do not have a place in Heaven."

"No," Marla responded again. Although her tone was quieter, Franz's shoulders twitched as he recognized what their friend Rudolf Tuchman had called her "sword steel" voice: hard, cold, inflexible, and barely restrained from cutting the pastor to ribbons. "I don't accept that."

"But all the authorities agree..."

"Then all your authorities are wrong."

"Even Martin Luther..."

"And he's wrong, too."

Pastor Nicolai was now staring red-faced at the very self-assured, very controlled young woman in front of him who was contradicting him at every point. If the man had not been such a fool, Franz would have felt at least a bit sorry for him. As it was, he squeezed Marla's hand in encouragement.

"But..." the pastor managed to utter before Marla cut him off again.

"These men you refer to are only men, Pastor. They can be just as wrong or mistaken as any other men, including the popes they abhor. And in this case, if this is what they all teach on this subject, then they're all mistaken. The Bible does not teach that Alison is in Hell, and I will not accept that from you or anyone else." Marla's tone was beyond cold now. In fact, icy failed to describe it.

Nicolai tried to expound his position again. Franz had had enough, and stood, shutting off the pastor's flow of words. "This conversation is over. Let me show you to the door, pastor."

Marla laid a hand on Franz's arm. "I suggest you spend some time meditating on Second Samuel, chapter twelve, Pastor Nicolai, particularly on David's reaction to the death of his child. Your authorities misinterpret what is being said there." She removed her hand, and Franz escorted the pastor from the room.

Franz led the pastor to the front door and held it open for him. As the pastor stepped through the door, he had a thought.

"Pastor Nicolai?"

"Yes?" The man turned, and Franz could see the light in his eye that perhaps the wayward musician was going to apologize to him. He had to bite his lip for a moment to keep from laughing.

"Are you married, Pastor?"

"Why...yes, I am."

Franz could see the confused look pass over the pastor's face.

"Is your wife a woman of wisdom?"

Now the poor pastor was very confused. "I believe so."

"Do you listen to her?" Franz hurried on before the pastor could respond. "I don't mean talk to her; do you *listen* to her?"

Pastor Nicolai still looked confused, but gave a slow nod.

"Then I suggest you ask her to explain to you what you did wrong here today. Good day to you, sir."

Franz closed the door, and turned to find that Marla had come up behind him. Her face was relaxed and her eyes were dancing. "That was cruel, love."

"No more than the man deserved." He folded his arms around his wife. Her arms went around his waist, and she laid her head on his shoulder. They stood that way for a moment, then he murmured, "I am sorry."

She leaned back head and looked at him. "For what?"

"For allowing that fool to come and disturb you, and for not

warning you what the Lutherans and Calvinists teach about..."
He couldn't finish the sentence.

"About children like Alison." Marla completed it for him, and
he nodded. "That's okay, dear." She raised a hand to his cheek for
a moment, then gave him an impish grin that brought warmth
to his heart. "Lennie came by last week, remember?"

Lennon Washaw was a Grantviller Methodist deacon who
resided in Magdeburg now. He was a good and kind man who
was a lay preacher for those up-timers who had gravitated to
Magdeburg, whether Methodist or not, who were not comfortable with the various down-timer congregations in the town. He
had spoken at Alison's funeral, and was held in high esteem by
both Marla and Franz. For all that Franz didn't agree with the
man on several points of doctrine, he knew and trusted Herr
Washaw to care for their welfare more than any of the Lutheran
pastors in Magdeburg—Pastor Nicolai in particular now being a
case in point.

"Yes?"

"Well, one of the reasons he did was to warn me of this very
thing. He knew that it was going to come up sooner or later,
and he wanted to prepare me for it."

"Ah." Franz began to smile in return. "And so you knew which
scripture to quote to a pastor."

"Yep." Marla giggled, hugged him tight, then released him.
"Now, aren't we supposed to be meeting Mary soon?"

Simon jumped up the steps of *Das Haus Des Brotes*. He opened
the door and hurried through, panting. He'd run the last few
blocks to the bakery because he thought he might be late. Once
inside, he looked for Frau Zenzi—Frau Kreszentia Traugottin verh.
Ostermännin, mistress of the bakery—but she was busy with a
late customer, so he stepped into the back, found the broom and
went to work.

The boy swept the broom across the floorboards of the bakery
with care. Frau Zenzi always inspected his work, so he needed
to do his best. He concentrated on the corners with special care.
The coarse twigs of the broom were hard to maneuver, especially
one-handed. Not for the first time in his young life he cursed
his right arm where it hung straight by his side, just as it had
for as far back as he could remember.

He couldn't remember just when he noticed that he was different from other children, that his right arm wouldn't work. But as far back as he had clear memories, it had always hung limp. He did remember crying about it when he was little, screaming about it. When he was older, he remembered praying about it. And then there were the times when he would sit and try by force of will to make it move. But no matter how he willed it, no matter how he strained, the response, always, was nothing. The arm hung there like a limb broken from a tree but still hanging by some shred of tissue or bark, just like now.

And of course, since the arm didn't work, the musculature had atrophied—withered—early in Simon's life, leaving it looking like nothing so much as a dead twig. He'd never known anything else. The left arm, however, since it had to do the work that the two healthy arms of normal people would do, was very well developed and strong. Other people were sometimes surprised by just how much Simon could do with his one good hand.

Simon stopped sweeping for a moment. He no longer grew angry with himself or his arm. It was what it was. He mostly just worked out ways to do what he needed to do one-handed. But sometimes he grew irritated at the way it flopped around, like it was doing now. He placed the broom between his legs, reached over with his left hand and with a practiced motion hooked his right hand and stuffed it in his jacket pocket. There, he thought. Now he could finish the sweeping without his arm getting in the way.

Just before he grasped the broom again, Simon looked at his left hand, closing and opening his fingers. If he ignored his right arm most of the time, the reverse was true of his left. It was never far from his thoughts. What would he do if he ever hurt that hand? It was a constant fear. Life was difficult one-handed—he could barely imagine the hell it would be if he had no hands.

Back to sweeping, he told himself. He swept the back area, then moved out to the front room where Frau Zenzi met her customers. She brushed by him as he swept along. Again, he took pains with the corners.

"Simon?" Frau Zenzi's voice came from the back of the bakery, and he could hear her steps approaching. "Are you done yet?" The mistress of the bakery appeared in the door from the rear.

"Almost, Frau Zenzi." One of the things that Simon really liked about the mistress was that she let everyone call her by her nickname. A large woman with a broad friendly face, she was not one to ordinarily stand on position. She was a caring woman, as well, who often would tend to the unfortunates of Magdeburg. In fact, she had taken a young blind boy named Willi into her household recently. Her husband, the baker Anselm Ostermann, would simply shake his head and smile whenever she added another person to her list of special people.

Simon was another of Frau Zenzi's special people. She had allowed him to begin sweeping the bakery every evening in exchange for some bread. At the age of twelve—he thought that was how old he was—Simon was determined to work for his food. No beggar he. And Simon did work. Frau Zenzi was never able to find anything wrong with her floors when he was done.

And so it was tonight. Simon finished cleaning out that last corner, then swept the pile of dust and flour and who-knows-what-else over to the front door with care. He flung the door open, swept the pile out the door, then leaned out to sweep it off the outside step. Once that was done, he closed the door and turned to put the broom away.

Frau Zenzi was standing behind him. She took the broom from him. "I will put that away." She smiled as she handed him two rolls. "Here. Take these and go, so I can bar the door. We will see you tomorrow."

Simon took one roll and tucked it inside his jacket, then took the other and gave a slight bow to the mistress. "Thank you, Frau Zenzi. And I will be here tomorrow."

Outside in the gathering twilight, Simon walked down the muddy street chewing on his roll. After walking a short distance, he stopped and sat on the front step of another building. He waited. The evening air was past chilly and moving toward cold. He pulled his jacket tighter around his chest.

The evening had not advanced much further when he saw what he was waiting for. A small dog, nondescript, brown with a white splash on the face, was nosing her way down the street, sniffing and rooting around, occasionally gulping something that she found. Stray dogs weren't common in Magdeburg, and the ones that were seen from time to time were pretty wary of people, as the city council would often set the knackers to hunting them. This one was obviously female, for her dugs hung heavy with milk. There were pups somewhere, waiting for her to return.

Simon tore a sizable piece of bread from his roll with his teeth, dropped the roll in his lap and took the fragment with his fingers. He gave a low whistle. The dog looked around, ears perked. "Here, Schatzi," Simon called. Schatzi, Simon's name for the stray, looked around, then trotted over to face Simon. She kept her distance, though, not coming in reach of hands or feet.

Simon held the bread out to one side, and whistled again. Schatzi edged in, tail between her legs, keeping an eye on his feet, until she could reach up and neatly nip the bread from his fingers. She scurried back several steps until she felt safe enough to stop and bolt the bread. That was the work of only a few moments, then she looked up at Simon again, head cocked to one side. After a moment, she whined a little.

"Sorry, girl, that is all I have tonight."

Schatzi, for all the world like she understood what he said, shook all over like a shrug. She turned and resumed her trail down the street, sniffing through the detritus of a day in the city, searching for anything that might feed her, no matter how noisome. Simon watched until she disappeared in the gathering gloom. He stood up, stuck the roll in his mouth again and brushed off the seat of his pants, then reached over and tucked his right hand farther into his jacket pocket with his left hand. Even though the arm was useless, or maybe especially because it was useless, he felt the cold with it.

Simon's path led in the opposite direction from Schatzi's. He kept looking around while he tore at the roll, chewing and swallowing as fast as he could. It wasn't unknown for others to take from him whatever he had. Being alone, small for his age and crippled on top of it, he was often an easy mark. Living on his own, as he had now for some time, could be very hard.

The last bite of roll went down with a bit of a struggle, as his mouth and throat had gotten very dry. He could feel it slowly working its way down his throat. A smile crossed his face at the thought that at least tonight he had eaten it all. He patted the breast of his jacket; there was even food for the morning. Although he hadn't made any money anywhere today, at least he had food. And a sheltered nook, if no one else had discovered it. He headed towards it with a jaunty step.

Steps sounded behind Simon, and before he could look around he was shoved to one side, almost falling in the street. "Out of the way, boy," said a harsh voice. He looked up to see two large men stride by him. There wasn't much he could tell about them in the dusk besides their size, but that voice was memorable.

More cautious now, Simon walked close to the buildings, keeping to the deeper pools of shadows. Ahead of him, the two men suddenly ducked into the mouth of a narrow alley. Simon stopped, nervous all of a sudden, and waited. After several moments passed without movement from the alley, he edged forward until he was almost at the corner. The temptation to peer around the corner was strong, but he resisted, listening instead. He could hear voices muttering, but the words weren't clear.

More moments passed. Simon looked around. There were other people in the street, but not many. On the other side of the street a man passed by, a shapeless hat pushed back on his head, jacket open, whistling tunelessly through his teeth for all he was worth. Simon winced; whatever the song was supposed to be, it bore a certain resemblance to yowling cats.

All of a sudden one of the alley voices, the voice he had promised himself he'd remember, that voice said clearly, "That's him." Simon pressed back against the side of the shop, but the men didn't look back as they launched themselves out of the alley and began pursuing the whistler. Both of them were holding knives.

Before he realized what he was doing, Simon screamed, "Look out!" Aghast at what he had done, he stood frozen by the shop and watched it happen.

The whistler spun in his tracks before the others could reach him. Simon had never seen a man move so fast. He dodged to one side, making one of the men block the other one. There was a *thock* as the whistler's fist flew out and smacked the jaw of the man in front of him. That individual stopped for a moment, stunned, dropping his knife. His companion tried to dodge around him just as the whistler delivered a kick to the first man's groin. With a yell that was more of a shriek, that unfortunate collapsed into a huddled mass on the street, tangling his companion's feet as he did so.

The second man succeeded in staying erect, but only by dint of some desperate footwork. He obviously knew what was coming, but by the time he regained his balance it was too late. The whistler's fist buried itself in his midsection. He folded over it with a groan but managed to hold on to his knife. But then the

whistler grabbed the back of his jacket and threw the man headfirst
into the wall of the building they were fighting in front of and
the knife went flying. This time the noise was a "thud" sound,
and the man slid down the wall to crumple senseless at its foot.

Simon stared, astonished. He'd seen many fights in the streets
of Magdeburg the last few years, especially in the rougher parts
of town where the rebuilding after the sack by Pappenheim's
troops was slow in happening. It was almost a daily occurrence
in his experience. But he'd never seen anyone dodge a sneak
attack and wreak havoc on dual assailants like the whistler had.
It amazed him.

Of a sudden, Simon became aware that the whistler was staring right at him where he stood in the shadows. He closed his
mouth with a gulp and stood frozen.

"You, boy." The whistler beckoned. "Come here."

Simon stood, lock-kneed, silent.

"Come here, boy. I will not hurt you." Unsure of what to do,
Simon took a hesitant step forward. "That's right, boy. Come on
over here."

One slow step at a time, much as Schatzi had approached him,
although he wasn't aware of it, Simon approached the whistler.
That worthy had picked his hat up off the street and was beating
it on his leg. Simon stopped an arm's length away as the man
crammed the hat on his head and pushed it back.

"You are the one who yelled, right?" The whistler cocked his
head and grinned at Simon. The boy's uncertainty dwindled and
a timorous smile crossed his own face. He nodded. "Then you
have my thanks. I would have beaten these two louts anyway,
but I would have taken some damage in the doing of it. Thanks
to you, they are on the ground and I've had a good warm-up."

The man in the street groaned and shifted a little, clutching
himself. The whistler turned and rather callously kicked him
in the head. Simon started, edging back. The whistler saw the
motion. "Nay, lad, you have got to know that when someone tries
to stab you in the back like this, you knock them down and keep
them down. You do not let them up; for sure as you do they
will try it again. Mercy is all well and good in the church when
the preachers talk about the Son of God, but out in the street a
man takes care of his own."

True to his own hard rule, the whistler bent down and rifled the pockets of the two assailants, coming away with three pouches. He sniffed at one pouch. "Hmm. Tobacky in this one, and a fair size wad from the feel of it. I know just where I can sell that for a pfennig or three. As to the rest, I doubt scum like this have more than a couple of coins to rub together, but we'll check it out later."

He picked up the knife dropped by his first assailant, examined it cursorily, and tossed it aside. "Cheap crap," he muttered. He didn't bother looking for the second knife.

He stood straight and turned to face Simon, who stood ready to duck or jump out of the way. Tucking his hands in his belt, he cocked his head to one side and studied the boy. Just as Simon started to feel uncomfortable at the close regard, the man jerked his chin down in a nod, reached out and clapped Simon on the shoulder. "Well, lad, it looks like you are my luck tonight. I'm Hans. You just come with me, and I'll give you a fine time." Hans started off, only to stop when Simon didn't move.

Simon didn't know what to do. He was glad that Hans seemed to be grateful to him, but the casually violent air about the big man made him nervous.

"Come on, boy. You don't have anyplace else to go, now, do you?"

"N-no," Simon stuttered.

"Then come on." Hans laid his big square hand on Simon's shoulder, and the boy found himself coming on despite his uncertainty.

Chapter 7

Hans led the way farther into the rough quarter of Old Magdeburg. Simon was familiar with every street in the quarter. He ran them all at different times. But Hans soon led him into streets that Simon didn't like to travel at night. They passed by people slumped in doorways. Others staggered down the street, taking swigs from coarse pottery bottles. Simon edged closer to Hans.

After one more turn into another dark street, Hans stopped in front of a door. "This is The Chain. Have you heard of it?"

Simon nodded, stomach sinking. The Chain was perhaps the worst tavern in the city. Fights were a frequent occurrence, and more than one dead body had been removed from the premises. It was said that the city watchmen, even the new *Polizei*, would only enter the place in groups of three or four. Simon had never been inside.

"Ah, it's a rough place, right enough. But you'll be safe with me." Hans pushed the door open and waved Simon in. Steps led down into a basement. At the bottom, Simon stepped into the barroom, afraid but hiding it from his new friend.

The room was dimly lit from a smoldering fire in a fireplace on the opposite side and a few guttering tallow candles on wall sconces. The air was smoky from the fire and candles and foul from the smell of too many unwashed bodies in a small space.

Simon coughed from the reek, then stumbled as he was pushed from behind. Hans stepped up beside him and scanned the room.

"Barnabas!" he shouted. A man across the room waved his hand. Hans faced him and held up two fingers, to which Barnabas responded with an upraised thumb. Hans clapped his hand on Simon's shoulder again. "Come on, lad. Barnabas has got seats for us, let us get some drink." Hans pushed his way through the seated crowd. Simon followed on his heels, as there was no way he could have made his own way through that mass of rough-spun covered backs.

Hans came to a thick board laid across a couple of barrels with a lamp at one end. "Hello, Veit, you old scoundrel."

"Hans, you lump of walking swine's flesh. I have not seen you in must be, oh, eight days now. What made you drag your stinking carcass in tonight?"

Simon stepped away when the tavern keeper so freely insulted Hans. He wasn't sure how the big man would respond, but when Hans laughed he relaxed.

"Oh, I need a purgative, so I figured I'd come by and drink some of your swill. That ought to have me puking by midnight." Both men laughed at that.

"So what's your poison tonight?" Veit asked after they settled down.

"Genever. The good stuff," Hans added as the tavern keeper turned back to the high table behind him. A moment later a blue ceramic bottle was set before Hans, stopper and neck wrapped in wax. Veit held his hand out. Simon watched as Hans pulled some coins out of his pocket, and counted them into the tavern keeper's palm. They both knew the cost of the bottle of spirits, because Veit was counting right along with Hans.

Hans counted out the final coin and reached for the bottle, only to find Veit's hand on it holding it down. "What's wrong?"

"Take back that Halle pfennig," Veit said.

Hans cursed. "You gave it to me, so you ought to take it back."

"I'm not saying I did or didn't," Veit replied. "But if you were in here drunk enough to take it, then you deserve it. Now give me dollars or honest silver or do your drinking somewhere else."

Simon was glad he couldn't understand what Hans muttered under his breath as he took back a blackish coin from the tavern keeper and gave him a different one in exchange. Veit removed his hand and Hans picked up his bottle. Then he looked over at Simon. "Thought I had forgotten you, eh? Boy, this is Veit Abend. Veit, this is . . . what *is* your name, boy?"

"Simon, sir."

"Sir!" Hans and Veit roared with laughter. "I'm no sir, boy. I'm just Hans, and that is good enough for me."

"Taking up with boys now, Hans?"

Simon stepped back as Hans' face went hard and cold all in a moment. He didn't want to be in the way if things got rough here. He'd already seen Hans in action once tonight.

Veit's laughter choked in his throat as Hans' hand flashed across the counter to grasp his jacket and lift him up on his toes. "You'll not say that again, Veit," Hans hissed through tight lips.

Veit's eyes were wide and his face was pale behind his scraggly beard. Simon knew his own eyes were just as wide and just as white around the edges.

"Sorry, Hans. I meant nothing by it. Bad joke."

The tableau stretched on for a long moment, then Hans relaxed his fist and let the cloth slide through his fingers. Veit settled back onto his feet.

"We will let it go at that," Hans said in a hard voice, "but you watch your mouth, Veit. A man can get hurt by saying the wrong thing." After a moment, he turned to Simon and said in a normal tone, "Now, boy, what do you want to drink? I'm buying."

Simon hesitated, then stammered, "Sm-small beer."

Hans frowned, but Veit held up his hand. "I keep some here for some of the doxies that come round in the mornings. He can have some of that, and I won't charge for it." The tavern keeper found a small mug on the back table and filled it from a keg sitting on the end of the table. "Here you are, lad."

Simon took the mug from the counter and looked up at Hans.

"Right. This way."

Again Simon followed close behind the bulk of the larger man through the press of bodies that seemed in the dim light to be clad in shades of gray. Hans pushed his way through without seeming to give a thought to those he was jostling. Following in Hans' wake, Simon heard mutters as he went by the men, but no one's voice was loud enough to catch Hans' attention. After what he had just seen at the counter, Simon was not surprised. People here apparently knew Hans—knew enough to keep on his good side, anyway.

Hans arrived at a table and kicked a bench out from underneath it. "Come on, boy, sit down." Hans himself dropped to the bench and carefully set his bottle on the table. "Barnabas, everyone, this is Simon. He is a small lad with a big name, and he is my luck. Stopped me from getting set upon by a couple of bully boys from over west of the Big Ditch. I recognized them."

Barnabas, a thin man with a narrow face, looked horrified. "Why, that...that is unheard of. They are supposed to keep to their side of the moat, and we keep to ours. That's the way it has always been...or at least since the sack."

Hans was busy scraping the wax from around the stopper and neck of his bottle of spirits. He didn't look up as he responded. "Maybe so, but just maybe someone over there is just a bit upset that I beat their man in the fights last week. Ah!" He got the stopper out and immediately took a big swig of the gin. He smacked his lips, smiled, and looked over at Simon. "Drink up, boy, even if it is small beer."

Simon took a sip from his mug. It was as bad as he expected from this place, but he swallowed it anyway. It was wet, and he was thirsty.

"Hans," Barnabas spoke up. "This is my cousin Karl, from Hannover." He pointed to a man who would make two of Barnabas. "I think I have told you about him before."

Simon studied Karl. From what he could tell, even in the dim light, the Hannoverian didn't really fit in here in The Chain. His beard was a neatly trimmed goatee with prominent mustaches. He wore a fine hat. His clothes, what Simon could see of them, were clean. No, not at all the appearance of the normal patron of this tavern.

"Sure," Hans said. "I remember you mentioning him. Good to meet you, Karl." He held his hand out across the table. Karl took it with a toothy grin. Simon could see their hands tense on each other. Karl's grin disappeared and his jaw set. There was a long moment of silence, then the clinch broke.

"So you are the famous Hans Metzger." Barnabas' cousin's speech was accented. His voice was nasal and harsh. It made Simon want to hunch his shoulders up around his ears.

Hans set the blue bottle back on the table with a *clack*. "There might be a few people have heard my name, aye, but I would not say I was famous."

"Oh, but to hear Barnabas say it, you are one of the most renowned men in all Magdeburg."

"Friend Karl, if you know your cousin at all, you know that he is liable to say most anything once he has had a mug or two of ale." A bit of the hard note had crept back into Hans' voice. Simon hunched down a little. He wasn't sure what was going on here and now, but he was pretty sure he didn't like it.

"Barnabas would have it that you are a very Samson." Karl's tone was more than a bit pugnacious by this point. Simon didn't understand why. "That you are renowned for your strength."

Hans took another gulp from his bottle. "Barnabas drinks too much. And I didn't know that he'd been to church enough to even know who Samson was." The men around the table laughed.

"But are you that man?" Karl's head was thrust forward, and he stared at Hans with intent.

Hans sighed. "What do you want? Are you looking for a contest with me on a night when all I wanted was a peaceful drink with my friends?"

Karl said nothing, just continued to stare at Hans.

Another sigh. "Fine. Here and now. Arm wrestling. But you will have to make it worth my while."

Karl sat back and blinked. Simon blinked along with him.

"Make it worth your while... What do you mean?"

Hans pulled two purses out of his coat pocket. They were small and worn, and from the way they lay flat on the table they didn't have many coins in them. Simon thought they were the purses Hans took from the men who had attacked him earlier in the evening.

"A wager. If I win, you pay me twice the value what's in these purses. If I lose, you get the purses." Karl opened his mouth to object, and Hans held up a finger. "You get the purses, and the knowledge that you beat Hans Metzger, the Samson of Magdeburg."

Karl sat back for a moment, then nodded his head. "Agreed."

With that, chairs and stools all around them scraped on the floor. The other men in the room had obviously been listening, and now they moved to where they could see what was going on. In a moment, their table was surrounded by a circle of observers. There was a murmuring sound, as side discussions happened and bets were made.

"You will have to move, boy." Hans stood and took off his coat. Karl did the same while Hans handed his bottle to Simon. "Hold on to that for me." Simon took it, but was forced to leave his mug on the table. "Nay, take your mug, too."

"I can't." Simon felt like he had ash in his mouth. "I only have one hand."

"Hummph!" Hans looked at him for a moment, then placed a hand on his shoulder. "Well, we can talk about that later. Meantime, you are still my luck, so stand over there where you can see everything and where I can see you."

Before he sat down, Hans turned his head toward the counter and bellowed, "Veit!"

The tavern keeper pushed his way through the circle. "What do you want?"

"Hold these." He handed Veit the purses and Simon's mug, then grinned at Simon and put his hat on the boy's head.

Hans took his seat across the table from Karl. The Hannover man plopped his elbow down on the table top and held his forearm up. There was an eager light in his eye. Hans took his time, rolling his shirt sleeve up with slow deliberation, revealing a hairy forearm corded with muscle.

"Otto," Hans called out as he laid his elbow on the table. "Call the count."

A man stepped out of the circle to stand by the table. As the two wrestlers joined hands he laid his atop theirs. "Begin when I count three. One . . . Two . . . *Three!*" With that, Otto dropped his hand and jumped back. The contest was on.

The muscles in Hans' arm sprang to hard definition. To Simon it almost appeared like there were sticks under the skin, the cords were so strong.

Karl snarled and grimaced, ducking his head as if he was clenching every muscle in his upper body. The joined hands began to move his way, his forearm forcing Hans' back and down. It was a slow movement, but steady, until the hands were maybe halfway toward the table. Then the motion stopped.

The hands stayed there for a long moment. Nothing Karl did moved Hans. No snarl or grunt affected him, no additional push moved him, no glare from fevered eyes touched him. Hans was rock steady.

Simon was so excited he was almost jumping up and down. He'd seen boys and young men arm wrestle before, but nothing like this contest. Here were two grown and very strong men pouring their all into the conflict, and the excitement filled the air around them. Simon found himself chanting, "Come on Hans, come on

Hans," while the men around him were all shouting and shaking their fists in the air. The roar in the tavern was almost deafening.

The boy almost missed it when it happened. He saw Hans' eyes narrow a little, then his hand turned a bit, forcing Karl's hand to twist on its wrist just the slightest amount.

The joined hands began to move again, only this time Hans' hand was moving upward and Karl's hand was moving back. Time and again the man from Hannover would grunt or snarl and try to stop the movement, only to fail. Hans made no noise but the breath whistling in and out of his nostrils. His hand made its slow and steady movement until it passed the vertical and started pushing Karl's hand toward the table.

The shouting redoubled, until Simon wondered if the building would collapse from the noise. He wished he had two empty hands, so he could cover his ears. At the same time, he continued to chant, "Come on, Hans!"

Back and back and back went Karl's hand. Hans showed no sign of elation or triumph; he continued pushing as if he were closing a door.

The end came suddenly. There was a *snap* sound, and Karl's hand smashed into the table.

"*Aaaah!*" Hans released his grip at Karl's scream and sat back, while the other man's face paled to what looked like a corpsely green in the dim light of the tavern and he grabbed his right arm above the elbow. Simon watched as the Hannoverian tried to move his arm and his face contorted with pain. "You son of a sow!" he shouted at Hans. "You've broken my arm."

Hans shrugged. "It was a fair contest. I did nothing to force that to happen. Everyone here will witness to that." Voices all around them were raised in agreement.

Barnabas was at his cousin's side, pulling on his sound arm and muttering something about a doctor. Hans held his hand up, stopping Karl in mid-rise.

"You lost," Hans stared into Karl's eyes. "You owe me. Veit, empty the purses on the table."

Simon had been right; the purses were almost flat. There were few coins in either of them. Two coins fell out of one; three out of the other. But the coins that fell out, now *that* caused eyes to widen all around the room. There on the table top lay three *Groschen* and two pfennigs. Simon sucked in his breath. He counted in his mind, twelve plus twelve plus twelve plus two—thirty-eight pfennigs worth. He'd never seen that much at one time.

Other minds had been doing their own counting. "Six *Groschen* you owe me, plus four pfennigs," Hans declared. "Pay up."

"I will do no such..." Karl began, only to be interrupted by a growl from the crowd. He looked around. Simon thought he turned even paler. The Hannoverian said nothing more, but reached under his jacket and dug out a purse with his left hand. He handed it to Barnabas and made a violent gesture toward Hans. Barnabas took the purse almost timidly, opened the drawstrings and rooted through the contents until he had counted out the bounty that Hans had won.

Hans looked over his winnings, smiled and nodded. Karl lurched to his feet and shouldered his way through the crowd, followed by Barnabas. Hans waited until the door crashed closed behind them, then stood. He pulled his coat back on, plucked his hat off of Simon's head and crammed it back on his own, then scraped all the coins together and poured them back into one of the purses.

"Well, lads," Hans bounced the purse in his hand, "not a bad night's work, eh?"

Some men in the crowd were grousing as they had to pay off on the poor bets they made, but most of them laughed. Simon heard a mutter sounding from all around him. "*Stark* Hans. *Stark* Hans."

Hard Hans indeed, Simon thought to himself. The hardest man he had known in his short life. The nickname sounded even harder because it was pronounced in the truncated form so often found in Amideutsch. In most German dialects the phrase would have been "Starker Hans."

"Veit," Hans called out. The tavern keeper looked his way. Hans held up a *Groschen* for all to see, then flipped it to him. "Ale all around."

There was a loud cheer from the crowd as it made a mass movement toward the serving counter. In a moment, Simon and Hans were standing by themselves amid a scattering of tables, chairs and benches.

"Well, Simon my lad," Hans said. "You've been my luck twice tonight. Here." He reached over, took the blue bottle from the boy, and tucked it in a side pocket of his coat, then handed Simon a pfennig. "Let's go home." He placed his hand on Simon's shoulder and they went out the door together.

Chapter 8

"Well, that was interesting," Marla said as she walked down the steps from the Simpson house, hands busy buttoning her coat to shut out the night-time chill.

Franz looked over as he stepped down beside her. "How so?"

"Oh, not that she's coordinating anything and everything she can to support the emperor. That's a given. For all that she says she's not political, Mary has been associated with power and influence for so long that if she's not breathing the atmosphere of politics she starts getting dizzy from the thinness of the air around her."

All their friends chuckled from where they had gathered around her and Franz. He held his elbow out to her, felt her take it, and they began walking back to their own house, friends trailing in their wake.

"And most of the ideas that she and Lady Beth put on the table are good, and reasonable. Parades—you'll like that," she twisted her head to look at Thomas Schwartzberg.

Thomas had finally made his way from Grantville to Magdeburg, having spent the last two years training some of the local musicians to copy up-time music from the many recordings that had come back through the Ring of Fire. Franz was delighted that his good friend had rejoined their little company.

"Parades, mmm," Thomas rumbled. "Sounds like opportunities

for marches." He gave a huge grin as the rest of the company chuckled. The amanuensis of up-time composers had developed a definite taste for up-time style symphonic band music. The others in the group, who were all involved with the Magdeburg Symphony Orchestra, poked fun at him, which he took in good nature. "I have one in mind."

"So what was interesting?" Franz prodded his wife.

"Oh, the plans for an opera, of course. Master Heinrich can do it..." Here Marla referred to Heinrich Schütz, the emperor's *Kappellmeister* for the court in Magdeburg, and the foremost German composer of the day. "...but can he do it quickly enough to be a help?"

Laughter sounded from all the group. "Master Heinrich is not one of your neurotic up-timer musicians," Rudolf Tuchman advised from behind them. "The man is one of the best of *our* day. He had to write a new cantata every week for weeks on end when the elector of Saxony was holding court. He will have *Arthur Rex* ready for rehearsal before you can believe it."

"I hope so." Marla was quiet for a few steps. "Funny, but for all that the Arthur legends are truly iconic in our literary history, even by my time there were few musical treatments of them, and none that were of the first rank. Well, except for Wagner's *Tristan und Isolde*, *Parsifal* and *Lohengrin*." Franz saw the expression of distaste cross Marla's face. It was apparent that Wagner was not her favorite composer. "But those only dealt with peripheral stories, not with the main legends. I hope *Arthur Rex* proves to be the exception to that rule."

They had arrived at their house, and Franz dug in his pocket for the door key. After a moment of fumbling at the lock, he swung the door open and they all trooped in, led by Marla. There was a busy minute or so of doffing coats and finding places to store them. Their friends all found places to sit or perch around their parlor.

Franz looked up as Marla stepped over to him. "If you don't mind, I'm going to let you guys talk about the orchestra programs without me. I'm...tired," she murmured. And to his eyes, she did appear to be wilting.

"As you wish. I will try to keep the discussion quiet in here." He squelched all the other things that rushed into his mind to say. It had been an eventful day; if she desired time alone, he would give it to her.

Marla kissed his cheek, then crossed through their friends,

smiling and speaking to them as she did. They all watched her leave the room, then turned as one to look at Franz, uniform sober expressions on nine faces: Rudolf and his brother Josef, Thomas, Hermann Katzberg, Isaac Fremdling, Paul Georg Seiler, and Matthäus, Marcus and Johann Amsel. Friends old and new, all close, all part of the nucleus of musicians committed to the future of music envisioned by Marla and Franz. All now looking at him with the same unspoken question on their faces.

"Yes, Marla is doing better," Franz responded. "No, she is obviously not back to her normal self from before the miscarriage. Frau Mary and Frau Lady Beth both tell me that she's doing well, but that it might be some time before she is fully recovered."

He withheld from them Mary's final statement on the matter to him: "And Marla may never fully regain her joy, Franz. To lose her firstborn like that, with no warning, is devastating. It can't help but change her. We'll just have to hope that it doesn't change her for the worse." Which was now his daily prayer.

Outside The Chain there was a bite of cold in the air. Simon pulled his jacket close around him with his left hand, checking to see that his bread was still tucked away.

The moon was shining full, and in the light Simon could see Hans look over at him. "So, your other arm is crippled?"

"Doesn't work at all," Simon said in a monotone.

"Did you hurt it as a younker, or something?"

"Born with it, I guess." Simon swallowed hard. "Been that way as long as I can remember."

They walked a few steps in silence, then Hans spat to one side. "Tough."

"Yah."

They walked a few more steps.

"Family?"

"No."

"Tough." Hans shook his head.

"Yah." The taste of ashes was back in Simon's mouth.

"Got a place?"

"Found a nook behind a chimney over in the new town. Stays warm there."

Hans shook his head again. "Not tonight. You're my luck; you'll come home with me. Meet my sister."

Simon still wasn't sure what kind of man this Hans Metzger was. He shook his head in return. "You don't have to do that."

A large hand landed on the boy's shoulder again. "I owe you, boy. You're my luck." The hand moved on to muss his hair. "Least I can do is give you a warm dry place to sleep tonight and food in the morning."

Simon felt the lump of bread in his jacket. Food in the morning would mean the bread could feed him later. And he could probably run away if he had to. He knew the ins and outs of the alleys and streets and ruins better than anyone. "All right."

"Good. Down this way."

Hans turned down a cross street. Before long they exited the old city, crossed the Big Ditch and were in a slightly more reputable neighborhood than the depths where The Chain was sited. Simon was tired. His feet were beginning to drag. It had been a long day for him, so he was very glad when Hans turned into an alley between two buildings.

"Come on, boy." Simon followed Hans' broad back up a flight of narrow wooden stairs. They arrived at the top, and he waited while Hans fumbled with a key in a lock. After a few moments, Simon heard his friend sigh in satisfaction and push the door open.

"Hans? Is that you?"

Simon's ears perked up at the sound of the voice from inside the rooms. It was a clear bell-like soprano that seemed to tease his ears, so unlike the voices of the vegetable sellers and barmaids that he saw on the streets.

"And who else would it be, Ursula?" Hans reached back and drew the boy into the room with him, then closed the door. Simon could make out a figure sitting in a chair with a candle on a nearby table.

"Oh!" Simon heard the surprise in her voice. "You have someone with you."

"Ursula, meet my young friend Simon ... I never did learn your other name, boy."

Simon felt a laugh coming up his throat, which he hurried to turn into a cough. "Bayer."

"Ah," Ursula said, "you are from Bavaria."

"Yes. I mean no." Simon was flustered now. "I was born here in Magdeburg. My father came from Bavaria, I think."

"Well, it is good to meet you, Herr Bayer. Please excuse my

appearance." The young woman was sitting in a robe, yellow hair plaited into a thick braid that hung before her shoulder. Simon was stunned by how beautiful she looked in the soft candlelight.

Hans dropped his hand from Simon's shoulder, ducked his head and shuffled closer to his sister. "I...uh...I forgot how late it was, and I wasn't thinking. Sorry, Uschi."

Ursula gave a warm smile up to her brother. "I know. It's all right." She lifted her hand. "Help me up, please."

Hans took her small hand with one of his and placed the other under her elbow. Simon watched as he gently lifted her from the chair. She came to her feet, then she...sagged. Simon almost jumped forward, afraid that she was falling. But then he could see that she was standing on her feet, she just wasn't straight. Her right shoulder was dropped, which meant that her hip probably was as well.

Ursula reached to the table where the candle was and picked up a cane that was hooked over the edge of the table. With that in hand, she lurched into motion. Step by laborious step she made her way to a door in one wall. She leaned on the cane as she reached to open the door, then pivoted slowly to look back at her brother and his guest.

"Good night, Hans, Herr Bayer."

"Good night, Uschi," Hans said. Simon's tongue was glued to the roof of his mouth. He could say nothing.

Hans sighed after her door closed and sat down in a chair across from Ursula's. He waved Simon to a nearby stool.

"It happened during the sack of the city," Hans began. "We were trying to get out, get away from Pappenheim's troops. I was able to force our way through the crowds, able to hold on to her and keep her with me. She was only fifteen, and so small, so delicate." There was a pensive expression on Hans' face in the candlelight. "I thought I could keep her safe, keep her protected. But there came a surge of the crowd and her hand was torn from mine. I turned and looked for her, I called for her, I started pushing against the flow trying to get back to where I lost her. Then I heard her scream."

The big man clasped his hands together, hard. "She had fallen, and before she could get back up some fool on a horse had ridden right over her. Her left leg was cut up, but her right...the knee was crushed, and the bones were broken in two other places."

Simon heard Hans swallow, hard.

"I almost went for him. I've never wanted to kill anyone, before or since, but him I wanted dead. Still do, for that matter. If I ever see his face, he's a dead man. But she screamed again, and I turned to her. I picked her up and carried her, out of the city and away to one of the villages. I didn't care where we went, so long as Ursula could find help."

Simon could see that scene in his mind; Hans cradling Ursula and walking as far as he had to go.

"It was months before she healed and could walk again. The leg didn't heal straight, and it's shorter than the other. You've seen what she's like."

Hans stared ahead, rocking his clasped hands. Simon said nothing, just waited.

"She's a saint, Simon. I know her leg hurts, but she hardly ever complains. And she never blames me, even though it's my fault she got hurt. She's a saint," he repeated. "She hardly ever gets out, because of the leg. It hurts her to walk, and she doesn't like people staring at her, but she does what she has to do. She takes in embroidery and sewing. She reads her Bible. And she's so good it almost kills me to see her like she is."

There was another long pause. Simon broke the silence. "Is . . . is that why you brought me here? To meet her, I mean?"

Hans looked into his eyes. "Yes. I mean, I thought . . . You've got a weakness," Simon's pride flashed a bit at that statement, but he forced it down, "I thought you would understand what she's going through." Hans looked down again. "You've been my luck tonight; I thought maybe you could be hers, too. Maybe even be a friend." Simon could see his hands twist together. "I think she may need a friend, maybe soon."

The big man looked up again with a strange expression on his face. Simon looked back at him solemnly. "If Fraulein Metzgerin will have me, I would like to be her luck, and her friend as well."

The biggest smile of the evening broke out on Hans' face. "Great! That's great, Simon. We'll talk to her about it in the morning."

They sat together in a companionable mood, neither speaking. At length, Hans rose and went through a door opposite the one into Ursula's room, returning with a thick blanket.

"Here. You can pull the two chairs together, or roll up in this on the floor for the night. We'll do something better if you stay over longer."

Simon took the blanket, marveling at how thick and warm it was. "Oh, this will be fine. I'll just roll up in front of the fireplace."

"Go ahead, then, before I blow out the candle."

Simon wasted no time in kicking off his wooden shoes. Suiting his actions to words, it was the work of moments to lay the blanket out in front of the fireplace and roll up in it.

"Good night, lad." Simon heard Hans blow out the candle. Darkness descended in the room, alleviated only by the glow of the banked fire in the fireplace.

"G'night."

Hans walked across the room in the darkness. The door closed behind him.

It had been an exciting day. Simon had never dreamed when he awoke in his cramped little nook this morning everything that he would do. New people to meet and adventures of a sort. He yawned, and fell asleep thinking that Fraulein Ursula was an angel. He'd never met an angel before.

Marla stepped into her study and pulled her lighter out of her pocket to light a lamp. She and Franz hadn't been able to afford a generator package yet, so they were still making do with lamps and candles. After getting the light started, she stared down at the old stainless steel Zippo for a moment. Odd how something that had belonged to her cigar-smoking grandfather and had almost been thrown away by her nonsmoking dad was now something that never left her possession, especially now that someone was producing up-time style lighter flints. She'd heard that the stuff they made it from came from India. She didn't care if it came from Antarctica, as long as she could keep using the lighter.

She looked around the room, knowing without hearing them that the guys were asking Franz how she was doing. Truth was, *she* didn't know how she was doing, so how was poor Franz supposed to know?

Some days Marla felt almost back to normal, that the miscarriage was past and over and done with; others, it was all she could do to get out of bed. And mood swings, oh my—on a bungee cord, it seemed like.

The worst thing was that she couldn't seem to focus. That was perhaps the most frustrating thing of all to her, that she just could not seem to finish anything. The room was filled with music books, all open to pieces that she had started to learn or review, only to drift away from them when something else caught her attention.

She didn't want to be that way. She was tired of being that way. She could feel a dull knot of anger forming in the pit of her stomach; anger partly at her circumstances, at the unfairness of life that had robbed her of her daughter, but also anger at herself, for drifting and not standing firm to start again.

Marla felt a snap of decision. "Enough," she said out loud. Order would return to her life, beginning with this room. Before she retired to bed tonight, this room at least would be clean and orderly again.

With that resolution, she began. Each book was picked up, place marked and closed, then returned to the waiting shelves.

As she worked, Marla's mind kept returning to what Mary Simpson had told them earlier in the evening, and some of the things she had heard from others about what was happening in Berlin. It worried her. She didn't want to live in a place and time that was ruled the way the reactionaries seemed to be headed. She definitely didn't want to ...

Marla realized she was standing stock still, frozen, hands locked on the last book she had picked up, unwilling to complete that last thought. She definitely didn't want to ... raise children under such a regime. The very thought made her angry.

Funny how finishing that thought gave Marla some release. Hard and painful as it might be to think about at the moment, she knew there would be other children. She even could see herself holding them. What happened with Alison would not be the end of her story as a mother.

She turned to put the book away, and the cover illustration caught her eye. The young waif on the cover with her blouse sliding off her shoulders morphing into the Tricolor always sent a chill through her. *Les Misérables* the musical had had a huge impact on her when she was first studying voice. She still loved it, and hoped one day to stage it at the new opera house, for all that Andrea Abati, her mentor, looked askance at it.

Opening the book again, Marla flipped through the pages slowly. "I Dreamed a Dream," "Castle on a Cloud," "Master of the House"; the songs flipped by one by one, until her fingers stopped seemingly of their own accord. She stared down at the title and the first line of the song, transfixed.

A slow fire began to burn within her as her mind raced. *Yes, this is the one.*

The fire bloomed. Yes, it had the message she ached to throw in the teeth of the Swedish chancellor.

Blossomed. Yes, the lyrics would need some adjustment and translation. *Surely there is a poet in Magdeburg.*

Brighter. Yes, although it was a man's song in the musical, she would make it hers.

Hotter, surging. Her hair seemed to float away from her head, the feeling was so strong.

Marla snatched up the lamp so quickly the oil sloshed. A moment later the study was dark and empty.

"So, we have *The Lemminkainen Suite* by Sibelius, *Mazeppa* by Liszt, Suppé's 'Light Cavalry Overture,' the Schubert 'Military Polonaise,' 'Procession of the Noblemen' by Rimsky-Korsakoff, and 'Stars and Stripes Forever.'" Franz looked up from his notes. "What else can we add to our concert slate that we can polish quickly?"

"We need a symphony," Thomas Schwartzberg responded.

"Suggestions?"

"Beethoven's Third," Josef Tuchman said.

"Good thought," Franz replied as he noted it down.

"I know we've already got Sibelius on the list, but his Third Symphony is beautiful," Herman Katzberg said, "and it has some stirring passages in it."

"I like that," Franz said. "It's a beautiful piece, and since Finland is connected to Sweden here and now, that would suit our purpose."

"Shostakovich's Fifth," Thomas countered.

"Too dissonant," one of the others said. "Even Frau Simpson's backers aren't ready for that one yet. It's way more dissonant than the Sibelius, or even the Vaughan Williams and Barber pieces we did back in '34."

"I agree with that," Franz added. "In a few years, maybe, but not now."

Thomas crossed his arms and leaned back in an exaggerated pouting pose. "But the fourth movement is so cool!"

"Bide your time, Thomas," Franz laughed, "bide your time."

Before any of the others could respond, the door into the back of the house flew open and Marla strode through. Franz managed to refrain from jumping, but some of the others didn't.

"Sorry to interrupt, guys, but I need something now." By then she was standing directly in front of Thomas, and she thrust an open music book into his hands. "Thomas, I need two arrangements of this song as soon as you can produce them—one for our Green Horse Tavern group, and one for full orchestra accompaniment."

Franz looked at his wife as Thomas scanned through the song. Her posture, the way she held her shoulders and her head, they spoke of resolution, of determination. A sense of excitement began to build in him. She looked at him and grinned, and his heart soared to see the fire in her eyes.

Thomas looked up. "A piece of cake, as you say. Two days for our group, two weeks for the orchestra, less if you have a recording for me to hear."

"I have the recording," Marla said. "You can hear it at the school tomorrow." She lifted her head and almost danced as she looked around at their friends. "Gentlemen, we are going to give Mary and the emperor all the support they could ask for, and we're going to give old Ox more than he bargained for."

"So what is the song?" Franz asked over the snorts and chuckles of the others.

The fire in Marla's eyes seemed to blaze even brighter. "We will give the people a voice with 'Do You Hear the People Sing'!"

Franz could only nod in agreement.

Chapter 9

Morning came. Simon came awake gradually, aware that someone was nearby. For a moment he panicked, until he remembered where he was. He opened his eyes to see Hans crouched by his feet, feeding sticks into the rekindled fire. A yawn came upon him without warning and tried to unhinge his jaw. When that was finished and his eyes were open again, he saw Hans looking at him.

"Good morning." Hans' voice was grumbly in the early morning air.

"Good morning," Simon replied. The tip of his nose was cold, so he reached up and rubbed it. Hans stood and walked over to a table in the corner, where he took cloths off a loaf of bread and a partial wheel of cheese. Simon unfolded the blanket—the nicest, warmest blanket he'd ever seen—and sat up, smacking his lips and rubbing his eyes.

"Hungry?" Hans asked over his shoulder.

"Yah, but..."

"There's a chamber pot in my room."

Moments later Simon walked back into the main room. As usual, arranging his clothing with only one hand took a bit of effort, but by backing up against the wall to hold things up he managed to deal with the buttons.

"Here." Hans handed him a plate of bread and cheese.

Simon sat on the stool and began eating just as the door to Ursula's room opened. Her progress was no faster in the morning that it had been the previous evening, but she finally made it to her chair and lowered herself with care. She sighed and hooked her cane over the edge of the table as Hans approached with another plate.

"I like this cheese," Ursula said with her mouth full. Simon smiled at the sight of her plump cheeks. "You need to get some more when this is gone."

"If I can remember who I got it from," Hans said as he brought two cups over, one for his sister and one for Simon. "This is the last of the small beer. I'll need to go get some here in a little while, so you're not left dry when I head out for work."

There was silence for a while as the three of them munched on hard bread and soft cheese. Midway through their repast, they heard the piercing whistle of the night soil man with his wagon. Hans stood while his cheeks were still bulging and went into his room. He returned with the chamber pot, went into his sister's room, then carried the two pots down to be dumped in the wagon's barrels. Simon grinned as he saw that even *Stark* Hans did not want to be confronted by the CoC and their mania for sanitation.

"All right," Hans said as he came back into the main room. "I'll go get the beer now. Nay, Simon," as the boy started to rise, "stay here. I won't be gone long." He picked up a small keg in the corner and left.

Simon and Ursula looked at each other. After a moment, Ursula gave a tentative smile, which Simon echoed.

Fraulein Metzgerin seemed even more like an angel today, Simon thought to himself. She was dressed in a forest green skirt, with a brown bodice and a cream colored linen blouse. Her hair was braided and wrapped around her head under a soft cap. A glint of humor was in her eye, and a flush was on her cheeks. All in all, she was the prettiest woman he'd ever seen.

Aware that he was almost gaping at her, Simon tore his gaze from the young woman and crammed the last of his bread into his mouth. He looked around the room as he chewed the bread, and noticed the traces of mud that he and Hans must have tracked in last night. "Um," he started, then strained to swallow the wad of bread in order to clear his mouth. "Do you have a broom?"

"In the corner," Ursula pointed. She had set her plate on the table next to her, and removed a bundle of cloth from a bag sitting beside her chair. Unfolding it carefully, she pulled a needle out of the cloth and started sewing.

Simon stood and crammed his feet into his wooden shoes. They were cold, and he shivered at their contact. He walked over to the corner and picked up the broom, then turned to address the dried mud.

It took him a few moments to find the balance of the broom. That was always a bit of a challenge for him. But he was sweeping away before long.

Simon decided that as long as he was sweeping, he might as well do a job of it, so he swept the entire room. He was well begun when Ursula spoke.

"Is your other arm hurt?"

He felt his cheeks flush a bit. "No. It's useless."

"An injury?"

"No. It's always been like this."

"Did Hans bring you here because of that?" She looked up with a frown.

"No...at least, I don't think that was the only reason." Now she had a quizzical expression on her face. "He calls me his luck."

Ursula chuckled, and now it was Simon's turn to feel confused. "My brother, for all that he is hardheaded about most things, is surprisingly superstitious. If something is lucky to him, he'll keep it around until it absolutely wears out and falls apart."

"Well, I hope that doesn't happen to me." They both shared a laugh over that comment.

Simon swept around the room, brushing all the dirt toward the outside door. He built the pile with care, then opened the door and swept it all outside onto the landing. It was the work of a moment to sweep the dirt off the landing, then he returned inside and placed the broom back in its corner.

"Do you have a family, Simon?" Ursula asked from where she was plying her needle.

"No, Fraulein Metzgerin."

Her laugh rang out. "Please, call me Ursula. You make me feel like an old maiden aunt." The smile left her face. "Not that I won't be an old maid someday. No one will marry a cripple."

Simon sat down on his stool. "Me neither."

"So what happened to your family?"

"Mutti and Vatti died before the soldiers came, along with my little brother Johann. The pastor came and put me in a family to foster me, because I had no uncles or cousins to take me in. That was okay, I guess, but then the soldiers came and we had to leave."

"That's when I got hurt."

"Hans told me last night."

Ursula sighed. "He would. He gives no thought that I might like some things to remain private." Sigh again. "Brothers."

"Anyway, when we came back, they didn't want me anymore. The pastor tried to find me an apprenticeship, but no one wants a one-handed apprentice. Especially a left-handed one. He found me another family to take me in, but they were hateful folk, so I left. I've been on my own ever since."

"So what do you do?"

"Whatever I can. I can carry messages and small packages. I can watch over things. I can sweep."

"You seem to be surviving."

"I do okay."

Simon stood up, restless all of a sudden. He wandered around the room, looking at different objects, wondering what it was like to be able to pay for rooms like this, and have your own things in them. His path took him by Ursula's chair, where he looked at what she was working on. He discovered she wasn't sewing, she was embroidering.

"That's pretty," he remarked.

"Thank you," Ursula replied. "It's a good thing I like to embroider, since that's about all I can do to earn money."

"Someone pays you to do this?"

"Oh, yes. I work mostly for Frau Schneider, seamstress for many of the best families in the city. Sometimes I'll do something for someone else, but Frau Schneider keeps me pretty busy."

Simon watched her for a while, watched the precise stitches being placed just so, watched as a bit more of the pattern was revealed. "I wish I could do something like that." His voice was very wistful. "To be able to make something beautiful, that would be...wonderful."

Ursula looked up at him. "Perhaps someday you will."

"Not with only a left hand I won't."

She started to say something, then stopped all of a sudden. A smile crossed her face. "Did you know that one of the heroes of the Bible was left-handed?"

Simon was startled. "Really?"

"Really." Ursula set the embroidery in her lap and reached over to the table, where she picked up a worn Bible. She handled it with care, opening it with a delicate touch. "It's in the book of Judges." She turned the pages, one by one. "Here it is." She cleared her throat and began to read:

> "And the children of Israel did evil again in the sight of the Lord: and the Lord strengthened Eglon the king of Moab against Israel, because they had done evil in the sight of the Lord. And he gathered unto him the children of Ammon and Amalek, and went and smote Israel, and possessed the city of palm trees. So the children of Israel served Eglon the king of Moab eighteen years. But when the children of Israel cried unto the Lord, the Lord raised them up a deliverer, Ehud the son of Gera, a Benjamite, a man lefthanded: and by him the children of Israel sent a present unto Eglon the king of Moab."

Simon listened as she read the tale; how Ehud bound a dagger to his right leg under his clothes, fooled the king into dismissing his guards by saying he had a secret message for him, and when they were alone stabbed him with such force that the handle of the dagger was hidden by the king's fat. The end of the story was eighty years of peace for Israel.

There was a moment of silence after Ursula finished reading. She closed the Bible and put it back on the table, then resumed her embroidery. "Of course, I always thought it was a little unfair for Ehud to trick the king like that. But then, I guess the king was not a nice man, so maybe it was all right." She giggled. "He must have been very fat, though."

Simon laughed with her, all the while marveling at the thought of a left-handed hero. A Bible hero, at that. His heart seemed to beat stronger at the thought of somehow following in Ehud's footsteps. He didn't know how he would do it, but somehow, someday people would tell stories about him like that.

The outside door opened as they were laughing. Hans stepped through with a small keg on his shoulder. He grinned at their mirth. He placed the keg in its corner and made it ready, then straightened and dusted his hands together.

"Hah! All done." He looked to Simon. "Well, boy, time for us to be about our work. Come on."

Simon stood and crossed to the door, where he turned back for a moment. "Goodbye, Fraulein Ursula. I'll see you another time."

"Goodbye, Simon. I'd like that."

Hans crossed to his sister and bent to kiss her cheek. "There's still water left from yesterday. I think you have everything you need. I'll be back late tonight."

"Another fight?"

"We need the money." Hans straightened.

She caught his hand. "Be careful, then. You know I don't like you fighting. You might get hurt."

"Don't worry. Careful doesn't win fights. I'll be the best."

Simon waited for Hans to move through the door, then he followed him with a wave to Ursula. At the bottom of the steps, Hans turned to him.

"I'm off to work."

"Where do you work?" Simon asked.

"At the Schardius grain factorage warehouse, down by the river."

"Can I come? Would they have work for me?"

"Probably not." Simon's face fell and Hans added, "But I will ask. Where will you be around sundown?"

"At Frau Zenzi's."

"The bakery?" Hans asked. Simon nodded. "Good. I'll meet you there. Here." Hans pressed a pfennig on Simon. "Get something to eat today. I'll see you later."

With a wave of his own, Hans was off down the street, whistling tunelessly as he dodged around a woman with a basket on her arm and then sidestepped a pile of dung. Simon watched him go, feeling a bit left out. He comforted himself with the thought that Hans had promised to meet him in the evening.

Simon squared his shoulders, and set out to face the day.

Chapter 10

Gotthilf looked up at his taller partner, and sighed. "Hey, Byron?"

"Mmm?"

"What are you looking for?"

It was one of the little things about partnering with the lanky up-timer that occasionally irritated Gotthilf. It was bad enough that the man was two hands taller than he was, but he would often start looking *over* Gotthilf from that rarefied height. And trying to figure out what Byron was looking at when they were in a crowd was a pure waste of time for the shorter German.

"Not a what," Byron responded.

That was another thing that sometimes ruffled Gotthilf's feathers. When the mood struck him, which was often, Byron became the very personification of terseness of speech, so much so that his name could become a synonym for laconic. Having meaningful conversations with him in those moments gave new meaning to the word exercise.

Gotthilf sighed again. "All right, who?"

"Mmm?"

"Byron!"

That jarred his partner, who looked down at him. "What?"

"Not what, who. Who are you looking for?"

"Oh." Byron grinned. "I'm trying to find old Demetrious."

"Ah." That explained it. They had spent most of the afternoon running down the stable of observers, informants and snitches they had developed and groomed over the last year, hoping that one of them had heard something they could use to put a crack in the silence surrounding the Delt case. So far, nothing.

Old Demetrious, though, if they could find him, just might have something for them. As Byron craned his neck and looked around the crowd in the market space, Gotthilf stood still and listened. Bit by bit he filtered out the sounds around him, until...

He grabbed Byron by the arm. "This way."

Most of the crowd made way for them. As much as the two men might not like it, they were developing a reputation in the city. Several high profile murder cases, most recently including the murders of several prostitutes, had made them..."notorious" was the best word, Gotthilf decided. That made moments like this easier, but also made keeping a low profile more difficult than it used to be.

Gotthilf elbowed his way through a throng of folks standing in a circle near a butcher's shop. In the center of the circle was Demetrious and his table, with another man facing him on the other side.

"Give the man back his pfennig, Demetrious," Byron growled. Gotthilf flashed his badge, and the circle began to break up and drift away. The mark grabbed his coin off the table and bolted.

Demetrious was almost as lanky as Byron. It was hard to tell how tall he was, because his shoulders were bowed. His face was leathered and creased with many wrinkles, some of them so deep Gotthilf thought they looked like knife cuts. White hair floated around his face in the chill breeze. His clothes were worn, but neat, and except for his fingerless gloves he might have been any old farmer come to town.

"Ah, Lieutenant," the old man sighed. "You surely have something better to do than come harass an honest citizen who is simply playing a game of chance."

Gotthilf gave an admiring glance at Demetrious' table. It was ingenious in its design, and well made in its craft. It was perhaps a cubit square, and a palm in depth, with legs that supported it well but could be folded up and away to make an easily carried parcel.

Atop the table were three wooden cups, upside down— Demetrious' "game of chance." Gotthilf had seen it before, and remained intrigued by it, although Byron insisted that the way Demetrious played, there was precious little chance in it.

"Citizen!" Byron snorted. "You're not a citizen until you start paying taxes."

Demetrious nodded at the touch. "Resident, then."

"Honest resident? Hah." Byron was playing to the few stragglers of the crowd. Gotthilf knew how his partner worked, and from the slight smile that tugged at the corner of Demetrious' mouth he was certain that the old man knew it as well.

"Show me your cups, then."

The two detectives bent their heads over the table as the old man tipped the cups up one by one. "Got anything for us about the Delt murder?" Byron whispered.

"Nay." Demetrious set the first cup down and picked up the second. "Only a breath here and there that someone very important has been dealing harshly with those who displease him."

"Any idea who?" Gotthilf murmured. The second cup was placed and the third lifted.

"Nay." The third cup was set down. "But you might look for a man named Hans Metzger."

"All right," Byron said loudly as he straightened. "Your cups are honest. But there'd better be a pea under one of those cups the next time we stop by."

Demetrious gave a slight bow. "As you command, Lieutenant."

Gotthilf waved a two-fingered salute as they turned away. Out of the corner of his eye he could see people drifting back to the table once it was clear the detectives were leaving.

Byron muttered something. Gotthilf poked him in the arm. "If you're going to make noise, say something intelligible."

"I was really hoping that old gypsy would have something more solid for us."

"Not in our cards or stars today," Gotthilf replied as they moved through the crowd.

"Yeah. No joke. Don't think I've heard of the Metzger guy." Byron pushed his hands into his jacket pockets. "Still, I suppose we'll have to follow up on the name, since it's the only lead we've got right now."

"True. And we will be able to tell Captain Reilly that we're pursuing our investigations."

"True."

Byron fell silent, and Gotthilf followed suit. Byron hadn't recalled the name Metzger, but it rang a bit of a bell with Gotthilf, and he worried after that thought for the better part of a block. Then it came to him.

"Metzger... I think he was the guy who got pulled in on that splashy drunk and disorderly arrest a few weeks ago."

"Oh, yeah..." Byron nodded. "Yeah, I remember him now. Big blocky guy, right? Looked like a warehouseman?"

"That's because he is a warehouseman."

"Who does he work for?"

"Mmm," Gotthilf thought for a moment. "One of the corn factors; Bünemann or Schardius, I think."

Those two names were familiar to both men, as they had investigated the murder of Paulus Bünemann earlier in the year. Schardius turned out to have no connection with the murder, but had impressed them both as being a sharp operator. Gotthilf wouldn't be surprised to hear that the man skated close to the edge of the law in his business.

After a few steps, Byron looked over at Gotthilf. "You don't suppose Schardius..."

Apparently Byron's thoughts were running in the same channels as Gotthilf's. He shrugged. "We'll find out."

After another long silence, Gotthilf asked, "Do you really think Demetrious is a gypsy?"

Byron chuckled. "Not full blood, no. But with that Greek name and his facial features and complexion, he's definitely not from around here. And he might be part Romanian, or Egyptian, or Armenian. Wouldn't surprise me if he came from Istanbul, even, although he doesn't look Turkish to me." He laughed again. "Not that I'm an expert on Turks, mind you."

Chapter 11

Otto looked up from the document he was reading at the sound of the tap on the door frame. When he saw Jacob Lentke standing in the opening, he stood and moved around the desk.

"Come in, Jacob, come in." He ushered the older man to a chair. "How goes your gout today?"

"Not badly, Otto. Not badly at all." Jacob waved a hand at the desk. "Sit, sit, my boy. What are you poring over so intently?"

"Oh, Father Christoff forwarded some documents from *Fürst* Ludwig that will be useful to me. He has granted me, or rather, the mayor of Greater Magdeburg, police authority over the properties of the *Stift* within the confines of the city."

Jacob's eyebrows rose. "The new city?"

"Not just the new city, but Old Magdeburg as well."

The older man's face adopted a grin that could only be described as evil. "That means you will have unquestionable authority over nearly half of the old city, which also removes it from the sphere of influence of the City Council. Hah! Can I tell them?"

Otto made a note to himself that one of these days he needed to find out just who on the council had offended Lentke, and just what they had done. Jacob was normally not a vindictive man, but this was not the first time he had indicated displeasure with the council.

"No, because the *Fürst* sent a copy of the documents to them as well."

Disappointment showed on Jacob's face, but he shrugged it off.

"Oh, well. That is still good news. But enough of that. I won't be long, must be someplace else soon, but I needed to leave this with you."

Otto picked up the leather folder that Jacob pushed across the desk to him. He opened and scanned the document it contained. "Ah, you finished the opinion already."

"Yes. It turns out that we each of us had a surprising amount of case material in our homes. Not enough to reconstruct the archives, of course, but enough to provide some useful precedents. And the review by Master Thomas Price Riddle from Grantville was useful, as well. The man has the clearest of minds and a most incisive wit. I wish his health was stronger. We of the *Schöffenstuhl* would be delighted if he could come to Magdeburg and spend some days with us in discussions."

"Discussions. Hah. I know you and your cronies," Otto smiled. "You would pick the poor man's mind cleaner than a wishbone at a feast-day meal. You would leave him without two thoughts to keep each other company."

Jacob smiled in turn. "Perhaps."

Otto turned back to the document. "So your considered opinion is that the chancellor has no legal standing?"

"For all of his prominent place in the Swedish regime, and for all that the emperor may have unofficially delegated imperial tasks and responsibilities to him from time to time, Chancellor Oxenstierna has no official position, standing, or authority in the USE, neither given by Parliament nor officially assigned by Emperor Gustav. Consequently, he has no basis to act as the viceroy for the emperor or as the regent for Princess Kristina in the USE." Jacob shrugged again. "It is very clear; he has standing in the kingdom of Sweden, but none in the USE. There is no rule or precedent that authorizes or condones his actions here."

"So he is outside the law," Otto stated.

"Indeed."

Franz took the broadsheet being passed out by the young woman from the Committees of Correspondence. She marched on down the street, pressing copies of the broadsheet into every hand that would take one, and a few that tried not to. Marla took the other side of it, and they looked at it together.

Marla had been surprised to find after they moved to Magde-burg that political cartoons were not a twentieth-century original art form; that, in fact, political cartoons were ubiquitous in the seventeenth century. The one at the top of the broadsheet was a typical sample of the current state of the cartooning art: sketchy, somewhat awkward art combined with savage satirical writing.

"Hmmph!" Marla snorted. "I need to have Aunt Susan send this guy some of my brother's comic books. Let him learn how to draw real cartoons."

"I don't know," said Franz. "I think he did well with the horns on the chancellor."

Chancellor Oxenstierna had been drawn as a Minotaur figure with sweeping horns; an obvious reference to the inevitable puns on his name that seemed to universally come to mind to both up-timers and down-timers alike. The Ox or *Der Ochse*, either way it referred to a bovine, and this particular figure was dressed in a fancy doublet.

All the figures in the cartoon were labeled. Franz wasn't sure if it was the artist or the editor that wanted to make sure that nothing was misunderstood, but it still brought a smile to his face.

"Hmm, that's the emperor lying on the bed," Marla puzzled out. "But who are all these people kneeling? Holy cow, this guy's lettering is atrocious."

"This one is 'Free Electorate,'" Franz said, pointing to the label. "That one is 'Freedom of Religion,' and the other one is 'Freedom of Speech.'"

"Who's the girl in the corner by the bed?"

Franz tilted the page, trying to get a better angle on the some-what muddled drawing. "I think that is supposed to be Princess Kristina."

"So what is it that he's got in his hands that he's aiming at the freedoms?"

"Well, judging from the caption, I think it is a giant scalpel." The caption read "Perhaps A Little Blood-letting Will Help The Emperor Regain His Senses."

Marla looked at him. "Scalpel?"

"You know they used to bleed patients?"

"Ick!" Marla thrust the broadsheet into his hands and started down the street. "I don't get it."

They spent the next few minutes arguing about whether the

drawing made any sense or not, walking along dodging other pedestrians, crossing streets, sidestepping wagons, carts, and the inevitable animal by-products. Wagon drivers were supposed to clean up after their horses, mules or oxen. Whether they did or not often depended on how visible a Committee of Correspondence member was.

Their badinage ended as they stopped before a familiar door. The sign above the door read *Zopff and Sons*, and through the small panes of glass set in the door they could see the printing presses the firm operated. Franz opened the door, and they stepped in, to be greeted by their friend Patroclus.

"Franz! Marla!" He advanced with open hands, albeit somewhat ink stained.

"Don't touch me," Marla warned. "Last time you got that ink on me, it took me two days to get it off."

Patroclus laughed. "All right, I will keep my hands to myself, then. But what brings you to see us? We do not have a commission from you at the moment, do we?"

"Nope," Marla said. "Although I think the Grantville Music Trust will have the next batch of music to be printed ready before long."

The younger of the two Zopff sons, Telemachus, came up behind his brother just as she said that. He made a face. "Music. All the fiddly little bits with the notes and stems and flags going just so. I would rather set ten pages of words, even in Roman type, than a single page of music."

Patroclus landed a backhand on his brother's biceps. "That music has kept us in sausage and ale the last couple of years, and you should be thankful for it."

Telemachus made another face and headed back to his press.

"So if you don't have a commission for us, what is the occasion for your dropping by?" Patroclus asked.

"I need a poet," Marla said. Patroclus raised an eyebrow, and she continued, "I have a song with English lyrics, and I need them translated into good German. But it can't just be a literal translation; a few of the lines will need to be modified to fit the modern circumstances. That's going to take poetic skill. So, I'm hoping you know a man we can contact."

"Hmm." Patroclus rubbed his chin, leaving a trace of ink behind. "A poet, who reads up-timer English, and is skilled at his art. And is in Magdeburg. I can think of several who can write doggerel, good enough for that." He nodded at the broadsheet that Franz was still holding. "But one who is truly worthy of the name poet?" He shook his head. "My mind is empty."

Telemachus turned around from the typesetting bench he was working at. "Logau might be able to do it."

Patroclus looked back at his brother. "Who?"

"Friedrich von Logau. You know, the guy who wrote that epigram you like so much:

> "Was bringt den Mann zum Amte?
> Vermutlich seine Kunst?
> Gar selten, was denn anders?
> Fast immer Geiz und Gunst."

Franz saw a hint of confusion on Marla's face. For all that she was adept at the Amideutsch that was common around Magdeburg and Grantville, and for all that she was better than adequate at the local dialect and in the specialized language of music, poetry was another level of skill she hadn't fully developed yet. He ran through the epigram in his head one more time, then translated it for her as:

> "What brings a man into public office?
> Presumably his ability?
> Very seldom, so what else?
> Almost always, greed and connections."

"Hah!" Marla's face lit up. "Okay, I don't know kielbasa from bratwurst as far as German poetry goes, but if that's his attitude, I think I like the man."

"The CoC like him," Telemachus said before he turned back to his work.

"I can see why. So where do I find him?" Marla turned back to Patroclus.

"He has been writing things for the *Times-Journal*." He shrugged. "Start with them."

Ciclope and Pietro moved to the side of the road and stopped to rest their horses. Magdeburg had been in sight in the distance for some time, but Ciclope saw no reason to exhaust the animals. They were pretty worn as it was. It had been a long fast ride from Venice, and there had not been much grain available for a lot of the way. And truth to tell, neither he nor Pietro were the most accomplished riders around, although they were somewhat better now than they were when they began the ride. Now that the end was in sight, he didn't begrudge their mounts a few moments of rest.

"So tell me again, One-Eye," Pietro muttered, "what are we going to be doing here? And why did we come all the way from Venice to do it?"

Ciclope hardly ever thought of his birth name. For years, ever since he had lost his left eye in a desperate fight, he had gone by the Italian form of Cyclops. It piqued his sense of humor; he was a solid bulk of a man, but not inordinately large, and the thought of being compared to a giant did make him smile a bit every now and then.

"Pietro, how many times do I have to tell you..."

"One more time. What are we going to be doing?"

Ciclope sighed. "I don't know. All I know is the boss got a request to send two men to Magdeburg who will not be known to the residents nor to the up-timers from Grantville, and who 'know how to handle difficult situations.'"

"Sounds to me like somebody is trying to be clever." Pietro spat to the off side of his horse.

"Perhaps," Ciclope nodded. "But the boss owes a favor to the guy who sent the request, so here we are. And we don't dare leave without doing the job."

Pietro shuddered. "Nay. I don't want to spend the rest of my life in this land of barbarians, and if we were to go south of the Alps back to civilized country, the boss would find us."

Ciclope reached up and adjusted his eye patch. "Sooner we get into town, meet the new boss, and get the job done, the sooner we can get back to Venice."

"Let's go, then."

The two men urged their horses back into motion, and headed for the capital of the USE.

Chapter 12

Friedrich von Logau sat in Walcha's Coffee House, doodling in his pocket notebook while his friends argued. Gathered around the table was a group of poets and writers from all over Germany, there to seek patrons and to partake of the capital city's *élan*.

"Lovecraft was the greater writer," intoned Karl Seelbach, Friedrich's fellow Silesian. Karl then proceeded to slurp his coffee, which evoked winces all around the table.

Friedrich drew loops around his latest attempt at an epigram.

> *In danger and great need,*
> *Irresolution brings destruction.*

It was rough, and he wasn't satisfied with it yet. So he listened to his friends while his mind worked under the level of the conversation.

"You've drunk so much coffee your head is addled," Johann Gronow retorted. "Anyone with a wit can clearly tell that Poe's skills were far superior to Lovecraft's, although he didn't write as much. Isn't that right, Friedrich?"

Gronow's Hamburg accent grated on Friedrich's Silesian ear just a bit, but he ignored it. "Don't be dragging me into your interminable verbal duels over which up-time author of old grandmother tales is superior."

Friedrich spoke with a smile, as he was the one who had put Gronow on the trail of both authors, with the end result being the creation of *Der schwarze Kater—Eine Zeitschrift*. Or *Black Tomcat Magazine*, as the up-timers more succinctly called it. Gronow was the publisher/editor of the two issues it had done so far, and his oft-spoken mission was to further the development of the art of macabre storytelling in German. Friedrich had it on good authority that Johann had written all of the first issue and most of the second issue except for the translations of two Poe stories.

His mind raised a thought at that moment, and he crossed out "Irresolution" and replaced it with "Compromise." He surveyed the result. Better, but still not quite right, somehow.

A sudden silence at the table caused Friedrich to look up. His friends were all looking behind him. "I wonder what *she* wants?" Johannes Plavius said. Friedrich turned in his chair and draped an arm across its back.

He knew who the woman was that approached with her husband shadowing her as he usually did. No one could move in the middle or upper circles of Magdeburg and not know—or at least know of—Marla Linder. Depending on one's beliefs about music, she was either famous or notorious, but she was never ignored. All agreed that her voice was spectacular.

Walcha's Coffee House was not one of her usual haunts. Friedrich watched her walk toward their table. Tall, with long black hair pulled back into a "ponytail," as up-timers called that odd hairstyle, she walked with assurance, as if she was so certain of herself and her place that she had no doubt of what she was doing. Which she probably didn't, he thought before he echoed Plavius' thoughts. "I wonder what she wants with *us*?"

"I believe we are about to find out," Plavius muttered.

Frau Linder came to a halt just beyond Friedrich's reach. "Good afternoon, *meine Herren*." Her Amideutsch had the unmistakable flavor of the Grantville up-timers, for all that her pronunciation was impeccable. Something about the tonal quality of the voice, he mused.

Greetings rumbled from most of the circle at the table. Friedrich contented himself with a nod of the head.

"I'm looking for Friedrich von Logau."

Although Friedrich did not react, he felt the gazes of his friends fix on him, and one of them must have pointed, for Frau Linder's eyes settled on him. A feeling not unlike staring at the muzzle of a loaded gun entered his mind.

"Herr Logau, I am Marla Linder, and this is my husband, Franz Sylwester." Herr Sylwester nodded his head in turn.

"I know who you are, Frau Linder. How could I not?" He felt the corner of his mouth quirk upward.

That seemed to fluster her for a moment, but she clasped her hands around the tube of paper she carried and settled. "I—we—have need of a poet. You have been highly recommended to us. Herr Adalbert, the editor at the *Times-Journal*, told us we might find you here."

"You have need of a poet." Friedrich made it a statement, not a question, and his voice was very dry.

"Yes. I have a song lyric written in up-time English that I need translated into German."

"A . . . song." Friedrich had trouble believing what he was hearing. He frowned. "You want me to translate?"

Frau Linder started to nod, then shook her head, which made for a very odd motion.

"Not just translate. I don't want a word-for-word literal translation. I need a German's poet's translations of the . . . the thoughts behind the English words. I need you to make the German lyrics sing like the English ones do."

"Ah." That was different. That, he could understand.

Friedrich had done some translating in his time. Most poets and men of letters did at one time or another in their careers. Translating words was usually easy. Translating the thought was always the challenge.

He held out his hand. "Let me see it."

Frau Linder placed the paper cylinder in his hand. He unrolled it, and started scanning the text. Midway through, he stopped, went back to the beginning, and read through again slowly, letting each word register in his mind.

He looked up at the woman. "I will not insult you by asking if you know what you are asking. But do you realize the kind of storm this could raise? Especially now?"

Frau Linder returned a grin that reminded him of nothing more than a feral cat showing its fangs. "Oh, I intend for it to do that," she breathed. "Exactly that." Her tone was not loud, but every man at the table heard it, and Friedrich felt the hair on his neck rise.

Friedrich looked at the short length of lines on the page. He read through them again, then folded the paper and put it in his inside coat pocket.

"Where can I reach you?"

"Messages can reach me at the Duchess Elisabeth Sofie Secondary School for Girls, at the Royal Academy of Music, or at our home." Herr Sylwester handed his wife a card, which she in turn handed to Friedrich. He looked at the address, then tucked that card into the same pocket.

"Give me a week."

"Sooner would be better, but if it takes a week, and it's good, so be it."

Herr Sylwester leaned forward and whispered in Frau Linder's ear. She nodded in response, then returned her focus to Friedrich. "How much?"

Friedrich was tempted to play word games with the woman, but in the end decided not to. "Nothing. I will do this just for the pleasure of being a part of it."

He was surprised when Frau Linder didn't remonstrate with him. She simply took him at his word, and nodded. "Within the week, then. Good day to you, Herr Logau, *meine Herren*."

Herr Sylwester nodded, having never said a word to the gathered writers, then turned and followed his wife. Friedrich felt his mouth quirk again. With Frau Linder for a wife, why would the man need to say anything? And from what Friedrich had heard, although he followed in his wife's wake often, Sylwester was no rudderless ship sucked along in an undertow. One could be quiet, and still be a rock of strength.

Friedrich turned back to his friends.

"Well?" Plavius demanded.

"Well what?"

"Aren't you going to show us the English lyrics?"

Friedrich made a pretense of considering this suggestion, before letting his face settle into a grin. "No," he said as he beamed at them. "You will hear them like everyone else, when *she* is ready to salvo them at the world."

"Salvo?" Gronow caught at that word. "You infer that it will be a momentous occasion."

"My friends, you have no idea. But you will remember that day, I doubt not."

As those around him erupted in expostulations, Friedrich looked back down to his notebook, and crossed out "destruction." He wrote in a simple word, so that the last line of the epigram now read "Compromise brings death." He read the line again, nodded, and put the notebook back in the breast pocket of his coat.

Bam!

Gotthilf walked up to the counter just as Byron fired his last shot. The action in the .45 locked back; Byron ejected the empty magazine and laid it and the empty pistol on the counter.

"Clear!" he called out to the range officer as he slid the ear protectors down to hang around his neck.

The range officer blew his whistle. Even though Byron was the only shooter in the range at the moment, the officer still yelled out, "Range is cold." After a moment, a young man ran out to grab the target off the hook, then ran back to the side and around the range perimeter to bring it to the lieutenant.

Gotthilf looked around his partner's arm to see the grouping. "Not bad, Byron."

Byron laid his hand on the spread. Nothing showed outside his palm. "Yeah, eight shots in a five-inch diameter at thirty feet. Not world class, maybe, but good enough for the guy's heart and lower left lung lobe to be hamburger." He put the target on the counter, then bent over and picked up his cartridge casings. "I almost forgot these. I've got almost a box worth that I need to get reloaded."

Gotthilf winced at Byron's description of the effect of the shots on a body. He couldn't disagree with it, but the thought still caused his stomach to lurch a bit. He covered for that by setting his case on the counter.

Byron started feeding stubby .45 cartridges into the empty magazine. *Click. Click. Click.* "Whatcha got, partner?" In a matter of moments, seven cartridges into the magazine, ram it into the handle, one cartridge into the chamber, release the action, throw the safety, and shove the pistol into the holster in the back of his belt, all the while looking with interest at Gotthilf's case.

Gotthilf flicked a particle of dust off the top of the polished wood. "Nothing you'd be interested in."

Byron grabbed for the case. "Anything that comes in a presentation case to a firing range interests me."

Gotthilf slapped his partner's hands away. "All right, all right! Don't get greedy." He lifted the lid of the case on its hinges, and unfolded the cloth from where it covered the contents.

"Ahh." That lengthy satisfied sigh from Byron made Gotthilf chuckle. "What?"

"You sound like a tad in the kitchen when the cook is baking pies," Gotthilf said.

Byron started to reach into the case, stopped, and looked to his partner. "May I?"

Gotthilf nodded. Byron completed his motion by pulling the pistol from its nest in the case. He held it in both hands at first, turning it this way and that to examine it in detail. "That's nice," he finally passed judgment. "Hockenjoss and Klott?"

"Of course," Gotthilf affirmed. He was very happy with the H&K .32 he'd been carrying for almost a year, so when he decided to look for another pistol he naturally gravitated to that firm's designs.

"Big bore," Bryon commented as he hefted the pistol. "Bigger than your other pistol." He held it out at arm's length, sighting down the range. "A bit heavy, I think. Nice balance, though."

"Forty-four caliber," Gotthilf nodded as he took two gunpowder flasks from his coat pockets and the small box of percussion caps from its slot in the presentation case. He staggered from the slap Byron delivered to his shoulder.

"All right! It's about time you got a man's gun."

"Give me that." Gotthilf plucked the pistol from Byron's hands, and swung out the cylinder to begin loading. "In truth, I wanted something heavier than the thirty-two, and I also wanted more shots."

"Wait a minute," Byron reached out and tapped the cylinder. "Seven shots? When did they come out with this one? Your thirty-two only has five."

"Uh-huh. New design." Gotthilf was pouring powder into the cylinder chambers, tongue sticking out from between his teeth. At that moment he envied Byron the up-time .45 cartridges more than ever. He knew H&K was making some cartridge weapons, and he lusted after one of them, but the price of the ammunition was so high he just couldn't justify it right then. Maybe in a few years. "I was in Farkas' gun shop a few months ago, and I talked with the master gunsmith of H and K when he dropped by, told him what I wanted. They've been making six-shot forty-fours for a while. I asked for more, and he came back to me with this."

"Hmm. Seven shots." Byron obviously mused on that for a while as Gotthilf finished loading the cylinder. "Okay. With a percussion cap system, it will take that much longer to reload, though."

"Maybe." Gotthilf started loading the bullets into the chambers one at a time. "Remind me to tell you what Herr Farkas suggested when I complained about that."

Byron stepped back when Gotthilf began placing the percussion caps on the chamber nipples. "That stuff makes me nervous, even in small doses."

"Relax. H and K switched to the French caps, the potassium... potassium chlorate. It's not nearly as sensitive."

Gotthilf swung the cylinder into place in the gun frame, keeping it pointing downrange. He reached into his vest pocket and pulled out the flat pill case he used to carry his wax ear plugs. Moments later, he was ready to shoot, and nodded to the range officer.

"Range is hot!" the officer yelled as Byron pulled his ear protectors back up.

Gotthilf waited for the range officer to give him the nod, took a two-handed grip, focused on the target through the sights, and began squeezing the trigger.

Bam!

Chapter 13

— A T & L TELEGRAPH —

BEGIN: MBRG TO GVL

TO: ATWOOD COCHRAN

ADDR: LOOK IT UP

FROM: MARLA LINDER

DATE: 14 DEC 1635

MESSAGE:

DOES YOUR PORTABLE RECORDING RIG STILL
WORK STOP IF SO, CAN YOU BRING TO MBURG
FOR A ONE SONG GIG PROBABLY ON OR AROUND
JAN 14 TO 16 STOP WILL PAY EXPENSES AND
GOING RATE FOR RECORDING OR IF TROMMLER
BUYS IN YOU CAN TAKE ONE FIFTH OF DEAL
STOP RESPOND BY TELEGRAPH STOP TELL
MARCUS HI STOP

END

Chapter 14

Simon's day turned out to be a good one. He ran messages for several merchants and delivered a package as well. At the end of the day, as he walked toward Frau Zenzi's, he had three pfennigs in his pocket, and that was after spending the one Hans had given him for a piece of grilled sausage on a stick. That and the remaining roll from yesterday, despite it being a little the worse for wear, had given him more of a day's meal than he could remember having since forever.

So he was in a good mood when he arrived at the bakery, whistling on his own as he claimed his broom and began sweeping.

"You seem happy," Frau Zenzi said as he worked.

"Yah. I made a couple of new friends yesterday, and pulled in a couple of coins today." Simon bent down to look under the edge of the counter to make sure he had swept it clean underneath.

"That is good," Frau Zenzi replied.

Simon continued sweeping. His good mood made the time pass swiftly, and before he knew it he was done. After he put the broom back in storage, Frau Zenzi gave him a roll. He gave a florid bow in reply, then exited the bakery with her laughter ringing in his ears.

He looked around, but Hans was not in sight yet. There was still a bit of light coming over the roofs of the western houses, so he might be a bit early himself. He sat down on Frau Zenzi's steps and bit into the roll. It was crusty and filled with flavor. Before he knew it, he was almost done. He was about to finish the last piece, when he realize he hadn't seen Schatzi yet today.

No sooner had that thought crossed his mind, than Simon saw her, nosing her way down the street. He whistled and she looked his way, ears perked. "Schatzi," he called, holding out the last scrap of the bread. As always, she approached him slowly, getting just close enough to grab the bread, then scooting back out of his reach to eat it. A few chomps and it was gone. She looked at him for a moment, then moved on her way, following her route, sniffing for the scraps of food that would keep her and her pups alive.

"What was that all about?"

Simon jumped. Hans was leaning against the front of the building next door, hands in pockets, watching him.

"She is the only creature I know who is worse off than I am. I always give her a scrap of my food when I see her."

Hans straightened. "Do you think that makes her yours?"

"I used to dream that it did, but no. She is too afraid to trust anyone."

"Hmmph. I know people like that, too."

So did Simon, and he nodded in agreement.

"I am surprised the knackers haven't caught up with her," Hans said.

Simon's gut twisted at that. He knew that the knackers were charged with clearing stray animals from the streets. "We do not see them around here very often. And Schatzi's smart, very smart. She would get away from them."

"That would not take very much smarts. One whiff of them and if she had any sense at all she would be running the other way as fast as she could." They both shared a laugh over that. Simon remembered the odor that clung to the last knackers he'd seen. Working with dead carcasses did not produce the finest of perfumes.

Hans turned. "Well, come on."

Simon hurried to catch up with him. "Can I ask you something?"

"Ask."

"What did you mean when you told Fraulein Ursula there would be a fight tonight?"

"A fist fight."

Simon was confused. Hans knew he was going to be in a fist fight?

Hans looked over at him and laughed at his expression. "For money, boy. A fist fight for money. See, there are men in town who arrange these, and other men in town, especially the well-to-do ones, come and watch them. Bets are laid on who will win, and a lot of money can change hands because of one of these fights."

"Ah." Simon nodded. "I have heard about those, but never saw one."

"Look, boy, Simon, you remember what it was like last night at the arm wrestling?"

Simon nodded vigorously.

"It will be like that, only louder and more excited. People really like this."

"Oh." Simon thought about it. "Do you do this often?"

"Every few weeks."

"Do you win?"

Hans laughed. "Every time so far. And with you as my luck," he reached over and tousled Simon's hair, "I am sure to keep winning."

Simon thought about that as they kept walking. He was Hans' luck. Okay, as the Americans said. He would be the best luck he could be.

Chapter 15

Magdeburg Times-Journal
December 14, 1635

The office of Mayor Otto Gericke made the following announcement yesterday:

"At the request of Fürst Ludwig von Anhalt-Cöthen, the Schöffenstuhl of Magdeburg, capital city of the USE, has reviewed the actions of Axel Oxenstierna, Chancellor of Sweden, in secluding the emperor, attempting to convene Parliament in Berlin, arresting Prime Minister Wettin, and attempting to assert authority over the government and citizens of the United States of Europe. The Schöffenstuhl has rendered their opinion, and it is being prepared for publication in full. In summary, the Schöffenstuhl today declared Chancellor Oxenstierna's actions to be illegal and unconstitutional, and further set forward that no citizen or resident of the USE owes the chancellor any obedience or recognition beyond that of common courtesy.

"It is our expectation that the USE Supreme Court in Wetzlar will issue a similar ruling when they conclude their deliberations on the issues."

The Times-Journal will bring you the full text of the judicial opinion as soon as it is made public.

✧　　✧　　✧

Ed Piazza, President of the State of Thuringia-Franconia, lowered the paper and whistled. "Well, now, that's certainly set the weasel among the chickens."

Those assembled in Rebecca Stearns' parlor all laughed. Gunther Achterhof's laugh morphed into an almost snarl. One of the chief leaders of the Magdeburg Committee of Correspondence, his views on political maneuvering tended to be very direct. "More like set the wolf among the sheep. Nothing plainer can be said to place the truth out in plain view."

"That is all to the good, isn't it?" asked Helene Gundelfinger. She was the vice president of said state of Thuringia-Franconia.

Gunther shook his head. "Sheep are dumb. Stoo-piid," he drew the syllables of the English word out.

Constantin Ableidinger, leader of the Ram movement in Franconia, grinned and responded, "Not all sheep, Gunther. Not all sheep."

"Maybe not," Gunther acknowledged sourly, "but too many. Just watch, this will make no difference to what is going to happen."

"Maybe not," Gunther's words were echoed by Rebecca Stearns, "but it will possibly make a huge difference to Michael's plans." Her husband Michael Stearns was now serving as the commanding general of the Third Division of the USE army. No one knew quite for sure yet what his plans to deal with this crisis entailed, but they all had faith that he had them.

"And afterward," Ableidinger rumbled. "As Michael has mentioned before, history is written by the winners. Being able to point to a judicial condemnation made before the fur—or rather, the lead—started flying can only strengthen us afterwards."

"Mmm." Gunther's expression was still sour. "Maybe."

Gunther Achterhof was not exactly a "glass is half full" kind of fellow.

Across town, behind the walls of the old city, three men met in the council room of the *Rathaus*, home of the *Regierender Rat*, the official city council and governing body of Old Magdeburg. One of them had just finished reading the same article from the newspaper. Three glum faces stared at each other.

"*Ach*," Georg Kühlewein huffed, "the chancellor will not believe we did not have a hand in this."

"Lentke is behind this. You know he is," said Johann Westvol,

Kühlewein's frequent and accustomed partner. "The others on the *Schöffenstuhl* would not have stirred if he had not rousted them out of their holes. I told you we should have brought him into this deal with us. If he stood to make the kind of money we are starting to gather, he would have kept his peace, but 'No,' you said, 'We need all the money we can get for ourselves,' you said. Now see where we are."

"Well, if you had not cheated him on that saffron deal, he would not have been so ready to seize an opportunity to heave a beam into our spokes." Kühlewein was getting red in the face and his voice was getting louder.

"Both of you just shut up." Spoken in a cold tone by the third man in the room, that phrase froze both Kühlewein and Westvol in place. Their mouths clacked shut, but the glares they focused on the speaker should by rights have set his clothing to smoldering.

"Better," Andreas Schardius said. "We do not have time for bickering and recriminations. Now, Georg, you're the mayor this year, correct?"

Kühlewein nodded.

"Then keep everything quiet and everyone in line. Do not give Lentke or Gericke or the *Schöffenstuhl* any more reason to look in our direction."

There was a mutinous look on Kühlewein's face. He was not used to taking orders from anyone, much less someone who was not a member of the *Rat*. "But..."

"*Do it.*" The ice returned to Schardius' voice. "Or I pull out of your little group, and take my money with me. Without me, you do not have a prayer of finishing the hospital wing on time, and you certainly will not skim off the money you expect to make on this deal."

Now there was a look of panic in both the other men's eyes. Westvol immediately acquiesced, nodding vigorously. Kühlewein was a bit slower in signaling affirmation, but he was no less firm when he did so.

"Good. And send a note to the chancellor and explain that you had nothing to do with the *Schöffenstuhl's* verdict. You are correct; he will probably not believe you. But if you do not send the message, he will begin to wonder even more about you. And we do not want that, now do we?" He gave a thin smile as the two men nodded in unison.

Chapter 16

— A T & L TELEGRAPH —

BEGIN: GVL TO MBRG

TO: FRAU MARLA LINDER

ADDR: SYLWESTERHAUS MAGDEBURG

FROM: ATWOOD COCHRAN

DATE: 14 DEC 1635

MESSAGE:

RIG STILL WORKS STOP BATTERIES STILL HOLD CHARGE WELL ENOUGH FOR ONE LONG SESSION OR TWO SHORT ONES STOP CAN TAKE TIME OFF FROM SCHOOL FOR GOOD CAUSE STOP IS THIS ONE STOP

ATWOOD

END

Chapter 17

Gotthilf turned away from the shift sergeant's desk and stepped over to where Byron was pouring a cup of coffee. "Sergeant Milich says Metzger works in Schardius' warehouse most days. He also says Metzger beat the charge, and is out on the street. Metzger has been keeping a low profile ever since, except that he does fight in the bear pit pretty often."

Byron sucked at the coffee, and made a face. "This stuff isn't any better than my mother's coffee, and that's pretty bad. So when's the next fight?"

Gotthilf smiled. "By coincidence, the sergeant says he may be fighting tonight."

His partner gulped the rest of the coffee down, shuddered, and said, "It's rumble time, then."

Gotthilf shook his head at yet another strange American idiom, and followed his partner out the door.

Simon walked with Hans out of the city, even beyond the exurb of Greater Magdeburg. He was uncomfortable outside of his streets, especially as it was drawing to full dark. It didn't take long, though, before they arrived where they were going.

"What is this?" Simon was mystified. All he saw was a big rectangular hole in the ground with timbers shoring up the sides and some bench seats around it.

"It's the bear fighting pit."

"Oh." Simon had heard of it, too, but he'd never seen it before. Somehow he'd always imagined it would be larger and...grander. He became aware of an odor as they drew closer to it. "It stinks."

"Yah. Lots of blood spilled in that pit, soaked into the ground." Hans chuckled. "Some of it even men's blood."

"Dog fight two nights ago," a stranger commented.

"Fresh blood, then," Hans said. Simon made a face.

More and more people were arriving, all men as far as Simon could tell.

"Hello, Herr Metzger," someone said from behind them. Simon turned with Hans to find two men: one tall and one short.

"Are you on the bill tonight?" asked the tall one. From his accent, he was an up-timer.

"On the bill?" Hans replied. Simon was confused as well.

"On the card. Are you fighting tonight?"

"Who's asking?" Hans sounded brusque to Simon.

"Lieutenant Chieske of the Magdeburg *Polizei*, and my partner Sergeant Hoch."

"Oh." Hans seemed taken aback. "I am at that, Lieutenant Chieske."

"Should be a good match, then," said the short one, who was clearly a down-timer.

"Yah, Sergeant Hoch. I will give the people their money's worth."

The two men nodded to them and walked on. Hans watched their backs for a moment, spat and muttered something Simon couldn't quite hear.

"Who are they, Hans?"

Hans looked at him with a sober expression on his face. "You know about the new *Polizei*?"

"Yah." Simon nodded.

"Those two are part of it. In fact, they are mostly leading it, from what everyone on the street says. And they have got a lot of the street people and hard men nervous. They are sharp-eyed and, so far at least, incurably honest."

"Why are they here tonight?"

"I don't know. Probably heard about the fight and came to sniff around the edges like your Schatzi, looking for whatever they can find."

Simon chuckled at the image conjured in his mind by Hans' words.

A man approached whose pointed nose and receding chin reminded Simon of nothing of so much as a ferret. "Time to get ready," he whined at Hans. Even his voice reminded Simon of a ferret.

"Right. Come on, lad." Hans led the way over to the pit and climbed down a ladder. When he got to the bottom he looked up at Simon. "Come on, now."

Byron saw someone he knew. "This way," he threw over his shoulder to Gotthilf, who followed him through the crowd. "Todd! Todd Pierpoint!"

An up-timer near one end of the pit turned. "Hey, Byron. What's up?"

"You just here for the fight?"

"Naw, I've got a stake in this."

"How so?"

"Tobias Dreher," Todd pointed to a weasely-looking down-timer who was walking with Hans Metzger toward the fighting pit. "He found a copy of *Sports Illustrated* that covered mostly boxing stories. Once he got someone to read it to him, he got ideas about starting a fight syndicate. Turns out there's been some sort of bare knuckle fighting around these parts off and on for quite a while. Anyway, he started looking for someone to work with him on it. He got pointed my way, and here we are. I do some general training of fighters at Karickhoff's gym, I referee, I put up some of the initial money, and I get half the profits."

"Wow. From one-time county welterweight champion to 1635's own Don King. In a few years I'll get to say 'I knew him when...'" Byron grinned and ducked as Todd swung a lazy roundhouse at him. "So, you make much from the bets?"

Todd's smile disappeared. "You being a cop, are you asking officially?"

"Not yet."

"Well, for the record, I don't bet on the fights. Conflict of interest, see?" Todd's head swiveled to find his partner. "Tobias, now, he might. He's never said anything to me about it." He looked back to the two policemen. "I haven't heard of anyone making book on these fights. So far as I know, it's just man to man here at the pit." He spat. "And I hope it stays that way."

There was a moment of quiet, then Byron said, "What's with the pit? I'd've thought you'd put a ring up."

Todd sighed. "You wouldn't believe how change-resistant some of these people can be. It took me weeks to get the fighters to understand why a raised ring would be good. They're used to the pit; they like the pit." He shook his head. "I finally got them to agree to use it if we built it. Now I've got to get the money together." Todd chuckled. "And it may not be square when it gets built. Might be more of a rectangle, like the pit is. Change-resistant, like I said."

"You got gloves and mouth protectors and everything going?"

"Working on gloves. The fighters we've got mostly don't like the big up-time style boxing gloves. I've had someone make up some of the padded five-ounce martial arts style ones that leave the fingers free, and some of the fighters have started using them."

"That include Hans Metzger?"

"Yep. And some of the guys have started using pieces of thick leather for mouth protectors, too. That works okay, but I'd rather have rubber. I keep hearing someone's bringing rubber in from overseas, but I haven't been able to chase it down yet. That would be better."

Todd looked over Byron's shoulder and waved.

"Gotta go, there's my cue. Watch the fight—it could be good."

Simon hadn't dealt much with ladders in his short life; a one-handed man is at a bit of a disadvantage on one. Of course, a one-handed man is at a bit of a disadvantage everywhere, he thought to himself as he reached for the left pole. A couple of moments later he was standing on the floor of the pit, pleased with himself that he had managed to scramble down the ladder without knocking it over or falling off it.

He looked up to see two men coming down the ladder at the other end of the pit. One of them began taking off his coat, followed by his shirt, which he handed to the other man.

Hans took off his own coat and folded it over one of the ladder rungs. His shirt went on top of it. His hat he dropped on Simon's head, grinning as it settled on top of the boy's ears. Then he dug a couple of leather gloves without fingers out of his coat pockets and tugged them on.

Without the shrouding of his clothing, Hans' body looked like a solid slab of muscle. His waist wasn't much narrower than his shoulders, which were wide enough. He smacked his fist into the palm of his other hand a few times, shook his arms, then stood waiting.

"What do I do?" Simon asked. He was nervous about being in the pit itself.

Hans looked over at him and grinned. "Just stand in the corner out of the way and wish me luck. I will take care of the rest of it."

Just then another man came down the ladder at the other end of the pit and moved to the center. "All right," he called out, in that distinctive up-time accent. "I'm Todd Pierpoint, and I'm the referee, the fight-master, for this contest. At this end of the pit, we have Hans Metzger." Scattered cheers broke out. "And at the other end, we have Pieter Sokolovsky." A couple of cheers and scattered boos. "This fight will be fought under the Markie of Cuiensberry rules..." or at least that's what Simon thought was said. It didn't make any sense to him. "...so there will be no biting, gouging, kicking, or blows below the belt. One infraction gets a warning. The second will stop the fight and give the win to your opponent. Do you understand?" Herr Pierpoint looked to Hans' opponent first, and received a nod. "Do you understand?" Now he was looking at Hans. Hans nodded.

"Good. This fight will be fought for ten three-minute rounds. The sound of the bell," he pointed to someone in the crowd and a bell rang, "will start and end the rounds. There will be one minute between the rounds. Now," Herr Pierpoint looked up at the crowd surrounding the pit, "the fight begins in two minutes." There was a rush of noise as the crowd members cajoled and argued with each other as they made bets.

Simon looked over at the other fighter. Sokolovsky was taller than Hans. His arms were longer, too. He looked soft, though; there was a bulge around his belly. Hans, by contrast, looked flat and hard. *Stark* Hans. The other fighter kept moving, picking his feet up and down, swinging his arms. Hans just stood there like a lump, waiting.

The two minutes passed quickly. Herr Pierpoint stepped to the center of the pit. "Are you ready?" The crowd packed around the pit roared as the two fighters nodded. Simon backed into the corner of the pit. "Begin!" Herr Pierpoint pointed up at the crowd and the bell rang.

Hans stepped forward, step, step, step, until he was close to the center of the pit. His opponent came forward at about the same pace. They started circling one another. Hans had his fists up in front of his face, Simon saw, elbows tucked in by his side. Sokolovsky was holding his fists in front of his chest with his elbows stuck out.

Simon started muttering, "Come on, Hans...come on, Hans..." over and over. The crowd was yelling and screaming.

The other fighter took a swing at Hans, a big wide looping swing of his right fist. Hans ducked the swing, stepped in while the other man was off-balance, and buried his own fist in Sokolovsky's gut. Then Hans slammed his other hand to the other man's ear. Sokolovsky was staggered, but manfully made a swing with his other fist. Hans ducked that one as well, then stepped back in to deliver another hammer blow to the gut.

The rest of the first round was like that. Sokolovsky would swing, Hans would evade the blows, then provide a punishing hit or two. By the end of the round, there were red marks and the beginnings of bruises on the body and face of the other fighter, but Hans stood untouched.

The bell rang. Herr Pierpoint stepped in between the two fighters and waved them to opposite ends of the pit. Hans came and stood by Simon.

"So, what do you think so far?" Hans asked.

Simon could barely hear him through the noise of the crowd. He was so excited he was bouncing on his toes. "You're better. You're beating him."

"Yah. This guy's no good. I will put him out next round, watch and see."

The bell rang for the second round. Hans put his hands up and moved forward deliberately. This round he started the action by throwing a punch at the face of Sokolovsky. The other man tried to duck but wasn't fast enough to evade it. It landed high on his left cheekbone.

Hans gave Sokolovsky no chance to recover. One punch followed another, body, body, head, body, head. His outclassed opponent tried to fight back, but Hans would either evade his swings or he'd brush them aside.

There was no retreat. The other fighter tried to step back and Hans stepped forward in pursuit. Always there was a punch coming, left, right, left. Simon could tell the other man was losing strength because his hands kept dropping lower and lower like he couldn't hold them up.

The crowd was still yelling when Hans put a fist in Sokolovsky's gut one last time, then put one to his jaw. His opponent's arms dropped straight down. He wavered, took one step, then stretched his length on the floor of the pit.

The crowd went wild while Herr Pierpoint counted to ten. Simon didn't understand why that was. But there was no mistaking the meaning when Herr Pierpoint lifted Hans' hand above his head and pointed to him.

Hans made a bit of a bow to each side of the pit, then walked back over to the ladder. Simon met him there with a huge smile on his face and handed him his shirt. After pulling the shirt on, Hans grabbed his hat and tousled Simon's hair. "I told you, you are my luck. With you around, I cannot lose." Simon's heart swelled with pride, a most unfamiliar emotion. "Come on."

Simon followed Hans up the ladder, coping with the lack of a hand better going up than he had going down. He managed to step off the ladder without needing Hans' offered hand.

Hans slung his coat over his shoulder, laid his arm on Simon's shoulder, and started pushing their way through the crowd. It was slow progress, as it seemed that at least every third man they encountered wanted to congratulate Hans on his win, or on how easily he'd defeated his opponent. Simon heard more than one voice murmur around them, "*Stark* Hans...*Stark* Hans..." One man even pressed some silver on Hans, saying that since he'd won his bet for him, he should share in the winnings.

Simon noticed that Hans kept his eyes moving over the crowd. Just as he was about to ask him what he was looking for, Hans muttered, "There he is," and steered them back toward the pit.

They reached a place where Hans could reach out an arm and grab a man by the shoulder. When he turned, it was Ferret-face. Simon had to swallow a laugh when he saw the man again.

"Tobias," Hans said, "pay up."

"All right, all right," the man whined. He pulled a roll of the new paper money out of his coat pocket and started counting bills into Hans' palm. "One thousand dollars," Tobias said, putting the now smaller roll back into his pocket. "Satisfied?"

"Yah. Let me know when you have another fight lined up for

me, after a week or so." Hans tipped a finger to his brow as the crowd started clumping around the pit for the next fight of the evening.

Simon tugged on Hans' sleeve as they stepped away from Tobias. "How much is that in pfennigs?" he asked.

"About ten *Groschen*, maybe a little more," Hans replied.

Simon's head spun. Ten *Groschen*; one hundred twenty pfennigs. Hans was nearly rich, with what he had won yesterday at the arm wrestling, and now this! Simon had never seen so much money at one time. "How much does the other man make?"

"A half of this, maybe a third." Hans' teeth flashed in his beard. "I don't know. I have never lost."

There was someone waiting for them as they neared the edge of the crowd.

"A good fight, Herr Metzger," Lieutenant Chieske said.

"Ach, it was a joke, Lieutenant." Hans hawked and spat. "That bum could not touch me. If Tobias does not find some better fighters, I will have to find something else to do. There is no fun in defeating the weak."

"Fun?" Sergeant Hoch asked. "You enjoy beating people?"

Simon bristled at the sergeant's tone. Hans turned and looked down to meet the shorter man's eyes. "What I enjoy, Sergeant Hoch, is the contest—the matching of strength to strength, skill to skill, finding the best. Tonight...I take no joy in tonight. I ended the fight as quickly as I could."

"And it's to be hoped that fool learns from his bruises and aches and pains not to do something like this again," Lieutenant Chieske offered.

"Or at least not until he has gotten a lot better at it," Hans agreed.

"Indeed. Well, good evening, Herr Metzger." With that, the two policemen nodded and moved on.

"So," Simon said, amazed at the calmness in his voice, "now what?"

"Now we go home to Ursula and let her know that her brother has won again." Hans shrugged into his coat. "Let's go."

Byron and Gotthilf turned and watched the fighter and his companion walk away into the darkness. "Sergeant Milich said he's connected to Schardius?"

"Yah. You think he can tell us what we want to know?" Gotthilf murmured under the crowd noise.

"Maybe." Byron tilted his head. "But it will have to seem like his idea. If he thinks we're trying to make him do it, he'll just clam up."

Gotthilf wasn't familiar with the last term. That wasn't unusual, since Amideutsch was basically German with stripped down grammar and conjugations and a boatload of American loan words. The dialect was very new and still very much in process of formation.

"Clam?"

"Okay, you know what a mussel is..."

Chapter 18

Ciclope and Pietro ducked into the tavern. It was filled with smoky haze, partly from the fireplace at one end of the room, and partly from an old man's pipe. Ciclope had to admit that the tobacco was aromatic—not that he had any experience to compare it with. Tobacco was still a novelty in northern Italy, and very pricey indeed.

They bought a couple of mugs of ale, then found an untenanted table in a back corner away from the fire. Without thought, they each sat with one of the corner's walls behind him.

Ciclope tried his ale, and winced. Not putrid, but not exactly something that he would have fond memories of, either. Ah, well.

"So, when does he show up?" Pietro asked.

"Keep your voice down or shut your mouth. The man will get here when he gets here."

The fact that he was so short with his partner was a mark of Ciclope's own nervousness. In truth, he himself was wondering how long they would have to wait. But the answer was the same for him as it was for Pietro; the man would get there when he got there.

Pietro had just returned to their table with their second round of ale when a man wearing ill-fitting clothes slipped into the chair across the table from Ciclope. Pietro started to say something, but Ciclope backhanded him on the shoulder as soon as he opened his mouth.

"Are you the pros from Dover?" the stranger asked.

Ciclope studied him for a moment before responding. Hard to see his eyes under the brim of the hat he was wearing, but his beard was very neatly trimmed and his hands looked rather clean for the kind of man his clothes would normally hang on. And that was the phrase his boss had told him to listen for, idiotic though it sounded. So this must be the new boss, the one that hired them to come to this God-forsaken hinterland of battlefields and howling Protestants.

"Aye, that is us," he responded when the stranger began to shift on his stool.

"You are who Signor Benavidez sent from Venice?"

"Aye."

The stranger's shoulders settled a little, as tension seemed to flow out of him. "Good. It took you long enough to get here."

"Travel from Venice in the winter is not the easiest thing to do, my friend," Ciclope said. "And Pietro ate some bad mutton in one inn along the way, and was sicker than a dog for days afterward."

Pietro gulped and looked queasy at the memory of it.

"Pietro—he is Italian?"

Ciclope wanted to shake his head. If this was the measure of the new boss, maybe he and Pietro had best pack up and head south again. "We *are* from Venice, you know."

"Of course, of course," the stranger quickly replied. "It's just that you will need to blend in with these Germans, you see."

Pietro spoke up in German. "Never fear, boss. I was raised in Graubünden, at the east end of the Swiss lands, so my Deutsch is as good as anyone's."

Ciclope chuckled. "If they speak Schwietzerdietsch, at any rate." That part of Switzerland had a very distinct dialect.

The stranger shrugged. "So long as nobody thinks he's Italian. And what about you?"

"Saxony," Ciclope said. "Dresden, to be exact."

"Oh." The stranger hesitated. Ciclope could guess why, given the news that had been circulating when they finally arrived in Magdeburg. Banér's army marching on the Saxon city had everyone talking.

"And no, I have no kin left there, and it would not matter if I did, as they all washed their hands of me when I left twenty years ago."

"Oh." The stranger brightened. "Well enough, then." He looked around furtively. "The reason why I brought you here..."

Finally, Ciclope thought.

"One of the building projects going on here in Magdeburg. I want you to hire on with the builder, and...keep him from succeeding."

"What do you mean?"

The stranger leaned forward over the table. "I do not care what you do, but I want that project to fail, quickly and spectacularly. I want the people involved in the project to suffer, and their reputations to be ruined."

"Does it matter if we hurt anyone?" Ciclope asked.

"Feel free."

Ciclope and Pietro looked at each other, and identical smiles appeared on their faces.

Logau wiped his pen's nib with a very stained cloth and set the pen aside with care. He leaned forward over the desk and pinched the bridge of his nose. *Done. Finally.* Opening his eyes, he lowered his hand and picked up the page in front of him, careful to not smudge the ink.

"Do You Hear the People Sing" translated into *"Das Lied des Volke."* And done in three days. Once Logau had arrived at his room and pulled Frau Linder's page from his pocket, he had been drawn into the work of translating the song, staring at the paper and alternating scribbling in a frenzy, balling pages up and throwing them over his shoulder, and staring at the wall with unfocused eyes. He knew he had thrown himself on his bed to sleep for a few hours at least once. He thought he had eaten. Surely he had.

No matter. He was done. Now to get this to Frau Linder and see what she would make of it.

Logau threw on his coat, plucked up his walking stick and gathered his hat. Halfway out the door of his rooms, he remembered to go back for the paper.

"Frau Linder!"

Marla stopped and turned to see Friedrich von Logau hurrying after her on the street. "Herr Logau," she greeted him when he caught up to them. Franz nodded, which Logau returned in acknowledgment.

The poet looked a bit worn to Marla. Wisps of hair stuck out at odd angles from under his hat, his coat looked as if it had been slept in, and his stockings were sagging from his breeches, all of which was intensified by the dark bags under his eyes. The burning gaze he directed toward her spoke more of a fever, though.

"I am glad to find you so quickly," Logau said. He reached into the breast of his coat and brought forth a page, which he presented to Marla with a bit of a flourish. She smiled at that. "Here is the translation you requested, Frau Linder. I believe that it will prove suitable. However," he pulled the page back with a bit of a smile as she reached for it, "I have decided I do have a price for this after all."

Marla looked at him with a small frown, wondering what he was after. "Very well, Herr Logau. State your price, if you will."

"I have three nonnegotiable demands. First, that you call me Friedrich. Logau sounds so stuffy, so . . . so pompous."

Marla smiled at that. "I can do that. Second?"

"I want to be with you when you first practice this, to hear it in case I need to change something. The words flow well on the paper, but that does not mean they will do so when mated with the melody."

"Agreed. And third?"

Logau gave her what could only be called an evil smile. "I want to be there when you sing this in public the first time."

Marla heard Franz chuckling behind her as she returned smile for smile. She held out her hand. "Agreed and done."

They shook hands, then she looped her hands through both men's arms. "Come with us, Friedrich. I have to make a stop at the telegraph office, then we'll go christen your words appropriately."

They strode off down the street with Marla humming "We're Off to See the Wizard." Neither man understood why she started laughing after a few measures.

Chapter 19

— A T & L TELEGRAPH —

BEGIN: MBRG TO GVL

TO: HEATHER MASON

ADDR: TROMMLER RECORDS

FROM: MARLA LINDER

DATE: 18 DEC 1635

MESSAGE:

HAVE A ONE SONG SPECIAL YOU REALLY OUGHT
TO BUY UP STOP WILL EITHER WRECK MY CAREER
OR TOP THE CHARTS STOP ATWOOD COCHRAN
WILL RECORD STOP YOU IN OR OUT STOP

MARLA

END

— A T & L TELEGRAPH —

BEGIN: MBRG TO GVL

TO: ATWOOD COCHRAN

ADDR: LOOK IT UP

FROM: MARLA LINDER

DATE: 18 DEC 1635

MESSAGE:

YEAH THIS IS ONE GOOD CAUSE STOP PITCHED
DEAL TO HEATHER AT TROMMLER STOP
EXPECT THEY WILL BUY STOP RECORDING DATE
SATURDAY JAN 19 STOP THIS WILL BE THUMB
IN THE EYE OF THE POWERS THAT BE STOP
YOU IN OR OUT STOP

MARLA

END

Marla looked at the two telegrams the delivery boy had just left with her, and smiled.

The first one read:

— A T & L TELEGRAPH —

BEGIN: GVL TO MBRG

TO: FRAU MARLA LINDER

ADDR: SYLWESTERHAUS MAGDEBURG

FROM: ATWOOD COCHRAN

DATE: 19 DEC 1635

MESSAGE:

CANT PASS UP CHANCE TO JAB THUMB IN EYE
STOP IN STOP WILL TAKE CUT OF TROMMLER
DEAL STOP

ATWOOD

END

And the second:

— A T & L TELEGRAPH —

BEGIN: GVL TO MBRG

TO: FRAU MARLA LINDER

ADDR: SYLWESTERHAUS MAGDEBURG

FROM: HM AT TROMMLER RECORDS

DATE: 19 DEC 1635

MESSAGE:

WE ARE IN STOP SEND DETAILS ASAP FOR
CONTRACT STOP

HEATHER

END

Marla looked up at her husband.

"You are really going to do this." Franz didn't ask a question. He knew who he was talking to; he made a statement.

"Uh-huh." She wrapped her arms around herself. She felt cold all of a sudden.

Franz said nothing more, but wrapped his own arms around her. She nestled in his embrace, and drew strength from him.

Part Two

January 1636

For changing people's manners and altering their customs
there is nothing better than music.
—Shu Ching

Chapter 20

A new pattern had settled in Simon's life. He arose each morning with Hans. They would share with Ursula whatever food was in the rooms, and then Hans would leave for his work at the grain factorage. True to his word, he had asked about work for Simon, but as with so many other places, there was no opportunity for a one-handed youth.

Simon would sweep the floor and clean up after their eating, wiping the plates off and stacking them in the little cupboard that stood in the corner. Then he would settle on his stool at Ursula's feet. She would pick up her worn Bible and read to him for a little while. Always it was something interesting, but Simon best liked the stories of the heroes from the Old Testament: King David, Joshua, the stories of the judges. Then they would talk about what she had read, wondering why the hero had done certain things and not done others, describing what they thought the characters in the stories looked like, sometimes laughing together over something silly one of them had said.

Ursula would always end the reading time by closing her Bible and putting it away, then picking up her current embroidery project. That would be the signal to Simon to go out and find what work he could.

✧　　✧　　✧

It was a Tuesday morning after the first of the year when Ursula all of a sudden noticed something that had always been in front of her.

"Simon, are those the only clothes you have?"

He ducked his head, feeling a sense of shame.

"Well, we cannot have that. Hans..." She turned to her brother, "Hans, Simon needs clothes. His shirt is almost cobwebby thin, his pants are tight and torn and much too short, his jacket does not fit around him. Tell your crew boss today that you have to take me to market tomorrow."

Simon discovered that although Ursula was normally the most agreeable of souls, when she chose to exert her will it was like encountering granite. It astonished him to see Hans, *Stark* Hans himself, nod his head and say, "Yes, Ursula," as if it was the most ordinary thing in the world for her to issue commands.

And on Wednesday, the world ordered itself to Ursula's intent. After they had eaten, she retired for a moment to her bedroom, then returned with a large bonnet on her head and wearing a coat over her dress. She stood lopsided and held her arms up in what was almost an imperious manner. Hans said nothing as he stepped up to her. There was a swirl of movement, then she was in his arms, one arm across his shoulders, the other holding her cane.

"Come along, Simon," she directed.

Simon started when Hans nodded at the door but stepped forward to open it. Hans moved through the doorway sideways, being most careful not to bump Ursula into the doorframe. When he started down the stairs, Simon came behind, closing the door with a loud thump. He clattered down the stairs, wooden shoes banging on the treads, and caught up with them at the bottom.

"Where to, Uschi?" Hans asked.

"Frau Anna's first. After that, we will see."

So Hans took off down the street, Simon following close behind. Before long, he was marveling at his friend's strength. He had seen men pick other people up before, but never for very long, and never when walking down the street, block after block. "*Stark* Hans, nothing," he muttered. "He should be called *Eisen* Hans." And indeed Hans seemed made of iron. There was no droop to his shoulders, no sagging of his arms. He carried Ursula as if she was only the weight of a feather.

"What did you say, Simon?" Hans called over his shoulder.

"Nothing."

Otto Gericke's rules for markets in Greater Magdeburg were considered liberal by the conservative bürgermeisters of Old Magdeburg. Due to the size of the population, markets were allowed three days a week, and were allowed in more than one location, such that after a while the various vendors started grouping together.

It wasn't long today before Ursula and her entourage arrived in the area of town favored by the sellers of secondhand clothing. It was one of Simon's favorite parts of town. People there would talk to him freely, and sometimes send him on errands.

Hans walked up to one particular cart and gently set Ursula's feet to the ground in front of it. His sister straightened herself as best she could, adjusted her coat, and faced the proprietress.

"Frau Anna," she said with a nod.

"Fraulein Ursula," came the response from what had to be the oldest woman Simon had ever seen. Under her scarf her hair was pure white, the skin of her broad face sagged in a very tapestry of wrinkles, and there did not appear to be a tooth in her head. But she stood straight and her alert eyes gleamed from their nests of wrinkles like those of a cuckoo. She also had a hearty chuckle, which sounded at the next moment.

"It's not that I'm not glad to see you, *Liebling*, but I wonder what has brought you to old Anna on this blustery day?" Simon had some trouble understanding her.

"Simon." Ursula beckoned with her free hand. He stepped around Hans to where she could lay her hand on his shoulder. "The boy needs clothes. Two shirts, two pants, two hose, a jacket that fits, and a coat."

Frau Anna looked Simon up and down. He straightened under her examination. "A scamp of a lad, I imagine he is." She chuckled again, reached out a wrinkled hand and patted his cheek. He bore the soft touch without flinching, he was proud to note. "Well enough, let me see what I have."

The old woman turned to her cart. Simon detected no rhyme or reason to the arrangement of the piles of clothes on the cart, but Anna's hands dove into the piles like otters into a river, surfacing every now and then to drape a bundle of cloth over the cart handles. One last time they appeared, and she began handing garments to Ursula.

"Simon," Ursula said again and pulled him around in front of her. He stood, bewildered, as she held shirts up against his back and shoulders and pants up against his waist, bending to see where they fell to. The two women muttered to each other, and Anna dove back into the cart to pull out yet another shirt. Ursula examined it with care, then nodded her approval.

Anna had a jacket for him as well, but when it came to a coat anywhere close to his size, she had nothing that a man would wear. "Sorry, *Liebling*, but I sold the last one I had not an hour before you came. But you might go down the way to old Herman's cart. He had some the last time I saw him. Just look them over good."

The old woman smiled, and just for a moment Simon got a glimpse of what she must have been like as a girl. That surprised him. He'd never thought before that old people had to have been his age upon a time.

"So how much?" Ursula asked. This commenced the bargaining over his new clothes. Simon listened, awe-struck, as the two women chaffered back and forth, eventually arriving at a sum that almost made him choke. It didn't seem to bother Hans, though, when Ursula waved at him. He stepped up, pulled a handful of money from his pocket, and counted a paper bill and a pfennig and bits of broken coins until Frau Anna was satisfied.

Frau Anna folded the clothes together, then tied the bundle with a bit of twine. She held it out to Simon. It took him a moment to realize that he was supposed to take it; he had never had a package of his own to carry.

Ursula said her farewells, then turned and limped down the street, Hans at her side. Simon followed behind, as usual, and noticed as he did so that Hans was very careful not to actually grab Ursula or hold her while she was walking but still managed to be close enough to provide instant support if she needed it.

Their progress was slow, but others would make way for them. Simon suspected this had more to do with Hans glowering at people than it did people giving way out of courtesy for Ursula's infirmity. He knew that if Hans had glowered at him, he would certainly have moved out of the way.

Ursula walked with her head held high, moving with an odd grace, despite her limp. They passed one vendor after another, from cart to ramshackle booth to oilskin laid on the ground.

Several of the vendors would speak to Hans or his sister. A few nodded to Simon as well.

They stopped in front of another cart. Simon assumed this must be old Herman's.

"Fraulein Metzgerin," a man stepped up and gave a short bow. "Herr Metzger." Hans nodded in return. Simon was ignored for the moment, which was just fine with him.

Old Herman did not look so old, at least not when he was compared with Frau Anna. His bushy beard and the hair that stuck out like a fringe from under his small hat were iron gray rather than snow white. His face wasn't as cross-hatched with wrinkles as the old woman's was; instead it bore deep furrows and seams. When his mouth opened, there were teeth present; not a lot, mind you, but still teeth peeped out from behind his lips. He was of middling height and of solid build despite his age.

"A coat," Herman said after Ursula had made known the object of their quest. He peered at Simon and beckoned him to come closer. "Hmm, yes, a coat for this lad. Have I seen you around here, boy?"

"Maybe," Simon muttered.

"Ah, well, with my memory I would not remember from one day to the next." Herman nodded several times with vigor, then started. "A coat. Yes, indeed, a coat." He turned and began rummaging through the piles on his cart. "No, not that one...nor that one, either...tch, definitely not that one..." Simon smiled as the old man kept up a running commentary. "Hmm...this one?" Herman held it up and stared at it, then tossed it back in the cart. "No. Keep looking."

After a few more minutes of searching accompanied by monologue, Herman pulled an item out of the bottom of the pile. "Aha! You just thought you would escape me." He shook it out, and it took form as a faded green coat of a size to perhaps fit Simon.

Ursula took the coat and examined it, checking the material and the seams. It passed her grudging judgment, so she held it out to Simon. "Here, try this on. Let's see how it fits."

Hans reached over and took the bundle of clothes from Simon, leaving him free to try the coat on. It took a few moments to get into it; sliding his right arm down the sleeve was a bit of a challenge, but with help from Hans to hold the front of the coat open he managed. He turned and faced Ursula.

"Mm-hmm." She touched a finger to her lips as she studied him, and reached out to adjust the lapels on the front of the coat so it would hang straight. A definite nod. "I think it will do. It is a bit large, but that leaves room for growing. Not a bad thing with a boy, I am told." She turned to Herman. "How much?"

Again the bargaining, again the back and forth, again ending in Hans pulling money from his pocket and counting it out. Simon's head was beginning to spin. How much money they had spent, just on him! He had never dreamed of that happening. He smoothed his hand down the front of the coat, feeling the warmth it gave him.

Ursula turned from accepting Herman's farewell, craned her head and looked around.

"What are you looking for?" Hans asked.

"Something...yes, over there." She pointed and led the way, stopping in front of a trestle with pairs of shoes on it. The woman who was there was tall and stooped, with hollowed cheeks and sunken eyes. She didn't look healthy to Simon, and after she gave a rheumy cough he edged away from the table.

"You need shoes, mistress?" the woman asked.

"For the boy," Ursula replied. Her gaze wandered over the table of secondhand footwear and finally lit on a pair of half-boots. "Hans," she said, putting her hand out to touch them, "measure these against Simon's foot."

The bundle of clothes got passed to Ursula while Hans picked a boot up, stepped around behind Simon and pulled his foot up to measure against the sole of the boot. Simon had to wave his arm wildly to maintain his balance while this was going on. He sighed with relief and shoved his foot back into its clog when Hans let go.

"They are a bit large, but I think they will do."

Ursula nodded and passed the clothing bundle back to Simon. "As with the coat, that is probably not a bad thing for a boy his age. He might actually wear them out before he outgrows them."

One more round of bargaining ensued, perhaps cut short by the woman's persistent cough. Hans hung the boots around Simon's neck and flashed a grin of triumph and congratulations at him. Simon was absolutely jubilant. Shoes! Real leather shoes, not clogs. He couldn't ever remember having leather shoes. He reached up to touch them, and managed to get a finger on them without dropping the bundle. He knew there was a silly grin on his own face, but he couldn't help it. *Shoes.*

Ursula turned to Hans. "We are done here, I think. Can we go someplace to sit and eat?" Simon thought it odd how her voice had gone all soft after being so firm earlier in the day.

Hans nodded and picked her up again. He gave her a moment to settle herself, then looked over to Simon, who was just enjoying the thought of his new belongings. "Do you know where the Green Horse is from here, lad?"

Simon thought for a moment, then nodded. "Yah. That way," he made an abortive move with his hand, but the package dragged it down.

"Lead the way, then."

Filled with joy and pride, Simon did lead the way, unerring in his path, arriving at the door to the tavern before much more of the day had passed. Hans set Ursula on her feet with his usual care, she settled her skirts, and they entered the tavern together

It was the middle of what was shaping up to be a very long day for his partner and himself, Gotthilf decided. They had made the rounds of their informants once again—nothing new there, not even from Demetrious. They checked with the patrol watchmen who had been keeping a particular eye on the warehouse of Andreas Schardius' corn factorage—nothing out of the very ordinary reported. They talked to the other investigators who had questioned the workmen who labored in that warehouse. Nothing at all noted.

"Three strikes and we're out," Byron muttered as they walked back toward the police house.

"I don't know," Gotthilf replied, thinking back over everything they had heard. One thing stuck out to him. "It strikes me that the answers of the warehousemen seemed to be uniform to an unlikely degree."

Byron gave a slow nod. "Yeah, now that you mention it, it did seem like they all gave more or less the same answers to the questions."

"That, and not a single word spoken against their work bosses or Schardius himself."

"Too right that's odd. Never met a workman yet who didn't have some kind of gripe against the men he worked for. It's like someone passed the word to watch what they said."

Their steps had wended their way toward the Green Horse in the new town. Gotthilf looked up and almost stumbled. "Byron, that's Metzger going in to the tavern."

Byron gave a sharp grin. "So it is, and that's the boy that was with him that night at the fights. Don't know the woman, though."

Gotthilf decided this was an opportunity for observation. He grinned back. "It's about time we had something to eat, right?"

"By all means, partner," Byron replied. "Let's duck into the tavern and grab a bite."

And so they did.

Simon opened his mouth to say something about the *Polizei* men coming in the door, but Hans looked at him from under lowered eyebrows, so he closed his mouth without saying anything. The three of them proceeded to have what Simon found to be a very pleasant luncheon. He finally sat back, unable to eat any more. Hans looked over at him and winked. "A good day, eh, lad?"

Simon nodded with another silly grin.

The three of them sat there for a while, just idly talking about various things that crossed their minds—usually whatever crossed Ursula's mind. Simon didn't say much, but his hand would reach up every few minutes and touch his new boots, which action would be followed by another smile.

The pleasantness came to an end for Simon when the two detectives finished their last flagons of ale, stood, and came toward their table. Hans looked at him again, so Simon didn't say anything. But he did shrink away from them a little. He couldn't help it. Men like that usually caused him problems.

"Good day to you, Herr Metzger." That was the up-timer speaking. "And to you, too, lad. I don't think I heard your name when we met the other night."

Simon had to clear his throat twice before he could answer. "S-Simon Bayer, sir."

The up-timer nodded, then looked back at Hans. The down-timer, however, was looking at Ursula. Simon startled to bristle, but Hans' hand grabbed his leg under the table, and he settled back.

"Good day, Lieutenant Chieske, Sergeant Hoch." Hans' voice sounded pleasant to Simon's ear, although the firmness of the grip on his thigh told him that Hans was not especially pleased by this encounter.

"And a good day to you as well, fraulein..." That was the down-timer sergeant. Simon startled to bristle again, only to feel Hans' fingers clamp almost to the bone on his thigh.

"Metzger," Hans growled. "My sister, Ursula Metzgerin."

Lieutenant Chieske nodded politely to her, but Sergeant Hoch stepped forward, gently lifted her hand where it lay on the table, and bowed over it, almost but not quite drawing it to his lips. "A pleasure, fraulein." He straightened with a pleasant smile on his face.

Simon bit the inside of his cheek to keep from gasping as Hans bore down on his leg. He'd have bruises in the morning, that was certain.

The sergeant stepped back, and Simon gave a sigh of relief as Hans released his leg.

"Just so you'll know, Herr Metzger," the lieutenant said, "we're looking into some odd events that have occurred near the river in the last couple of months."

Hans grunted.

"If you happen to think of anything unusual you've seen or heard, you might let us know."

Hans grunted again. Simon saw the lieutenant's mouth twitch a bit.

"Well, we've got to get back to work. Enjoy the rest of the day Herr Metzger, fraulein, Simon." The sergeant started when his partner tapped him on the shoulder. They both nodded, then turned away. Simon looked to see Hans following their departure with a hard-set mouth and narrowed eyes.

"A nice man, that Sergeant Hoch," Ursula said with a bit of a smile. "The other one was a bit brusque, though."

Hans grunted. Simon looked to him, then said to Ursula, "He is an up-timer. They are all a bit odd; some more than others."

"Ah. An up-timer. I see." Ursula looked toward the door. "Do you know, I think that is the first up-timer I have met?"

"And please God, it will be the last," Hans muttered. "They are nothing but trouble."

Simon had no reply to the last statement.

The whole encounter had cast a pall over the afternoon. They soon arose to return to their rooms.

"What was that all about?" Byron asked, disturbing Gotthilf's thoughts.

"What was what all about?"

"You made a big deal over Fraulein Metzgerin back there," the up-timer pointed out. "You don't normally do that. So what was it all about?"

"Two things," Gotthilf answered distractedly. "First, it occurred to me that leaving her with a positive memory of us might be to our advantage. And second, I think I've met her before, or at least seen her . . . but I cannot remember where or when."

He staggered a bit when he was unexpectedly clapped on the shoulder by his partner. "Ah, you'll remember it sooner or later," Byron said. "You always do."

Gotthilf hoped so. This was like having an itch in the middle of his back—he couldn't reach it.

The rest of the day passed in a fog for Simon. He knew they had to have returned home, because he woke in his usual place the next morning. He knew he had to have changed clothes, because he was wearing some of the new clothing. He knew that he had to have gone to Frau Zenzi's and swept, because a loaf of her bread was on the table. But all he could remember was the sheer joy of having new-to-him clothes. And shoes. Especially the shoes.

Chapter 21

"Good morning, Frau Simpson," the man waiting in her parlor said as Mary Simpson entered the room. She made a lightning assessment with a single glance, a skill that had served her well since early in her days in Pittsburgh. The man was of middling height, middling years, middling size, dressed well but not with ostentation.

"Good morning, Herr Schardius," Mary responded. She waved to a chair opposite the small settee she preferred for her seat. "Please, sit with me. Coffee will be here in a moment." She could hear Hilde coming down the hall with the tray.

Hilde entered the room and set the silver coffee service on the low table in the center of the seats. Then, after looking to Mary for direction, retreated to a corner.

Mary leaned forward, poured the coffee, and offered a cup to her visitor. "What can I do for you, Master Schardius?"

"Perhaps it is more what I can do for you, Frau Simpson." He took a sip from his cup, smiled, and leaned back in his chair. "I understand from some of my friends and associates that you, or rather, the Royal and Imperial Arts Council, intend to produce a new opera soon."

"As it happens, your friends and associates are correct; we will be staging a new opera entitled *Arthur Rex*." Mary set her own cup down and steepled her fingers below her chin. "*Kappellmeister*

Schütz is writing it even now. He says he will be done soon, so we are preparing for the production."

"Good." Schardius looked into his cup for a moment. "I am here to offer to underwrite a portion of the production. I appreciate great music. I spent some time in Venice a few years ago, you see, where I was able to hear Monteverdi's works in the Cathedral, and occasionally at some noble's house. I even managed to hear the first performance of *Il Combattimento di Tancredi e Clorinda*."

Mary was impressed despite herself. "I envy you that, Master Schardius."

He shrugged. "It was good, and it certainly instilled in me a hunger to hear music of that scale. It is a hunger that, until recently, has mostly gone unfed." Mary raised her eyebrows, and Schardius nodded. "Yes, the music that has been presented during the last two years by your band of musicians from and through Grantville—that has fed the hunger, yet at the same time heightened it. I have seen almost every performance, great and small, and I want more, both in amount and in kind. So here I am, willing to pay for what will feed my insatiable appetite." Another shrug. "Business has been good, this year."

"And what do you want for your support, Master Schardius?"

His eyebrows rose for a moment, and his head tilted a bit, as if he were considering her seriously for the first time. After a moment, his expression evened itself out again, but for the sharp glitter in his eyes.

"As I said," Schardius replied, "I am hungry and thirsty for great music, so I would expect to be allowed to observe rehearsals."

"I think not," Mary said. "The director would never stand for it."

"Twenty percent," Schardius offered.

Mary shook her head.

"Twenty-five."

"No."

"Thirty percent," Schardius said, and a hard tone had entered his voice for the first time.

God, Mary thought, *he's serious about this. And I can't afford to lose that much revenue. Surely Amber will understand that.*

"You will not sit on the stage or in the wings," Mary said as gracefully as she could. "Only in the audience seats or one of the boxes."

"Agreed."

"And you will not interfere with the director, or her instructions to the cast."

"I wouldn't dream of doing so. I simply wish the pleasure of observing. I think we are witnessing a new moment in the arts."

Mary could hardly quarrel with that, since she thought the same herself. No one in Europe, not even in Italy, has ever seen the sort of opera—*grand opera*, it was rightly called—that was about to be performed in Magdeburg.

"Very good, Master Schardius, we will accept your generous offer." She stood and held her hand out.

He came to his feet, and took her hand in his. "Have your man of business send an accounting of what is needed to my office at the Schardius corn factorage and warehouse. I will send the money as soon as I can after I look it over."

"Thank you." Mary thought that he might be a bit surprised when it turned out that her "man of business" was Lady Beth Haygood.

"And with that, I must return to my office. Today promises to be a busy one for me, but I did want to speak with you today." Schardius turned away, then turned back. "Oh, will Frau Linder be one of the singers in the opera?"

"Well, casting has not been done yet," she said, "but I would be very surprised if she isn't."

"Splendid!" Schardius said.

Mary smiled in return. She had long experience with patrons of the arts. Even the most hard-bitten businessmen and financiers could turn into fanboys when presented with attractive female performers. Occasionally that could become a bit of a problem, but it was usually harmless enough. And there was no denying that such enthusiasms tended to open wallets still wider.

She rose to her feet. "Hilde, show Master Schardius out, please."

Simon was developing a reputation as a reliable messenger and delivery boy. His new clothes made him a bit more presentable in the eyes of the businessmen of Greater Magdeburg, and he found himself in some demand. Even so, he never neglected Frau Zenzi. Every day he would appear at the bakery's door not long before sundown to do the sweeping.

One day the door to the bakery opened just as Simon was reaching for the handle, and he looked up to see two familiar figures coming out of the bakery. Startled, he hesitated for a moment, then stepped down and to one side. They came down the steps and turned to face him.

"I know you," the short one said—Sergeant Hoch, Simon reminded himself. "You're Hans Metzger's young friend, aren't you? I've seen you at the fights."

Simon fought the urge to duck and straightened instead. "Yes, Sergeant. Hans calls me his luck, so I go with him to all the fights."

"You must be good luck," Lieutenant Chieske laughed, "because I haven't seen him lose yet."

"And you won't," Simon replied fiercely. "Hans is the best."

Both men nodded. "He is indeed," Sergeant Hoch said.

"Tell me your name again, boy," the tall up-timer said.

"Simon. Simon Bayer."

"Well, Simon, no fighter stays on top forever. There comes a time where, if nothing else, age will slow him down. There's always someone younger, faster, stronger, just waiting for that to happen."

"Did you have fights in the up-time?" Simon asked, intrigued.

"Oh, yes. And they were a big deal, too. Men would fight at the town and state level, men would fight at the national level, men from different countries would even fight at the world level," the up-timer said. "Todd Pierpoint used to fight when he was young, back before the Ring of Fire." Lieutenant Chieske grinned. "Even Mike Stearns used to fight professionally."

Now Simon was really surprised. "The prime minister used to be a fighter?"

"Former prime minister," the up-timer corrected. "And yes, he did, until like I said, he ran into a man who was younger and faster. He might not have been stronger, but he was younger and faster, and according to Mike, he just about took Mike's head off."

"Huh." Simon thought about that. A man who called Emperor Gustavus by his first name used to fight like Hans did. His mind swung in circles as he tried to grasp that. "Was he a world fighter?"

"No!" Chieske laughed. "Mike was never *that* good. But even now, when I'm sure he's slowed a step or two, I wouldn't want to face him. The point is, your friend Hans won't always be able to fight like this. There will come a time when, even if he doesn't lose, he starts getting hurt. That will be the time when his friends

will need to talk him out of fighting. Friends like you, maybe."
The up-timer gave Simon a sobering look.

Simon didn't want to think like that. He wanted to think that
Hans would always win, would always come out of his fights
with barely a mark on him. But Lieutenant Chieske's words
crawled into his mind, settled in the back of it and wouldn't
leave. He looked away, then made himself look back to the
policemen and nod.

Faint expressions of surprise and respect crossed their faces,
and they nodded in return as if to an equal. With that, they
took their leave.

Simon looked at their backs, disquieted. After they rounded
the corner, he turned and went into the bakery. He said nothing,
just went to where the broom was stored and started sweeping.
A few minutes later, Frau Zenzi came into the room.

"Oh, good, Simon, you're here. I didn't hear you come in."

"Yah. I came in after the policemen left." He continued sweeping while he talked. "Frau Zenzi?"

"Yes?"

"Do you know those two policemen?"

"Oh, yes, for some time now."

"Are they good men?"

Frau Zenzi stopped what she was doing and straightened up.
"Yes, they are. They saved my Willi." Willi was the blind boy
that Zenzi and her husband had adopted several weeks ago. He
usually worked in the back of the bakery. Simon remembered
some kind of to-do over his coming to them, but none of the
details would come to mind. "They protected him and brought
him to me. They come often to see Willi. They are good men,
for all that one of them is an up-timer and the other one is the
son of a patrician family." Her voice was rock solid, so much so
that you could have used her statement for a foundation stone.
"Why do you ask?"

"Oh, no reason," Simon replied. "It's just that they keep coming
around my friend Hans, and I cannot figure out why."

"Hans. Is he the man that meets you outside the shop some
nights?" Her tone was disapproving.

"Uh-huh." Simon kept his head down as he swept.

"Simon, he looks to be a hard man, one who knows things
and people that you should not know."

He stopped and looked her in the eye. "He is not like that, Frau Zenzi. He is a good man. He has a job and he works hard at it. He's got a crippled sister at home that he takes care of. He takes care of me, too. He is not an evil man, or wicked."

Zenzi's expression was still doubtful. "If you say so, Simon. But mind you, if you ever need someplace to come, if trouble comes, you come to me."

Simon ducked his head again. "Yes, Frau Zenzi."

She stared at him a while longer while he swept, then left the room. When he was done and had put the broom away, she gave him a loaf of bread, tilted her head with a wry expression, and patted him on the shoulder without a word. He left the bakery wondering what that was all about.

Byron looked down at his partner. "Any chance the boy could tell us anything?"

"Could, maybe," Gotthilf replied. "That's if he knows anything at all. He appears to be a recent acquaintance for Metzger, after all, and why would Metzger tell a young boy like that anything? But if the boy does know something, whether he would say anything or not is another matter. He seems to be very attached to Metzger, and I doubt he would say anything without talking to him first."

"Okay." They walked along in silence, eyes moving this way and that, watching the street around them. "But we've got to get a break somewhere. If we don't find a lead soon, the captain's going to tell us to move on to another case."

"Yah."

Chapter 22

Logau cursed as he trotted down the street, feet crunching on the gravel, one hand holding his hat on his head and the other grasping his walking stick. He was supposed to have met with Frau Marla and her friends a quarter-hour ago, and he was late. It was his own fault, too. If he hadn't started doodling with another epigram, he would have been there in plenty of time. Of course there wasn't a cab for hire within sight. And he'd come away from his rooms with his evening walking stick, instead of his morning walking stick.

Some days the world just conspired against him, he was sure of it.

He was headed for the Royal Academy of Music, which was located across a plaza from the new opera house in the southwest corner of the Neustadt section of Old Magdeburg. Rather than take one of the narrow bridges across the Big Ditch into the Altstadt, then have to cross it again to get to the Neustadt, he turned north on the boulevard that paralleled the canal and followed it, dodging women waving broadsheets and newspapers for sale, wagons, carts, drays, animals and swearing teamsters alike until he got to the crossroad that ran through a gate in the rebuilt city walls into the Neustadt.

Once he was through the gate Logau slowed to a fast walk. It would not do to arrive at the rehearsal out of breath, after all.

He adjusted his jacket, flicked a bit of lint from his lapel, and tilted his hat to its proper angle just as he reached the steps to the academy.

Inside the building, not having a clue where he was to go, he stopped a student. "Can you tell me where to find Room Six?" he asked.

"Down this hall, turn right at the first cross-corridor, then about halfway down it on the left," the young woman replied.

"My thanks. I'm to meet Frau Linder there."

"In that case," the student laughed, "just follow your ears after you turn the corner. She's already in full voice."

Logau touched his walking stick to the brim of his hat in acknowledgment, and the young woman dropped a curtsey before scurrying on her way. He made his way to the designated corridor and rounded the corner. No sooner had he done so than he realized why the young woman had laughed. The unmistakable sound of Frau Linder's voice filled the hallway, even though the door to Room VI was shut. "They need to invent a way to deaden the sound," he muttered to himself.

He knocked on the door just as the singing stopped. A moment later, the door was opened by a young man Logau didn't recognize. "Ah, Friedrich, you're here," Frau Linder said. "Let Herr Logau in, Rudolf. He's playing a part in this." The young man stepped aside, and Logau entered the room, doffing his hat as he did so. There was a table conveniently by the door already burdened by coats, so he laid his hat atop the pile. He unbuttoned his coat, but left it on, as he was still feeling the chill from his brisk walk.

Marla came and took him by the arm. "Everyone, this is Friedrich von Logau, writer, poet, and epigrammist. He's the wordsmith who gave us the German words for this song. Friedrich, let me introduce you to the guys."

Friedrich paid close attention as Marla introduced the men in the room: the brothers Tuchman, Rudolf and Josef, who smiled and nodded; Thomas Schwartzberg, tall and lanky, who gave an easy grin; Hermann Katzberg, short enough to almost be a dwarf; Isaac Fremdling, dark and intense, standing with arms crossed; Paul Georg Seiler, dour but still giving a nod; and three of the Amsel brothers, Matthäus, Marcus and Johann, alike as three sons of the same parents could be, with only the difference in their years providing any solid clue as to which was which.

These were the men in Marla Linder and Franz Sylwester's inner circle. He noted them and made sure he knew the names and faces. These were the men who had come to Magdeburg and coalesced into a nucleus of musicians around which the new music seemed to pour out like water from a fountain. It behooved him to know them, and know them well.

"My thanks to you all," he responded to the introductions. "I am here to simply see how my words fit with the music. Do not let me stop or interfere with anything." He looked around for a chair, but saw they were all occupied. There was only a stool in one corner. He strode over and took a seat, resting his chin on his clasped hands atop his walking stick.

For the next half hour he was a silent witness to a master at work. The Amsels and Paul Georg Seiler were also just observers, but the others played the music, three violins, two flutes, and a harp. Marla worked with them as separate groups first: beating time; leading them to phrase certain notes together; adjusting the tempo here, the volume there; cajoling, urging, driving them to achieve a fusion of sound. Friedrich noticed that both Franz and Matthäus Amsel were making notes along the way.

At the end of the half hour, Marla brushed an errant strand of hair out of her face, looked at them all, and said, "All right, let's try it together. English first."

She stepped to one side and Franz stepped forward. "One, two, three," he counted. The three violinists began, playing unison notes, low-pitched and regular on the beat. At the end of the second measure, Marla opened her mouth.

"Do you hear the people sing..."

Logau sat, transfixed. He almost forgot to breathe. God above, the woman's voice was like nothing he had ever heard. He had heard her sing from a distance once, but to be in this room, to sit almost within arm's reach of her, and to hear her sing so... so indescribably. For once, he, the man of words, had no words at hand that could describe such a sensation.

The song was short, and all too soon Marla's voice ceased sounding. Logau twitched and sat up straight, taking a deep breath.

"Good," Marla said matter-of-factly. "We'll work the parts some more later, but that was good. Now with the German words, so Herr Logau—Friedrich—can hear his work and judge its fitness. From the top, gentlemen."

Again Franz gave the count; again the violins began the low rhythmic pulsing. Again Marla's lips opened, and beauty poured forth.

Logau forced himself to ignore the siren song of Marla's voice and concentrate on the words. Image followed image: angry men singing, men who would no longer be slaves, men responding to the sound of the drums, all for the sake of tomorrow. Then came the verse calling these men to stand forth and be a part of reaching that future.

The chorus of angry men sounded again. It was followed by the second verse calling men to sacrifice and martyrdom. And then the chorus again, the final time, flutes skirling and violins somehow evoking martial airs.

The last line rang out, and the song again came to a close. Logau closed his eyes for a moment, calming his heart. He opened them again, to find the gaze of all the others fixed on him.

He licked his lips, for a moment uncertain. "Frau Marla, are you sure..." He cleared his throat and tried again. "Are you certain you want to sing this song, now, the way things are?"

"Now, yes, by all means now," Marla replied forcefully. "This song was made for this time. I will stand before the face of the chancellor and throw this in his teeth if I must. Just watch me."

Logau looked around the room, suddenly aware that he was an alien in this group. Thomas and Hermann echoed Marla's smile. The others, even Johann Amsel, who was not much more than a youth, wore hard-eyed expressions. He was struck by the resemblance to a painting he had once seen of Alexander the Great surrounded by his captains. He saw in this room that same edge, that same ferocity, that same obdurate hardness that was in the faces of the captains in that picture. Being on the receiving end of those stares was not a comfortable sensation.

He stood, gave a slight bow to Marla, and addressed her formally. "As you will, Frau Linder." He was not astonished to hear that his voice was a bit unsteady. He stepped to the table and collected his hat, then turned to face them all again. "And do you know when you will unleash this upon an unsuspecting world?"

Marla's face softened, the smile slipping away. "On January 19th, at the Green Horse Tavern."

Logau gave a final nod. "I will be there." He settled his hat on his head, touched his walking stick to the brim. "Good day to you, Frau Linder, *meine Herren.*"

After the door closed behind Logau, Marla sighed and looked around. "That's all for today, guys. Can we meet at our house in two days?"

There were murmurs of assent as the others cased instruments and gathered coats. They left quietly, leaving Marla standing with Franz. He set his violin on the table and came and stood behind her, wrapping his arms around her beneath her chin and resting his hands on the opposite shoulders. She leaned back against him, drained, almost exhausted, and pressed her hands against her face for a moment. "Am I crazy to be doing this?" She dropped her hands and turned in his embrace to rest her head on his shoulder. "God, Franz, I..." Her voice broke, and she could feel tears forming in her eyes.

"Shh, shh," Franz said. His hand rose to cup the back of her head, beneath the rubber band that was holding her ponytail. "If you feel it needs to be done, then it is not a crazy thing."

"It's just that...I don't know...I never cared about politics in my whole life, but what the chancellor wants to do...that world would kill me. I couldn't live in it. And it would kill my babies. I've already lost Alison. I can't...I can't..." Marla gulped.

"Shh," Franz said again. His embrace strengthened, until she felt for a moment as if she were held in oak. "It is enough that you feel this must be done. We will do it; for you, and for Alison's memory."

Chapter 23

Ciclope walked up to the gate at the construction site. "You looking to hire anybody?" he asked the burly man standing there with a clipboard in hand and a shallow helmet on his head.

"Might be. You have any special skills?" The burly man spoke in a gravelly voice without looking up.

"I am strong, I can use a shovel or a pick, and I have laid a course or two of stone in my day."

"We will be laying brick. It is not the same."

Ciclope shrugged. "I can learn."

The man looked him over, seeming to pay more attention to his hands than anything. He looked back to his clipboard as he jerked his thumb over his shoulder. "Go see Heinrich, the mason boss. He should be over by the brick supply in the northeast corner. Tell him I said to give you a try."

"And you are?"

The man looked up again. "I'm Leonhart Kolman, head crew boss for Schiffer Construction. Remember that name."

"Got it." Ciclope nodded.

Kolman focused on the clipboard and jerked his thumb again. "Get moving."

Ciclope got. Once he was through the gate and past the crew boss, he slowed his pace and looked around. Pietro had hired on two days earlier as a general laborer, and had spent last night describing the layout of the construction site to him. Right: brick pile to the northeast, sand for mortar to the southeast, lumber pile to the northwest, and the excavation site to the southwest. Lots of men hurrying across the site in different directions. And that derrick pointing up to the sky swinging a cable with a load of barrels hanging from it must be the steam crane.

The arsenal masters in Venice must be rubbing their hands at the thought of getting one of those, he thought to himself. Whether the arsenal workers would accept it was another question.

Ahead he could see a group of men gathered together by the great mound of bricks on pallets. One was talking and gesticulating, the others were gathered around him. That was probably the mason boss.

Ciclope squared his shoulders and headed for him. He needed to convince the man to keep him on, or he and his partner would have a much harder time figuring out where to do their sabotage.

Maybe those months he spent apprenticed to that sot of a mason in Dresden all those years ago would come in handy after all.

Every day after he swept at Frau Zenzi's, Simon would give a scrap of food to Schatzi. Most nights he would then go back to the rooms and spend the time nibbling on whatever food was on the table that night while Hans and Ursula talked, or while Ursula would read the Bible aloud to them.

But on some nights, perhaps every fortnight or so, Hans would meet him when he was done and they would go to the bear pit. The quality of Hans' opponents did improve somewhat, but no one that Simon had seen gave the hard man a real challenge.

Tonight was one of those nights. Hans was waiting on him when he stepped out the door. "Come on." He pounded a fist into the opposite palm. "It's fight night."

"Okay." Simon kept on the lookout for Schatzi as they walked down the street, but there was no sign of her in the dimming evening light. He hoped the little dog was okay.

The walk out to the bear pit went quickly. Neither of them spoke much. Hans was in a good mood. His battered hat was shoved back on his head, letting his hair escape its confines. Simon looked over at his friend, walking along with his shoulders back and his hands tucked in his belt, whistling. Hans seemed immortal, indestructible.

The crowds had already begun to gather when they arrived.

Simon saw Lieutenant Chieske and Sergeant Hoch walking among the voluble men. The lieutenant raised his head a bit when he saw Simon, then winked at him.

"Hans!" someone called out, which caused them to veer away from the pit. Simon's eyes followed their new direction to see a man approaching with several companions. He was of middling height and build, shorter than Hans and definitely not as wide, dressed very well with a large gold ring on one hand. "Hans," he exclaimed again in a resonant baritone, "I have been hearing of your exploits in the pit, and have come to see for myself." He clapped a hand on Hans' shoulder.

"It is good of you to come, Master Schardius," Hans replied with a quick bob of the head and shoulders. "I hope you won't be disappointed."

So this was Hans' employer, Simon realized, the very prosperous corn factor whose warehouse Hans labored in during the daylight hours. He looked at the man with fresh interest, only to be somewhat disappointed. Somehow he'd expected a man of Master Schardius' wealth and reputation to be...larger, somehow more impressive.

"I shall only be disappointed if you lose, Hans." The merchant squeezed his shoulder, then turned back to his friends. "Now, who will take my bets on *Stark* Hans? Anyone for even money? No? Then what odds will it take..."

The merchant wandered off. Simon noticed that Hans' hands were fisted by his sides. "Hans? What's the matter?"

Hans stood motionless for a long moment, then heaved a long breath in and out. "Nothing. Come on." He turned back toward the pit. Simon followed, hearing the murmurs of "*Stark* Hans" all around them.

They climbed down the ladder into the pit, where Hans, as usual, took off his jacket and shirt and placed them on a ladder rung. His hat went on Simon's head. The gloves went on his hands. He swung his arms a bit, but was staring off toward the crowd instead of his opponent. Simon grew concerned.

"Hans." No reaction. "Hans!" Still no reaction. He reached out and touched his friend. Hans started and looked over at him. "The fight, Hans. Look at him," Simon pointed to the other end of the pit, "not all those overstuffed pigeons who came to see you beat him."

Hans looked at him for a moment, then a slow smile crossed his face. "Pigeons, huh?" He looked at the crowd again, then back at Simon. "Mayhap you're right, boy. And you're my luck, so I'd best listen to you." His gaze went down the pit and locked on the other fighter. "So, let's be about this."

Just then Herr Pierpoint came down the other ladder and moved to the center of the pit. Simon didn't listen as the up-timer went through his usual before-the-fight routine, focusing instead on the other fighter. Whoever he was, he looked to be more of a challenge than the last few men Hans had faced, especially poor Sokolovsky. He stood erect, head up and eyes staring at Hans. There was no fat around his middle; he was lean, and a bit taller than Hans. Simon shivered all of a sudden. Hans might have to work for this one.

Herr Pierpoint pointed to the timekeeper and the bell rang. Hans stepped forward, and the fight began.

In the event, Simon needn't have worried. This fight was more of a contest than any that Simon had seen before, true. The other fighter was good enough to land a number of solid body blows, and early on he managed to thoroughly blacken Hans' left eye. But in return, Hans' relentless pounding just wore the other man down. He dropped in the seventh round.

The crowd went wild—as Simon had come to expect. But even for a fight night crowd, they were very exuberant. He looked at the people leaning over the rail, shouting and pounding on each other. At the same moment, he caught a whiff of the old blood smell from the pit itself. And in a moment of insight well beyond his years, Simon saw that the people cheering for Hans would most likely have been cheering on the dogs in the bear baitings that used to occur in the pit. That almost made him want to throw up, and he only kept his supper in his stomach by gulping hard a couple of times and taking deep breaths.

Hans walked over to Simon after Herr Pierpoint lifted his arm in victory. He was breathing deeply and flexing his hands, but there was a smile on his face. "That was a good fight," he said. "That man knew what he was doing." A touch to his left eye brought a wince, but didn't dim the smile. "A good fight," Hans repeated. He started whistling again as he donned his clothes, finishing off by plucking his hat off Simon's head and giving the boy's hair a ruffle.

Up the ladder they went. Simon had been up and down the ladder so many times over the last few weeks that he'd learned how to balance himself to get on and off at the top and didn't even think about it now.

"Now, where's Tobias?" Hans was looking around.

"Ferret-face," Simon muttered. Hans heard him and laughed.

"There he is." Hans pointed and they pushed their way through the crowd, accepting congratulation and claps on the back as they moved. In a moment Hans had Tobias by the arm and was watching him count out bills.

Simon counted along with them. "...ten, eleven, twelve." Twelve hundred dollars! Hans was making even more money for each fight. It still amazed Simon that people would pay to see a fight, despite all the proof he had received over the last weeks.

"Twelve for tonight," Hans said as he pocketed the money. "Next time it's fifteen."

"Fifteen!" Tobias almost screamed. "That's robbery!"

Hans shrugged. "The people pay to come see me. If you want me in your fights, the price is now fifteen hundred dollars."

Tobias' eyes nearly popped out of his head. This increased his resemblance to the weasellike ferrets to such an extent that Simon had to bite the inside of his cheek to keep from bursting out laughing. They left Tobias wordless and huffing.

"There you are, Hans." The crowd parted to let Andreas Schardius and his friends through. "You are indeed the Samson of Magdeburg. Congratulations on your win tonight. May it not be the last."

"Thank you, Master Schardius," Hans said. Simon could hear a strained note in his voice.

The merchant waved a hand. "I'm so glad you didn't disappoint me, Hans. If you had lost, well, it would have been costly." With that, he turned and walked away.

Simon was alarmed. Hans' hands were fists again. He laid a hand on Hans' arm. "Hans...Hans...pigeons, remember."

After a moment the fists relaxed, but this time there was no smile. "No, Simon, not a pigeon. Not that one. A kestrel, maybe, or better yet, a carrion crow." Hans spat as if clearing his mouth. "Come on."

Byron and Gotthilf looked at each other from where they stood on the fringe of the crowd.

"Interesting," Gotthilf said.

Byron nodded.

✧   ✧   ✧

The torchlight around the bear pit dimmed behind them. The moon was in half-phase, riding high in the sky, so their way was lit before them. Simon was perplexed, and finally worked up his courage to ask a question.

"Hans?"

"Hmm?"

"Why is Master Schardius not a pigeon?"

Hans spat again. "The preachers say that we are God's flock, the sheep of His pasture. They might as well say we are the pigeons in His roost. Sheep and pigeons are both stupid, messy, nasty creatures, helpless for the most part. That probably describes most people—certainly the ones you and I know." They walked a few steps farther on. "But there are always those who prey on the flocks. Call them wolves, or hawks, or carrion crows..." Hans kicked a rock out of his path. "...but they batten on the misery of others. And some of them..." Simon heard the smack of a fist into a palm. "...some of them feed on pain. And *Master Schardius*," loathing dripped from the title, "he is one of the worst. He misses no opportunity to increase his wealth at the expense of others. I know that he brings stolen property into Magdeburg on his barges. I know that he cheats his customers, giving them short weights when they buy his grain. And I know that he delights in tearing at people to cause pain or to receive gain, and if he can do both at once then he is a happy man."

Simon walked beside his friend, trying to absorb everything that had just been said. "But...but he seems so nice and friendly."

"Does he? Think about what he told me before the fight. Think it over carefully."

Simon recalled the words the merchant had spoken. One phrase in particular stood out in his memory, *I shall only be disappointed if you lose, Hans.* He thought of the expression on the merchant's face, of the tone of his voice. A realization dawned in his mind.

"He ordered you to win."

Hans spat. "Yah. Ordered, and threatened."

Simon shuddered. "Threatened?"

"Oh, I know the words seem mild. But there was a warehouseman who did something to 'disappoint' the good master some time back. One day he didn't come to work, nor the next day. The day after that he was found floating face-down in the river."

"You think..."

Hans was silent for a moment. "Not that it would have done much good, the words of such as us against the word of one of the richest men in Magdeburg."

Simon was very confused. What was Hans talking about? And if Master Schardius was such a bad man..."So why do you work for him?"

Hans was silent for a long time. Then he said: "I was never able to read or write. The school master would write the letters down, but when I tried to read them they twisted around. So I ended up working for Schardius. I don't like him, but..." He shrugged. "He pays his warehouse men better than anyone else for that kind of work, and in turn we do some other work for him now and then."

"Other work?"

"Never mind. You don't need to know right now. It's just... I needed the money," Hans muttered. "I still do. It's the same reason I fight. I need the money to take care of Uschi."

"But you make enough money to take care of her from your job, don't you? And she makes money with her embroidery." Simon was confused.

"It's not enough," Hans said. "If something happens to me, she needs money set back, money to keep her. I failed her once; I'm not going to fail her again; never. That's why I fight."

Simon had trouble understanding. "What could happen to you?"

"I may have seen something I shouldn't have seen."

Hans stopped suddenly and placed both hands on Simon's shoulder. "I'm not going to tell you to forget what I just told you. I know you won't. But for the sake of your safety, and for Ursula's, keep it behind your eyes. Don't open the gate of your mouth and let it out." He dropped his hands and started to turn, paused as if a thought had struck him, then turned back. "Unless something happens to me."

"Nothing will happen to you," Simon protested.

"Maybe it won't. But if it does, you go to the policemen, Chieske and Hoch. Especially Chieske. No one else. They're the only ones who look to be honest, and that up-timer Chieske is a hard man himself. Nobody will turn him. You tell them what I said. But no one else. Understand?"

Simon nodded.

"Promise?"

Another nod.

"Good. Now, I need something to get a bad taste out of my mouth."

It was not many more minutes before they were at The Chain. Hans walked up to the counter and slapped coins down in front of Veit. "Genever." Veit produced another of the blue bottles from the table behind him. Hans grabbed it and headed toward a table. Veit turned a spigot and pulled a mug of small beer from its cask and handed it to Simon.

"Fight not go well?" Veit nodded towards Hans where he was sitting alone at a table.

"He won in seven rounds. He's happy with the fight. It's something else that's chewing on his insides." Simon was faithful to his promise and left it at that.

"Right. If it gets worse, give me the high sign. A moody Hans is not good for the establishment." Veit winked.

Simon went over and took a seat on the bench next to where Hans was cradling the blue bottle between his palms.

It was some time later that they wandered back to their rooms. Ursula was happy to see them home in one piece. She was not, however, happy about the black eye Hans had received. She let him know in very clear and concise language the extent of her unhappiness, with the aid of a finger pointing in his face. Simon was somewhat surprised to see his friend just stand with a smile on his face and let his sister upbraid him, but he was beginning to understand that Hans would give Ursula anything and everything he could, including being her target if that was what she needed.

When she at length ran out of words and emotional steam, Ursula threw her hands up in the air and exclaimed, "You great lunk, you don't even care that you got hurt, do you?"

Hans shook his head, still grinning.

Ursula started laughing. "Oh, Hans, what am I going to do with you?" He held his arms out, and she stepped into his embrace. "I love you, you know."

"I know," Hans said, his face gone serious.

"It just bothers me that you fight so much."

"I know," Hans repeated. "But we need the money."

"Do we really?" Ursula pushed back from him. "Or is that just your excuse to fight?"

Hans took the money Tobias had given him from his pocket and placed it in her cupped palms. Then he drew himself up. "I'm good at it, Uschi. I like it. And I'm going to keep doing it, to provide for you." He spread his hands, shrugged, and turned to his room.

Ursula looked after him and took a step, then stopped. Her shoulders drooped. After a moment, she put the money in her own pocket, then reached over to the table, picked up her cane, and made her way to her own room. "Blow out the candle, please, Simon," she said over her shoulder in a dull voice.

Simon waited for her door to close. His blanket lay folded on his stool. He sat long enough to take off his boots, then picked up the blanket. Blowing out the candle, he moved to his space in front of the fireplace. A moment later he was rolled up in the blanket, and moments after that his eyes drifted closed.

Chapter 24

Ciclope actually saw what he believed was the first puff of smoke. He had glanced at the wood yard from a distance as he walked by carrying some tools to the brick yard. He glanced around quickly. No one else had that particular angle of vision on the wood. He almost sagged in relief, but steeled himself to keep trotting with the tools and not look around.

After some discussion, he and Pietro had agreed to try to set a fire. The wood was costly, so any amount of destruction would work toward their ordered goal. But even though it was costly, it was mostly left unattended. That played into their hands nicely.

Pietro had convinced Ciclope that he could get in and out of the wood yard without being noticed. Ciclope knew his rail-thin companion was adept at getting into and out of places without being noticed. He had been a thief, after all, and from all accounts he had been a successful one. Unsuccessful thieves didn't last very long in Venice. If the doge's guards or the city watch didn't grab them in the act, the other thieves would rat them out to the guards. It reduced competition among the thieves and gave the guard something to brag about, which meant they'd be a bit less vigilant for the next little while.

But Ciclope had still had his doubts as to whether or not Pietro could get into the wood yard, at least without being noticed by someone. Apparently he could.

So Pietro still remembered how to move like a thief, Ciclope mused to himself as he neared the brick yard. He'd buy the little runt a mug of ale. Now, had he remembered how to set a fire so that it would catch fast and burn hot?

A shout sounded from behind him. He looked around to see flames spreading along the top of the wood piles. From the smoke that was rising, it looked as if the fire was well and truly set.

Looked like Ciclope owed Pietro two mugs of ale.

"Look out below!"

Ciclope jumped back with the rest of the gang he was with just a moment before a barrel's worth of water splashed over the flaming timber stack they were attempting to pull apart.

"Now!" shouted Leonhart Kolman as the steam crane swung the barrel back toward the Big Ditch to refill it for the next dump. The gang leaped in with their tools and poles as the flames momentarily died down and tipped the top of the pile over to the ground on the other side where the charred timbers and boards sizzled in the pools of water and mud. They spent a couple of minutes making sure that the fire in that stack, if not totally quenched, wouldn't at least return to a conflagration for some time. Then Kolman looked around, pointed to another stack, and yelled, "Come on!"

Ciclope cursed to himself as he allowed most of the others to get ahead of him. He had to show willingness in this emergency, but at the same time he didn't want the efforts to be too successful. The crew boss was entirely too good at his job.

"Get out of the way!" someone yelled from behind Ciclope. He jumped to one side just as a stream of water shot past him to splash against the stack the gang had been headed toward. His internal cursing redoubled as he realized that the fire company had finally managed to get their balky steam engine running well enough to start their pump sucking water out of the moat to feed their erstwhile limp hoses.

"I think that has it."

Ciclope looked up from where he was trying to clean his mud-encased shoes to see Leonhart Kolman talking to the head of the fire company. Both men drooped with weariness. But then, they were no different from anyone else in the construction site. Firemen were slowly dragging their hoses out of the way of the construction workers trying to shovel and rake the charred bits of wood together.

Pietro looked toward Ciclope from the gang he was mustered with. He tilted his head to one side just a fraction of an inch, and a hint of a smile crossed his face; more of a smirk, actually, and it was gone almost as quickly as it appeared.

Ciclope raised his chin by the same distance. *Good job.*

Pietro looked away.

"Stop those men! Now!"

An up-timer by the sound of his accent. Ciclope turned his head to catch a glimpse of a clean—or at least not sooty and mud-soaked—man charging from the main gate of the site toward the leaders. An older man dressed in restrained down-timer finery followed behind, picking his way with care.

Kolman tipped his helmet to the back of his head. Ciclope had observed the man for long enough that he knew this meant the crew boss was about to level some unsuspecting soul.

"Who are you and what are you doing in my construction yard?" Kolman demanded.

"I'm Bill Reilly, Captain of the Magdeburg *Polizei*, is who I am, and it's not your construction yard right now, it's the scene of a possible crime, and your men are destroying possible evidence. Now shut it down!"

Ciclope forced himself to stand still. For all that the up-timer was practically nose-to-nose with the crew boss, Ciclope was still in his range of vision, and he wanted to do absolutely nothing that would draw himself to this man's attention.

"But..." Kolman tried to interject.

"*Now!*" Reilly roared.

"Do it," the well-dressed down-timer said as he arrived at their sides.

"But Master Gericke..." the crew boss tried again.

"Do it." Gericke's words were cold and. "This is a public project, and until the fire company, the *Polizei*, and I are satisfied that there is nothing criminal going on, this area is under the control of the *Polizei*."

Kolman took his helmet off his head and slammed it into the mud, then turned around and began yelling and waving his arms and pulling the construction crew away from the smoldering heap of the wood yard.

Reilly pulled a watch whistle from his pocket and blew a long blast on it. The shrill tone hadn't ceased sounding when several of the *Polizei* entered the construction site carrying short poles with cruciform bases and lots of cord. As Ciclope watched, they began cordoning off the wood yard at Reilly's directions.

Ciclope looked to where Gericke and the fire company head were talking. So that was the famous mayor, he took note. At first glance, he seemed to be not much more than just another burgher. But Ciclope was pretty sure the mayor was a hard man, for all his polish. He eavesdropped on the conversation for a moment.

"Hard work," Gericke observed.

"Aye," the fire company head replied. "And in fairness, it would have been a lot worse if the Schiffer people had not improvised a water hoist and dump out of the Big Ditch. Master Gericke," the man sounded like a man arguing a case before a judge, "we have got to have a better steam engine and pump. We near enough lost everything today because we couldn't get that balky bitch of an engine to run reliably. This time it was a pile of wood. Next time it will be a house with children in it...or a church."

Ciclope saw Gericke wince at that last.

The saboteur had observed in the city's taverns that the quickest way to get a group of Magdeburgers frothing mad was to mention how Pappenheim had caused almost all their churches to be burned to blackened shells of masonry. Sad drunks, quiet drunks, jolly drunks; all would transform to narrow-eyed lunatics ready to perform a double orchidectomy on Pappenheim with a rusty broken razor and without the benefit of the new-fangled anesthetic if they only had the opportunity. A very Old Testament attitude. And that was the men. What the women proposed was beyond the Old Testament, and made even Ciclope shudder.

Suffice it to say that the Magdeburgers were sensitive about their churches.

Gericke took a deep breath. "The city cannot pay for it. But have your owners come talk to me. Maybe something can be worked out."

Ciclope faded back as that conversation ended and Gericke started looking around. He didn't want to catch that man's attention either.

Not a bad day's work, he thought to himself as he joined the throng of men heading for the gate. Not bad at all. A pity no one was seriously hurt, though.

Chapter 25

Magdeburg Times-Journal
January 15, 1636

A fire broke out yesterday at the construction site of the new surgical wing of the Magdeburg Memorial Hospital in Greater Magdeburg. It was contained and quickly put out by the local fire company, assisted by the members of the construction crew. According to Captain Bill Reilly of the Magdeburg Polizei, injuries were minor, consisting mostly of burns, although one workman was knocked out when he ran into the path of the crane hook just as it started to swing. His workmates picked him up and ran him right next door to the hospital, where he is currently still under observation.

Johannes Kretzer, spokesman for the Schiffer Painting and Contracting firm, managers of the construction project, indicated that the fire was contained to the lumber stores. "We salvaged much of the timber," Kretzer said. He acknowledged that this would be a setback to the project, however.

No cause of the fire has been determined as of press time today.

✧   ✧   ✧

Andreas Schardius opened his eyes when Johann Westvol finished reading the article aloud. Westvol and Georg Kühlewein stared back at him; Westvol blankly, Kühlewein with a thunderous expression. Neither of them said a word. That was just as well, Schardius thought to himself. He was not in a mood for their typical idiocy. He had heard up-timers talk about Tweedledum and Tweedledee, but he hadn't really understood that until after he had embroiled himself in the affairs of these two men. They weren't even bright enough to say "I'm Dee."

Well, perhaps they were better than that—they had been effective bürgermeisters before the sack of the city, after all, in a venal sort of way—but not much.

"You realize, of course, that this fire may have ended your tapping the revenues of this project." Schardius knew how to deal with untoward events. He was a very successful trader, after all, with all that was implied by that label. So his voice was calm, and steady, and had just the right touch of firmness to it. "At least for a while." He watched the reactions of his partners carefully.

Westvol was predictable. His eyes widened, for all the world like a five-year-old spoiled child who had just been informed that his greatest wish was not only not going to be granted, neither were any of the other wishes on his current "If you love me you will get me this" list.

"But the newspaper said they put the fire out quickly and salvaged the wood..." Westvol began.

"Shut up, Johann," Kühlewein growled. "He's right. It doesn't matter what the article said, Leonhart Kolman told me they lost nearly half of the wood outright, and a lot of what's left is only usable now to feed the steam engine in the crane. You know the price of wood these days... especially the long timbers we had to have brought all the way from the mountains."

Praise be to God, Schardius thought to himself with more than a touch of sarcasm. Kühlewein just took the lead to be Dee. There might be hope for the man after all if he could recognize reality when it stepped up and slapped him in the face.

Westvol looked like he was going to cry, until his face lit with a sudden smile. Schardius had been waiting for that.

"And no, you can't file a claim against the accident insurance, Johann."

"Why not?" the bürgermeister asked with a note of petulance.

"Do you remember when we were drawing up the project plans and you insisted on the high deductible on the insurance to hold the premium costs down?" Schardius drew his eyebrows together in a serious frown.

"Yessss." That was drawn out slowly by the hapless Westvol, who was bright enough to see what was coming.

"Well, the cost of the damage is only just a bit more than the deductible."

"Oh. Then why did we buy the insurance, then?"

"Because you insisted we should."

Westvol had no response to that, which was just as well. Schardius extended his frown to the fuming Kühlewein, who glared back but didn't say a word.

"So what are we going to do?" Westvol finally asked.

"We are going to order more timber, pay the costs of the fire company, and have Kolman beat into his people that this cannot be allowed to happen again."

The meeting tailed off in repeats of that theme. But underneath it all, Schardius had two thoughts. First, a question—was the fire an accident? And second, a desire—if it wasn't, he really wanted to hurt somebody.

Georg Schmidt was delighted. "Ha! Take that!" he declared, smacking the paper with his hand.

His secretary, Stephan Burckardt, looked around the edge of the office doorway.

"Did you need something, sir?"

"No, Stephan, I do not. The newspaper has given me all I needed." The smile on his face felt as if it was stretching stiff muscles; which it might have been, given how less than happy he had been of late.

Schmidt gestured expansively. "Go, Stephan. You and the others take the rest of the day off—with pay. Go. I will see you tomorrow."

Stephan's head disappeared from the doorway almost as if it had been a figment of Schmidt's imagination. It reappeared a moment later long enough to say, "Thank you, sir," then disappeared again.

Georg looked back to the paper, reading the article one more time, smiling as he heard the troop of feet in the hallway headed out the front door.

"Ha!" he exclaimed again. "You think you can beat me, Kühlewein? You and your money man? Oh, no. You will pay for cheating me out of my contract. You will pay dearly."

He crossed to the window and stared out it, clasping his hands behind him.

"A good start," he murmured. "A good start."

This attacked the project, which would hurt all of the consortium who got the project contract awarded to them. But he really wanted to hurt Andreas Schardius. If he hadn't poked his nose into Schmidt's business, the other members of that consortium couldn't have won the contract. So it was Schardius, he decided, more than any other, who deserved to be ruined.

He rocked back and forth on his feet, smiling. His Italian servants would deal with Schardius, he thought, despite all the hard men surrounding the other merchant. Indeed they would.

Otto Gericke read the article and frowned. He made a note to send an official commendation to the fire company, followed by a note to remind himself to ask Captain Reilly when the *Polizei* would be able to determine if the fire was an accident.

There was a long pause while Otto tapped the pencil against his lips. God Above, he hoped that this didn't stir up the Committee of Correspondence. That was the last thing he needed right now.

Gunther Achterhof lowered the newspaper.

No one in the room stirred when he looked up. But then, they all knew him, so they all had a good idea of what his reaction would be to the article about the fire.

Gunther started to crumple the paper in one fist. Then, stopping himself, he laid the paper down on the table and smoothed it out. It was the gesture of a man capable of savage fury who was keeping it under control.

He tapped his fingers on the table for a few seconds, ever so gently. "Will," he said after some thought. "Go to the construction site. Offer some help to the site manager with cleaning up. If he does not accept that, which he probably will not, explain to him that his project is very important to the CoC, and we will be keeping an eye on things in the future. And remind him—gently—that we will object if all the ash and scraps are thrown into the Big Ditch." Will grinned and bobbed his head.

"That water is not clean, but there is no reason to make it worse than it already is."

"What if he asks what to do with it?"

Gunther shrugged. "Burn it in his steam engine. No-brainer, as Frau Marla would say."

He rose, and the others rose with him. "Meanwhile, I will go have a quiet conversation with our esteemed mayor."

Stephan Burckardt stopped in The Chain for a mug of ale as a token of celebration. He didn't much care for the place; the locals who frequented it were a pretty rough crowd. But it was earlier than usual, and most of them would still be working, so he took the chance. It wasn't often at all that he was given any kind of reprieve from work. Master Schmidt begrudged him even Sundays and the holy days of the church calendar, and usually managed to find a way to make him spend part of those days laboring at his desk. Stephan didn't dare complain to the church authorities. All that would accomplish would be angering Schmidt to an alarming degree. Stephan didn't know what Schmidt would do in that situation. He did know two things, however: Schmidt would not let what he perceived as a challenge to his authority go unanswered; and without a doubt Stephan would not enjoy that answer.

The ale was as bad as always. That was the other reason Stephan came to The Chain. It was the lowest of the low, as far as places to get a mug of ale or beer went. Even though it was located in Old Magdeburg, which most people tried to pretend at least was the home of the best people and the upper society—which thought caused Stephan to bark a bitter laugh—it represented the very dregs of Magdeburg society. And the ale, Stephan confirmed with a sip, was no better than the social ranking of the local patrons. But it was cheap, which was a sterling virtue in the eyes of the overworked and underpaid secretary.

Stephan's thoughts rolled back to Master Schmidt, while he slowly lowered the level of fluid in his mug. The master had been in a most unusually good mood this afternoon. Whatever caused it must have been in the newspaper, as he had been snarling until the paper hit his desk. But the only thing that was remarkable in the news was the fire at the hospital project. And why would that make the master happy?

Chapter 26

Gotthilf sat on the window seat, staring out into the night, trying to scratch the itch in the middle of his mental back. He heard someone move up behind him.

"A pfennig for your thoughts."

That was his younger sister Margarethe. Without looking around he held his hand out.

"What?"

"Where's the pfennig?" he queried.

"Oh! You!" Margarethe slapped his palm. "That's all the pfennig you will get from me. I think you spend too much time with that up-timer fellow you call your partner."

Reflected in the small panes of glass he could see multiple images of her sticking her tongue out at him. He spun quickly and ran his palm across her tongue before she could react to his motion.

"Ick!" She jumped back and scrubbed at her mouth with the back of her hand, then stuck her tongue out again as he laughed at her.

After Gotthilf quit chuckling, she said, "No, seriously, what are you thinking about so hard? You haven't moved from that seat for over an hour."

"Nothing you can help with, Margarethe."

"Maybe I can, maybe I can't, but we won't know until you tell me."

"No," Gotthilf said, "you can't help..." A sudden realization struck him. "Actually, maybe you can. I met a young woman the other day, a bit older than you, perhaps."

"Ah," Margarethe interjected with a sly grin. "Is this something I need to tell Mother or hide from her?"

"Neither," Gotthilf said, while shuddering a bit from the thought of his busybody mother linking a woman's name—any woman's name—to him. "It was in connection with a case we are working, not social at all."

"Oh. Okay."

He could see that Margarethe was disappointed there wasn't some angle she could use to dig at him a little. He continued with, "Anyway, I met this girl, like I said, and she looked familiar to me, but I cannot remember where I have seen her before. I have been wracking my brain for days now, and nothing. It is driving me moon-silly."

"That's not a drive, that's a short putt," Margarethe spouted.

Gotthilf looked at his sister in disbelief. "What did you just say?"

"Didn't I say it right? It's an up-time joke. I learned it from a girl at school. Isn't it funny?"

"Do you even know what it means?"

Margarethe frowned a little at his lack of reaction. "No."

Now Gotthilf chuckled a bit. "Margarethe, don't try to tell up-timer jokes unless you really understand them. You can't tell them right if you don't, and depending on the joke you might find yourself in trouble. Besides, I get enough of that from Byron." He shook his head. "Anyway, before you so rudely interrupted me, I was telling you about the girl. Her name is Ursula Metzgerin."

"Metzgerin, Metzgerin," Margarethe mused. "Ursula..." She looked down at the floor, brow wrinkled, mouth pursed. Gotthilf thought about swiping his fingers across her lips, but refrained.

After a moment, she looked up. "There was an older girl in my catechism class a few years ago. Her name was Ursula, and I think her last name started with an M. She only came a few times, then someone said she was going to another church and attending catechism there."

With that clue, Gotthilf thought back to the times when he walked his sister to catechism. Sure enough, a recollection surfaced of a younger version of Ursula, blond hair shining, coming out of the church door while he waited on Margarethe.

He jumped to his feet, grabbed Margarethe by the waist and swung her in circles in the air, proclaiming "That's it!" over her loud protests. He set her feet back on the floor, and flung his arm around her shoulder.

"Thanks, Margarethe. That is a big help." Their mother appeared in the parlor doorway and motioned them to come to dinner. "You're a pretty good sister, you know...even if you can't tell a joke."

"Gotthilf?"

"Yes?"

"What's a putt?"

For the next several days Ursula was her usual cheerful self—or at least she seemed to be. Simon wasn't so sure, though. There was a shadow in her eyes, and he thought her eyes followed Hans as he moved around the room more than usual. But her voice was bright and she laughed a lot, so maybe he was imagining it.

One day, after Hans left for his job at the grain factorage, Ursula picked up her Bible as had become their custom. "Well, what shall we read today?"

Simon plopped down on his stool. "Samson. I want to hear about Samson." He had a desire to know everything there was to know about Samson.

She opened the Bible and started turning pages. "There's still his last adventure to tell."

Simon hugged his knees with his one good arm, waiting.

> And it came to pass afterward, that he loved a woman in the valley of Sorek, whose name was Delilah. And the lords of the Philistines came up unto her, and said unto her, Entice him, and see wherein his great strength lieth, and by what means we may prevail against him, that we may bind him to afflict him: and we will give thee every one of us eleven hundred pieces of silver.
>
> And Delilah said to Samson, Tell me, I pray thee, wherein thy great strength lieth, and wherewith thou mightest be bound to afflict thee.

"Don't listen to her, Samson," Simon muttered. He could already see the way this story was weaving.

And Samson said unto her, If they bind me with seven green withies that were never dried, then shall I be weak, and be as another man.

Then the lords of the Philistines brought up to her seven green withies which had not been dried, and she bound him with them.

Now there were men lying in wait, abiding with her in the chamber. And she said unto him, The Philistines be upon thee, Samson. And he brake the withies, as a thread of tow is broken when it toucheth the fire. So his strength was not known.

Simon listened to Ursula read the story. As Delilah continued to ply Samson and Samson continued to respond to her, it crossed his mind more than once that Samson did not seem very smart. Finally the story wound to the now-obvious climax.

That he told her all his heart, and said unto her. There hath not come a razor upon mine head; for I have been a Nazarite unto God from my mother's womb: if I be shaven, then my strength will go from me, and I shall become weak, and be like any other man.

And when Delilah saw that he had told her all his heart, she sent and called for the lords of the Philistines, saying, Come up this once, for he hath showed me all his heart. Then the lords of the Philistines came up unto her, and brought money in their hand.

And she made him sleep upon her knees; and she called for a man, and she caused him to shave off the seven locks of his head; and she began to afflict him, and his strength went from him.

And she said, The Philistines be upon thee, Samson. And he awoke out of his sleep, and said, I will go out as at other times before, and shake myself. And he wist not that the Lord was departed from him.

Ursula stopped.

"That can't be all the story," Simon exclaimed.

"I thought we could read the rest tomorrow."

"No!" He leaned forward. "Please, I need to hear what happens."

She looked at him for a moment, then said, "All right," and resumed reading. Simon listened as the end of the story rolled out.

But the Philistines took him, and put out his eyes, and brought him down to Gaza, and bound him with fetters of brass; and he did grind in the prison house.

Then the lords of the Philistines gathered them together for to offer a great sacrifice unto Dagon their god, and to rejoice: for they said, Our god hath delivered Samson our enemy into our hand. And when the people saw him, they praised their god: for they said, Our god hath delivered into our hands our enemy, and the destroyer of our country, which slew many of us.

And it came to pass, when their hearts were merry, that they said, Call for Samson, that he may make us sport. And they called for Samson out of the prison house; and he made them sport: and they set him between the pillars. And Samson said unto the lad that held him by the hand, Suffer me that I may feel the pillars whereupon the house standeth, that I may lean upon them.

Now the house was full of men and women; and all the lords of the Philistines were there; and there were upon the roof about three thousand men and women, that beheld while Samson made sport. And Samson called unto the Lord, and said, O Lord God, remember me, I pray thee, and strengthen me, I pray thee, only this once, O God, that I may be at once avenged of the Philistines for my two eyes.

And Samson took hold of the two middle pillars upon which the house stood, and on which it was borne up, of the one with his right hand, and of the other with his left. And Samson said, Let me die with the Philistines. And he bowed himself with all his might; and the house fell upon the lords, and upon all the people that were therein. So the dead which he slew at his death were more than they which he slew in his life.

Simon sat back on his stool. He had never imagined it would end that way.

Ursula put her Bible away and took out her embroidery. "Not a very happy ending, is it?"

"No," Simon muttered.

"I don't like to read that story much because of that." She pushed the needle through the cloth. "But sometimes, you know, we need to be reminded that the things we choose to do don't always end up the way we intend for them to."

Simon took a deep breath. "Yah. I see that."

"Good." Ursula focused on her work.

It was obviously time for him to go find work. He opened the door, but looked back at Ursula before he stepped through. Ursula's head was bent over her embroidery. She didn't look up when he left.

"Come in, Marla." Mary Simpson herself met Marla at the door of Simpsonhaus. "Have a seat, dear. Coffee?"

Marla settled into a chair in Mary's parlor, nodding to Andrea Abati, Heinrich Schütz, and Amber Higham as she did so.

"Coffee would be nice." She hunched up a bit in the chair. "It's still cold outside." It wasn't just the cold. Today was not one of her better days, although she had managed to hide that from Franz. He had a major rehearsal with the orchestra today, but he would have called it off if he had seen her starting to waver.

Within moments a cup was passed to her. Marla cradled it in her hands for a few moments to savor the warmth before taking her first sip.

"Ah." She felt the warmth trickle down her throat and spread through her body. "That helps."

Marla set her cup on the nearby side table, picked up her document case, and pulled out the manuscript of *Arthur Rex*. That she placed on the coffee table centered between all the seats. Then she sat back and picked up her coffee cup, still appreciating the warmth of the cup. She *really* hated being cold. And the warmth helped with her other problem as well.

"So, what do you think?" Amber Higham asked, interlacing one hand's fingers with those of Heinrich Schütz, her husband.

Marla took a sip before she replied.

"It's good." She saw a line appear between Amber's eyebrows, and hastened to say, "It's very good."

"Do I hear a 'but' in your voice?" Heinrich asked with a smile.

"Well . . ." Marla dragged the syllable out.

Heinrich chuckled. "Masses I have written, and motets. Opera, however, is a somewhat new thing for me, especially one of this . . . magnitude, shall we say. You, despite your youth, know more of them than I do. So, please, give me your thoughts on this. I promise not to rage if you butcher my sacred cow." He chuckled again.

"I wouldn't do that," Marla protested, in the face of everyone else's smiles. After a moment, she smiled as well. "All right, but I need more coffee first." She leaned forward and held her cup out for Mary to refill.

Settling back with a freshly filled steaming cup wafting warm vapors past her nose, she began. "My main observation is I think it needs more passion and tension, especially between Merlin and Guinevere early on and between Guinevere and Nimue in the last act. Second, the vocal styling is too . . . too restrained, too soft. It needs more bite, more edge to it. The last thing is, am I correct you are thinking of me for the role of Guinevere and Master Andrea," she nodded at him, "for the role of Nimue?"

"Yep," Amber replied, "you called it."

"The music is too similar for those roles," Marla said. She sipped at the coffee again, trying to get the butterflies in her stomach under control. Despite her acquaintance and friendship with Amber, she felt intimidated by Schütz. She was still getting used to the idea, even two-plus years after she arrived in Magdeburg, that someone who was in the encyclopedia as "The Father of German Music" would value her opinions. "There needs to be a distinct differentiation between the styles, the themes, and the timbre of their music."

"What do you mean?" Heinrich spoke up, gaze intent on Marla.

"As I read the libretto," Marla began, then interrupted herself with, "and that's a near-brilliant piece of work, by the way. Who wrote it?"

"I worked with Johann Gronow," Amber said. "He's the editor of—"

"*Black Tomcat Magazine*," Marla interjected. "He's also the friend of Friedrich von Logau, who just worked on a small project for me. They're both good."

She finished the coffee and put the cup down, holding up her hand in negation when Mary pointed to the coffee pot again.

"Anyway, as I was saying, when I read the libretto, I was hearing Guinevere as earth and fire: very emotional, all strings and brass and percussion. Nimue, on the other hand, came across to me as air: ethereal, not particularly passionate, with woodwinds as her sound."

"Ah," Heinrich sighed. He sat in thought for a long moment, then said, "That is what I was missing. I need to contrast those two women more. I see it now, and I see how to rework it." He gave a seated bow to Marla. "My thanks, Frau Marla. You have been of great assistance."

Amber flashed a smile at Marla, and she relaxed a bit.

"My turn," Amber said. "Any thoughts on staging?"

"You're asking me?" Marla asked in confusion. *What is this, pick on Marla day, or something? Where does it say, I'm the expert here?* "You're the professional director and stage manager. I should be asking you."

"Come on," Amber insisted. "I know something had to have popped up in your brain. Let me have it."

"Okay." Marla thought for a moment. "Only two things at this point in time: first, I think Nimue needs to be played in a very androgynous manner."

"That won't be difficult," Andrea observed from his chair with a chuckle, joining the conversation for the first time. He looked toward Amber. "Much the same thought had occurred to me— make a virtue out of necessity, as it were." His grin flashed for a moment. "I just hadn't had time to bring it up yet."

"Noted." Amber actually did write it down in a small notebook. "What's the other thing?"

"Please don't make the costumes too heavy."

From there they descended into a detailed discussion of costume designs and proposed staging. It was nearly an hour later that Mary finally brought the conversation to a close.

"All right, we're good to go then. Master Heinrich will make his revisions as soon as possible, and we'll get the parts passed out as soon as he does. We're shooting to begin rehearsals by February 5th, and we have money from a supporter that will get the sets and costumes under way."

There was a general bustle as the others stood and took their leave. Marla remained seated, staring at the coffee table where the manuscript had been, tired and numb.

There came a touch on her shoulder. She looked up to see Mary there, looking down at her. No words were spoken, but she could see the expression of sympathy on the other woman's face, and the tears began welling up in her eyes to match the sudden surge of grief from the void under her heart.

Mary took a white linen handkerchief from a pocket and handed it to Marla, then sat down in the chair next to hers and wrapped an arm around her shoulder.

Marla wept. She bit down on the handkerchief, but still small moans of grief escaped her. The tears coursed down her cheeks, and she trembled as if she were badly chilled. The thought touched the edge of her mind that she *was* chilled; not to the bone, but in the soul.

She had no idea how long she mourned within the curve of Mary's arm. It felt like hours, but doubtless was not more than a few minutes. The tears slowed; her ragged breathing calmed.

Taking the handkerchief from between her teeth, Marla unfolded it and wiped the moisture from her face, rubbing fiercely to remove the feeling of the drying tracks of the tears. Then she clasped it between her hands in her lap.

Mary took her arm from Marla's shoulder.

"Not many people here know it," Mary said, "but Tom could have been a second child. I had a miscarriage before I had him."

Mary's voice was quiet. There was no sense of claiming some identity in a sisterhood of suffering; no sense of one-upmanship in her words. Just a simple statement of fact. But it was enough that Marla released her clasp and reached a hand out to Mary, who grasped it tightly.

"How ..." Marla husked, "how do the down-timer women bear it, seeing half or more of their children die?"

"The same way I did," Mary responded. "One day at a time; one hour at a time; sometimes one minute at a time."

Marla looked at the older woman, saw the strength in her, and drew on that strength to stiffen her own resolve. She was going to make it through this torrent, some way, somehow.

"Thanks, Mary."

"Any time, dear. I have lots of handkerchiefs."

Chapter 27

Ciclope and Pietro were back in that same tavern. It was still filled with smoky haze from the fireplace at one end of the room. Ciclope missed the old man and his pipe, though. It would have made the haze a bit sweeter.

They bought their ale, then looked for a table. The one they used last time was occupied, but they found another where they could put their backs against a wall and watch the door.

Ciclope tried his ale. It hadn't improved in their absence. It still tasted of mold and dirt. If he didn't know any better, he'd have sworn there was a bit of stable straw floating on top of it.

"So, when does he show up?" Pietro asked.

"Don't start that," Ciclope said. "Same as last time. The man will be here when he gets here."

And in fact, it wasn't long before their "patron," wearing what looked to be the same ill-fitting clothes, slipped into the chair beside Pietro.

"That was a good start," he said without wasting any time. "What will you do next?"

Ciclope took advantage of the moment to study him some more. His German was the local dialect, and under the baggy and slovenly clothes he was still too neat and clean for the kind of man he was attempting to portray. No ink on the fingers, so he was well-to-do enough to pay someone to do his writing. No hint of perfume. He didn't walk forthright like a soldier, nor like an absent-minded scholar. So, he was a burgher, a merchant of some kind.

The patron shifted on his chair, and Ciclope set his thoughts aside for the moment. "Well, we can't do the trick with the wood again, if for no other reason than they don't have much of it left right now. Maybe after they rebuild their stocks."

"I do not want them to 'rebuild their stocks,'" the other man hissed. "I want them ruined now!"

Ciclope raised his hand. "Calmly, calmly, boss. It does no good if you attract attention, now does it?" He drank off the last of his ale, suppressing a shudder at the taste.

Setting the mug down, he began running a finger around its rim.

"We have started weakening scaffolding. There should be some falls soon. We've also started rumors that the place is unlucky. Between the two, the workmen should start getting goosy soon, and they'll start drifting away."

"I want them ruined!" the man insisted in a whisper.

"There's only so much we can do at one time, boss," Pietro said.

"He's right," Ciclope confirmed. "We can't pop a big thing every week. They would start looking for people right away."

The patron's mouth twisted. "Very well," he said in a low tone. "But I want to see results soon."

"You will, boss," Ciclope assured him. "You will."

Clouds of fine dust arose from the ash in the hospital construction site as they walked through the wood yard, stinging Gotthilf's eyes and coating his tongue, giving the flavor of smoke to every breath he took. He followed Byron along with Karl Honister, the detective who was being given charge of the investigation. They all trod carefully through the destruction wrought by the fire. He looked up to see Dan Frost waving from the bucket he was standing in. Said bucket was thirty feet in the air at the end of a chain lifted by the derrick of the steam crane. The former Grantville police chief was now an independent consultant on policing and investigation. Luckily, he'd been available right after the fire happened, and quickly responded to Mayor Gericke's call.

"He says more to the right," he reported.

"I guess Dan *can* see the burn pattern better from up there than from ground level," Byron said as he adjusted his heading in the desired direction. "That's good, because the sooner we let the builder have access back to this yard, the sooner they'll quit bugging Mayor Gericke about it."

Before long they heard a blast from Dan's old police whistle, his signal to stop. They froze in place, waiting for the crane to lower the former police chief to the ground. In a couple of minutes he joined them, moving to the lead of their little group.

"It's like I expected," Dan said as he stepped forward slowly, eyes on the ground. "I never got any formal training in fire and arson investigation, but you pick up stuff by watching the real experts work a case. Anyway, the fire definitely started in this area. We need to see if we can figure out what started it."

"Are you suspecting arson?" Byron asked.

"If we were still up-time, absolutely. Here and now, no, not really. The whole idea of risk insurance for this kind of project is just starting, so I doubt that the idea of arson for fun and profit has really occurred to anyone yet." Dan bent over and poked at something on the ground, then straightened without picking it up. "But I still don't want to rule it out until we've checked every bit of this area. So step carefully, gentlemen, and keep your eyes peeled."

Gotthilf turned and made his way back to the watchmen standing behind the rope that cordoned off the wood yard.

"Gather 'round, men." Gotthilf waited until they had circled around him. "Okay, here's the word. Walk single file through the scene over the steps that we made in the ashes until you get to where Herr Frost and Lieutenant Chieske are standing. Once you're there, spread out where Herr Frost tells you to and start looking at the ground. Anything that is not ash or a bit of burnt wood, stand still and call out. Either Herr Frost or Detective Honister will come check it out. Don't move again until they tell you to. Everyone got that?"

Heads nodded all around the circle.

"Good. Get out there."

Honister stepped up beside Gotthilf as the watchmen started down the path.

"So what are we really looking for?"

Gotthilf turned his head toward the other detective. "Herr Frost will not rule that this fire was not arson without a detailed examination of the scene. This is the fastest way to do that. You are looking for anything that looks as if it might have started a fire: a match, gun powder, a magnifying lens; anything at all that is not wood or ash needs to be examined."

Honister's father and Gotthilf's had occasionally joined forces on business dealings, so the two young men were slightly acquainted with each other even before they both ended up in the detective group.

Gotthilf smiled a bit as he observed the other man's clothing. Honister was a bit on the dapper side, and he had dressed especially so today.

"You are going to wish you had dressed differently before the morning is out."

Honister gave a rueful nod, then asked. "So what do you think?"

For all that Gotthilf was the youngest detective in the Magdeburg *Polizei*, he was well-respected by his peers; a respect he had earned, he admitted to himself.

"What do I think? Honestly, I don't know what to think...but something about this fire does not feel right."

Honister stared at him for a moment, gave another nod, and touched the brim of his hat with a finger before turning and following the watchmen into the crime scene.

Gotthilf waited where he was. After a couple of minutes, he could see Byron make one last comment to Herr Frost and then head his direction. "Back to Metzger?" he asked when his partner stood beside him taking futile swipes at the fine particles of ash clinging to his clothing.

Byron straightened. "Yep. Back to Metzger."

Stephan Burckardt sighed as he tied a ribbon around a file folder and carried it from his desk to the filing cabinet in the corner. It was one of Master Schmidt's special files—as the red ribbon color indicated—one of the files that only Stephan and the master were supposed to see. The men who updated the regular ledgers knew that they weren't supposed to touch any folder tied up with a red ribbon. In fact, Master Schmidt had made it very clear that anyone other than Stephan who tried to look in the red ribbon files had better leave Magdeburg. And those who had been in the office for very long took that statement seriously.

He turned away from the cabinet after locking it. To be honest, he hadn't seen anything in those folders that was particularly risky. Nothing that couldn't be found in any master merchant's files, he supposed, based on things he'd heard other secretaries and accountants say. But Master Schmidt's rules were iron hard.

Stephan tested the door to Master Schmidt's office. Locked, as usual. The master never forgot to lock it. He closed and locked the door to his office, walked down the hall and out the building, then locked the front door.

Dark again. It had been so long since Stephan had seen the sun. Master Schmidt demanded he open the building just as the predawn light was filtering into the eastern sky, and he very seldom got to leave before dusk was well settled. He turned up his collar, shoved his hands in his coat pockets, and trudged down the street.

Franz was waiting when the river boat from Halle tied up at the dock and threw its gangplank up. Two scruffy looking men, one swinging a live chicken by its feet, disembarked first. Then the man he was waiting for appeared, treading with care up the springy plank. Franz didn't blame him for the care, because the case the man was carrying was absolutely irreplaceable up-time technology. Once the passenger had both feet on the ground, Franz stepped forward.

"Herr Cochran, I see you made it safe and sound."

Atwood Cochran—music teacher, guitarist, radio personality, and, not least, friend—grinned at him. "Don't call me that, Franz. People calling me 'Herr' is like calling me 'Sir'—I look around for my dad."

Franz returned the other man's grin. "Well enough, Atwood. Let me take one of those bags," and he reached for one.

Atwood hastily handed him the other bag. "I'll keep this one, if you don't mind. It's not that I don't trust you, or anything, it's just that..."

Franz laughed. "You would not trust your own mother with that recording equipment right now, admit it."

Atwood laughed, and said, "You're right."

"This way," Franz motioned. "We should be able to catch a cab pretty quickly."

Atwood followed him over to the nearby street. When a pony cart stopped in response to Franz's hail, he chuckled.

"That's not exactly what I imagined when you said 'cab.'"

"Heavy wagon, light wagon, large cart, small cart, everyone

just calls them 'cabs,'" Franz said. "Something we picked up from you up-timers."

"As long as it saves my feet and gets me and my duffle where I want to go faster than walking, you could call it a Range Rover for all I care." The music teacher carefully placed his case on the floor of the cart. After he clambered in, he kept the case between his two feet.

Franz tossed the other bag into the cart, then climbed up to sit opposite Atwood.

"Where to, Mac?" the cab driver tossed over his shoulder in understandable English.

"Nine Musikstrasse. Sylwesterhaus."

"Got it. We'll be there in fifteen minutes."

With that the driver shook the reins and clucked to the pony, which leaned into his collar and harness to start the cart rolling with a lurch.

Atwood wasted no time in asking the question that Franz expected to hear from him. "So, how are things with Marla?"

Since Atwood was one of Marla's long acquaintances, Franz didn't brush him off with a perfunctory response. "We were very worried about her for some time after we lost the baby, but now she is almost her old self again. Some days are better than others, of course," he shrugged, "and she is still a bit... fragile, you might say. But all things considered, and by the grace of God, she is doing well."

"Good," Atwood said quietly. "That's good to hear."

They rode in silence, surrounded by the noise of Greater Magdeburg as the driver directed his pony through the crowded streets with skill, a certain amount of panache, and a great deal of vulgarity of tongue which he unleashed on anyone who even looked as if they might get in his way.

Atwood laughed again. "He reminds me of the cabbie I got on my last trip to New York City. I guess they're a universal breed."

Franz chuckled. "That may well be. I know they sprang from the ground almost immediately in the greater city, rather like Mayor Gericke had sown dragon's teeth in the lands round about."

Atwood leaned forward, elbows on knees. "So, enough chit-chat. What's this all about?"

Typical up-timer bluntness, Franz thought to himself. No dancing around a topic with this man.

"It is Marla's idea, and she has seized upon it with a passion as strong as any I have ever seen from her."

The up-timer's eyebrows rose and his lips pursed for a moment before he spoke.

"That would be saying something, I believe. Ever since I've known her, that girl could be so single-minded at times she would border on obsession."

"Obsession." Franz turned that word around and around in his mind. "I would judge she is not obsessed...yet." He shrugged again. "But single-minded? Oh, yes."

"She didn't tell me in the telegrams what she was planning on performing."

Franz felt a wry smile cross his face. "She has decided to sing 'Do You Hear the People Sing?'" He paused for a moment. "In German, mind you."

Atwood sat back. "From *Les Misérables*?"

Franz nodded.

"Seriously?"

Franz nodded again.

"Does she realize what she's letting herself in for, especially right now?"

Franz couldn't help it; he burst out laughing. After a few moments, he sobered again. "Ah, friend Atwood, that is the question everyone asks. And the answer is, yes, she understands what the consequences could be. But that is part of what is driving her, you see, the fact that such consequences are even possible."

"Hmm." Atwood crossed his arms and thought for a moment. "Okay, I can see that. And I understand her telegrams a little better now. So it's damn the torpedoes, full steam ahead, huh?"

Franz didn't understand the full import of Atwood's allusion, but he got the general idea. "Indeed. In two nights at the Green Horse Tavern, Marla intends to cause a turmoil in the city, in the province, and even unto the entire USE."

"All right," Atwood said as the cabbie pulled the pony to a stop in front of Franz's house. "I've come all this way; I'll see it through."

They swung down from the back of the cart. Franz hung back to pay the driver as the door to the house flew open and Marla stepped through to greet her friend and erstwhile teacher.

✧   ✧   ✧

"Freeze!" Honister snapped. The watch patrolman stopped in surprise, his fingers but a fraction of an inch from picking up the white object that had attracted his attention. "Stand up and back away."

Honister looked around for a moment. "Herr Frost! Over here, please."

Dan was at his side in a moment. "What is it, Karl?"

Honister just pointed at the ground in front of him, and what was sitting in the shelter of several bits of charcoaled timber.

"Son of a..." Dan breathed after a pause. "Good catch, Karl. Now, get the photographer over here. I want pictures before we even think about touching anything."

The photographer stepped through the ashes, and after judging the light began taking pictures of the evidence.

"So did I see what I think I saw?" Karl asked Dan in a low tone as they watched the photographer.

"I'm afraid so. It appears I may have been wrong."

Chapter 28

For several days, Samson's end was never very far from the front of Simon's mind. He would worry at the tale like a dog with a scrap of bone. How could a hero be so stupid? If Samson was God's hero, why did God let him fall the way he did? Wouldn't it have been better for the people if he had beaten the Philistines instead of being captured?

Never far from those thoughts was the reminder that so many people called Hans "the Samson of Magdeburg," which in turn would remind him of what Lieutenant Chieske had told him might result from Hans' boxing career. As soon as those thoughts crossed his mind, he would shake his head violently and do anything he could to change what he was thinking about. But eventually his thoughts would circle back to Samson and the cycle would start over again.

And so Simon found himself walking by St. Jacob's church, the *Filialkirche* that served the poorest district of Magdeburg. Thoughts of Samson were running through his brain as he looked in the doorway to the shadowy interior of the church.

Simon had not attended church since before the sack of the city by Pappenheim's troops. But now, for the first time in what was literally years, Simon felt an urge to enter a church; this church, in the most downtrodden area of the Magdeburg that was being resurrected from the ashes of the old city. With hesitance he walked inside and stood in the shadows, waiting for his eyes to adjust. After a few moments, he stepped forward with care, setting his feet down so that there was little noise as he made his way down the center. About halfway down, where he was just beginning to make out the details of the crucifix hanging on the wall behind the podium, he tripped over the edge of a paving stone that was protruding up from the floor by just enough to catch the toe of his shoe. Only by great exertion did he manage to keep himself from stretching his length on the floor. The resulting noise echoed through the building.

"Who's there?"

Simon froze. If he'd known there was anyone in the church, he wouldn't have entered. What to do?

There was a shuffling sound as a figure moved from the front of the nave into a beam of light from one of the few windows. "Who's there?" The voice was that of an old man. Simon relaxed. "Is there something I can do to help you?"

"No," Simon replied. "Um, I just...I was just passing by... and, um..."

"And you wanted to see the inside of the church?" The speaker resolved into the figure of a stooped old man with flowing white hair and beard and dressed in rusty black clothes.

"Well..."

"It's all right, son. There is nothing happening today. The wedding that was scheduled for this afternoon has been postponed."

The smile on the old man's face prompted Simon to ask, "Why?"

The old man chuckled. "Well, it seems that the bride's mother invited the groom to dine with the family, and fixed a special dish. In the middle of the night the poor man awoke with stomach pains, and could not even clamber out of the bed before his bowels released. I understand it was rather noxious."

Simon giggled.

"Well may you laugh, boy. But the groom accused his mother-in-law-to-be of attempting to poison him, and his betrothed began throwing everything at him that she could get her hands on because of the insult dealt her mother."

"So, they are not going to wed?" Simon said around another giggle about to escape.

"No, they will probably marry after the heat of everyone's anger cools off. But I wager it will be some time before the groom eats his bride's mother's cooking again."

That did it. Simon's giggle escaped, followed by several chortles and even a guffaw or two. When his hilarity began to settle, the old man spoke up again.

"Did you come just to hear the latest gossip from an old preacher, lad? Or did you have some question on your heart?"

"Well..." Simon began, dragging the word out. The old man smiled encouragingly. "...it's Samson, you see."

"Ah, Samson," the old man nodded. He gestured with a gnarled hand. "Come, let us sit and discuss Samson." When they had settled on the steps leading up to the podium, he faced Simon with faded blue eyes framed with wrinkles peering out from between his bushy white eyebrows and his beard.

"So, lad...what is your name?"

"Simon, sir."

"And I am Pastor Moritz Gruber." He nodded. "So, Simon, which Samson are we to talk about?"

Simon was perplexed. "You mean there is more than one?"

The old pastor gave a hearty chuckle. "I meant did you want to talk about the Samson of the Bible or some other Samson?"

"The one in the Bible, please, sir."

"Do you have a question, then?"

"Well..." Simon hesitated, then poured out in a rush, "why was Samson such a fool? Why could he not see that Delilah was playing with him? Why did he tell her his secret so she could tell the Philistines and they could capture and blind him?" He stopped, breathless.

Pastor Gruber reached up and ran rheumatism-twisted fingers through his beard. "Yes, indeed, those are good questions." At least he wasn't laughing at him, Simon thought to himself.

"The first thing you must know, young Simon, is that all men, even the greatest of heroes, have flaws. Only our Saviour is without flaw or imperfection. Even the greatest heroes of the Bible have flaws. Why, King David..." Pastor Gruber stopped for a moment. "But then, you are asking about Samson, not David." He coughed for a moment, a deep wet sound. "Let us just say that Samson was a good example of a flawed hero."

"But he was so strong, and so great, and so mighty," Simon protested.

"The ancient Greeks tell us that the greater the hero, the deeper his flaws, the worst of which was arrogant pride, what they called *hubris."* The old man raised a hand. "And certainly that seems to be true of Samson. I have often thought that Samson was not a very smart man, myself."

Simon was stunned. He'd come to the church looking for answers, only to find that the pastor had some of the same thoughts he had. That left his mind reeling for a moment. "But Delilah..." he finally said.

"Ah, the harlot Delilah," Pastor Gruber replied with a small smile. "How old are you, lad?"

"Twelve, I think."

"Have you started looking at girls yet?"

Simon sat back, startled and embarrassed. It was strange to him. Girls caught his eye recently in a way they never had before. Not that any would look at him, not once they saw his arm.

"Never mind," the pastor chuckled before Simon could respond. "If you have not yet, you will soon."

The old man sobered. "The attraction of a man for a woman is a gift from God, but it is also one of Satan's greatest temptations. For some men, women are a weakness. They cannot stay away from them, especially if they are not their own wives. Samson was that way, if I read the scriptures correctly." He sighed. "A man who has a weakness for women is disarmed when he meets one who is a subtle schemer and conniver like Delilah."

"So why didn't God tell Samson to leave her alone?"

"But he did, Simon. Samson was what they called a Nazarite, and he had rules that he was supposed to live by." Pastor Gruber clicked his tongue. "He knew what God wanted from him. But Samson was a very proud man, so he did what he wanted."

"Why didn't God stop Samson from meeting Delilah?"

"You will have to ask God that question someday, young Simon, for I have no answer." The pastor chuckled again. "In fact, I have my own list of questions. But consider Samson's end." He closed his eyes and quoted from memory.

"And Samson said, Let me die with the Philistines. And he bowed himself with all his might; and the house fell upon the lords, and upon all the people that were therein. So the dead which he slew at his death were more than they which he slew in his life."

"What do you mean?" Simon asked.

"At the end," Pastor Gruber mused, "after he had failed, Samson remembered what God had called him to do. He called out to God, and God rewarded him for it."

"Rewarded? Being killed is a reward?" Simon's questions were impassioned.

"All men die, Simon." The old pastor pointed out the door of the church. "Kings die, merchants die, soldiers and generals die, doctors and lawyers and farmers and bakers all die. Even old pastors die." He laid a hand on his own chest. "No one escapes death, not even our Saviour. Cheating death is never within our grasp, as much as some people try to do it." He lowered his hand. "No, lad, what matters is how you die. Sometimes that matters even more than how you live. That was certainly so in Samson's case. 'So the dead which he slew at his death were more than they which he slew in his life.' Despite his arrogant pride, it is not a bad epitaph for a hero who died defending his people."

Simon sat back, slumped. "I...I don't know. I never thought of it that way. It just seemed so...so stupid, the way things happened."

Pastor Gruber gave his gentle smile. "But scripture says that the ways of the Lord are foolishness to men."

They sat in silence together for some time. The old pastor seemed to know when to quit talking, letting the boy's mind work through everything that had been given him. At length, Simon straightened.

"I need to think about this." He faced Pastor Gruber. "Can I come back and talk with you again?"

Again the gentle smile bloomed in the middle of the white whiskers. "Of course, young Simon. I am here most days. The senior pastors don't let me preach much these days...my voice isn't what it used to be, I'm afraid, and I am a bit absentminded at times. But they do not mind my spending time here where I can be a hand and a voice for those poor souls in this part of the city. And if there are weddings or such scheduled, we will find a quiet corner, you and I."

Simon stood and awkwardly bobbed his head. "Thank you, Pastor Gruber. I think you have helped me."

"The Lord helped you, lad. I am just an old man waiting for my days to end."

"Well, thank you anyway." Simon walked to the doorway of the church, then turned to look back. Pastor Gruber stood in another beam of light from a window and raised a hand in farewell. Simon waved back, then plunged back into the streets of Magdeburg.

Chapter 29

Franz gave the downbeat for the next-to-the-last song of the night, what Marla referred to as her mother's favorite ballad, "Those Were the Days."

During the slow verse, Franz looked around as his bow made the slight tremolo under Marla's voice. The Green Horse was standing room only tonight, as the up-timers would have said—if any had been able to get in, that is. But with the exception of Marla and Atwood, the crowd tonight was all down-timers.

Some he recognized: the table at the front where Friedrich von Logau and Johann Gronow were planted with several of their friends; the CoC men who were scattered throughout the crowd; even the cabbie who had brought Atwood from the pier to the house had managed to squeeze in and was standing in a corner with a couple of friends.

Marla was winding up the verse. Franz stopped the tremolo, poised to put a foundation of broad bow strokes under the beginning of the chorus. He could see her take the deep breath that led into it. And...now!

"Those were the days, my friend,"

They were off. For all that the lyrics seemed a bit maudlin in their constant dwelling on the past, even in German translation, Franz couldn't deny that the chorus could almost raise a corpse. It was a chorus made for singing along, and sure enough, at the end of the second verse, when they hit the chorus, half the men in the tavern were singing right along with Marla, from Logau and his pals to the cabbie in the back corner.

When they hit the chorus the third time, everyone was singing, even Franz, who, as he had remarked before, had the voice of a raven or crow. It was the only time he allowed himself to sing in public, when the public was being so loud he couldn't be heard.

After the last verse, Marla cycled through the chorus three more times, the last two on the "Lai, lai" syllables. If it was possible, the roar from the crowd got even louder. Franz cast a sideways glance at the walls. He didn't think it was possible for them to bulge, but...

Marla took to a high note on *"Oh..."* and held it. Even over the roar of the men her voice penetrated, and within a short time they had all quieted. She glanced sideways at Franz, who gave a nod back. With that, she drew the song to an end with *"...yes, those were the days!"*

The players all snapped to a halt with her, and there was a bare moment of silence before the patrons of the tavern erupted into applause; claps, shouts, whistles, and very quickly, a rhythmic stomping of feet. This went on for a timeless moment. Franz's ears were starting to ring when Marla held her arms up at an angle, and just stood there.

Bit by bit the noise died down: first the stomping; then the whistling; then the shouting; and finally the clapping slowly faded away. A roomful of flush-faced men, hot and sweaty, sat and gazed on Marla. Franz had to chuckle to himself—it was a good thing that he wasn't the jealous type.

At last Marla lowered her arms. Franz knew she was going to say something, but he didn't know for sure what would come out. For that matter, he wasn't sure she knew what she was going to say.

"Thank you," Marla began. Someone in the back of the room started to clap again, but she held up a hand. "Please, just listen to me for a few minutes."

The noise died down. Franz watched as she brushed her hair back behind her ears. At this moment, he was perhaps prouder of Marla than he had ever been in his life. He didn't—couldn't— know what she had been through the last few months. His own grief had been bad enough, but it wasn't even a tithe of what she had felt; he knew that much. And yet now she stood before these men, mostly rough working-class men, to try to do something she thought was very important. He tucked his violin and bow under his arm and clasped his hands behind his back, crippled left cradled in whole right, squeezing them together as hard as he could as he breathed a silent prayer for the woman who had proven herself to be far braver than he.

"I'm not very fond of politics," Marla started again. A chuckle ran through the room. "I mean, I find them boring, and tedious, and most politicians are stuffy people. At least they mostly were up-time, and except for Mike and Ed, they mostly are down-time, from what I can see." The laughter got louder.

"But," she stopped and swallowed, "every once in a while something happens that forces people like me to pay attention. Every once in a while someone does or says something so wrong, so raw, so evil, so...I don't know...hellish, maybe, that even people like me will take a stand."

The room was utterly quiet. It seemed as if the mob of men sitting and standing cheek by jowl were all holding their collective breath, hanging on Marla's every word. Franz even found himself not breathing, until he noticed and let his air out.

"I'm talking about what's been happening in Berlin," Marla continued.

If it was possible, attention in the room got even sharper.

"I'm not a wordsmith. I'm not a philosopher, or preacher, or poet, or playwright. But I can recognize good words when I see them, and I found some in an up-timer song. So I give you tonight—tonight and every night—'Do You Hear the People Sing?'"

Marla bowed her head for a moment, then raised it again. She took a deep breath, then nodded without looking around. Franz gave the nod to the others, and they began the low unison tones that gave Marla the foundation for the beginning.

"Do you hear the people sing?"

Franz was awe-struck. He knew just how good a musician, how fine a singer, his wife was. And he had heard her rise above even her usual superlative level of performance before. But tonight, tonight she had elevated to another plane entirely; or perhaps a different world. He could hear the passion in her voice, he could hear the joy that she was pouring out like a very fountain, but tonight there was a keenness, a honed edge to her. She stood still as she sang, unlike her normal flowing movements; hands outstretched, no movement other than the rise and fall of her chest and diaphragm.

At the end of it, when Marla had finished pouring forth her soul like a fountain of liquid diamond, it was as if the voice of heaven had stopped; the world seemed darker and poorer for it. She stood there, breast heaving as she gulped air in, hand shaking as she tucked a loosened lock of hair back behind her ear again.

There was one thought on the minds of every man facing her. Franz could see it in their eyes. But only one had the courage to say it. There was a stir as men moved—or were moved—out of the way to allow Gunther Achterhof to reach the front. He nodded to Marla, which Franz knew was equivalent to a genu-flection from a lesser man, and said in a quiet voice, "*Wieder, bitte*—again, please."

Marla nodded in return.

The room was quiet as she regained her breath, waiting with a hard singleness of purpose. After some moments, she looked over to Franz and lifted a hand. He looked to their friends, gave the nod, and began again.

The second time through was not as intense as the first time. It couldn't help but be lesser. No singer could give at that most extreme level for very long. Oh, Franz could tell that Marla still felt the passion for the song, and she still gave it a superlative performance, but the unique edge was missing. She was just Marla with the angelic voice now, rather than being the Sword of Music, or of God. But that was still enough.

Men throughout the room mouthed the words, trying to com-mit them to memory. These were words that would change men's lives. Franz knew it, and they could sense it.

The song came to an end a second time. There was a brief moment of silence, until Logau began rapping his walking stick on his table top in a slow regular beat that matched the pulse of the song. Hands and feet quickly followed suit, until the building rocked from the regular percussive slam of sound.

Marla faced the men. Franz could see her shoulders beginning to shake, so he handed off his violin to one of the Amsel broth-ers and went to guide her to a stool. Gronow leapt up from his and shoved it forward with alacrity. Franz looked up and caught Gunther's gaze. He drew his hand across his throat sharply.

Gunther got the point as if they had discussed having a special signal. He gave a piercing whistle, then yelled, "Out! The evening's over. Remember it, but go home now."

CoC men coalesced from all over the room, forming a barrier between Marla and her friends and the rest of the crowd. The tavern emptied; amidst shoving and protesting, granted, but it emptied.

Franz waved Gunther over, and handed him a piece of paper from his pocket.

"She said you would want this."

Gunther took it with upraised eyebrows.

"Words," Franz explained.

Gunther unfolded it enough to see the first verse of lyrics to the song, and flashed a tight smile to them all. "She is so right. Thank you, my friend." He shook Franz's hand. "My friends." He swept his gaze around the rest of the group. "Frau Marla." He nodded again to her. "This will mean quite a lot to the people."

There was a stir in the doorway, someone trying to go against the flow. Whoever it was managed to penetrate the crowd, until he bounced off of the CoC men.

Franz had just drawn Marla to her feet, ready to take her home. He looked around at the disturbance, and caught a glimpse of a familiar face being pushed away.

"Let him through," he called out. A moment later, Andrea Abati squeezed through the barrier of muscle and hurried over to take Marla's hands.

Marla looked up at him—one of the few down-timers who was taller than she—and her mouth quirked a bit, as if she was trying to smile.

"Did you hear me, Master Andrea?"

"I wasn't able to get inside, but I was able to stand in the doorway and hear you." He was very serious, and he swallowed before he spoke again. "Oh, child, what have you wrought?"

Franz could see the iron determination on Marla's face, as weary and drained as she was.

"What I must, Master Andrea. What I must."

Franz arose early the next morning. By some miracle of scheduling, Atwood had managed to arrange for a ride on a river boat leaving Magdeburg that day, even though it was Sunday. By the time the sun was shining over the city walls, Franz and Atwood were walking out the front door to catch a cab for the river dock. Atwood allowed Franz to carry the duffle, but the up-timer still insisted on carrying the case with the precious recording rig.

A couple of men leaning against the front of their house straightened as they came out the door. Atwood frowned a bit, but relaxed when Franz greeted them.

"Klaus, Reuel. It has been a while since I've seen you."

"Aye," Klaus nodded. "Gunther said after last night that we should stand watch again for a while."

"Watch?" Atwood asked.

"I am sorry, I forgot to introduce you. Herr Cochran, meet Klaus Meissner and Reuel Traeger, two of the staunchest members in the ranks of the Committees of Correspondence." Atwood held his hand out. "Guys, this is Atwood Cochran from Grantville, Marla's good friend." They smiled and shook hands with the up-timer.

Klaus snapped his fingers. "I almost forgot." He started digging through his pockets. "Gunther wanted you to have this right away." He grinned in triumph and produced a much folded sheet of paper from his coat and handed it to Franz.

Franz unfolded it to produce a broadsheet. The caption blazoned across the top read:

Ein Ruf zu den Waffen

Atwood looked over his shoulder. "I still have trouble reading the heavy scripts," he said. "What does it say?"

"A Call to Arms," Franz translated. He gestured to the balance of the broadsheet. "And here are the words Marla sang last night."

Atwood whistled. "That was fast work, to get this out so quickly."

Klaus grinned. "Gunther had the press crew up out of bed as soon as he got back to the Arches last night. Told them he didn't care what they had to do, he wanted this on the streets by dawn." He chuckled. "They did it, too."

Franz tried to hand the broadsheet back to Klaus, who held up a hand in refusal.

"That's for you and Frau Marla, Herr Franz. Gunther insisted you have one of the first copies. 'That's little enough,' he said, 'for what she has worked for us.'"

Franz nodded his thanks, folded the broadsheet back up with care, and placed it in his own jacket pocket.

"Herr Franz," Reuel spoke up, "you tell Frau Marla that we heard her sing last night, and we really liked it. But that last song," his expression became very sober, "that last song was something special. You tell her that for us, and tell her that... just tell her that."

"I will," Franz assured him.

"There's already men kicking themselves that they were not there to hear her last night," Klaus added.

"Oh, tell them not to worry," Atwood spoke up with a grin. "I recorded the song on tape, and I'm going to play it on my music show on Voice of America in a week."

Klaus and Reuel looked at him wide-eyed. "Does Gunther know that?"

Atwood's grin grew wider. "Since I just now decided to do it, I really doubt that he does."

"'Scuse me," Klaus said. He stepped out into the street and whistled shrilly. Another man trotted up from a block away. "Will, you stay here. I have to get word to Gunther." And he sprinted down the street.

A cab approached, attracted by the whistle. Franz flagged the cabbie down, and he and Atwood clambered up into the wagon with the baggage. The cabbie clucked to his horse, and they rolled off with a final wave to the CoC men.

"Keep watch?" Atwood repeated his question. "Why do you have CoC toughs loitering in front of your house like they're keeping guard on it?"

"Because they are."

Atwood frowned. "Give."

"When we first came to Magdeburg, the CoC kept an eye over us because we were important to Frau Simpson. But after Marla started singing the Irish songs in the tavern, well, those songs spoke to them and they watched over her because the songs were important to them. And to keep her from being harassed in the tavern, until people learned who and what she was."

"Oh, yes," Atwood chuckled. "I got a good belly-laugh when I heard what she was doing. You do realize that most of those songs were from the Catholic side of that particular disagreement, don't you? The thought of a bunch of mostly Protestant Germans singing music written by mostly Catholic Irishmen just really tickled my funny bone. Still does."

They chatted about nothing consequential for a few blocks, until Atwood pointed to one side.

"Look at that."

Franz followed the other man's finger and saw a young woman handing out broadsheets to grasping hands, broadsheets that had a familiar looking caption on them. He leaned back, as he began to absorb the reality of just what might come of Marla's song.

Friedrich von Logau sauntered into Walcha's Coffee House later that day, pleased with himself, which wasn't an unusual condition, and pleased with the world as well, which was a bit more irregular. He seated himself at his accustomed table, waving a hand at the serving maid and holding up one finger. His cup of coffee appeared almost before he could lower his hand.

He was midway through his first cup, doodling in his pocket notebook again as he mentally masticated on a new epigram that was refusing to take proper shape, when the door opened and Gronow and Plavius came in. They were arguing over something; not an unusual state of affairs for them. They broke it off when they saw Friedrich, however, and almost marched on him, wasting no time in crossing the floor and setting into chairs on each side of him.

Logau made a slow studied gesture of pulling out his pocket watch and checking the time. "Well, I would have said good morning, my friends, but according to this the morning has fled and afternoon is upon us." He closed the cover of the watch and beamed at them. "So good afternoon to you, instead. What took you so long?"

"*Ach,*" Plavius said, "the pastor was long-winded in his homily this morning, and the choir had a new cantata to sing by *Kappellmeister* Schütz, which was so long I wonder if he got confused and decided to write an oratorio instead."

Gronow waved a hand in dismissal of all that. "Friedrich, you knew, did you not, what that woman was going to do last night?"

Logau pursed his lips and nodded.

"And you purposely and intentionally did not tell us beforehand."

Now Logau could feel his facial muscles stretch as the very broad grin fought its way onto his face despite all he could do to repress it.

"You son of a syphilitic sow," Gronow exclaimed in English,

sitting back as the serving maid slid a cup of coffee in front of him.

"Nice alliteration," Logau commented, still smiling. He was enjoying this.

"No," Plavius contradicted his friend. "You should not insult good swine that way. Myself, I would say he is more of a scrofulous, flea-infested, pox-ridden cur."

Logau put his pencil down, and applauded.

"Well done, my friends. You have risen to new heights—or is it depths—of invective. Well done, indeed."

He stopped clapping, and let the smile slip from his face. "Yes, I knew what she intended to do. And having heard her rehearse it once, I thought I knew what to expect."

Logau remained silent after that, until Gronow set his coffee cup down with a clank and said, "Well?" Logau looked at him with his eyebrows raised. "What did you expect?" Gronow's voice dripped with impatience.

"I really do not recall, now," Logau replied, "but what we heard was far more than I expected. Gods and little demons," Plavius frowned at his blasphemy, but Logau continued on, "if she had called for a march on Berlin after that song, I would have been in the front rank. Me; resident skeptic, Stoic, and curmudgeon in training after my august father. I am not at all sure that the wax of Ulysses would prevail against the siren's voice of Frau Linder."

Plavius checked his coffee cup in its motion to his mouth, and returned it to the table. "Along that thought..." He reached inside his coat and drew a page out that he handed to Logau. "The CoC girls were handing these out this morning. Doing a brisk trade, they were."

Logau unfolded the page into a broadsheet. It was a momentary shock to see the words he had penned for Marla in print under a screaming banner. But then the reality of who had to be involved sank in, and a sardonic smile crossed his face.

"Of course. It was to be expected that the good Gunther Achterhof would not let this opportunity slip."

The conversation turned after that to questions of what Gronow would publish in the next issue of *Black Tomcat Magazine*, as well as their various projects, such as Gronow's libretto for the opera *Arthur Rex*. It turned, that is, until Gronow himself jerked upright coughing and spewing coffee from his mouth.

Logau leaned back to make sure that none of the spew landed on his clothing. He frowned at his friend. "Coffee is for drinking, not breathing. And what, may I ask, brought on this fit?"

Gronow held up a hand until he finally could clear his throat and get a breath of air. "It just dawned on me—she's going to sing Guinevere in my opera!"

Logau began to laugh at the panic-stricken look on his friend's face.

Chapter 30

Magdeburg Times-Journal
January 21, 1636

Editorial—On the Notes of Angels
by Friedrich von Logau

It was my extreme good fortune to spend a good part of my evening last Saturday night in an establishment called the Green Horse. I and some of my friends had gone there to hear the up-timer—no, she would object to my characterizing her in that manner—to hear that most accomplished of musicians, Frau Marla Linder, hold court. She and her band of Companions took the field, if you will allow me to mix metaphors, and salvoed song after song at those who were seated before her. Slow songs, fast songs; serious songs, funny songs. And she had us all in her hand, going where she directed, laughing and crying in turn.

Those of you who have heard *of* Frau Linder, but have not actually heard her, may think to brush aside the oft-heard statement that she sings with the voice of heaven. Do not do so. If you have been reading my columns here, you know that I seldom permit hyperbole to go unchallenged. Therefore, be suitably impressed when I say that to call her voice angelic or heavenly is not an insult to heaven or an overstatement of her gifts as a musician. I have been to Rome. I have heard the finest voices in the world there, and in Florence, and in Venice. And I say to you, that she is not their equal, but beyond them—*ne plus ultra*, if you will.

I could end this article at this point, with a paean to the good Frau Linder. But in all truth, I told you all of that in order to now tell you this story, with words that cannot help but be inadequate to the task. Saturday night, at the last, Frau Linder proved to be an outstanding general as she unveiled her greatest stratagem which had been held in reserve all evening. She sang a song: a song that was flavored with bitterness, and rue, and gall; a song that stirred the blood of everyone there and called for blood; a song that fired the soul and chilled the spirit; a song that, although no names were named, called for all the Germanies to stand forth; and she aimed it at Berlin. She aimed it at the heart of Chancellor The Ox, and the herd that has gathered behind him. Like Diana the Huntress she stood forth, aimed, and loosed. And she loosed no shaft of Eros, but rather of Eris; Mars himself would not be shamed by what was sent forth that night.

In the light of day, I marvel at Frau Linder: for her voice, for her passion, for the hard steel of her convictions. At the risk of evoking the anger of the pastors, I will paraphrase Our Saviour: "I have not found such passion, no, not in all the Germanies."

As for Saturday night, let me end this rumination with another paraphrase, this time from the English playwright William Shakespeare:

> *And gentlemen in Germany, now a-bed*
> *Shall think themselves accursed they were not here,*
> *And hold their manhoods cheap whiles any speaks*
> *"I was there that night, to hear Frau Linder sing."*

Andreas Schardius lowered the paper and stared at the wall opposite his desk. He laid a finger from nose to chin, thinking.

After a moment, he removed it and nodded. "Interesting," he said. "So the angel is not ignorant of where she is, after all."

He leaned back in his chair and thought some more.

In his youth, Schardius had spent some time in northern Italy, mostly at Venice and Florence. He had enjoyed both cities and their societies greatly, but even now, years later, Florence called to him. It was there he had seen Francesca Caccini, *La Cecchina*, the nightingale of the Medici court. She was a few years older than him, and wasn't exactly beautiful, but she was a most exciting person to be around, in several senses of the word.

And he had lusted after her; there was no other word for it. He had wanted to possess her so badly he had ached. But even as a near-callow youth, and even in that state of constant arousal, he had retained enough wisdom to understand that she was under the protection of the Medici family, which was a line that he had dared not cross.

He had eventually left Florence with his lust unslaked. But to this day, the sound of an attractive woman singing could send a thrill up and down his spine. And now, in the person of Marla Linder, he might be able to attain his desire, his longing.

That thought caused his breath to come a little faster.

Karl Honister finished reading the article out loud, and looked over the top of it at Byron. "Frau Linder is some connection to you, isn't she?"

Byron shrugged as he signed off on a report. "Wife's sister."

"Is she always so...ah, direct?"

Gotthilf snorted. "Try strong-willed. She's full-blood sister, after all, to the woman who married him," he jerked a thumb at his partner, "of her own free will, and holds her own with him."

"Point," Honister said as Byron grinned. The other detective sergeant pulled a paper out of his coat, and unfolded a broadsheet. "But I have met Frau Linder the elder, and I don't think she would have seen this come out from something she did."

Byron took the paper, and Gotthilf read over his shoulder. The hair on his neck stood up as his eyes scanned down the lyrics on the page. "Wow," the down-timer said.

"Nope," Byron said after he handed the page back to Honister. "Jonni might be stubborn and hardheaded, but she's never been in her little sister's league. And even though she didn't write the words, that's pure quill Marla on that page. No give to her, once she's decided." He scanned over and signed another report. "I'm not much of a praying man, but from time to time I thank God for sending Franz Sylwester along four years ago."

"What do you mean?" Gotthilf asked.

"You've met Marla. Try to imagine her without Franz in her life." Gotthilf considered, and twitched his shoulders in a sudden chill. "Yah."

Grantville

Atwood was so wrapped up in the music that when it came to an end, he had forgotten where he was. It was an occupational hazard for a disc jockey. It took a moment before he realized it was time for him to talk again. He quickly flipped a switch on the board and leaned forward to the microphone on the table.

"Once again, that was the *Little Fugue in G*, written originally for organ by Johann Sebastian Bach and transcribed for orchestra by Leopold Stokowski. I hope you enjoyed that; it's certainly one of my favorites."

As he was talking, Atwood was flipping switches and checking that the cassette player was cued up. It still amused him from time to time that he was a radio disc jockey to half of Germany.

He flipped a last switch and spoke into the open mike. "I promised you something very special at the beginning of the evening. Tonight we have a recording of someone here in Germany, made only a week ago. I predict that you will either like it or hate it, but you will not be able to ignore it. So, here is Marla Linder and her friends, with 'Do You Hear the People Sing?'"

Atwood pressed the play button on the cassette deck. After a moment the music began to flow from the control room monitor speakers. He leaned back and just listened, a large grin on his face.

He had the professional musician's ability to divorce himself from the effect of the music while he appraised the performance. It was especially hard to do for this recording, though, and not because he'd been involved in producing it. Marla's performance was beyond her usual excellence; it was so spot on it was like it was the sonic equivalent of a laser beam. And for a live recording, with the equipment available, it was pretty darn good, if he did say so himself. His Sony rig was near top of the line when he got it, and for Marla he had opened his last virgin chromium dioxide cassette tape package, over which he would never record. That sound was as clear and as pristine as anything that would be produced for generations, probably. The folks at Trommler Records had practically slavered over it.

And wouldn't it just set the fox in the henhouse, though? Most down-timers still didn't get the full power and impact of radio. The nobility for sure didn't get it. This recording would drive the point home like a ten-penny nail smacked by a sixteen-pound sledge hammer.

Assessment over, he surrendered himself to the music. All too soon it was finished. He leaned forward again. "There is nothing I can say after that. I hope you enjoyed it. And if you did like it, you might drop a line to the folks at Trommler Records. They're going to put out a record of that song. It should be available soon.

"Thanks for being with us this Sunday evening for *Adventures in Great Music* on the Voice of America Radio Network, sponsored by the Burke Wish Book, where you can order anything you need or want. I'll see you next Sunday evening.

"I'm Atwood Cochran, and good night."

Magdeburg

Gotthilf threw a hand up in front of Byron's chest and brought his partner to a halt.

"What's up?" Byron asked, looking around.

"Sssh," Gotthilf whispered. "That's Fraulein Metzgerin up ahead."

Byron caught sight of the woman limping along the street, leaning heavily on a cane. "So it is. Want to go talk to her?"

"Actually, I do," Gotthilf admitted. "But by myself, I think." Byron looked at him with raised eyebrows. "I might get more out of her that way."

His partner shrugged. "Whatever. I'm good with that. I'll head back to the station. I've got more reports to read anyway."

They parted company, and Gotthilf trailed along behind the woman for about half a block, then he eased up beside her.

"Fraulein Metzgerin?" He gave a partial bow, touching the brim of his hat with two fingers.

"Oh!"

The young woman lurched in surprise, and Gotthilf hastily reached a hand out to grab her elbow and help her keep her footing. As soon as he could see she was stable, he released her and stepped back to give her room.

"Oh," Fraulein Metzgerin repeated in a more normal tone of voice. "Sergeant Hoch, is it not?"

"Yes, Fraulein. I saw you in the street alone, and wondered if something was wrong."

"No," she replied. "I looked out a little while ago, and the sun was shining, and since it was, I decided to walk down to Frau Diermissen to get some purple thread."

"Purple thread?" Gotthilf asked as he kept pace with her slow steps.

"Mm-hmm." Fraulein Metzgerin didn't say anything for a moment as she negotiated a tricky patch of the street where a puddle had formed across part of what would have been her best path. Gotthilf stood ready to help her, but she placed her cane carefully, and stepped with care across the slick gravel, arriving at the other side without mishap.

Once there, she resumed her conversation. "I do embroidery, you see, for Frau Schneider and other seamstresses."

"Frau Schneider, you say?" Gotthilf tucked that connection away in his mind. You never knew when little bits of information like that could prove to be useful. "My mother speaks very highly of her."

"And she should," Fraulein Metzgerin said with a smile. "I think she is the best of them. Certainly she is the best I have worked with."

"So, you needed some purple thread for work you are doing for the good Frau Schneider," Gotthilf continued. "But could you not have sent your young friend Simon Bayer for it and saved yourself the steps?"

Fraulein Metzgerin stopped, and looked at Gotthilf. He noticed with part of his mind that her eyes were level with his, and they were not at this moment friendly. In fact, they seemed rather cold.

"Sergeant Hoch, I am a cripple. That does not mean I am stupid. You dance attendance on me for a reason, and it is not because of my fair face or form." Gotthilf thought he detected a trace of bitterness; but only a trace. "If you have something to ask me, ask it."

Gotthilf tilted his head and observed her for a moment, then nodded. "As you say. Yes, we..."

"The *Polizei*," she interrupted.

Gotthilf nodded again. "The *Polizei* have been looking at your brother. Not that we suspect him of a crime," he hastened to add as her eyes widened. "But he has been known to associate with men that we are interested in."

"So why have you not asked your questions of him?" Fraulein Metzgerin asked, her voice oozing tartness.

Gotthilf shrugged. "Because the time is not right. We do not know enough to know what questions to ask."

Fraulein Metzgerin stared at him with hard eyes for several moments, then faced forward again. "Men!" she muttered as she started down the road again.

Gotthilf continued to keep pace with her. They walked in silence for some time, until he said, "We have met before, you know."

"Yes, at the tavern several days ago." Her tone now bordered on acerbic. It was obvious that she was no longer enjoying their conversation.

"No, actually it was back before the sack. And perhaps I misspoke a bit; we did not actually meet, but we did see each other."

Ursula stopped again, and the expression she turned on him was dark enough to be called thunderous.

"Do not attempt to delude me, Sergeant!"

He held his hands up in a peace gesture. "On my honor, our paths have indeed crossed on occasion when I accompanied my sister to her catechism classes."

"Your...sister."

"Margarethe Hoch. She is somewhat younger than you, I believe, but I do recall seeing you at least twice." As he said that, the image of a younger Ursula Metzgerin crossed his mind. "It was before the sack of the city, of course."

An expression of sorrow and pain crossed Fraulein Metzgerin's face. "Yes. Of course. So much there was before the sack of the city." She faced forward and resumed her progress.

Their mutual journey ended at a flight of wooden steps up the outside of a building. Fraulein Metzgerin turned to face him once again.

"I remember Margarethe Hoch. A sweet girl." She paused for a moment. "Those were good times. Give her my greetings, please."

"I will," Gotthilf said. "May I help you in any way?" he continued, as she set foot on the first stair tread.

"No," Fraulein Metzgerin responded. "There is nothing you can do to help." She looked back over her shoulder with a smile. "But thank you for asking."

And with that, she began her slow ascent up the stairs, one tread at a time, using her cane and the railing to pull herself up over the obstacle that her right leg presented. Gotthilf waited at the bottom, watching, until she had attained the landing outside her door. She pulled a key from a pocket in her jacket, unlocked the door, and entered in without looking at him.

After the door closed, he heaved a sigh, and stood staring at nothing in particular for a long moment. That last smile—that was the face of the girl he had seen before the sack. That was the face of the woman who might have been, before her body was wrecked by God-knows-what horrible accident. It was the face of a woman that he was beginning to find very interesting, God help him.

He looked up to see a *Polizei* patrolman walking down the block toward him. He stepped away from the stairs and beckoned to the man. It was one of the older hands, so they recognized each other.

"Good afternoon, Sergeant Hoch," the patrolman said. "Is there something I can do for you?"

"Do you know the people who live up these stairs, Phillip?"

"Aye. That would be Hans Metzger, a warehouse worker and sometime fighter in the contests held out at the old bear-baiting pit; his sister Ursula, the cripple; and some boy that seems to have moved in with them recently."

"The boy would be Simon Bayer, and no, I don't know if he is really from Bavaria."

"Is there something you need from them, Sergeant?"

"Yes, uh, no. Not from them. What I want is for you and your mates to keep an eye on Fraulein Metzgerin. See to it that no one bothers her."

"Right. Keep a protective watch on the Fraulein. I will pass the word to Bastian and Johann. They usually walk the other shifts on this patrol. Anything else?"

Gotthilf hesitated for a moment, then said, "Also keep an eye on her brother. If you notice anyone spending a lot of time with him, I want to know about it. If he has any unusual visitors, I want to know about it. If he disappears for any period of time, I want to know about it."

"Right, sir. Will do."

"That's all, Phillip. Send word to the main station if anything comes up I need to hear about."

The watchman touched the brim of his hat in salute, and moved on down the street. Gotthilf looked up at the door into the Metzger apartment, feeling as if he had perhaps betrayed a friend.

Part Three

February 1636

Let me write the songs of a nation,
and I care not who makes its laws.
—Dónal Ó Conaill

Chapter 31

Magdeburg

Right in the middle of the big Act III duet between Guinevere and Arthur, Marla started coughing. It was more than a small cough. It bordered on a paroxysm; cough followed cough followed cough. The rehearsal ground to a halt around her, and after a moment, Amber Higham picked up a bottle and brought it to her.

Marla finally got whatever it was in her throat cleared out, and took a breath. She felt light-headed after all that, and she must have looked pale, because Dieter Fischer—not the radio preacher, the other one, the singer—who was singing the role of Arthur took her by the arm and led her back to her stool. Amber handed her the bottle of purified water, and she sipped at it, then held the cool ceramic of the bottle against her forehead.

"Better now?" Amber asked.

She took another sip of water, then nodded.

"Yeah. I don't know what caused that, but it's over."

Amber studied her with practiced eyes, and evidently came to a decision, because she announced, "That's all for today, folks. We'll pick back up tomorrow afternoon at one o'clock. And Dieter," she pointed a finger at the baritone, "don't forget your music again."

"Yes, Frau Amber," he muttered against the laughter of the other singers in the room.

"You don't need to do that, Amber," Marla protested. "I'm okay now, we can keep going."

"Nope," Amber said. "The care and feeding of performers—especially you temperamental singers—is part of my job description. You're starting to droop, but you're not the only one. We'll call it a day, and pick it up from there tomorrow. Now go home and drink some tea or coffee or a hot toddy or whatever to rest your voice. Git!"

Marla got, along with the others. Amber in full director mode was not to be gainsaid. And in truth, she was tired. Fatigued would be a better word, actually. But it was a good feeling.

Ever since the night she sang The Song (as she thought of it) at the Green Horse, she had felt different—more...something. Assured wasn't the word, and neither was peaceful or well. Centered, now...that might be the right word. She still hurt from her loss, she still grieved at times, but she didn't feel totally off-balance all the time, as if she was swinging from one extreme to another on an emotional bungee cord. It was like when she first met Franz, after the Ring of Fire happened and she'd lost her parents and her brother. She'd been more than a bit moody then as well, and he had given her a center to rest on. Now, in a very strange way, that performance had done the same thing for her.

Or maybe she was just a bit dotty, to use a phrase her Aunt Susan would say, and it was just that enough time had passed for her to turn the corner, or crest the hill, or pass through the valley of the shadow of death, or whatever metaphor was most appropriate. Either way, she was thankful for the change.

By now her musings had carried her through the front door of the Royal Academy of Music, where they had been rehearsing. She finished buttoning her coat, and shifted her load of books to her left arm.

She looked up as Klaus and Reuel stirred from where they leaned against the front of the building. "Ah, there you are, my faithful shadows." The two men grinned at her, but didn't speak. She pointed across the small plaza. "To the opera house, to find my husband. The orchestra is rehearsing today, and we got done early."

"Yo, Karl," Byron called out. Gotthilf tagged along with his partner as Detective Honister changed directions and came their way. "I hear the final report on the fire investigation was turned in yesterday. Did Dan say it was arson?"

Karl Honister shook his head. "No, he stopped just short of that. He listed it as the most likely possibility, but he also said that it might have been an accident due to carelessness. The oil can that we found was one that belonged to Schiffer, after all."

Gotthilf snorted. "That is analogous to saying God is at fault because He created all things; therefore He created the wood, the oil, fire, and the idiot that brought them all together."

Byron laughed out loud. "Good one, partner." Gotthilf grinned in reply.

Honister smiled. "Indeed. Myself, I think the candle stub we found is probable proof of intent."

"Yah," Gotthilf replied. "I have trouble believing that that particular piece of evidence was there simply by random chance or negative serendipity."

The other two men nodded in agreement.

"I think Captain Reilly agrees," Honister added. "He told me to do more digging into this, see if I can find a suspect either way." He looked at Magdeburg's two best detectives. "Any advice for me on this one? I do not mind admitting it is somewhat outside of my experience."

"Just one thing," Byron said. He looked to his partner.

"You should know this one," Gotthilf picked up the cue. "I learned it at my father's knee, and you should have learned it at yours—follow the money."

"Arson?" Andreas Schardius pinched the bridge of his nose. "They think that someone set the wood stock on fire *on purpose*?" He lowered his hand and stared at Georg Kühlewein and Johann Westvol. His stomach began to roil; not an uncommon occurrence when he was in the presence of these two.

"Not necessarily," Kühlewein said. "They did say that it could have simply been an accident on the part of one of Schiffer's employees."

Schardius' mouth twisted in reaction to that thought, but he didn't say anything for a moment.

"Do you know who is doing the investigation?"

The other two men looked at each other, then Kühlewein said, "Someone named Honister, I believe."

"Ah, Phillip Honister's boy," Schardius said. "He's of good stock; he'll do it right. At least it's not Chieske and Hoch."

He'd had contact with those two during the investigation of Paulus Bünemann's death last year. Bünemann was a fellow corn factor, and the two detectives had had the temerity to consider him a suspect in the crime. Not respectful; especially since he hadn't been involved in it at all. Not that he hadn't thought about it occasionally, but he'd decided a long time ago that thoughts didn't count, except in Sunday sermons.

Kühlewein and Westvol looked back at him with lowered eyebrows, obviously waiting for a reaction that they weren't sure they wanted to experience. He took a deep breath, then let it out slowly.

"Fine. Maybe it was an accident, or carelessness, or simple stupidity. I am not sure I believe it, but let's say it was. We cannot afford—Can Not Afford," making sure they heard the emphasis in his voice, "to have another such event occur."

Both the other men nodded their heads with vigor. They understood that losing big money was a Bad Idea in more than one respect.

Schardius leveled an index finger at Kühlewein. "Therefore you, Herr Mayor Kühlewein, will stress to Leonhart Kolman there must be no repeats of this event. Feel free to loose the flensing knife of your tongue and flay him in slow inches."

Kühlewein nodded, with a hard set to his mouth and no compassion in his eyes.

"And you," Schardius shifted the finger to Westvol, and sighted down it like a gun barrel. "You will say nothing, and do nothing, of any sort out of the ordinary." Westvol nodded, opened his mouth, then closed it again.

Schardius sighed. "Spit it out, man."

"What about the newspapers?"

Schardius sat up straight. "Oh, do *not* tell me you have been talking to newspapermen!"

"No, no," Westvol hastened to assure him. "One reporter tried to interview me about the *Polizei* report on the fire, but I told him I could not spare the time right then. But he will try again, I am sure."

Westvol looked nervous at confessing this, but for once Schardius was not angry with the man; he was actually delighted with him.

"Good. Perfect, in fact. And in the future, if newspapermen contact either of you about anything dealing with this contract or project, just tell them that you have no comment and that the partners in the project will make a joint statement soon."

He was going to leave it at that, but decided he'd best make sure they knew what he expected. "And if they do contact you, you will tell me about it immediately. Understood?"

Both men nodded. Schardius had to suppress a snort at the thought that the race to be Dee might be even again.

"So, how are rehearsals going?" Mary Simpson asked, as she passed a cup of coffee to Amber Higham. They were in Mary's parlor again. That was her usual place for small meetings. She said the informality relaxed everyone.

Amber didn't care. The combination of good coffee and the heat emanating from the cast iron heater in the corner made the parlor one of her favorite places in Magdeburg during the winter. February had proven to be even colder than January so far, and January had not been warm by anybody's definition. She remembered one of the science guys back in Grantville talking about a Little Ice Age. From the sensations her toes were reporting, it wasn't particularly little.

"Rehearsals are going well," Amber replied, in her usual precise use of the English language. "In fact, we are actually a bit ahead of schedule in terms of learning lines and notes. I'm going to start blocking in another day or two."

The two women sat in companionable silence for several moments, just sipping coffee and enjoying the moment.

Mary finally set her cup down. "So, give—how is Marla doing?"

Amber shrugged. "As far as I can tell, fine."

She had been keeping strict watch on the young woman. Amber knew all about dealing with grief and stress; not from having lost a child, but from a particularly messy and tempestuous divorce after she'd caught her first husband in the costume room with the latest ingénue—again. Character assassination was the most civil of the techniques his lawyer had leveled against her, until she finally agreed to a rather less-than-equitable settlement just so she could get it over and done with. Then she'd retreated from Chicago to Grantville, where she licked her wounds for longer than she liked to admit. So, yeah, she knew something about grief.

"She's focused, staying on task, and she's learned—or learning, rather—in short order a part that might have challenged Beverly Sills." Amber shrugged again. "Only problem I see is that she's still a bit short on stamina. I have to rein her in, keep her from pushing too hard."

"Good." Mary seemed to relax a bit. "I hated to draft her so soon, but if we were going to have a prayer of pulling *Arthur Rex* off, we had to have her."

Amber nodded. "Oh, yeah. Heinrich outdid himself with this one. There are parts of it that sound like Puccini and Verdi rolled into one. But that rewrite of the two lead women's roles—killer stuff, in more ways than one."

Mary busied herself in pouring more coffee for the two of them, and then sat for a moment, staring at her cup but not drinking. Okay, Amber thought to herself, she's got something to tell me, and she's either not sure how to say it or she doesn't like what she's about to say. Either way, that's not good.

"I've had a request," Mary finally started. When she lifted her eyes, they weren't exactly pleading, but they did ask for understanding. "One of our backers—the merchant who's footing half of the production costs, actually—wants to watch the rehearsals when you start in the opera house."

Amber blew air through her lips. She was right. This wasn't good news. She really, really, really didn't like having producer types hanging around her rehearsals. The performers needed to be focused, and that was hard enough to achieve without the distraction—and often, the interference—of people with a vested interest in the production at hand.

On the other hand, in the theater world, the Golden Rule was "those who have the gold make the rules." It was just a fact that sponsorship and special privileges went hand in hand. And it wasn't the first time this had happened to Amber in her career as a director.

"All right," she sighed. "I don't like it, but I'll let him watch from the audience or one of the box seats, not on stage. But if he gets disruptive or tries to interfere, I'll kick his august and wealthy butt out the stage door."

Mary smiled. "Thanks, Amber. That's all I can ask for. And that's what I told him. I think it will really help in getting the production publicized."

"Hope so. By the way, have you nailed down yet just exactly

when opening night will be? I have a need to know that, you know?"

Mary laughed. "Yes, I have. First night will be March 25th."

"March 25th?" Amber searched her memory. "Not the first day of spring. Old beginning-of-the-year day?"

"Nope," Mary responded with a grin. "But I did ask the pastors what would be the best day in March for the debut, and they came back with the 25th. Seems for Lutherans that's the Feast of the Annunciation, and it's the most important feast day in March, so that's what we went with."

Amber shrugged again. "Maybe I need to get Heinrich to include 'When the Saints Come Marching In' in the overture."

The meeting ended in laughter.

Chapter 32

Pietro nudged Ciclope.

"There he comes now."

Ciclope waited for a moment, then looked around with a casual air and let his gaze seemingly by accident pass over the average looking down-timer who was walking by. His eyes ended up looking up the street beyond the man, and he didn't look back until after the man had passed them by. Only then did he look back to Pietro.

"You are sure he's the one?"

"*Si*. Head accountant for Schiffer. I found out from three different people, and they all said he is the one in charge of the payroll."

"Come on," Ciclope said, as he pushed away from the wall and turned in the direction the accountant had gone. "I just hope you did a better job of disguising your questions than you did your fire."

"That was not my fault!" Pietro complained. "There wasn't supposed to be anything left there."

"Quiet," Ciclope ordered, and his partner, wonder of wonders, obeyed—at least to the extent of dropping off into unintelligible mutters.

Now what, Ciclope began wondering, could they do with the accountant and paymaster?

Franz Sylwester stumbled in the parlor, tripping over furniture that his early-morning bleary eyes could barely see. He did

202

manage to avoid dropping the lamp, but only at the cost of a bruise on his shin that was going to hurt later.

Whoever it was who was playing tympani riffs on their front door was noticeably impatient. He would barely allow for a couple of breaths before resuming his hammering. There was a glimmer of light coming in through the parlor window curtains, so if it was not dawning yet, it wasn't far from it. Franz not being what Marla called a morning person, he was not happy about being aroused from some of his best sleep of the night.

He finally made it to the door, set the lamp on the nearby table, and pulled the bolt and yanked open the door in a single motion.

"Who the..." Franz stopped in mid-tirade as he realized that a large fist hung directly in front of his nose. After a moment, the hand dropped, and he recognized the man to whom it belonged.

"Thomas?" It was Thomas Schwartzberg, one of his best friends for years, and an intimate member of the musicians who had coalesced around Franz and Marla. "What the devil are you doing here at this hour?"

"I need to talk to you, Franz. It is important."

Before Franz could respond, from behind him he heard, "Franz? Who is it?"

He looked behind him to see her standing in the doorway to the back part of the house, belting her robe about her waist.

"It's me, Marla," Thomas spoke over Franz's head from his advantage of height.

"Well, don't just stand there, Franz. Let the man in."

Feeling more than a bit put-upon, Franz opened the door wider and stepped out of the way for their friend to enter. After closing the door, he picked up the lamp and led the way to where Marla was settling onto a chair. Franz set the lamp on another table and settled himself on the sofa. He pointed to another chair.

"Sit."

Thomas placed his hands on the back of the chair in question and leaned forward. Before he could open his mouth, Franz snarled, "You woke us up almost in the middle of the night. I am tired, and not at all happy about the manner by which I was roused. I refuse to get a crick in my neck staring up the length of your oversized body." He stabbed his finger at the chair again. "So sit!"

Thomas released the chair back, stepped around it, and sat,

all without a word. He then looked at the two of them, hands on his knees, silent.

Franz wiped a hand over his face. "*Ach*, my friend, my very dear friend, forgive my rudeness. I am not at my best in the morning, and especially so when awakened so abruptly."

Thomas smiled, and it was like the dawn of the sun, teeth gleaming in the lamplight. "Well I know it, Franz, and I will forgive if you will forgive my beating a tattoo on your door before a white hair could be told from a black."

Franz waved a hand. "Forgiven, forgiven. Now, what drives you to chance the anger of the dragon so early?"

Thomas leaned forward, elbows on knees and excitement evident in every line of his face.

"I need the orchestra, Franz—or at least the wind players."

"Why?"

"Frau Simpson commissioned me to write a march as part of the program she described some time back. I have been working on it. But last night she sent me a note, saying that it needed to be ready to perform at a moment's notice." Thomas' face was animated, and his hands were waving around.

"She gave no explanation as to why?" Franz asked.

"None."

Franz crossed his arms and leaned back as he thought. "I have heard no rumors that would explain that."

"Nor have I," Thomas agreed.

"Me neither," Marla contributed through a yawn.

"But whatever it is, it must be important," Thomas rushed on. "This is my chance, Franz, my chance to make an impression! Help me, I pray."

Franz had known Thomas for years, and never had he heard such a note of pleading from his friend. He thought for a moment.

"The orchestra is somewhat ahead of where we absolutely must be in the learning of *Arthur Rex*. I think we can allow you some time. At least a half an hour for several days; perhaps a full hour, depending on how things flow."

Thomas' face lit up again with the biggest smile Franz could ever remember seeing on his face. He leaned forward and stretched out his long arms to snatch Franz's hands and shake them both.

"I thank you with all my heart, and so you prove yourself to be the greatest of friends. Thank you, thank you, thank you."

Thomas looked for all the world like a man who had just been told his first son had been born alive and healthy. Franz winced at the thought, but it was appropriate for Thomas, for every composer seemed to have a paternal (or in some rare cases, maternal) instinct for his works.

"You're not going to have much of a band with only the winds from the orchestra," Marla observed. Franz caught a glimpse of a broad smile on her face as well.

"True," Thomas shrugged. "But I will take whatever I can get. And even a brass quartet would get the piece heard."

"Here's a thought for you: there are people from Grantville in Magdeburg who play instruments. I can give you a couple of names, and maybe they can think of others. If they don't have their horns with them, a telegram to Marcus Wendell and he'll have something playable on a train headed for Magdeburg in twenty-four hours. That would bulk up the ranks."

"Wait, wait," Thomas said. He pulled a pad of music paper out of a capacious coat pocket. Franz could see the top page was covered with music notes, with whole sections of the page crossed out.

Franz almost laughed at what happened next: Thomas' hands began acting like two squirrels chasing each other around a tree, diving into one pocket after another. "Pencil, pencil...I know I have a pencil...I never leave the room without one. Where is it?" His voice descended to muttering as his hands continued the chase.

"Aha! Here it is!" Thomas produced the pencil in triumph from a pocket that Franz knew had been plunged into at least three times before the pencil was finally found. Thomas poised the pencil over the pad. "Names, please."

"Dane Stevenson and Dallas Chaffin. They were both here in Magdeburg the last I knew. Dane plays tuba, and Dallas is a percussionist. And they might know of some others."

Thomas wrote the names in the margin of the page with care, then looked up. "Anyone else?"

"You might ask Lennie Washaw as well. He's in touch with most of the up-timers in Magdeburg. He could know of some other players."

Thomas noted all that before carefully restoring both pad and pencil to their accustomed places. He stood, and gave a short bow to them both.

"I thank you again for your grace and kindness, and for the good advice. I shall pursue these names immediately," with a pat for the pocket where the pad was resting.

"Uh, Thomas," Marla responded in one if the driest tones Franz had ever heard her use, "you might want to wait a little while to do that. Most people don't like to be hammered awake at the crack of dawn, or to talk to strangers before they've had their morning coffee and brushed their teeth."

"Oh. Right." Thomas looked a bit nonplussed, then shrugged. "Okay. Good-bye." He shook hands with them both, and charged out the front door before Franz could stir from his chair.

Marla finally broke down in giggles, and Franz felt himself chuckling along with her.

"Is he always like that?" Marla asked. "I mean, I don't think I've ever seen him like that before."

"Thomas is a man of strong passions," Franz replied, "but even for him that was a side of Thomas I have not seen. Must be part of becoming a composer."

"Must be," Marla said. She stood up. "Well, come to bed, love, and let's see if we can get a bit more rest before the day truly begins."

Chapter 33

Simon Bayer charged up the steps to the rooms that Hans and Ursula shared with him. He burst in the door, to find Ursula sitting in her chair, reading her Bible.

"Here you are, Ursula," he said as he presented her with a roll fresh from *Das Haus Des Brotes*. "Hans said to bring this to you now, and he would bring more when he comes home tonight."

"Thank you, Simon." She set her Bible on the side table, tore the roll into smaller pieces with her fingers, and began eating it. "I thought Hans would be fighting tonight."

"Naw," Simon said. "Herr Todd and Herr Tobias said the bear pit is filled with snow and ice, and the new place still is not ready, so they had to cancel this week. But they promised they will be ready soon."

His excitement must have showed, because Ursula sighed and shook her head. He looked at her with a frown. "Aren't you proud of Hans, Ursula? He has never been beaten. Men call him the Samson of Magdeburg."

"I am glad that he has not been hurt," Ursula replied after a moment, "and I am glad that he has found something that he likes to do. I just wish that he was not hurting people to make this money."

Simon had to think about that a bit. "But he does not hurt them bad. It's just like in play, you know. It's not like he is trying to kill them or anything. He is not a soldier."

Simon's opinion of soldiers was shaped by his elders' recollections of the sack of Magdeburg by Pappenheim's troops. In his mind, he often thought of them as some species of devil, led by Pappenheim direct from the right hand of Satan, eight feet tall, with horns and bloody fangs.

He saw a trace of a smile on Ursula's lips.

"Yes, Simon, he is not a soldier. Thank you for reminding me that there are worse things for a young man strong in body to do than to occasionally pummel someone."

Simon mulled that one over, and decided that it was a positive statement.

"Well, I have to get back on the street," he said. "The candler told me if I came by this afternoon he would have three different packages for me to deliver, and I do not want to leave him looking for someone else."

Ursula waved a hand as she finished the roll. "Then get on with you, and stay out of trouble."

He grinned at her, then charged back out the door and rumbled down the steps.

Ursula stared at the door, feeling a lump in the back of her throat. Yes, it could be worse. But the reality was bad enough. She had never seen Hans fight; God willing, she never would. But she knew his strength—who better than the sister that he'd carried from place to place without complaining? And she knew the size and hardness of those hands that were still remarkably gentle when he picked her up. The thought of that strength, those hands, hitting someone on purpose, with the intent of driving them to the ground, made the bread she had just swallowed turn to a leaden lump in her stomach.

She stared around the room. Even with the shutters thrown open, it suddenly seemed gray and dim. The room seemed to be closing in on her. A sudden urge to see the sky struck her, so strong that she was on her feet and shrugging into her coat without remembering her usual struggle with the cane.

Moments later she was outside the locked door and moving down the steps at a pace that, while not as fast as Simon's rapid rumble, was still faster than she could remember moving in oh-so-long.

At the bottom of the steps, breathing hard, Ursula looked

around. Even though the day was overcast, it still seemed light to her. People hurried by, wagons rattled as they passed, it was a scene of welcome activity. And the cacophony of sound—shouts, bits of singing, creaking carts, whistles—it all fell on her ears as energizing as the most lustily sung hymn at church.

Ursula suddenly realized that she was tired of sitting alone every day. The stories that Hans and Simon would share of their work and travels within the city made her hunger to see more. So she picked a direction and started walking.

One of the city watchmen passed her going the other way, swinging a truncheon from a wrist strap. She knew what he was by the funny cut of his coat and the odd tint of green cloth from which it was made. Simon had described it to her before, and Hans had made her laugh with his attempt to describe just what shade of green it was. All in all, she decided, acknowledging the watchman's touch of his hat brim while examining his coat with an expert's eye, puke green was—sadly—perhaps a very accurate judgment. It had to be a dye from Lothlorien Farbenwerke. No dye from before the Ring of Fire could be that strong, that vivid, and that repulsive all at the same time. If she had to bet, either the dye or the dye-work had to be a mistake, and whoever made the cloth found a way to sell it to the city government.

For some reason that thought cheered her immensely, and she continued down the street with a smile on her face. She didn't see the watchman turn and watch her for several moments, then pull out his constable's whistle and blow a series of notes.

"Here he comes." Pietro's whisper caused Ciclope to stir where he leaned against the alley wall.

"Is he by himself?"

"One guard."

Ciclope stood straight and rolled his head around, listening to his neck crack and pop.

"Anyone looking this way?"

"No," Pietro muttered as he pulled his gloves on. These were the very thin gloves he'd used back in Venice when he would enter homes by second floor windows; thick enough to protect his hands—barely—yet thin enough that he could almost feel the lettering on a coin through them. Even now, some years since he had last essayed an unheralded visit to a rich man's home, they were still his favorite gloves to wear when something outside of society's normal rules was to be attempted.

The accountant—Ciclope still hadn't bothered to learn his name—was a man of regular habits. He walked the same way to work every day, at the same time. He went home at the same time every evening. And every Friday he walked from his desk at Schiffer's main office to the hospital work site, carrying the workers' payroll in a satchel. Most of the workers engaged in building the hospital addition still had little faith in the modern post-Ring of Fire proliferation of checks and drafts. They were used to dealing in cash, and they wanted to be paid in cash. Hence the accountant's weekly trip.

This alley was along the accountant's accustomed path, along a bit of a jog to the street so that part of it was not in full view from every direction on the street. So the two saboteurs set their little snare up in it.

"One man with him," Pietro repeated in a whisper after hazarding one last peek around the corner of the building. "Big guy, on the street side. Our pigeon is walking on the inside."

"Right," Ciclope said. "Let's do this and get out of here."

They were standing with their backs against the wall that would remain out of the accountant's view, watching for his shadow to appear. Ciclope's eyes were pointed to the ground just outside the mouth of the alley, but he actually heard footsteps before the shadow came into view. The big guy must be big, he thought to himself.

The shadows came into view. An instant later, Pietro made his move. The wiry Italian was much stronger than he looked to be, and the accountant found his arm grasped by a hand like steel that yanked him through the air into the alley. His surprised squawk died just before it could issue forth when something round and harshly aromatic was crammed into his mouth.

Ciclope made his own move as soon the accountant flew by him, stepping out to grab the guard by his arm. Although he was a strong man in his own right, Ciclope didn't attempt to duplicate Pietro's feat. He settled for simply spinning the very surprised guard into the alley, following through with the motion to slam a shoulder into the man's gut, which stopped that shout before it could proceed any farther than the inhale. The big man's "Oof!" was punctuated by a surprised look and a gurgle as Ciclope slammed a knife into the guard's chest, very expertly, at such a place and angle that it pierced his heart. He was dead before he even knew what happened.

Ciclope released the knife and let his target drop. He turned from the corpse to where Pietro had dragged the accountant. The victim was almost purple in the face, wheezing and gagging, pawing at his throat with his free hand.

"What's with him?"

"Bruised bulb of garlic in his mouth," Pietro muttered in a distracted fashion as he tried to force the lock on the satchel, which turned out to be chained to the accountant's wrist.

Ciclope winced in momentary sympathy. "Waste of garlic," he muttered, then took another knife from an inside pocket. "Cut the handle out." And he proceeded to do exactly that. It took a moment—even a very sharp knife will not slice leather like it was paper—but it was a very, very sharp knife, so it didn't take long before Pietro was holding the satchel and the accountant was free to bring both hands up to his mistreated mouth and throat.

"Sorry," Ciclope said to the accountant, "nothing personal. It's just business, you understand."

That very same very sharp knife found its way into the accountant's heart. Ciclope released it, grabbed Pietro by the arm, and headed for the other end of the alley as the accountant slumped to the ground behind them, no longer concerned about the burning garlic in his mouth.

Pietro tried to twist around. "Your knife!"

"Leave it," Ciclope said. "I never understood why you and the others insist on using expensive knives for this kind of stuff. You don't need a good knife for this. Cheap and sharp works just as well, and you can leave it behind so no one ever sees you with it again."

Pietro had no reply to that observation.

Ciclope missed the blood. He had wanted to see blood, but it wasn't safe this time to wait for it.

Gotthilf looked up when he heard the constable whistle code for *sergeant come!*

He and Byron were still trolling for leads among their informers, and were walking in one of the less affluent areas of Greater Magdeburg. He noted that they actually weren't far from where

Hans Metzger lived. He was about to remark on that when the sound of the whistle registered.

Byron got it, too, and looked to his partner with a raised eyebrow. *Should we?*

Gotthilf responded with a shrug. *Why not?*

So they pivoted in lockstep and walked toward the sound of the whistle. Half a block, turn left at the corner, and walk down to arrive at the watchman's side just as the sergeant over this patrol sector rode up on his horse.

"So, Georg," Byron said to the sergeant, a watchman who had been part of a couple of their previous investigations before his promotion, "I see you got tired of the shift sergeant's desk. How goes the patrol sergeanting?"

The horse wasn't much better than a nag, but Georg kept both hands on the reins anyway. He grinned as he responded, "Just fine, Lieutenant. Thanks for asking. Sergeant," he nodded to Gotthilf.

Byron turned his attention to the patrolman. "So, you called this meeting. What's up?"

Gotthilf took pity on the man, who was the very same Phillip with whom he had conversed about watching the Metzgers. "He means, why did you signal?"

The confusion on Phillip's face faded. "I did not know you would be in the area, Sergeant Gotthilf, but Fraulein Metzgerin just left their rooms, so I thought to check with Sergeant Georg here to see if he wanted her followed."

"Was she with her brother or that boy, Simon?" Gotthilf asked.

"No, she was alone."

"Which way?"

Phillip pointed down the street in the direction they were facing. "That way, maybe five minutes ago."

"My thanks," Gotthilf said. He looked up at Byron. "Staying or coming?" Ye gods and little fishes, as he'd heard one up-timer say, he was starting to be as stingy with words as Byron was.

Byron waved a hand. "You go. I'll keep trying to find Demetrious."

"Right." And with that, Gotthilf took off down the street.

Marla and Franz stopped midway between their separate destinations. They leaned toward each other for a kiss, made somewhat cumbersome by their coats. The day was colder than it had been for the past few days, and they were bundled into their heaviest garments. She lingered with the kiss, regardless, warmed inside by the intimacy of the moment with her husband, albeit they were outside in plain view of all the passers-by.

When they broke apart, Franz blinked at her. "My," was his only comment.

She smiled at him, and pointed at the opera house. "Get to work," she said. "Your orchestra awaits."

They parted company, and she headed for the Royal Academy of Music building, the first of several planned for the complex around the opera house. Today, the biggest room inside was housing the rehearsal for *Arthur Rex*.

She checked her watch as she walked through the outer door. "Eep! I'm late." By the time she walked into the room, she had her coat, hat, and scarf off, and she was tugging her gloves off with her teeth. Everything got plopped in a pile on a table by the door.

Thankfully this room, while not exactly warm by up-time central heating standards, was much warmer than the great out-of-doors. She waved at Amber, where she was talking to some well-dressed—in a relatively sober manner—down-timer. Hermann Katzberg raised his chin at her from where he was playing through one of the aria accompaniments on the rehearsal hall piano, so she headed his direction.

"Hey, Hermann."

"Good morning, Marla," he said as he finished a percussive run up the keyboard, ending with a chord that almost shivered in the air. Then he repositioned his hands and looked up at her. "The usual?"

"Yep."

Hermann played through a series of chords to help her establish the sound of the piano in her mind again. Marla had perfect pitch. She had never met anyone else with perfect pitch, but speaking for herself, she had found it as much a curse as a blessing. Any performance that was not perfectly in tune was to her like listening to fingernails scraping on a blackboard. Perhaps even more so. She had never been able to communicate even to other musicians just how torturous that could be.

Likewise, it took some effort on her part to blend with instruments whose tuning had drifted off the mark. She could do it, but she had to spend some time listening to the instrument to set its tuning in her mind. And unfortunately, her mind seemed to reset itself back to the "normal default tuning" every night when she slept, so she now had a morning ritual of listening to Hermann play the piano until she could mesh with its tuning. Then she would warm up with her vocalises, at which time she was ready to begin the rehearsal. It was a bit time consuming, but by getting in early every morning, it worked.

She turned and faced Hermann, placed both hands on the piano top, and opened her mouth.

Amber Higham heard Marla beginning her warm-ups. That was good. Now if she could only get this man out of Her Rehearsal Space, maybe they'd be ready to start on time.

"One more time, Herr Schardius," she started again, holding on to her temper with both hands, "when I agreed to let you view the rehearsals, I meant after we moved to the opera house for the final rehearsals. We are too early in the process and we have such a restricted amount of time to prepare, I can't allow any distractions for my people right now.

"And trust me," she held up a hand as he opened his mouth to interrupt, "you would be a distraction on the order of an elephant trying to hide under a table."

Actually, if all the performers were of the caliber of Andrea Abati and Marla, it probably wouldn't have been that big a deal if the merchant had hung around. Professionals of the up-time theater were used to strangers being around while they were rehearsing. But over half of her performers were basically rank amateurs, and none of them, Andrea and Marla included, had performed an opera of this magnitude before, so yeah, it was a big deal. She crossed her arms, leaned forward slightly—a dominance trick she had learned early in her acting career—and focused her strongest and most draconian glare on the merchant who was intruding into Her Rehearsal Space.

Schardius seemed a bit distracted himself now, listening to Marla's voice make even the warm-up vocalises seem like works of art. After a moment, he shook his head in a sharp motion, then focused back on Amber. Her glare was unrelenting, and he seemed to finally get the message that he was not going to be spending the morning watching the rehearsal.

"Very well, Frau Higham." For all that he had to be angry and frustrated—or at least disappointed—the cool tones of his voice revealed no such thing. He might have been discussing the morning weather, for all the passion that was in his voice. "But I shall hold you to your word. When you move to the opera house, I will be there to watch."

Amber gave him a short nod, but did not change her posture or release her glare.

After another long consideration of Marla at work, the merchant sauntered to the door, looked around one final time, and left.

Amber dropped her arms. Finally! They could get on with rehearsals. She picked up her notebook off a nearby table and leafed through it until Marla finished warming up. At that point, Amber raised her voice.

"Okay, everyone, gather 'round." In a matter of moments, the cast scheduled for this rehearsal was standing in front of her. "Right. We're going to pick up where we left off last rehearsal. Hermann," she looked over to the piano, "start with the interlude before the big Act Two duet. Dieter, Marla, you're on. Everyone else, step over there until we get to your piece."

Over the sound of movements, Amber finished with, "Once we finish the run-through of Act Two, we'll work on the blocking again. We're down to less than six weeks, folks. Let's make every moment count."

Everyone was in place. She looked to the piano again.

"Okay, Hermann, hit it."

Chapter 34

"Halt!"

The three laughing apprentices came to a sudden stop in front of a short man with a very loud voice who was obstructing their path with his hand upheld.

"Sir?" Martin asked. He was the oldest, tallest, and loudest of the trio, so he took the lead in most everything they did. At the moment, he was acting a bit pugnacious.

"You," the hand suddenly became a spear with a finger that rammed under Martin's breastbone. "Get back there and pick up the woman you just knocked over."

Such was the tone in the man's voice and the expression on his face that there was no hesitation. Martin spun and hurried to assist the young woman who was struggling to arise with the aid of her cane.

"You and you," the pointing finger now aimed at the two younger members of the trio, "stand there against the wall." The pointing finger moved, and so did they, as if attached to it.

The older youth meanwhile had lifted the young woman by main strength, and set her on her feet, all the while apologizing profusely. He was now hovering over her, hands almost outstretched as if he was about to try to dust her off, but couldn't figure out a way to do it that wouldn't get him in more trouble.

"That is enough," the man called out. "Get back over here with your friends." In a moment, there were three nervous faces in a row, looking back at him.

Gotthilf frowned fiercely. "I am Detective Sergeant Hoch, of the Magdeburg *Polizei*." He pulled a case out of his coat pocket, and flipped it open.

Two of the faces went ashen at the sight of the snarling lion badge now displayed in front of their noses; the youngest boy's face lit up and he leaned forward just a bit. "Cool," he breathed. That word had become almost as ubiquitous among the youth of Magdeburg as *okay* had. One of his friends elbowed him, and he straightened in a hurry.

The boys watched as the sergeant put his badge away and took out a small notebook and pencil from an inside pocket.

"Names."

The stammered responses were jotted down in the notebook.

"Martin, Phillip, and Johann. The three most common names for boys in Thuringia. Why could your parents not have had some sense of originality?"

The pencil stopped.

"Masters."

Those names were also jotted down in the notebook. The boys' eyes watched as the notebook was closed and returned to its resting place. If anything, the boys were looking even more nervous.

"Now, what are you doing running loose on an afternoon when you should be at work?"

The two younger boys looked at the hapless Martin. "It, um, it is the commemoration of the Lord's Presentation. Our masters were called to the guild halls, and said we could take this afternoon off."

"And what were you going to do? Besides get into trouble, that is."

Again the glances, again Martin had to speak. "We thought..."

"Yes?"

"We heard about the fights out at the old bear pit," one of the younger boys—Phillip—piped up.

"The fights, huh? And what do you know about them?"

"That Hans Metzger is the best fighter," Johann said.

"Is not," from Phillip.

"Is too!"

They both shut up as a red-faced Martin almost knocked them down with nudges from his elbows.

"Hans Metzger, huh?"

Nods from all the boys.

"Well, you had better pray that you *don't* meet Herr Metzger, since that was his sister you sent sprawling in the dirt and gravel."

Three faces suddenly achieved a corpselike pallor.

"Somehow I do not believe your masters would countenance your running wild in the streets of the city, knocking young women off of their feet."

The sergeant's expression had just gone from stern to flinty.

"And I hate to think what might happen to anyone who Herr Metzger thought had given his sister less than the respect he believes she is due."

Two sets of eyes were very wide; young Phillip's were half-closed, and he wavered a bit as he stood there.

"I suggest that you go provide your most profound apologies to Fraulein Metzgerin, then get out of my sight. Is that clear?" He pointed toward the young woman, who was standing where Martin had left her, leaning on her cane. The boys timidly approached her. Each bowed in turn, and attempted to apologize to her, stammering all the while and casting sidelong glances at the sergeant.

"Enough," the sergeant finally directed. "Now get."

The boys vanished.

Gotthilf looked at Ursula Metzgerin, and felt a smile spread across his face in response to the one that was lurking around the corners of her mouth.

"Quite the taskmaster you are," she murmured.

"Are you all right?" Gotthilf asked as he stepped closer.

"Yes." She lifted a hand from her cane and waved it in the air. "In truth, it was more a matter of I tripped myself. They barely touched me. And you, stern face of authority that you are, you..."

She paused, obviously looking for a word.

"I read them the riot act?" Gotthilf contributed. "Lowered the boom? Chewed them out? Gave them what for?"

Ursula tilted her head and furrowed her brow.

Gotthilf laughed. "Those are all up-time figures of speech meaning I berated them thoroughly."

Her expression cleared, and she laughed.

"Yes, you did that well."

They stood, smiling at each other, and Gotthilf thought to himself that Ursula stood in beauty. Oh, not that she was the most striking woman he had ever seen. His father would call her "presentable at best," and his mother would probably sniff at her, but something about Ursula as she stood there in the weak winter sunlight caught his regard.

That was the moment when he finally admitted to himself that he was intrigued with this working class girl—woman. It was a moment of light, of expansion, of ebullience.

And the next moment it all came crashing down in shards in his heart and soul. She was the sister of a suspect under investigation. He could not act on his interest. Could not. He almost shuddered at the thought of what Captain Reilly would say about that—never mind what his partner would say.

"Are you going after more embroidery thread?" he asked, in an attempt to move past the moment.

"No," she replied. "Just out getting some sun and air. But I think I have had enough of both for the day, so I will return to our rooms now."

"Then have a good day, Fraulein Metzgerin." Gotthilf touched a finger to his hat brim, and forced himself to stand in place and watch her limp back the way she had come.

Ursula called herself fifteen different kinds of fool as she hobbled back to the rooms. She was not a stranger to attraction to the opposite sex. Before the sack, she had had contact with boys of her own age, had felt the stirrings of interest, of emotion, of what might have become the beginnings of passion. Then the sack happened, and the wrack of her body. Since then, the only man she had seen for more than a few moments had been her brother.

Of all the men to be attracted to, it had to be one of the *Polizei*. And not a watchman, either, but a sergeant. And he was from a well-to-do family. His clothes would tell that to anyone with an eye for fabrics and tailoring, like her. And she really did remember his sister from the catechism classes.

Dreams; the thought that someone like him might find her interesting, poor and broken as she was.

Dreams dry as dust. What did she have to offer him?

✧   ✧   ✧

Magdeburg Times-Journal
February 6, 1636

Magdeburg Polizei Captain William Reilly appealed to the public today for assistance in solving a brutal double homicide committed on February 4. The two men, both employees of Schiffer Painting and Contracting, were found stabbed to death in an alley off of Kanalstrasse in Greater Magdeburg. When last seen at the company headquarters, they were carrying the week's payroll for the expansion building project at the Magdeburg Memorial Hospital. The payroll was not found at the crime scene.

"It seems obvious that robbery was the motive for the killings," Captain Reilly stated to reporters today. "If anyone noticed anything unusual around that alley on the afternoon of the 4th, please let us know. Likewise, if anyone sees someone flashing a lot of cash around."

Chapter 35

Franz walked into the auditorium from the rear audience entrance. It was early in the morning, and he was confused for a moment that some of the players were already on the stage and playing. Then he recognized Thomas Schwartzberg standing in front of them waving his arms in a simplistic conductor's pattern. So, by process of deduction, those who were on the stage must be the players Thomas had recruited to play his march.

He smiled when he remembered Thomas asking him for advice on how to conduct. "Just give them a good solid beat," he'd replied. "You can't go far wrong if you do that much." And from the look of it, Thomas had taken that advice to heart.

The piece they were playing was recognizably a march; at least to someone who had an ear for up-time music, which definitely included Franz. He stood in the back of the hall and listened to them run through it. Thomas' experience in notating up-time music from recordings had definitely shaped his style in this first work as a composer.

Low brass was very prominent in the march, which was something that would sound strange to the typical down-timer. Tubas and sousaphones and baritone horns were all unknown here-and-now. Franz suspected that one of the reasons was just the economics involved. A dozen trumpets could be made from the brass used in a single sousaphone; maybe more.

The rumble of low-pitched drums also stood out, which was another sound the down-time residents hadn't heard before. In fact, as the music crested to the final climax, it resembled thunder. Franz smiled at that. It would be an ominous sound to many of those who heard the march, he thought to himself.

After Thomas concluded his rehearsal and the musicians began to scatter—some to their day jobs, some to different chairs on the platform for the orchestra rehearsal—Franz walked up beside him.

"Oh, hello," Thomas said after a quick sideways glance.

"Nice job," Franz said. "It's starting to sound good."

"Thanks," Thomas said. "It took longer than I thought it would, but it's finally getting there."

"So are you ready?" Franz asked.

"Is it time?"

Franz let a mischievous grin surface when Thomas reacted in wide-eyed panic. "No, no, nothing like that."

"Don't do that!" Thomas slumped in relief as he continued, "Still, I wish whatever it is would hurry up and happen."

"Me, too," Franz replied, "if for no other reason than so you'll settle down."

Karl Honister looked at the naked knife blades the blacksmith was holding. His name was Erhard Misch and he was a friend of the Honister family.

"Very cheap knives," the smith said. "I punched out the rivets—they were soft brass—and took the hand grips off." He nodded at the pieces of wood lying on the table standing to one side. "The blades are steel, but not very good grade steel, and not forged all that well."

"So can you tell me where they came from?" Honister took one of them and turned it over in his hands.

"Not from around here," Misch replied.

"How can you tell?"

"I know the work of every smith in and around Magdeburg, and no one does work like this."

"Right." Honister said. "So what else can you tell me about them?"

"Made by the same smith, probably in or near Venice."

"Venice?" Honister looked up from the blade.

"Yah." The smith pointed with one very large and very grimy

finger at a mark on the blade he held. "No maker's mark on either blade, but that's a symbol used by a lot of people in Venice."

Honister held his hand out for the other blade, and looked at both of them closely. Sure enough, there was a similar mark on the first blade as well.

He looked up at the smith. "Anything else, Erhard?"

Misch spread his hands. "Looks like young journeyman work to me, maybe even made on the sly and sold for drinking money. Even the wood for the grips is cheap pine."

Honister set the blades on the table next to the grip pieces. "So what are two cheap knives from northern Italy doing buried in the chests of two dead men in a Magdeburg alley?"

"Good question." Misch picked up a towel to wipe his hands. "Got an answer?"

"Nay. That's why you are the detective and I am but the blacksmith."

"Thanks a lot," Honister said sourly over the smith's chuckle.

"I want the money," the mysterious boss hissed as he leaned over the table in the tavern.

"No," Ciclope murmured in return. "We took the money, we keep it."

"You fools!" The boss's whisper almost could be termed a scream; for all that it was barely audible. The expression on his face and the tone to his voice both expressed agitated anger. "You can't spend it. You can't even be seen with part of it. The *Polizei* will be looking for anyone who has more than two or three of the bills and asking some very pointed questions of them—questions I do not think you want to be faced with."

Ciclope ran his finger around the rim of the mug sitting before him. It was still full of ale, which was still as noisome as ever. He was minded to have Pietro start a fire in this place. If there was ever a waste of space, this tavern was it.

"Half," he said as he drew a line on the table top between them to test the boss, who placed his head in his hands and muttered something Ciclope didn't catch.

The boss lifted his head. "You idiots really do not understand just how much danger you are now in. I do not fault you for what you did. I applaud it, to be truthful. But the up-timers have a very dim view of murder, and they will really be on the hunt for you. If they get even a hint that you might have some of that money, they will be on you like flies on the turds floating in Venice's canals."

Ciclope considered that, and reluctantly came to the conclusion that the boss probably knew what he was talking about. The man had had a lot more contact with up-timers that he had, after all.

"All right," he conceded. "You take the money in exchange for money we can use, good silver from Venice or Amsterdam." The boss seemed to choke, which was almost—but not quite—enough to make Ciclope laugh. "After all," he continued, "we have expenses, too. And we deserve some...compensation...for our work."

The boss seemed to have his breathing back under control, although his face was perhaps a bit darker. It was hard to tell for sure in the shadowed interior of the tavern.

"I cannot exchange all of it. I doubt that anybody in Magdeburg has that much silver on hand, except..." The boss's expression twisted. Ciclope noted that the man apparently knew how to hate. And given the reasons why he and his partner had been called to Magdeburg, that gave him some idea as to who the unnamed source of silver might be.

"And having that much silver would be almost as dangerous as having the paper money," the boss continued. "I can get you maybe..."

Here came the offer, Ciclope thought.

"...maybe enough for one part in ten."

Ciclope gave the man marks for sheer arrogance. "I was thinking more like three parts in four," he replied. "Maybe even five parts in six."

The boss choked again, and this time Ciclope did smile; just a bit, a narrow blade's edge of a smile, but a definite smile. The boss saw it; his color seemed to pale a bit.

They bargained back and forth, before finally settling on three parts out of ten.

"It will take me some time to gather that much coin without arousing suspicions," the boss said. "Two, maybe three days. I will look for you here when I have it, and we can make the exchange elsewhere."

"Agreed." Ciclope nodded to the boss.

After the boss left, Pietro looked over to Ciclope. "He will try to cheat us, you know."

"I know," Ciclope said. "That is why you will leave in a moment and follow him. I want to know where he goes, and I especially want to know who he is. Be discreet." He gripped Pietro's forearm hard. "Do *not* let him see you, and do not attract attention. Right?"

"*Sì.*"

Pietro left the table and drifted out the tavern door. Ciclope frowned, which scared away a couple of burly types who were looking for a table to sit at. What could they do next to disrupt the building project? They needed something big; something flashy...*Hmm*...

The watcher had observed the whole exchange from where he sat in the corner, collar pulled up and hat pulled down.

Interesting, he thought. Unfortunate that he couldn't have heard the conversation, but now that he had seen the connection, perhaps he could dig the rest of it up.

Gotthilf was already at the *Polizei* shooting range when Byron finally showed up. When his partner walked in he had the cylinder of his new-model, seven-shot H&K .44 revolver swung out so he could check the loads and the percussion caps.

"Ready, partner?"

Byron appeared to be in a brisk mood this morning, wasting even fewer words than usual. Gotthilf responded with a nod.

Byron stripped the magazine out of his up-time Colt .45, and laid both on the counter beside Gotthilf's. He then dug his ear protectors out of his coat pocket and laid them on the counter as well.

The up-timer touched Gotthilf's revolver with a fingertip. "Didn't you say something about Herr Farkas telling you about a fast loading technique for this thing?"

Gotthilf just smiled, and pulled two extra revolver cylinders out of his pocket, lining them up on the counter in front of him.

"What the...?"

Byron picked a cylinder up and examined it closely, using a finger to feel inside one of the chambers, then to touch the caps on the back of the chambers.

"Is that wax?"

"Yes," Gotthilf said as he pulled his earplugs out of his own pockets. "Herr Farkas gave me the idea when I picked up the pistol at his shop: a very thin layer of wax poured into the chamber after the load is finished, and over the cap after it is installed. It is waterproof, so it helps keep the loads dry, and it will help keep things in place unless the cylinder is dropped or thrown at someone. Of course, it may take a bit more work to get the gun clean after shooting it."

"And can you change cylinders quickly?"

Gotthilf shrugged. "Watch and see." He nodded to the range officer, who blew his whistle and yelled, "Guns down." The other shooters immediately laid their guns on the counters and raised their hands for a few seconds. After looking around, the officer pronounced, "Range is cold."

Gotthilf held up three fingers. The range officer nodded. "Three targets in lanes six, seven and eight."

The target spotter ran out from behind his barrier, posted three man-sized targets side by side, and scurried back to his safe spot.

The range officer looked around. "One shooter," he yelled. "One shooter only."

Gotthilf put his earplugs in. He looked to the range officer, who nodded and announced, "Range is hot!"

Picking up the big revolver, Gotthilf swung the cylinder out one last time for a check, then returned it to its seated position with a *click*. He took a two-handed stance, focused on the center target over the sights, and began squeezing the trigger.

Bam! Bam! Bam! Bam! Bam! Bam! Bam!

Gotthilf hadn't just pulled the trigger as fast as he could. There had been aim involved, even though he was shooting quickly. He popped the cylinder out of the frame, triggered the release into his left hand, snatched a fresh cylinder off the counter and loaded it, then swung it back into the frame. In a moment, it was lined up with the left target, and he began squeezing the trigger again.

Bam! Bam! Bam! Bam! Bam! Bam! Bam!

The smoke from the black powder was getting thick around his position, despite the electric fans that were blowing air into the space. Gotthilf repeated the drill to replace the cylinder, even faster this time, and took aim at the right target.

Bam! Bam! Bam! Bam! Bam! Bam! Bam!

He laid the revolver down on the counter, smoke wisping from the barrel. The ranger officer blew his whistle again. "No shooting!" After a moment, he blew it again. "Range is cold. Clear the targets!"

The target spotter ran out, grabbed Gotthilf's targets and ran them up to him, then ran back to his place behind the barrier.

Everyone gathered around as Gotthilf laid the targets out side by side. Byron whistled.

"Good shooting, partner. Twenty-one shots in less than a minute, and most of them landed in the center of mass, except for this one," he pointed to one that grazed the head outline of one of the targets, "which probably took off an ear, and that one," Gotthilf winced at the hole in the groin area of the outline, "which I figure has the guy singing soprano now."

Laughter and ribald jests broke out around them. A couple of the other shooters clapped him on the back before they headed back to their own positions, talking about what they had seen.

"...got to get me one of those..."

"You know how much they cost?"

"...don't care...give up beer if I have to..."

"So that's a lot of firepower," Byron said over the background conversations, nudging the big revolver with a finger. "You really think you need that much?"

"That and more," Gotthilf said, pulling three more cylinders out of his pockets and setting them on the counter. "I have a bad feeling about what's brewing in Magdeburg."

Byron whistled.

Amber Higham strode down the hall accompanied by Andrea Abati and Hermann Katzberg. She arrived at the knot of her people milling around in the hallway, and said, "What's going on? Why aren't you in the room getting ready for rehearsal?"

"Someone else is in the room," Dieter said. "Listen."

And when she stopped and paid attention to the noises floating through the hallway, sure enough, she could hear the sounds of the rehearsal room piano being played. Played loudly. Being hammered, actually.

"Classical stuff," she remarked. "Not Bach. Doesn't sound like Chopin. Liszt? Brahms?"

"No," Hermann said with a grin. "The last movement of Beethoven's 'Moonlight Sonata.' And by the piece I know who's in the room. Go ahead and go in. She will not notice."

Amber opened the door and stuck her head through the opening, whereupon she glimpsed the back of Marla Linder, ponytail swaying behind her as her hands flashed up and down the keyboard, alternating rolling arpeggios with crashing chords. She opened the door wide and motioned everyone into the room. They all gathered in the back of the room behind the piano, and simply watched the artist at work. Amber remembered Mary saying something about when Marla practiced the piano she shut out the entire world. Sure seemed like she was this morning.

In another minute or so, the piece came to its ending as Marla played arpeggiated runs up and down the keyboard, leading into the final statement of the theme of the piece, followed by several percussive chords. She took her hands off the keys, but held the sustain pedal down and let the final chord resonate in the room.

The clapping started as soon as Marla released the pedal. Her head jerked around, and Amber thought she blushed. She stood quickly, edged out from between the piano and the bench, and said, "Oh, come on now, stop it. I was just practicing."

"Maybe so," Amber replied, "but your practicing is better than most folks' performance." She waved everyone forward to start preparing for the rehearsal.

Marla snorted, which amused Amber. It wasn't a ladylike snort. But then, with Marla's diaphragm, a lot of air would get moved at a moment like that.

"Not hardly," Marla said. "I lost three months. I'm as rusty as a piece of old barbed wire. I'm starting to get my singing chops back, but I've still got a ways to go with the piano, so I'm grabbing every chance I can to practice. And let's not even talk about the flute."

"That sounded good," Hermann contributed from where he was arranging his music on the piano. "I did not hear any clunkers."

"Oh, I've quit making the easy mistakes," Marla said with a grimace. "Now I've got to quit making the hard ones."

"Enough about the piano." Amber spoke firmly. "Now is the time for the voice."

The vocalists warmed up quickly, and they swung into the rehearsal.

Voices were clear today, and everyone seemed to have plenty of stamina. Even so, Amber didn't push them too hard. After a solid morning of rehearsing, she finally called it to an end.

"Okay, listen up, everyone." When they were grouped in front of where she sat on her stool, she said, "Good rehearsal. Last one for a couple of days. Today's Friday. Tomorrow we start fitting costumes. I want the soloists here in the morning, chorus in the afternoon. Everyone got that?"

Nods from all the group.

"Good. Spend Sunday with your friends and family, because that's the last time you get to before opening night. Monday we start rehearsing in the auditorium at the opera hall. It's going to be long days and even longer nights for the next few weeks. Things are going well, but don't let up on it, okay?"

Grins from some, sober looks from others, but nods all around again.

"Great. See you tomorrow."

She waved at them, and they scattered.

Left by herself in an empty room, Amber sagged on her stool for a long moment, pushed her glasses up into her hair, and scrubbed her hands across her face. Lord, she wasn't getting any younger, and boy, could she tell it. The last few weeks before any premiere were always horrendous, but even at the height of her professional acting and directing days she'd never had anything as important as this show resting on her shoulders. Some big shot investor's money, yeah. The reputations of the actors, sometimes the reputations of the writers, yeah. But never anything that could potentially affect the future of a nation. And she was doing it with the equivalent of one and a half seasoned professionals and a bunch of serious but newbie amateurs.

Amber scrubbed her face again, dropped her glasses back on her nose, and got back on her feet to start gathering her stuff.

One thing about it, she thought to herself. If she had to do something like this, at least she was working with dynamite material. She wasn't a fan of opera, as such, although she did like Gilbert and Sullivan. But Gronow's libretto was stellar. And although she was not the consummate musician that Marla and Andrea Abati were, even she could tell that Heinrich, her husband, had written a very good score.

Amber shrugged her coat on, looked around the room one more time, and closed the door firmly behind her. One step closer to opening night.

Chapter 36

Stephan Burckardt carried the leather bag in and set it down on his employer's desk with a thump.

"That's the last of it, Herr Schmidt."

Schmidt loosened the neck of the bag, reached into it, and pulled out a handful of silver coins. He looked them over, then tipped his palm and let them slide back into the bag, which he then retied.

"Took you long enough," Schmidt snarled. "I needed it three days ago." He leaned back in his chair. "Be gone. But be here early in the morning."

Stephan didn't need to be told twice that he could leave. His keys were in his hand before he was out of Schmidt's office. One trice to lock the file cabinets; one trice to shovel papers into a drawer and lock his desk; half a trice to grab his hat and coat off the pegs they hung from; and he was out the door before the master could change his mind.

Outside, he looked around, trying to decide whether to head across the Big Ditch to his room and get a good night's sleep, or to the nearest tavern for a mug of ale. He licked his lips. Sleep sounded good, but so did ale, and seemingly without a conscious decision his feet took him in the direction of The Chain. It had been a long few days. Surely he'd be okay for the length of time it took to down a mug. And Master Schmidt had released him early enough that he'd still have plenty of time for sleep after taking a mug's worth.

Before long he came to the low doorway into the tavern and ducked through it. Once inside, he looked around, saw that the crowd was still light. He released the breath he had been holding, relaxed, and headed for the counter where Veit the bartender was serving up mugs of ale.

A minute later, Stephan was seated at a scrap of a table in a back corner, elbows propped on the top and sipping at the ale. Sipping because it was better than Veit's usual lot, and actually could be allowed to pass over the tongue slowly without inducing disgust or nausea or comparisons to the inside of one's oldest boot.

Stephan wanted nothing more than to just let his mind empty out, but it kept worrying at Master Schmidt. He wasn't sure what was going on, for the master was being remarkably tight-lipped about it, but he was certain that something out of the ordinary was in the wind. If for no other reason than the fact that the master had had him gather as much coin as he could quietly manage, exchanging what USE paper scrip was on hand with a few of the other merchants and those guild treasuries who could be trusted to keep their mouths shut. It wasn't the first time that a merchant of Magdeburg had needed solid coin, after all, and it probably wouldn't be the last. Stephan knew who would keep a closed mouth, and that was who he had approached. Of course, one usually paid a premium when one desired quick service, but the master knew that as well as Stephan did, and had actually seemed satisfied in a sour sort of way at the sums that had been amassed.

But why? Stephan kept circling back to that question. Unfortunately, every time he arrived at it, the answer was still "I don't know," and that would start the process all over again.

Something was going on.

"Friend, you look like you're at the end of a long day," someone remarked. Samuel Heilbronner looked up in startlement to see a stranger sitting on the stool across the table from him. He'd been so wrapped up in his beer he hadn't even perceived the man approaching.

He shook his head to clear his head, and shrugged. "Yah, a long day. But then, every day is long, right?" He raised his mug and sipped.

"True, true," the other man said with a chuckle. "At least for those of us who have to work for our bread and salt and hope the masters and foremen have the money to pay us at the end of the day."

They chatted back and forth, commiserating with each other on the evils of working for an uncaring boss, and congratulating each other on having won out so far by simply surviving. They had a friendly argument about the merits of Samuel's job as a ledger poster for Master Georg Schmidt, and the other fellow's job as a bricklayer.

The other man bought the second round when Samuel discovered his mug was empty, so it was only fair that Samuel bought the third. And somewhere after that he kind of lost track of a lot of things.

When he was awakened the next morning by his wife, his head was throbbing to the beat of a demon's hammer and the taste in his mouth was beyond foul. And as he stumbled down the streets toward the bridge across the Big Ditch, he muzzily wondered what had become of his new friend... or even what his name was. He remembered it started with a P. Peter? Paulus?

Schardius looked around the main foyer of the opera hall. Good, no one was in sight. He slipped a key out of his pocket, walked over and unlocked a single door at the far end of the foyer. After stepping through it, he locked it again.

He smiled in the darkness at the thought of how surprised Frau Higham and others would be if they knew he had that key. It was amazing what a few pieces of silver could buy from someone low enough in the social ranks that everyone forgot about him... like the building custodian.

Schardius pulled a Grantville device from his pocket, cranked the handle several times, and smiled again as light bloomed in the darkness from the flashlight. He'd paid good money for the battery-less flashlight. Good money. And this wasn't the first time that he'd found use for it.

Directing the light ahead of him, he continued his explorations of the nonpublic areas of the opera hall.

"Take a deep breath, dear."

Marla obliged the seamstress by expanding her diaphragm to its maximum, which of course caused her waistline to also expand.

The seamstress' hands fluttered around her torso, checking the fit and making sure the cloth draped right.

"Right, dear, you can relax now."

Air whooshed out of Marla's lungs. The seamstress smiled as the expired breath made the frills of her cap flutter a bit.

"Move for me, please, how you would on the stage."

Marla decided she was getting a bit tired of being this woman's puppet—she wasn't nearly as personable as Frau Schneider, the seamstress who made most of Marla's clothes. But she stalked grandly back and forth a few times as directed, humming one of the big arias; then stood and made several of the grand gestures that the part of Guinevere called for.

"That's good, dear. Did you feel anything binding on you?"

The seamstress looked to be older than Aunt Susan, Marla thought, maybe even as old as her grandmother. She'd let her get away with "dear," but if she started using the down-time equivalent of "Hon," things would commence to get fractious, as Aunt Susan used to say.

"I think I did," Marla said in response to the question. She moved her left hand and arm in a somewhat contorted gesture. "It felt tight in the shoulder right..." She stopped in mid-movement. "...there."

"Hold there, please."

The seamstress stepped up close and peered at the fabric of the costume, running her fingers up and down the seams.

"Ah," she said. "I see the problem. It will be easy to fix. Thank you, dear, you can take that one off now." She turned away and called to another woman, "Frau Ballauf."

Marla stepped behind the partition screen with alacrity as the other two women bent their heads in conversation over a clipboard. That was the last costume she had to try on. It had been a long morning, and she was ready to get back into her jeans and sweater.

Amber Higham had mobilized the production dressers for the costume fitting. Marla turned her back to the other young woman, who began unbuttoning the buttons down the back of the costume. After a moment, Marla was able to shuck the top of the costume forward and begin loosening the waistband of the skirt. Another few moments, and she was free of all that cloth, skinning her way back into soft worn denim and her favorite bulky yellow sweater.

"Thanks, Sophie," she said as her head popped through the top of the sweater. "I think we're going to need all the practice we can get dealing with this stuff. The costume changes are going to be fun," she rolled her eyes to match her sarcastic tone, "especially the two in the third act."

The dresser smiled as she gathered up the skirt to clip it onto the special hanger made for it. "You will do fine, Marla."

"That's *we*, partner," Marla replied as she ran her fingers through her long hair, fluffing it out a bit. No ponytail today; she wasn't in the mood for it for some reason. "I won't be able to do it without you."

"Schardius, your time is coming, and that, soon," Georg Schmidt snarled, slipping as he ducked into an alley. It took him a moment to regain his balance; then he went on, unaware that he had been overheard.

Marla gave a quick wave to the dresser and stepped out into the main room again. She spotted Amber standing by the door and headed that way.

"Hey, Amber."

"Marla."

She settled in beside the director and leaned back against the wall. "So how's it going?"

Amber grunted. "You tell me. Can you live with the costumes?"

"Yep." Marla grinned. "They're actually not too bad. I was afraid they'd be skin-tight or something, and these folks have never heard of Spandex."

"Good." The woman that the seamstress had talked to came up to them, carrying her clipboard. She nodded to Marla, and Amber said, "Sorry, I should have introduced you. Frau Ballauf, this is Marla Linder. Marla, this is Frau Frontilia Ballauf. She's my new administrative assistant and stage-manager-in-training. I borrowed her from Lady Beth Haygood at the school."

"Stole, actually, after I had only been there two days," Frau Ballauf said dryly. "Frau Haygood felt she had been—how did she put it—strong-armed after your conversation."

"She'll get over it." Amber waved a hand in a pooh-pooh gesture. The two women had a quick conversation about a couple of the items on the clipboard, then Frau Ballauf nodded to Marla again and turned back to the controlled chaos in the room.

"Frontilia?" Marla whispered with a giggle. "That sounds like something out of a bad Star Trek movie. Can't be from any part of Germany I've ever heard of."

"She's actually from the Vogtland."

Marla tilted her head at that.

"Southwest of Dresden," Amber clarified.

"Ah." Dresden, Marla had heard of. Anyone in Germany who possessed a spark of awareness had some idea of where Dresden was. The siege of that city by a Swedish army was, after all, one of the top three topics of conversation/arguments/disagreements in Magdeburg. "So what's she doing here?"

"Her husband had a distant relative who owned property rights of some kind in Magdeburg. It took a while after the sack in 1631 for him to hear that his relative had died in the sack, and that due to the deaths of some other kinsmen elsewhere, he was probably the heir. She said he dithered about it for quite some time, but he finally decided to come to Magdeburg to claim the property."

"Sounds kind of like what Mrs. Dreeson went through a couple of years ago," Marla said.

"Yeah, similar set of circumstances. Just dawned on me, there's probably been a lot of that happening all over, between the fighting and the plagues. Anyway, you'll have to sit down with Frontilia and get her to give you the whole story over a glass of wine someday. Suffice it to say that while her adventures with her husband on the trip here weren't quite as exciting as Ronnie Dreeson's, they exacted their toll. They got here a few months ago, and they no sooner arrived and got settled into a rooming house than he dropped dead from a heart attack. He was standing talking to her one moment, the next he was lying on the floor, gone."

"That's terrible," Marla said, horrified at the thought of anyone losing a mate like that.

"Yeah. And to top it off, after the funeral, when she finally tracked down someone who could tell her where the property was actually located, it turned out it was one of the lots that Gericke condemned in the emperor's name to build one of the big fancy boulevards in the Old City. She had to hire a lawyer—some guy named Lentke, if I remember correctly—but she did screw some money out of Mayor Gericke as compensation for the loss of her husband's rights."

"She sounds tough," Marla said.

"Believe it. She might not knock Ronnie off her throne as Queen of the Tough Old Broads," Marla could hear the capital letters in Amber's tone, "but I'd say she's a candidate for Crown Princess. Anyway, the money she got wasn't enough to go back home on or even live here for very long. She had worked with a school back in her home town, so when she somehow found out about Desfig"—that was how Amber pronounced the acronym for the Duchess Elisabeth Sofie Secondary School for Girls, where Marla taught music—"Lady Beth hired her right away."

"And then you poached her before I could even meet her at the school," Marla grinned.

"And then I poached her," Amber agreed with her own grin. "And it's a good thing I did, too. The woman is an organizational genius. Even at this late date she's going to make my job easier."

"Cool."

Marla leaned back against the wall again. Frontilia, huh? Well, it wasn't the prettiest of names, but one thing was for certain; if someone called it out, there wouldn't be half-a-dozen or more heads turning around like there would be if you called out Anna or Elizabeth. More power to her.

Schardius flicked his light across the sign on the door. Women's Dressing Room.

Aah.

He stepped into the room, and shone his light around. Several small shallow tables with mirrors on the wall. A few of them had placards with names on them. He walked down the room, reading them, until he found one in particular.

Marla.

"Georg Schmidt?" Ciclope murmured to Pietro as they approached the work site that morning. "You're sure?"

"Yes," Pietro muttered back. "This guy came out of the same place of business that the boss went into after he changed his clothes in that other house. I followed him to a tavern and got him drunk. He was a cheap drunk, too." Pietro spat to one side in emphasis, but the redness in his own eyes indicated that the clerk may not have been all that wimpy.

"Georg Schmidt," Ciclope murmured again. "Well, we'll just have to see what we can make out of that."

Someone tugged on his jacket and he spun around, fist cocked to level what he suspected was a pickpocket. Instead, he saw a skinny boy holding up a folded piece of paper in his left hand. There was something odd about the boy's stance.

"What do you want?" he snarled, lowering his fist.

"Man paid me to give this to you."

The boy's voice wavered a bit, but Ciclope had to give him points for standing his ground.

"You sure it's for me?"

"I don't see any other one-eyed men around," the boy replied cheekily.

Ciclope snatched the paper out of the boy's hand.

"Man have a name?"

"No."

"What did he look like?"

"Old…almost as old as you, a little bit fat, soft hands."

Ciclope exchanged glances with Pietro. That fit Schmidt. He turned back to the boy, but he was gone, weaving through the press of workers heading for the construction site. He crammed the note into his pocket.

"Aren't you going to read it?" Pietro nagged.

"Later," Ciclope muttered. "Not out here in front of everyone. Get to work."

He took his own advice and headed into the gate.

Chapter 37

Simon closed the door to *Das Haus Des Brotes* behind himself as he stood on the top step. He heard whistling, and looked up to see Hans leaning against the next building over, hat tilted back on his head and hands in his pockets. Simon tucked his roll into his pocket and trotted down the steps to meet his friend.

"So, is the new ring finally ready?" he asked, eyes alight with eagerness.

Hans broke off his whistling. "Yah." He nodded.

"And are you on the list, the..." Simon searched his memory for the word, "...the program?"

"Yah."

Simon grinned. "Well, what are we waiting for? Let's go!"

Hans grinned back, and pushed off the building. They had taken a few steps down the street when Simon stopped and said, "Wait!" Hans looked on in puzzlement as Simon looked up and down the street. After a moment, the boy shrugged, reached into his pocket to tear a piece off his roll, and bent to lay it on the ground right in front of the wall of the building.

"There." He stood and brushed his hand off on his pants leg. "Now we can go."

Hans grinned for a moment, then turned and led off down the street again. "You know, you care more about that dog than you do for people."

Simon caught up to the big man and settled into place to Hans' left. That left his crippled arm between them, and kept his left arm to the outside. He never really thought about it when he did it; that was just his preferred way to travel with company. He tucked his good hand behind his belt and swaggered a bit.

"Not more than for you and Ursula, and not more than Frau Zenzi and her husband." He shrugged again. Well, maybe Pastor Gruber, too. "At least Schatzi's never tried to hurt me."

"Rough day?"

"Yah."

Hans grunted. After a few steps, he said, "Sounds pretty lonely to me."

Simon swallowed the lump that suddenly appeared in his throat. "Yah."

Hans reached over and wrapped his arm around Simon's shoulder. Simon leaned into it, savoring the wordless contact.

They reached the intersection with the road that led to the bear-baiting pit, and Simon started to turn into it.

"Hoy!" Hans called as he continued straight through the intersection. "This way, remember?"

"Right." Simon wanted to smack himself for forgetting they were going to the new location, but he focused instead on catching up to Hans. "So, are you ready for this fight?"

"Yah." Hans looked over with a wide grin. "Very ready. It's been too long since the last one. I've been about to tie myself in a knot for the last few weeks."

"Yah, I know."

Simon ducked as Hans took a slow swipe at the back of his head. That big strong hand just barely ruffled his hair; he was thankful that it was just in jest. Having seen Hans fight for real, he knew that a real blow from the fighter would have left him crumpled and broken.

They bantered back and forth as they walked to the new site for the fights. It was a bit farther out from the Old City than the bear-baiting pit had been. The owners of the land the pit was on had sold it when someone had offered them more for the rights than they would ever see from the various fights that got staged there. That had put the fight promoters on the hunt for a new site, and it had taken a while to first find it, and second, negotiate for the rights to build a ring. Then they had to build it, and getting the funds raised for that hadn't been the easiest task in the world, either.

Although Hans had seen the ring, Simon hadn't yet, but he knew that even though they called it a ring, it wasn't round. Another weird thing that up-timers did, he supposed.

"And there it is," Hans said as they crested a bit of a rise. He pointed to the ring, which sat between the small hillock they stood on and another one on the other side.

There was a roof of sorts over the ring itself. Hans started down the slope. Simon followed in his steps. As they drew nearer, he could see more details about the ring: rectangular, almost square but not quite; sturdy posts in the corners, three courses of heavy ropes suspended and stretched along the sides between the corner posts, floor painted red.

There were already people milling around the ring. A genial outcry began when they spotted Hans descending the hillock.

"*Stark* Hans! *Stark* Hans!"

Hans waved at them as he drew closer. Simon could see the big grin on his friend's face when men stepped up to him and slapped him on the back or grabbed his hand to shake it. They finally made it to the side of the ring, where they were greeted by Todd Pierpoint.

"Hans! Good to see you, man! Come this way."

The promoter guided them to a bench in a roped off section of seats. "This is where you will wait for your fight. We have three fights tonight, and you're the main attraction, so you'll fight last."

"Sounds good," Hans said as he took his seat at the end of the front row much like Simon imagined a king would seat himself on his throne; slowly, and with deliberation. Simon sat to Hans' left almost as an afterthought. Herr Pierpoint's down-time partner Tobias Dreher called for him from the opposite end of the ring, so he left them to their own devices to answer that call.

After a few minutes, two other fighters made their way to the ropes and joined them on the benches.

"Where are the other guys?" Hans asked one of them.

"Down at the other end," came the response with a jerk of a thumb.

The next little while was amusing to Simon. The crowd around the ring was growing larger by the minute, and almost every man who joined the throng made his way by the roped-off area. Most just looked at Hans and nodded. Several spoke; a few offered their hands. It was almost as if Simon's imaginary king were receiving the worship of his subjects; at least, that's what it seemed like to Simon as Hans smiled at all and sundry.

Simon also found it humorous that few of the passers-by seemed to notice the other fighters.

At one point there was a lull in the traffic, and Simon nudged his friend. When Hans leaned over, Simon said, "Just remember they're all pigeons or crows," at which Hans' smile got larger, "and either way that means they're hungry. They all want something from you."

Hans sobered and he looked down at Simon. "Why are you so cynical, boy?"

Simon reached over with his left hand, pulled his limp right hand out of the coat pocket where it had been resting, and held it up between them. Hans' eyes narrowed for a moment, but then he got the point. His lips tightened and he looked away, but then his gaze returned to Simon's face and he clapped his hand on Simon's leg. "Happens you're probably right, lad, you're probably right."

"Yah." Simon didn't say anything else, just tucked his useless hand back into its nest and sat staring at nothing, eyes burning but cold at heart. It really had been a rough day.

It wasn't long after that that the evening's program began. Herr Pierpoint jumped up on the edge of the ring, bent and stepped through the ropes, then reached over them to take a short rod connected to a wire from his partner Tobias. He held the rod up to his mouth, and began speaking.

"Good evening, and on behalf of TNT Promotions, welcome to our new facility."

Simon jumped. It seemed like a giant was shouting at him from all directions. He craned his neck around, trying to see where the sound was coming from. Hans pointed at a black metal horn thing hanging from the edge of the roof. Once Simon realized that sound was coming out of that, he next realized there were four of the horn things; one hanging from each side of the roof. He looked at Hans.

"They're called speakers," Hans said. "Up-time stuff. They use electricity and make sounds loud, or louder."

"Oh."

What would the up-timers think of next?

"You're late," the man Ciclope now thought of as Georg Schmidt hissed. "And where's your partner?"

"I got your note this morning," Ciclope said, "but we couldn't leave the project until close to evening. We have to keep them thinking we're workers they can rely on, remember?"

The note had directed them to come to an out-of-the-way nook between buildings near the market area where secondhand dealers of everything gathered. They were to bring their "exchanges" with them.

"And I had to send Pietro back for the merchandise. You don't think we're stupid enough to carry it around, do you? Especially after the way you browbeat us the last time we met ... Herr Schmidt."

The other man froze for a moment, thereby confirming Pietro's research.

"What ... what do you mean? That's not my name."

Ciclope chuckled. It was remarkable how such an innocuous sound could at the same time have such an evil tone to it.

"Oh, come now. Surely you didn't think you could keep us in the dark forever. You are Herr Georg Schmidt, brother-in-law of Mayor Otto Gericke, bürgermeister of Old Magdeburg, successful merchant—and the man who hired us to come and commit murder and arson on your rivals."

Schmidt flushed dark red and seemed to swell up. A long moment passed while he looked around, but then settled when he realized no one was close enough to have heard Ciclope. "All right. So you know who I am. Now what?"

"Oh, no change. You tell us what you want done; you turn us loose to do it." Ciclope watched relief move across the other man's face. "Except..."

"Except what?" Schmidt bit the response off.

"Except you pay us twice what you said you would for the paper money."

Schmidt's eyebrows drew together in a fearsome frown, and he tried to stare Ciclope down. But Ciclope had out-stared better—tougher—men than the merchant more than once. Schmidt finally folded. "All right," he said in a surly tone.

Gotthilf looked around the crowd at the new fight location. It was already being called an arena, although to him it looked more like a barn without walls. The crowd was really thick tonight; he and Byron were having trouble making their way through it.

"We've got a good program for you tonight," Herr Pierpoint's voice boomed out from the speakers. "Three fights, every one of them between modern-day gladiators."

Byron had managed to get to the edge of the ring and catch up with Tobias, Pierpoint's down-timer partner. Gotthilf caught up with them just as Tobias realized he had company. The promoter nodded to them, but his attention was mostly still on watching his partner in the ring.

"TNT Promotions?" Byron asked.

Tobias grinned. "Tobias and Todd. His idea." He jerked his thumb at the ring, where Pierpoint was still talking.

"Ah." Byron pursed his lips. "I was expecting some kind of joke about explosive fights or bombshell contests."

Tobias snickered. "He is saving that for the broadsheet advertisements that will start going out next week."

Gotthilf suppressed a groan. Up-timers seemed to have a predilection for low humor that equaled if not surpassed the worst of down-time excesses in that area. Puns in any language or style just caused him mental indigestion.

Pierpoint finished introducing the fighters and referee for the first fight, ducked through the ropes, and pointed to the bell man. The bell clanged, and the fight was on.

Simon and Hans watched the first two fights from their seat on the bench. The first one was a five-round contest that wasn't much of a fight: two skinny youths standing in the center of the ring throwing haymakers at each other and dodging with little attempt at blocking or any other technique. Hans and the remaining fighter muttered to each other all the way through the first round, but by the end of the second round they were grinning at the two hapless fighters, all the while making snide comments to each other that Simon sometimes had trouble understanding.

When one of the fighters actually managed to knock the other down, they both stood and cheered, laughing.

At the end of that bout, the other fighter on the bench shucked his jacket and shirt off while he was waiting for Herr Pierpoint to finish announcing the winner of the first fight and then introduce his fight. Hans helped him on with his gloves, then held up a fist.

"Good luck, Gus."

The other fighter tapped Hans' fist with his own.

"Thanks, but hopefully I will not need it."

With that he stepped up to the ring as his fight was announced.

Hans leaned back and spread his arms along the back of the bench.

"You know him?" Simon asked.

"Yah, Gus Bäcker is a good guy."

"You ever fight him?"

Hans chuckled. "Once. It lasted two rounds. Ever since then Gus has stuck with fighting guys his own size."

The second fight was on the schedule for eight rounds, but it ended in the fourth when Gus knocked out his opponent, who had proved to be somewhat better than the tyros of the first bout—but not much. He ducked out of the ring hardly breathing hard. Hans held his fist up again, and again Gus tapped it.

"Good fight," Hans decreed.

"Every win is a good fight," Gus grinned.

"Yah."

Hans stood and began taking his own jacket and shirt off. He draped them over the back of the bench, then dropped his hat on Simon's head. Simon looked up at his friend from under the brim of the hat and held up his own fist.

"Luck."

Hans tapped fists with him. "Luck from my luck. I'm sure to win."

Gus returned the favor as he helped Hans with his gloves. When they were fitted to Hans' satisfaction, he alternated pounding his fists into the opposite palms, standing and waiting for the announcing of his fight.

Hans didn't have to wait long. It was only a minute or two before Herr Pierpoint was announcing the last fight of the evening.

"Fighting out of the green corner, the challenger in tonight's main event hails from the Western Isles of Scotland. He stands five feet eleven inches tall and weighs two hundred twenty-five pounds. He is the best fighter in the Marine guards. Give it up for Anselm MacDonald of Clanranald!"

The other fighter was a bit taller than Hans, Simon saw when he climbed into the ring at the other end, though perhaps not as big overall. His red hair was like a flame atop his head, and when he grinned his front teeth were missing. There was a loud burst of applause and yells of "Go, Anse!" from a group of men in boots and buff coats standing at his end of the ring, and he raised an arm in salute.

"Fighting out of the red corner," Herr Pierpoint began while Hans climbed up to the ring, "here is the premier fighter in Magdeburg today. He stands five feet nine inches tall and weighs two hundred thirty-five pounds. He is undefeated in his professional fighting career, with a record of sixteen wins and zero defeats, with fourteen of the wins coming by knockouts. Give it up for the Samson of Magdeburg, Hans Metzger!"

Pierpoint pointed to where Hans was stepping through the ropes, and the crowd exploded, roaring and cheering and clapping in a flood of sound. Simon stood up on the bench and yelled along with the rest of them.

Hans stood in the center of the ring and grinned, turning to each of the four sides and pointing to the crowd there, which resulted in even more cheering. It took a long time for the noise to die down.

"Interesting," Byron said.

Gotthilf looking to his partner. "What?"

"The man's no Muhammad Ali, but he's certainly learned how to work a crowd."

"What..." Gotthilf started to ask the obvious question, but just then the bell rang and the fight began. "Oh, never mind."

Ciclope looked around as Pietro approached, whistling a song from the gutters of Venice—or what would pass for gutters among the canals of that city. He saw that his partner had a drawstring bag slung over one shoulder.

"So, what's to do?" Pietro asked as he joined the little tête-à-tête.

"Herr Schmidt, here," Ciclope jerked a thumb in the man's direction, "has agreed to double our take of the payroll money."

"Shh!" Schmidt said, looking around, then relaxing a bit when he realized still no one seemed to be close to them. The anger on his face was still very evident, however.

"That is very good," Pietro said, slinging the bag to the ground and rubbing his hands together. "When do we get it?"

"I have the amount we originally agreed on here," Schmidt muttered, shifting position a bit so they could see a bag behind him. "But it will take some time to get that much again. I can't get too much too fast from any one person, or it could cause someone to start thinking and asking questions."

"Fine. Give us that much, then," Ciclope kicked Pietro's bag forward and reached for the other bag. "We can wait for the rest...for a while." His tone made it clear that it had best not take any longer than absolutely necessary.

Ciclope hefted Schmidt's bag. It had a very satisfying weight to it, and emitted a clink when he shook it a bit. He handed it to Pietro, whose face immediately put on a very large grin. A thought crossed Ciclope's mind, and he looked over at Schmidt from under lowered eyebrows.

"A word, Herr Schmidt."

Schmidt glared back.

"We may not be master merchants like your august self, but we are not ignorant. We can count—quite well, actually—and we know how much we should be receiving in that bag. If the count is off by more than a handful of coins," Ciclope focused a wolfish grin on the merchant, "why, we will have to come visit you."

Ciclope let the silence broaden for a long moment.

"And we do know where you live."

Schmidt's face tightened. He stood motionless for moment, not saying anything. Finally, he just shook his head and pulled a small sack out of a pocket of his ragged coat and handed it to Pietro.

"Always nice doing business with a man who understands the realities of life," Pietro cracked.

Simon watched keenly as Hans stepped up to face the Scot MacDonald. Gus slid over to sit by him.

"So, you are Hans' luck?" the other fighter asked.

"Yah," Simon replied, eyes on the action. "At least, that is what he calls me."

"That's good," Gus said. "A fighter can be good, but he still needs some luck on his side."

They both winced as the Scot unloaded a flurry of punches. Hans ducked some, and took the rest on his arms. After that moment, MacDonald stepped back and starting circling Hans, who circled in turn.

"The Scotsman is stupid," Gus said.

"Why is that?"

"He is wearing those big heavy gloves."

"The ones like mittens that Hans won't wear?" Simon looked at the hands of the Scot, and sure enough, that's what he was wearing.

"Yah. He probably thinks that they'll help him hit harder, the *dummkopf*." Gus spit in the dirt. "That will not help him."

"Why not?" Simon looked over at the other fighter.

"Hans wears what Herr Pierpoint calls the MMA gloves. His hands will be faster. You'll see."

The first round ended. Hans came over to his corner and leaned back against the ropes, waving a hand to Simon. He didn't even seem to be breathing hard.

The bell clanged, and Round 2 began.

"Ah," Gus said.

"What?" Simon asked, alarmed.

"No, it's good. Look at how the Scot is moving."

Simon watched. At the end of the second round, he still hadn't seen what Gus was seeing. It wasn't until most of the way through the third round that he finally got it. "The red-haired guy is flat-footed. He does not move on his toes like Hans does."

Gus nodded.

"Yah. That's one thing that Herr Pierpoint keeps hammering into us, that we need to be on our toes. It's all about speed, and you can do everything faster when you're moving on your toes. You watch, pretty soon now Hans is going to hand this guy his head."

Gus seemed to be lacking as a prophet, however, throughout the first four rounds. Hans seemed to be content to let the big Scotsman try his whole arsenal. Straight jabs, uppercuts, hay-makers, cross punches; he wasn't able to tag Hans with many of them, and those that did land didn't seem to faze the German.

In the rest period after the fourth round, Simon turned to Gus and asked the question that had been on his mind most of the evening.

"Why are you helping and supporting Hans? Didn't he beat you?"

"Like a drum," Gus said with a big grin. "But he was not mean about it, and he helped me up off the ground after it was over. And he's Our Hans," he said, waving his hand round the arena. "Everyone watches Hans. And when he goes up against someone from outside Magdeburg," pointing at the redhead across the ring, "then we all are for him. The Scotsman may think he's a hard man, but compared to Hans..." He shook his head.

"*Stark* Hans," Simon said, looking back to the ring as the bell rang for Round 5.

"Yah."

The two fighters approached each other from their opposite corners. They started their circling again, until all of a sudden MacDonald lunged forward with a straight punch. Hans must have let his focus drift for a moment, because the punch crashed through hands he raised just a fraction of a second too late and connected solidly with his jaw. Simon leapt to his feet as the crowd roared.

"What happened? What happened?" he shouted, shaking Gus' shoulder.

"I don't know, Simon," Gus shouted back through the crowd noise. "But whatever that big oaf did, Hans has really had his bell rung."

Indeed, the German was back-pedaling around the ring, head ducked, hands in front of his face, elbows tight to his sides, weathering a storm of punches from the big Scot, who was obviously trying to finish Hans off. But before too long, the storm began diminishing as the Scot was unable to sustain the frenzied pace. By the end of the round, he was almost plodding, and Hans was back to ducking and flicking off anything that came close to connecting.

The end of the round bell rang. Hans came back to his corner and leaned back against the ropes. He didn't turn around, but Simon could tell from the tension in his shoulders that he was angry.

He tugged on Gus' arm. "Come help me up."

For a moment the other man didn't move, a confused expression on his face. But as Simon gestured to the ring with his hand, understanding dawned, and he took Simon around the waist and lifted him up to the apron of the ring.

Hans' head swiveled to look at Simon, who gulped at the set

expression on his friend's face. For the first time, he began to really understand just how hard *Stark* Hans could be.

Simon still shuffled sideways until he was close to the fighter. He raised his fist up between them. "Luck," he said.

Hans stared at him for a few seconds, then a slight smile appeared and he reached out and tapped Simon's fist with his own. "Luck," was the reply.

Simon turned and hopped down off the ring apron, supported by Gus' strong arms. He went back to the bench, but instead of sitting he stood up on it so he could get his best view of the ring. He had a feeling something was about to happen.

As it turned out, he was right. Hans glided out of his corner, met MacDonald in the center of the ring, and proceeded to give the Scot intensive instruction in the art of pugilism as practiced in Magdeburg. Punch followed punch, measured and administered with a precision and a force that was almost like watching an up-time repeating firearm in use.

"See, see!" Gus said, grabbing Simon by the shoulder. "I told you his hands would be faster."

Simon could see it. Hans' fists would flick out and back, so fast it seemed that he couldn't have hit the big Scot. But the red marks on the body and face of MacDonald told the tale, as did the blood flowing from his nose and from the cut above one eye, matting in his moustache and beard.

Simon had never heard the word juggernaut, but if he had, he would have agreed that it was a good description of Hans in this round; advancing inexorably, with nothing to deter or divert him from his goal, which appeared to be nothing less than the demolishment of one Andrew MacDonald of Clanranald.

The end came suddenly when Hans blocked a haymaker, stepped forward and buried one fist right below the sternum of the hapless Scotsman. MacDonald froze for just a moment, almost paralyzed, and in that moment Hans landed a thunderous blow on the point of the chin hidden behind the red beard.

The big Scot was straightened up by the punch; his eyes rolled up in his head and he crashed backwards onto the floor of the ring.

The crowd erupted in cheers as the referee waved Hans to his corner, and began reciting the count. Simon, elated, counted along with him.

"*Eins!*

"*Zwei!*"

Gus started yelling out the count in concert with Simon.

"*Drei!*

"*Vier!*"

By now others around them were counting with them.

"*Fünf!*

"*Sechs!*

"*Sieben!*"

The entire crowd was shouting along with the referee now.

"*Acht!*

"*Neun!*

"*Zehn!*"

Hans came out of his corner for the obligatory holding up of the winner's hand. He turned and waved to each side of the ring, then returned to the near side of the ring, stepped through the ropes and hopped down to the ground.

Gus immediately began helping with removing the gloves. Simon picked up Hans' shirt and handed it to him as soon as his hands were free, following it with the big man's coat.

Hans plucked his hat off of Simon's head. Simon grinned up at him; Hans grinned back and held out a fist. "Luck."

Simon tapped it with his own fist. "Luck."

"Luck indeed," Gus said. "Wish I had a luck like that."

Hans draped an arm around Simon's skinny shoulders. "You find your own luck. Simon's mine." Simon beamed in pride.

And with that, they took off to find Herr Pierpoint and collect the winnings for the evening.

"Well, I guess we have an understanding," Ciclope said to Schmidt. "A good evening to you, Herr Schmidt."

He started to turn away.

"Wait!" Schmidt hissed.

Ciclope turned back slowly, a serious frown forming on his face.

"What are you going to do next?" Schmidt asked. "I have the right to know."

"Ah," Ciclope responded. "Next? Pietro, tell the man what we have in mind."

The Italian did so, in a rapid mutter. Schmidt's eyes grew wider and wider, and toward the end he began to smile. After Pietro was done, he clapped his hands together.

"Wonderful! If you manage that, I will increase the money from two parts in three to three parts in four!"

Ciclope smiled in turn. "Get the money ready, Herr Schmidt. It will take a while to get put into action. Pietro has to find some tools, first; but it won't be long. And I promise you, it will set Magdeburg on its ear when it happens."

The watcher nodded to himself. Confirmation.

Chapter 38

— A T & L TELEGRAPH —

BEGIN: GVL TO MBRG

TO: FRAU MARLA LINDER

ADDR: SYLWESTERHAUS MAGDEBURG

FROM: HM AT TROMMLER RECORDS

DATE: 6 FEB 1636

MESSAGE:

YOU ARE A PROPHET STOP NUMBER ONE WITH
A BULLET STOP DOING A THIRD PRESSING OF DO
YOU HEAR THE PEOPLE SING STOP ORDERS KEEP
POURING IN STOP HEARD THROUGH GRAPEVINE
THAT RECORD PLAYER CO HAS SOLD ALL UNITS
ON HAND AND IS BACKORDERED OUT WAZOO
STOP YOU HAVE PROBABLY MADE US ALL
WEALTHY STOP OR AT LEAST WELL OFF STOP
CONGRATS STOP WHAT TO DO FOR ENCORE STOP

HEATHER

END

Marla looked up from the telegram, a bit bewildered. "But I didn't do it for money."

Confused himself, Franz took the telegram from her and read it. "Ah," he said after being enlightened. He handed the telegram back to Marla. "Did you expect to be ignored?"

"Nooo..." Marla drew the word out as her eyebrows drew down into a frown.

Franz smiled and he spread his hands. "Well then, it was inevitable, I fear, that after delivering such a message you would become either famous or infamous. Of the two, I really think famous is the better choice."

"But I didn't want the focus to be on me!" Marla looked like she wanted to stomp her foot. Her frame of mind was not helped when Franz started chuckling. She swung a slap at him, which missed by two feet.

Franz sobered. "Dear, most people can't separate a message from its messenger. If they like the message, they will like the messenger. But the reverse is also true. Be thankful they are buying your records. They could be shooting at you."

"Huh." After a moment, her frown eased. "I suppose you're right. And it's not like all the money is going to be mine. Atwood and Trommler are going to get a good piece of it."

"Right. So by doing well, you're doing some good for others at the same time."

"Right." Marla's expression could now be called resigned. "A rising tide floats all boats, or something like that."

Franz chuckled again. "Only you, dear, would put up such a struggle against people wanting to give you money."

After a moment, Marla smiled at Franz, and he felt the usual warmth of that smile flood through him. Just to tease her, he frowned.

"What?" Now she looked concerned.

"So what are you going to do for an encore?"

Mary Simpson stopped short and turned to face Gunther Achterhof.

"Are you certain?"

"From the lips of Frau Abrabanel herself, less than a quarter hour ago."

"Two days?"

"Yah."

Mary stood up straight, let out a determined sigh, and nodded to Gunther.

"Tell her we'll be ready."

Chapter 39

Gotthilf looked up at a nudge from Byron.

"There he is."

Sure enough, Hans Metzger had appeared out of the street that ran by the Schardius corn factorage warehouse and all the other businesses that lined the river. They had been watching for some little while. The other warehousemen had mostly left some time ago, but Metzger for some reason was running a little behind the rest. No matter, Gotthilf thought to himself. In fact, it might be to their advantage if others didn't see what was going to happen in a moment.

Metzger had his hat pushed back on his head and was ambling along with his hands in his pockets and whistling tunelessly. His carefree attitude came to an abrupt end when Byron hissed at him from the shadows.

"Metzger!"

The whistling stopped, and the big man's head swiveled to look at them. A wary expression dropped onto his face, and his shoulders hunched a bit. "What do you want?" he asked in a mutter.

"We need to talk."

"Now?"

"Now."

Metzger looked around.

"Someone will see us."

"I'm not worried about that," Byron chuckled. "Are you?"

Metzger stood still for a moment, then reluctantly stepped into the mouth of the alley.

"What do you want?"

Gotthilf picked up the conversational thread.

"We are not looking at you for anything, so rest at ease on that score. No, we want to ask you some questions about your employer."

"Master Schardius?"

Aha, Gotthilf thought as Metzger visibly tensed. *Jackpot, as Byron would say.*

"Yes."

"What do you want to know about?"

Even under his loose-fitting clothing, Gotthilf could see almost every muscle in Metzger's body tense up. The man obviously knew things he didn't want to make known. The question was, were they the same things that he and Byron wanted to know?

Franz Sylwester stood outside the imperial palace in the Altstadt in Old Magdeburg, waiting in the cold along with most of the residents of the city for the arrival of Princess Kristina and her consort. He looked over at Marla and smiled. She was swaddled in so much clothing that it was almost a miracle she could move. He mentally recounted the layers: thermal up-timer underwear, doubled wool socks, heavy boots, jeans, her heaviest velvet divided skirt, two sweaters, a green down-filled jacket formerly her father's, heavy gloves, a triple layer knit cap—pink with green and purple blotches—pulled down low over her forehead, and matching heavy scarf wrapped round and round her neck and face. Her gloved hands were in her jacket pockets, and he could barely see a glint of her eyes in the narrow gap between the lower edge of the cap and the top of the scarf.

"What are you laughing at?"

Her voice was so muffled by the layers of scarf that he almost didn't hear her.

"You."

"So I hate to be cold. Sue me."

Franz laughed and wrapped his arm around her waist. She snuggled against him. For all that she was a humorous sight, he didn't begrudge Marla her attempts to stay somewhat warm. She did chill easily, he knew, and once she got cold it took forever to warm her up. He still remembered the ride on the river boats when they first came to Magdeburg over two years ago—had it really been that long? She got soaked in the rain because she wouldn't stay in the shelter but had to be near the crate containing her precious piano. By the time they got to Magdeburg, he was almost beside himself with worry over her health, she had drooped so badly.

Marla wasn't the only one who seemed to be wearing everything they owned as they stood out in the cold February air. Most everyone in sight seemed to have on as many layers as they could fit into, but no one looked comfortable. Red noses and hands on ears seemed to be the order of the day. Franz felt sorry for the Marine guards in their new and ridiculously elaborate uniforms. He hoped that all the gilt and braid that weighed down their coats added warmth, but from the looks on most of their faces he suspected that was not the case.

But the people he felt sorriest for were the players in Thomas Schwartzberg's little band—or at least, the horn players.

Thomas had managed to amass a group of fourteen brass players and six drummers; some from the Magdeburg Symphony Orchestra, and some from the community. Trumpets, trombones, the wildly misnamed French horns, and tubas, combined with two snare drums and four tenor drums. Not a patch on the full-blown high school field band that Grantville mustered for festivities and parades, but still not bad. And for all that they were a "pick-up" group, as Marla put it, they had really cohered into a solid ensemble that could put forth an amazing volume of sound.

But today the poor brass men were being tested to their limits. The temperature was well below the point where water would freeze, and there was a bit of a north breeze blowing. There was nothing they could do that would keep the brass warm. In fact, Thomas had fretted over what the cold would do to their intonation and timbre if the parade happened on a cold day—like today, for example. Dane Stevenson and Dallas Chaffin, the two most experienced up-time bandsmen of the group, had just shrugged.

"It happens," Dane had said. "You just do your best. Don't bother trying to tune once you go outside. Just blow and go. And trust me, if it's that cold, no one is going to be listening critically. They're all going to be thinking about how soon they can get to a warm spot or can get a hot drink."

"Yep," Dallas had confirmed. "Been there, done that. Just make sure your players haven't had too much gin or schnapps beforehand trying to turn their blood into antifreeze."

The two young up-timers had laughed together after that, obviously sharing a memory of some kind. Franz reminded himself that he wanted to hear that story one day.

The six drummers and two cymbalists, on the other hand, were all smiling a bit. Dallas had had a late brainstorm and come up with several small iron pots which he filled with lit charcoal and placed in front of their feet right when they took their positions. His excuse was that they had to do something to keep the leather drum heads at least sort-of warm, or they might become so brittle in the cold that they'd break when played. Franz wasn't sure he believed it, but the drummers had all agreed loudly and longly, and as a consequence were all enjoying some slight amount of warmth. In fact, he noticed that the brass players had sort of curled back around the drums as much as they could, trying to pick up some bit of the warmth for themselves.

Thomas Schwartzberg's head swiveled to the right and cocked as if he was listening to something. A moment later, Franz could hear it, too; the sound of cheering as the vehicles of the princess' cortege drew nearer. Within moments, the people near him started cheering and waving flags and banners and sashes in the air.

The cars in the procession were moving at a slow pace, allowing plenty of opportunities for everyone who lined the streets to say they saw the princess, whether they really did or not. As the procession neared, Franz could only see various large fleshy men in the princess' car. That stood to reason, he supposed. Princess Kristina was only nine years old, after all.

The cheering redoubled in volume as the princess' car pulled up to the area where the greeting committee and the honor guard were standing. The first man out of the car came out of the front door. He was very tall—perhaps even taller than Emperor Gustav—and was very large to boot, to the extent that the up-timer shotgun he carried in one hand seemed almost a toy of some kind. A more imposing, deterring guard Franz couldn't imagine. He looked around alertly for a moment, then rapped once on the glass of the rear door.

The door opened, and people started clambering out of the rear seat. Thomas turned and faced the band, pulled a baton out of one sleeve, and poised his hand in the air. As one, the brass players pulled their right hands out of their coats where they had been holding their mouthpieces in their armpits to keep them warm, plugged the mouthpieces into their horns, and applied them to their lips. All their eyes were on Thomas, who was watching the car out of the corner of his eye.

The first man out was an obvious politician, but not one that Franz had seen before, so he suspected it was someone from one of the northern or western cities where the Committees had a strong presence. The man who followed him out to stand and straighten slowly was dressed in rich—but not gaudy—finery, and looked somewhat rumpled. By default, that had to be Prince Ulrik. Finally, the slight frame of the princess slid across the seat and out the door. When her face came into view, the crowd erupted into cheers. At the same moment, Thomas sketched a four-beat and launched the band into musical motion.

Byron spoke again, drawing Metzger's attention. Gotthilf thought the man tensed even more. It wouldn't have surprised him if Metzger's hands had drawn into fists and raised before his body. Whatever his perception of Byron, he was definitely at least wary of him.

"We're looking into several corpses found floating in the river, remember?"

"Yah."

Metzger obviously wasn't going to volunteer anything.

"We've received tips..." Gotthilf began.

"Tips?" Metzger looked confused.

"We've heard rumors," Gotthilf started over, "that someone influential in the city is having people killed who are...not meeting his expectations."

"Murdered because they disobey or won't keep their mouths shut." That was Byron's contribution. Gotthilf reminded himself that being blunt might work to their advantage with this guy.

"So? You think I had something to do with it?"

Metzger's face was giving nothing away.

"No," Gotthilf said. "Not that we know of. But your boss, on the other hand..." He let the pause build until Metzger's eyes shifted. "We hear rumors that Schardius is the one ordering these killings."

That wasn't an out-and-out lie, Gotthilf rationalized to himself. It did, however, stretch the truth to the point of dismemberment. If it got the man to talk, well, it was worth it. But his hopes of Metzger's lips unlocking were quickly dashed.

"I know nothing about anything like that."

"Word on the street is you do." Byron being a blunt object again. Gotthilf watched Metzger's face pale, and his fists did clench this time, for all that his features otherwise didn't change.

"Then the street lied."

"Look," Gotthilf intervened before the two big men went toe to toe and nose to nose, "we are looking for the truth. If the rumors are wrong, fine. Tell us what is the truth, and we will move on."

"I have nothing to tell you," Metzger insisted.

"Now who's lying?" Byron jumped back in.

Metzger's face went red, and his fists started to rise, but he stopped them before they got waist high. He looked at Byron, then he looked at Gotthilf.

Gotthilf could see how hard his partner's face was. From the tension he was feeling in his facial muscles, he suspected that his own face was similarly aligned, and his hand wasn't far from the butt of his pistol.

Metzger broke. His fists dropped and his shoulders slumped.

"I can't tell you anything," he said in a weary tone of voice.

"Can't?" Byron said in a stern tone. "Or won't?"

Metzger shrugged. "Does it make any difference?"

"Not really." Gotthilf offered that. "But give me this much—is there something to tell?"

Metzger hesitated, then realized that his hesitation was answer enough, so he nodded.

"What are you afraid of?" Byron demanded.

Metzger remained silent.

The silence grew to a long moment. It was finally broken by Byron.

"All right, we can't make you talk. But you hear me, and hear me well, Herr Metzger: if one more person dies because you kept your silence, I will be all over you like stink on a knacker. I'll be the first face you see when you leave your rooms in the morning, and the last one you see when you close your door at night. I'll be picking your change up off the bar when you order a drink. I'll take the last swig out of your bottle of gin. I'll be watching you load and unload at the Schardius warehouse. I'll hand you your towel at your fights. And all I need is one mistake on your part; just one, and you'll be so deep in trouble you'll need a miner's lamp just to figure out how deep you are."

Gotthilf almost stared at his partner. That was more words than he'd heard out of him at one time since the beginning of their working together.

Metzger stared at Byron, then shifted his gaze to Gotthilf.

Gotthilf gave a firm nod. "Believe it."

The big down-timer shifted gaze between the two partners several times. His mouth tightened and twisted. "You do what you have to do," he said. "Are we done now?"

Gotthilf looked at Byron, who shrugged.

"Yah, we are done." Gotthilf waited until Metzger had started to turn to leave their confrontation. "But do not be surprised if we call you in for more discussions."

Metzger turned back. "If you keep this up, it will be my body you find in the river."

"Your choice," Byron said coldly.

The band began pouring out the strains of Thomas' work. He had entitled it the "Vasa March" in honor of the emperor's dynasty. His explanation for that was he was honoring the emperor's valor on the field of battle. Franz was a little skeptical that that was the reason; or at least, that it was the only reason. Musicians had for generations flattered those in power in order to reach positions of security and support. Franz had done something similar almost two years ago, when he had renamed the up-time Brandenburg Concerto No. 3 to be the Vasa Concerto No. 3. It was a custom, even a fact of life, for musicians. Looking through Marla's eyes, he thought that might change in the next generation. He hoped so, but right now he wasn't holding his breath.

The march was loud, and vigorous. In the music from before the arrival of Grantville, low instruments usually just provided a foundation for the treble instruments to dance above. Franz was intrigued to hear that Thomas had written his march to feature the low brass. They were the ones actually declaring the primary themes, only to be echoed by trumpets and horns.

And the percussion, oh my. Franz had to chuckle at some of the expressions on the nonmusician faces around him. Most down-timers never heard anything more than a small hand drum played by a traveling musician at fairs and markets when the sprightly dances were performed. The sound of rapid, heavy, orchestrated drums was as utterly foreign to them as... well, as an electric guitar would be, he supposed. It was only about four years ago, after all, that he himself had learned about them, and he still had some recollection of his initial reaction to them. "An avalanche of cacophony," he had described it to his friends... or something like that.

But he set those thoughts aside to listen to Thomas' march. The low brass combined with the constant rolling patterns played on the tenor drums gave a sensation of listening almost to thunder—a thunder that throbbed and pulsed, a thunder that ebbed and flowed, a thunder that filled the square before the palace, yet didn't cover up the sound of the higher brass or drive the Magdeburgers out in pain.

The music came to a crashing end. Thomas lowered his baton and looked toward Franz and Marla. They both gave him an up-time thumbs-up, and he grinned in delight as he thrust the baton back into his sleeve and joined them.

The speeches began. Franz leaned over to Thomas and muttered under the louder noise. "Well written, and well done."

Thomas flashed another grin at him.

Franz learned something that afternoon: even politicians will bow to the weather, if it is severe enough. Every speech was mercifully short, even those of Prince Ulrik and Princess Kristina.

The big surprise came at the end of Kristina's speech.

Gotthilf watched as Metzger left the alleyway. He looked over at Byron, and was surprised to see a slight smile.

"What are you grinning about?"

Byron chuckled a bit, even though the smile faded. "We've got him. He'll talk to us."

"I hope so. You were pretty hard on him there at the end."

Byron looked at him from under lowered brows.

"He knows what's happened, and he won't tell us. That makes him complicit at best, if not an outright accomplice. You know what kind of man he is. Do you think he'd listen to the voice of reason?"

As much as he didn't want to say it, Gotthilf had no choice. "No."

"He'll talk to us," Byron repeated. "It's just a matter of when."

"I hope you are right," Gotthilf replied. "I really do not want to be in the room with Captain Reilly if they find another floater in the river."

"Yeah."

There was a long moment of silence, broken eventually by the up-timer.

"But it could be worse."

Gotthilf dipped his head and looked at his partner from under his own lowered eyebrows.

Byron pointed south toward the palace. "We could be on parade duty."

"Point."

"I'm having a party, and everybody's invited!"

There was a bare moment of silence before the cheering redoubled after the princess' statement. Franz's jaw dropped, and he looked over at the Magdeburg powers that be, who were beginning to cluster around Senator Abrabanel. He had noted her hanging back, letting all the other notables take the front ranks and present themselves to the princess, her consort-to-be, and to the crowds. After a moment, his mouth closed and he started to chuckle. It was obvious now to anyone with eyes just who held the reins today. All eyes turned to the senator, who started handing out marching orders. Attendant after attendant, most of them young women, left her presence with quick steps, some scattering in different directions but most heading into the palace.

Franz was jolted when Marla grabbed him by the arm and started dragging him through the crowd.

"Where are you going?" he asked in exasperation.

"Inside," she snapped back, voice still muffled by the scarf.

"What?"

She stopped and turned to face him. "There's a grand piano in that palace, the one that Girolamo Zenti rebuilt and presented to the princess over a year ago. In the madhouse that's getting ready to flow into the palace, I don't expect anyone to be thinking about it. I want in there now to protect it. Now come on!"

Franz now matched his wife stride for stride. Marla's head was swiveling around, looking through the crowd.

"There!"

She changed course slightly. In a moment, Franz saw the slight figure of Mary Simpson appear out of the crowd as she won free of the crush around the princess.

"Mary!" Marla called out. The admiral's wife looked around and headed their direction. Marla didn't even give the older woman a chance to speak, blurting out, "The palace piano! We need to protect it."

Mary said not a word, but turned and headed not for Rebecca Abrabanel, as Franz expected, but instead for the sergeant in charge of the Marine Guard. That worthy, already looking a bit nervous at the thought of the mass of people getting ready to invade his turf, bent down to listen to her.

Franz couldn't hear what she said over the crowd noise, but from fingers pointing first at Marla and then at the palace, he got a pretty good idea of the conversation. The conclusion of the short conversation was the detaching of one of the guards into Mary's charge. He followed her across to Marla as the sergeant turned his gaze back to the crowd.

"Private Brodie here will take you to the piano. You might open it up and start playing something. I suspect that Rebecca will appreciate that touch."

Brodie them a nod, then turned and headed for the palace with his SRG carried across his body. Marla and Franz followed close behind, following the wagging shako as the crowd moved out of the private's way.

Once inside, Marla pulled the cap from her head as they followed the private and shoved it and her gloves in her jacket pockets. Next came the scarf, unwound and stuffed into a sleeve of the jacket to keep it from wandering off. She handed the jacket to Franz as they walked through the double doors into the great room of the palace, and made a beeline to the piano, which was set to one side. While she was propping up the lid and opening the keyboard cover, Franz looked over to Private Brodie.

"Our thanks. My wife is protective of any piano, but that one is one of a kind. She'll guard it like a mother sow with one piglet."

"Well, if it is that important, maybe I should stand guard," the private said with a wink.

Franz winked back. "Well, I am certain that the palace staff would appreciate the reinforcement over this rare and costly instrument." He sobered. "Seriously, it does sound like a good idea."

"Just you remember to say that to my sergeant if he comes looking for me in here where it's warm," Brodie said with another wink.

Franz laughed, just as Marla started playing "Jesu, Joy of Man's Desiring."

Hans Metzger stalked through the streets of the poorest quarter of the old city. God Above, what was he going to do? If the *Polizei* were going to start coming after him, whether they thought he had a hand in the floaters' deaths or not, Schardius was going to start getting nervous, and that meant his own days were possibly numbered. One on one, two on one, even three on one he wasn't worried about dealing with any attackers, be they thugs or even true hard men. But he was under no illusions about Schardius hiring as many bodies as was needed to overwhelm him. Or even just give one of them a pistol and shoot him in the back some night.

But his greatest fear wasn't for himself. He would take his own chances, and after surviving the sack he figured he was living on borrowed time anyway. But what would he do about Ursula? Ursula, and Simon now? How could he protect them?

Hans started across the east bridge between the Altstadt and the Neustadt. He stopped at the crest of it, and stared over the side at the water flowing from underneath it in the Big Ditch.

What was he going to do?

The water gave no answer.

Chapter 40

It was a long afternoon, and by the end of it Marla was ready for it to be over. She had played most everything she knew, from classical to pop to hymns. Fortunately their friends had started showing up one by one, and she was able to change off with Hermann and Thomas. She was back at the keyboard at the end of the party, however. Most everyone had left by the time she started the Beethoven. She'd almost begun playing it several times during the day, but had held back until now.

She laid her hands on the keys, and waited. For all that it was considered by some up-time authorities to be a lesser work because of its popularity, to Marla, Sonata No. 14 in C sharp minor, Opus 27, No. 2—the *Sonata quasi una fantasia,* most commonly known as the "Moonlight" or "Mondschein Sonata"—was quintessential Beethoven. Even more than Chopin, it was the piece that had made her want to study piano at an early age. It was the first adult piece she played in its entirety in a recital. And it was the first piece she had brought back to her exacting standards after her ... hiatus.

Eyes closed, head bowed, Marla breathed in and out, and when the moment felt right, lifted her hands and began.

The opening slow arpeggios poured from her long fingers. Even though Marla was focused on the music, a small thought surfaced in a corner of her mind: she never did understand why the nickname of the piece was "Moonlight." To her the opening movement, with its long quiet flowing themes, was much more evocative of water. Her mouth quirked at the thought that it should have been the "Moonlake" Sonata.

Releasing the thought, Marla poured herself into the music, and for several minutes just let the *adagio sostenuto* of that first movement ebb and flow in tempo, ebb and flow in volume, ebb and flow in spirit. At length, the conclusion arrived, and she closed in the soft final chords; peaceful, cleansing, cleansed.

Without more than half a breath, she tripped on to the *allegretto* movement, one that had always felt like a stately dance to her, albeit one with a lilt. Eyes still closed, fingers still unerringly finding the keys, she felt her lips curve in an involuntary smile. It was impossible not to smile when playing such a light-hearted piece.

All too soon the second movement was over, and this time the pause between it and the third movement was even shorter, lasting only long enough to lift the hands from the closing positions and place them to begin the great rolling arpeggios of the *presto agitato*. Fingers flashed as she began at the bottom and rolled up to crashing chords, again and again. Interludes came and went, but always the return to the arpeggios, always the return to the hammered double chords, always the impact of the keys hitting the bottom of their travelings as she treated them almost as percussive instruments.

The final arpeggios rippled and ran down and up the keyboard to an extended trill, a final quiet interlude, then a last outburst of ripples ending in the ultimate chords. She held her hands on the keys as the final sound resonated from the piano, then snatched them away.

"Ha! Nailed it!" she exulted.

Applause sounded around her, and her eyes flew open. She had forgotten where she was, and for a moment she was horrified to see the princess standing close by and clapping madly, with Ulrik behind her with his hand on her shoulder.

Not that Kristina was the only one applauding. The color climbed Marla's face as she stood to face Mary, and Rebecca Abrabanel, and others of the political elite of Magdeburg and the USE. She inclined her head and shoulders, fuming a little on the inside. Just her luck that she had given what amounted to a mini-recital dressed like a bag lady in everything she owned.

Marla could tell from his expression that Franz, that rat, was holding in laughter. She shot him a look that told him he would pay for not warning her. His response was a further tightening of the lips to repress chuckles that she was certain were threatening to burst forth.

She had to straighten hurriedly, as the princess stepped forward and gravely offered her hand.

"You are Frau Linder, the one who teaches music at the girls' school, yes? I saw the Christmas concert there. Not last year," Kristina corrected herself, "but the year before."

"Yes, you did. I remember seeing you."

Kristina retrieved her hand after the handshake. "I liked that then. I liked this now. Can you teach me to play like you do?"

Marla got serious. "That would depend: how badly do you want to play, Princess?"

The girl cocked her head and a furrow appeared between her eyebrows. Marla continued.

"I started when I was six, and I practiced five or six hours a week. By the time I was your age, I was practicing eight to ten hours a week. When I was fourteen, it was twelve or more hours a week. And now," she looked the princess directly in the eye, "I try to get twenty hours a week of practice in."

Kristina looked appalled. "I have to do that much to learn to play the piano?"

Marla shook her head. "No, but you didn't ask me if I could teach you to play; you asked me if I could teach you to play *like me*."

She could almost see the wheels turning behind the princess' eyes. And she could see the moment when Kristina understood the difference.

"You mean that to be really good at it, I would have to work really hard at it for a long time."

Marla smiled. "Yes."

Kristina walked over and ran her hand along the side of the piano cabinet. "This is my piano, you know."

"Kristina," Ulrik said.

"Well, really my father's, but Signor Zenti presented it to me because Papa wasn't here when he brought it down the river from Grantville. So it's kind of like mine."

That would have been December 1633, Marla remembered; the same month she had made her "debut" recital in Magdeburg.

She ran her own hand over the keyboard cover. "Yes, Girolamo Zenti did a really good job of rebuilding this piano. It's pretty cool, actually." Her eyes strayed to Prince Ulrik. "The framework and the mechanism are all from an instrument that came back through the Ring of Fire, but the cabinet and case, in all its beauty, is down-time work, from one of the best instrument makers alive. Best of both worlds, you might say."

Heads nodded all around the room, as the point was taken. Even Prince Ulrik pursed his lips and nodded to her.

"I knew Signor Zenti a long time ago, when I was very young," Kristina announced, running her hand over the side of the piano again. "He was in Stockholm, making harpsichords for my father and mother. I used to go to his workshop and watch. He wouldn't let me touch anything, but he would talk to me and explain what he was doing. Sometimes he would let me hold his tools. That was fun."

Marla heard the plaintive note in Kristina's voice. It dawned on her that being the royal heir to Sweden may not have been the easiest way to grow up, especially in the last few years.

Ulrik cleared his throat.

"Ah, Frau Linder, I understand that you sing, as well."

"Yes, Prince—"

Ulrik waved his hand. "Just Ulrik, Frau Linder. Save the titles for formal occasions, which..." he looked around to where servants were beginning to clear up some of the detritus of Kristina's impromptu party, "...this most certainly is not."

The prince reached inside his jacket pocket and brought out a much folded piece of paper, which he proceeded to unfold and stare at for a moment before he turned it around and handed it to her.

"They tell me you have some connection with this."

Ein Ruf zu den Waffen, the banner read. The ubiquity of the CoC broadsheets no longer surprised Marla, but that didn't mean she was pleased.

"God, I'm getting tired of seeing this," she muttered to herself, forgetting for the moment who else was near.

"What was that?" Ulrik asked.

Marla looked up, not exactly flustered but not sure what to say.

"Ah...yes. These are the words to a song I sang a few weeks ago here in Magdeburg. It was an up-time song." Her voice didn't quite trail off.

"A song," Ulrik said. "Would you sing it for me...for us?"

"Now?"

"If possible."

Marla looked around. Thomas was standing nearby; she beckoned to him and pointed to the piano bench. As Thomas folded himself behind the keyboard, she looked back at Ulrik.

"Yes, it's possible. Give me just a moment to prepare, please."

Marla beckoned to Franz as well, stepped away from the prince, and turned her back on everyone long enough to grab the waistband of her heavy sweater and yank it over her head, revealing a snug black turtleneck sweater beneath it. She thrust the heavy sweater into Franz's waiting hands, yanked her fingers through her hair to try to impart a hint of order to it, and moved over to face the curve of the piano. He wanted this song, of all songs, she thought to herself as she placed her hands along the top of the cabinet. He wanted this song? He'd get it; no holds barred.

"Give me the chords, please," to Thomas. He obliged her, and she softly sang wordlessly for a few phrases, warming her voice at least a little. Fortunately—or at least, semi-fortunately—the demands of the song were more emotional than technical. And right now, she had enough of an edge on that she wouldn't have any trouble pushing the song through.

Holding a hand up, Marla turned and faced those who had drifted over and gathered around the piano. It was mostly the politicians, but there were a few of the servants in earshot.

She dropped the hand, and Thomas began the introduction. Came the moment, and Marla began to pour out her voice, and her power, and her edge, and her soul. Not like she did the night she sang it in the Green Horse...different, somehow... but still way more than she had ever done with any other song, even Master Carissimi's "Lament for a Fallen Eagle." And today she had a visible focus.

"Do you hear the people sing..."

The music staggered Ulrik. Short, not flowery or ornate, it seemed barely worthy of the description "song"...until one considered the voice, and the message.

A most remarkable voice, he thought to himself as he struggled to be objective. But the words; ah, the words as sung by that voice—razors, every one of them. He had read the article by that writer, Logau. He now had a new appreciation for Logau's metaphor of the archer, as he felt at the moment as if Marla were indeed Diana the Huntress, with her eyes fixed on him as her lawful prey.

For all its power and impact, the song wasn't very long. Less than three minutes in Thomas' arrangement, from beginning notes to final chords. Yet, as with all weapons, it wasn't how big it was that mattered, it was how sharp it was and how it was used. Where previously the song had been aimed at Berlin, today Marla aimed it right at Prince Ulrik. And at the end, she saw that she had reached him. Something—some narrowing of the eyelids or slight drawing together of the brows—something Marla's poker-playing daddy would have called a "tell"—told her that a touch had been made.

There was silence after the final chord. Even the irrepressible Kristina was subdued for a moment.

Ulrik looked around, and took in the expressions of those who listened: the sober faces among the leaders; the nods and quiet smiles of pride on the faces of the other musicians; and just for a moment, savage smiles of glee on the faces of some of the servants before they turned away.

He took a deep breath, then nodded to Marla. "I believe I understand why everyone was talking about this in Luebeck. I also understand why my father has ordered three Bledsoe and Riebeck pianos for his palaces."

He refolded the broadsheet and restored it to his coat pocket. "And you, my dear Frau Linder, sing very well indeed."

The formidable songstress nodded in return.

"I shall play the flute," Kristina announced firmly, momentary subduing expired.

Ulrik looked to his charge with interest. "Why do you say that, Kristina?"

"Well," the princess said in a voice of reason, "I will never be able to sing as well as she can." She tilted her head toward Marla. "And we won't be able to carry a piano around with us when we travel, so I will never be able to practice enough to play it well. But I can put a flute in one of my bags and play it wherever we are."

"Marla can play the flute, too," one of her musician friends—the short one—said matter-of-factly from where he stood in front of that part of the crowd.

Kristina stomped her foot. "That's not fair!"

The room exploded in laughter.

Ciclope looked up with a guttural snarl when someone slid onto the unoccupied stool still sitting at the small table he and Pietro were sharing in the tavern. The stranger, no one he had met before, held up a hand in simultaneous greeting and remonstrance.

"We have a mutual acquaintance, *meine Herren*." The stranger's voice was low, both in pitch and in volume.

Ciclope glared at the man, and he could see Pietro aiming a sharp stare from his position as well. If looks were weapons, this idiot would be lying on the floor bleeding from multiple wounds.

Seeing they weren't going to speak, the stranger continued, "I am an associate of your paymaster." Ciclope's mouth shaped the name *Schmidt*, but no sound was uttered.

The stranger nodded. "Indeed." He leaned forward, elbows on the table, and lowered his voice even more. "That person's associates are not certain just how well he has communicated how important it is that your next task be undertaken with, ah, zeal. We think it would be best if the effect were as great as can be accomplished. To that end, we are willing to pay you this additional sum to 'enhance' your work, as it were."

He slid one hand across the table, and when he slid the hand back there was a small purse lying before Ciclope.

"Take that in good confidence that we will approve of anything done to improve the results of your next task. And we will be in touch again."

The stranger nodded again, stood, and left, leaving Ciclope and Pietro to stare after him with furrowed brows.

Ciclope laid his own arm on the table, and knocked the purse into his lap as he did so. After another minute or so, he said back with both hands in his lap. He opened the purse and dumped the contents into one hand, then rapidly counted them back into the purse. He looked to Pietro.

"Fifty."

Pietro pursed his lips.

Then Ciclope pulled one of the coins out of the bag and set

it on the table between them, screened from casual viewers by one hand. His eyebrows went up when he saw the denomination of the coin.

"Fifty *Thaler*?" Pietro whispered. Ciclope nodded. The Italian grinned, and said, "You know, suddenly I feel like doing a really good job at work."

Both men laughed.

Later that evening, alone in his room, Ulrik contemplated the depths of a Venetian glass wine goblet, swirling the rich red contents slowly while he thought about the day. All things considered, everything had gone well. No, they had not gone well; they had not even gone as well as could be expected; they had for the most part gone as well as he could have desired.

He and Kristina were safe in Magdeburg, which had by no means been a certain thing. Flying, after all, was still a very new and, to be truthful, somewhat risky thing in the here-and-now. Oh, the rewards had far outweighed the risks, he admitted, but that was not the same as saying that the risks of their trip had been eliminated.

More than safe, they were welcome in Magdeburg. Which had also been by no means a foregone conclusion.

Ulrik had counted on Kristina being welcome. She had, after all, been the—what was the phrase Admiral Simpson had used?— the "poster child" of the first great flexing of the commoners' strength after the Battle of Wismar. So her warm reception had been no surprise.

On the other hand, he had been prepared for his own welcome to be scant and cool. It had been a relief that it had been otherwise. Oh, he had no illusions—every one of those leaders and politicians who had been smiling out in the biting cold today had serious reservations about him, and what he might portend. But they were all following Rebecca Abrabanel's lead, even the ranks of the Committees of Correspondence behind Spartacus and Gunther Achterhof. They were willing to talk, and reason, and negotiate—at least, as long as he operated in good faith.

The wine was every bit as good as what his father had laid down in his cellars, Ulrik decided after another sip. He wondered how that had happened, after Pappenheim had purportedly not left two stones of Magdeburg touching one another some four years ago.

His mind returned to the thread he had been turning in his mind for much of the evening. Yes, he and the princess might have the—nominal—support of the leaders in Magdeburg. But that support ultimately rested on the commoners, and he now realized that those people were not perhaps as controlled as he had assumed.

Frau Linder's song still left him unsettled. And he could tell that the song had touched everyone in the room this evening. From leaders on the one hand to servants on the other, everyone had been touched...but the touches had been different. And what he had seen in the eyes and faces of the servants, just for that brief moment, had been chilling.

It would have been a serious concern if it had only been performed here in Magdeburg. But the up-timers had recorded it, and it had been played over the radio, not once but many times now, and Trommler Records was supposedly selling as many records of the song as they could make.

Ulrik's father, King Christian IV of Denmark, was greatly enamored of the many technological marvels brought back by the up-timers. Many a scholar rejoiced over the knowledge available in Grantville. And many of the radical philosophers wrapped themselves in the egalitarianism of the Americans. But who would have thought that music might shake the foundations of Europe?

Ulrik spent much of the night pondering that thought, and how the radio and the records just might be as much of a social lever as the SRG rifle.

Chapter 41

Ulrik came around the corner and managed to sidestep in time to avoid running into Baldur Norddahl. He and Caroline Platzer, Kristina's favorite guardian, had arrived a day or two earlier, having had to travel from Luebeck on the ground instead of by air as the princess and her consort-to-be had done. The burly Norwegian was studying a broadside with a wide grin on his face.

"Have you seen this one?" He held it out to Ulrik.

The prince glanced at it.

"Yes. That's the one that Caroline insisted we keep from Kristina. She said it was a bit raw, even for the current times."

Ulrik had to admit, though, the drawing of a minotaur figure with widespread horns ravishing a female from behind was certainly attention-getting. Clothing in disarray, she was bent over the walls of a city. The label "Magdeburg" pointed to both the city and the woman, making an obvious play on the German word for "maiden."

The CoC must have a new cartoonist, he thought. The maiden's face was recognizably that of Wilhelm Wettin, complete with moustache. And little touches about Oxenstierna-as-minotaur, such as the tongue lolling out the side of his mouth, indicated an artistic vision that had been lacking in some of the earlier broadsheets that had lampooned the Swedish chancellor. Nonetheless, the point of this new cartoon was as savage and sharp as any he had ever seen.

Baldur pulled it back and looked at it a moment longer. "Girl's ugly, though."

Ulrik snorted as his sometime-lieutenant folded the broadside with care and stowed it in a jacket pocket. Before he could say anything else, one of Kristina's ladies came around the corner and almost ran into him, much as he had encountered Baldur minutes earlier.

"Oh, there you are, Prince Ulrik. Frau Platzer says that you should come to the palace radio room now, please."

Ulrik looked at her with raised eyebrows.

"Did she perchance give a reason as to why I should come?"

The lady dipped in a bit of a breathless curtsey. "Only that I should say 'it's starting.'"

"Ah. Indeed."

With that, Ulrik headed for the radio room. He didn't break into a run—quite—but Baldur had to stretch his shorter legs to keep up with him.

Caroline handed the prince the message sheets that the operator had written so far as soon as he came through the door. The most recent sheet was snatched up by Rebecca Abrabanel as soon as the operator's pencil was lifted from it. Caroline read over her shoulder, and handed it to Ulrik as soon as they were done with it.

Ulrik saw immediately that Mike Stearns was making his break. The text of the first message sheet, directed to Chancellor Oxenstierna and repudiating him in elaborate and fascinating detail, made that abundantly clear. About the only thing Stearns had left out of the indictment, Ulrik thought to himself, was a charge that the chancellor had stolen the royal chamber pot and misappropriated its contents.

The second message, directed and offering support to Princess Kristina, produced a surge of relief in Ulrik's heart. He had hoped, expected, counted on this happening. But until it did, there was always that faint chance that something would go wrong. Now, however, the die was cast; the almost frighteningly competent Stearns had committed himself to support the dynasty against the chancellor. A smile crossed his face as some of the tension he had been living with released.

Ulrik looked up to see Rebecca Abrabanel gazing at him.

"You planned this, didn't you?" he asked.

Rebecca nodded. "Not in so much detail. There is not a lot we could do to coordinate between Magdeburg and an army somewhere in the field. But we've known for months that Wettin was losing control of his factions, and Michael himself made it clear to us that our only reasonable course was to support the dynasty against the reactionaries. Provided, of course, that the dynasty would in turn give us at least some recognition."

She shrugged. "We didn't know exactly what Michael would do, or when, but we knew it had to follow those general lines, so we prepared, and waited, and moved when we could."

"Even down to Frau Linder and her songs," Ulrik commented.

Rebecca shook her head. "No, that was totally unexpected. Not even Mary Simpson saw that one coming, or the effect it would have. Serendipity at work, perhaps."

"Even so," the prince acknowledged, "I believe I would rather not be at odds with the good Frau Linder. Where others use words as rifles, sniping at one another, she combines them with music and makes siege guns out of them."

The next message was completed, and it made its way through the circle of hands. Ulrik read through the message to the legitimate parliament, then passed it on to Baldur. "So now we just wait to see if your husband's strategy works," he concluded.

Baldur snorted, looking up from the message forms.

"Stearns against Banér? That's like pitting a hungry wolf against an old blind boar. The boar may gnash his tusks and squeal like mad, but the wolf will be eating ham and bacon and chops before long."

Ulrik would remember that comment in the days that followed.

Chapter 42

Magdeburg Times-Journal
February 24, 1636

SIEGE OF DRESDEN LIFTED!

THIRD DIVISION TRIUMPHANT!

BANÉR BLOWN TO BITS
BY HANGMAN REGIMENT!

Otto Gericke looked over the top of the paper at his head judge after reading the headlines.

"Well?"

"If I were the Swede," Jacob Lentke intoned in his best judicial manner, "I would leave for Stockholm now. If he waits to pack his bags, it may be too late."

Otto considered that for a moment, then shook his head. "He won't do it, though. Too much pride at stake."

Jacob nodded sadly. "And probably more people will die before he is finished."

Chapter 43

Magdeburg Times-Journal
February 28, 1636

EMPEROR AWAKES!!!!

THE OX GORED FOR TREASON!!!!

DR. NICHOLS FLIES TO BERLIN

EMPEROR TO RETURN TO MAGDEBURG!!

Gotthilf looked around him at the people celebrating in the streets, then looked over at his partner's profile. Byron's craggy face was closed up, expressionless, as his eyes scanned their surroundings.

"Well?"

"No doubt it's a good thing for the country," the up-timer said after a moment.

"Yah." Gotthilf agreed wholeheartedly. "Maybe things will calm down now."

"Not the way to bet," Byron said. "People haven't changed any, and we still have at least two murderers and an arsonist running loose."

"Point," Gotthilf sighed.

He checked his gun.

Part Four

March 1636

When modes of music change,
the fundamental laws of the state always change with them.
—Plato

Chapter 44

Magdeburg

> And when Ahithophel saw that his counsel was not
> followed, he saddled his ass, and arose, and gat him
> home to his house, to his city, and put his household
> in order, and hanged himself, and died, and was buried
> in the sepulchre of his father.

"Stop," Simon said. Ursula quit reading and waited while Simon
thought through everything that she had read from II Samuel
about the rebellion of Absalom against King David.

"This is going to be another one of those stories where I'm
not going to like the ending and probably won't understand
everything that's going on, isn't it?" he finally asked.

Ursula smiled a bit as she placed a ribbon in her worn Bible
and closed it. "That's possible," she said.

"But why did this guy Ahith...Ahith..."

"Ahithophel."

"Yah, him. Why did he—when he was such a friend of King
David, why did he take the other guy's side?"

Ursula shook her head. "I don't know. The story doesn't seem
to say. It certainly doesn't seem very nice, does it?"

"No," Simon muttered.

Ursula picked up her latest embroidery project. "You'd best get out and make your rounds. I've got to get this done for Frau Schneider today."

Andreas Schardius leaned forward in his chair, crossed his arms on the railing at the front of the opera house box, and rested his chin on them. It was fascinating to watch as Frau Higham drilled her performers for the stage performance of *Arthur Rex*. The best singers in Magdeburg and its surrounding environs had become part of the cast, many of them quite familiar with large choral works and pageants. But this largest of large scale work in a true theatrical setting was taking most of them to a newer level of performance than anything they'd previously experienced. The discipline needed to walk and gesture and sing at the same time, to hit a mark on the stage at the same word in a song—the same syllable—every time, was something new to them, and Frau Higham had labored with them in what she called "blocking" to get them used to it.

Schardius had not been there for all of it, of course. He was a businessman who liked music, not a musician who dabbled in business, and the requirements on his time were many and consuming. But he had seen pieces of the effort now and then, when he had been able to slip into the opera house and watch. The performers had progressed from Frau Higham walking them through a narrative, sometimes physically taking singers or chorus members by their arms to move them to the right spots, to "walk-throughs" where they would recite their lines as they stepped through the evolutions of the story, to finally arrive today at the first rehearsal where they were trying to put it all together.

It sent chills down his spine to see this piece coming into focus. It promised to be so far beyond the Monteverdi productions he had seen in northern Italy that it was all he could do not to laugh and exult out loud.

He stifled that reaction, though. Frau Linder—Marla—was entering this scene in the second act, where as Guinevere she confronted Arthur about his infidelity.

Once again Simon was haunted by a Biblical account as he went about his normal routines. No matter who he talked to, what errands he was running, Ahithophel's story wasn't far from his mind. And so, sometime in the afternoon, when his steps took him past St. Jacob's, he turned them to the doorway of the church.

There was a large family party exiting the church as he drew near. Since there was a bundle of cloth carefully cradled in a young woman's arms, it wasn't hard to guess that there had been a baptism earlier that afternoon. He stood and watched for a moment as the happy family gathered in the chill March air and chattered, men shaking hands and women gathered around the beaming mother, breaths frosting in the air.

After a moment, Simon shivered and craned his neck, looking this way and that for Pastor Gruber. Just as he was about to give up and leave, he heard a call.

"Simon!"

He looked in the direction of the voice, and there the old man was, walking around the edge of the crowd. The old pastor crossed the intervening distance to join him and took him by the arm.

"How are you, lad?"

They walked off together, around the family and toward a small door into the church building.

"Fine, I guess," Simon said.

"So, did you just come by to see an old pastor today, or did you have something on your mind?" Pastor Gruber held the door open to let the boy in, then closing it behind himself.

Simon found himself in a narrow room with a small desk in one corner, and various robes and cloaks hanging from pegs on the wall. Pastor Gruber slowly settled himself in the only chair and pointed at a nearby stool.

"Have a seat, Simon, and tell me what is on your heart. Did you ever settle the matter of Samson in your mind?"

Simon sat, keeping his hands in his pockets due to the chill air even in the room.

"I think so, sir."

"So," the pastor repeated, "what brings you by today?"

"Well, it's King David."

"Ah. David the king, the man after God's own heart. And have you discovered that he had feet of clay, as Samson did?"

"No, sir...I mean, yes, sir, that whole Bathsheba thing."

"That whole Bathsheba thing, indeed," Pastor Gruber said in a very dry tone. "Is that what is plaguing you today?"

"No. I think I understand that. But...it's Absalom, you see."

"Ah." The old man nodded. "I see. Yes, a very tragic story. It is always a horrible thing when a son rebels against his father, whether the father is a king or a shoemaker."

"No, that part I understand," Simon replied. "It's the other guy."

The pastor's eyebrows climbed his forehead like fuzzy white caterpillars. "Other...guy?" The American word seemed to perplex the older man.

"You know, the king's friend, Ahith...Ahith..."

Understanding dawned in Pastor Gruber's eyes. "Oh, you mean Ahithophel."

"Yah, him. If he was the king's friend, if he had worked for the king all those years, why did he turn against him like that when Absalom..."

"When Absalom rebelled."

"Yah."

The old pastor stroked his beard for a moment, staring at Simon.

"You know, lad, you ask interesting questions. Come; let us see if we can find an interesting answer." He reached inside the breast of his coat and brought out a small and much worn Bible. Laying it on the desk, he opened it with care and began gently turning pages. "I think the answer begins in the story of David and Bathsheba."

A few more pages were turned.

"Here we are. Chapter eleven, verse three, of Second Samuel. Come see, Simon."

The boy got to his feet, and went to stand beside the pastor. A gnarled and bent forefinger traced a line of words.

"See, here it says, *'And David sent and inquired after the woman. And one said, Is not this Bathsheba, the daughter of Eliam, the wife of Uriah the Hittite?'* So Bathsheba was the daughter of a man named Eliam."

The old man thought for a moment, then flipped a few more pages.

"Ah, yes, I thought this was here. Look, Simon, here in chapter twenty-three, verse thirty-four it says this: *'Eliam the son of Ahithophel the Gilonite.'*" Again the crooked forefinger traced the words as they were read.

Pastor Gruber closed the Bible, rested his misshapen hand upon it, and looked into Simon's face. "So, lad, if Bathsheba was Eliam's daughter, and Eliam was Ahithophel's son, what was Bathsheba to Ahithophel?"

Simon didn't have to think very long. "His granddaughter."

The old pastor beamed at him for a moment. "Right!" Then he sobered. "Do you think, Simon, that Ahithophel might have been just a bit angry with King David for committing adultery with his granddaughter, having her husband murdered, and contributing to the death of her first-born son, his great-grandson?"

Simon was already nodding. "Yah. Now I understand it. But why did he wait so long to hit back at the king?"

"Well, lad, Ahithophel was a king's councilor, and they don't think like other men. There might be several reasons why. But I think—just thinking about the kind of man that Ahithophel proved to be—I think he waited until he could do something that would really hurt the king, as much as he himself had been hurt. And supporting Absalom's revolt would have hurt King David very badly."

Simon thought about that. He could see that.

"Okay."

Pastor Gruber held up a hand.

"What lesson would you receive from this, Simon?"

Simon thought about that for a moment.

"Be careful who you trust?"

The old man gave a rheumy chuckle.

"Yes, that is certainly one lesson that could come from this story. But the more important lesson is this: everything you do has consequences. King David never realized that slaking his lust with Bathsheba would result a few years later in one of his sons driving him from his throne and coming within but a few minutes of killing him. But it did."

"I'll never do anything like that," Simon avowed.

Pastor Gruber chuckled again. "Like as not, lad, like as not. But you or your friends should always be thinking about what could happen from the choices you make. Sometimes people make choices that could make other people die later on."

The pastor gave a beatific smile in the middle of his white beard.

"But enough of that, lad." He looked out the window. "That gaggle of noisy townsmen is gone, and there's still daylight left. You'd best get about your business. But come by and see this old pastor some time, eh?"

"I will," Simon promised.

He headed out the door and down the street, off to his next

stop on his rounds. But in the back of his mind, now, the word *consequences* was rolling around.

Ciclope entered his room, to find Pietro waiting for him. "Now what?" he asked.

"I've got the last of the tools I need," the thief said, holding up a drill and large bit. "But I need you to hold the wood while the bit turns."

Ciclope reached over to the shelf on the wall, tore a piece of bread off the end of the loaf that sat there, and crammed it in his mouth. "What you want me to do?" he mumbled around the stale crust.

"Sit here," Pietro pointed to a scrap of blanket on the floor. Once he did that, Ciclope was handed a piece of tree limb about as wide as the palm of his hand and as long as his forearm. "Hold that up, and keep it from moving."

Ciclope rested the butt end of the log on the floor. "What is the blanket for?" He wrapped his hands around the log.

"To catch the shavings, so we don't have to try to sweep them up."

Pietro set the bit point in the center of the other end of the log, leaned on the top of the drill, and began turning the handle. The bit turned twice, then the cutting edge sliced into the wood, and the log tried to turn with it.

"Wait!" Ciclope snapped as the bark tore into his hands. Pietro stopped, and Ciclope pointed at the table. "Hand me my gloves."

Once he had the leather cushioning his hands, Ciclope wrapped them around the log again. "Okay, now try it."

He had to squeeze hard at first to hold the log still, but after a few turns the bit was well seated and cutting smoothly, and he was able to relax his grip a bit.

Ciclope waited a few more turns. The bit was not making great progress into the wood. "Going to take a while at this rate."

"*Sì.*"

"How many do you think we need?"

"At least three," Pietro grunted out.

"Three!"

"*Sì.* Maybe four."

"Will the drill last that long?"

Pietro sniffed. "Stole a file, too, so I can keep it sharp."

Ciclope looked at the little pile of curled shavings that was beginning to form on the blanket at the bottom of the log. The bit was making progress into the log, now that it was through the driest part of the exterior. "It's still going to take a long time. You'll only be able to do so much before you give out."

"*Si.*" Pietro stopped "Fifty passes. Your turn."

"My turn? Who says it's my turn?"

"The money we'll get when it's done," Pietro said.

Ciclope couldn't deny that. He let go of the log, clambered to his feet, and took the drill from Pietro. The thief pulled on his own gloves, squatted on the blanket and grabbed the log.

"Go."

Ciclope started turning the drill. It was harder than it looked. He leaned into it.

"One," Pietro counted.

Chapter 45

Byron Chieske looked up from the report he was reading.

"Hey, Karl. What's up?"

Detective Sergeant Honister ran his fingers through his hair. "I've reached the end of my rope, Lieutenant, or my ladder, or whatever that up-time figure of speech is. I've been trying to find some trace of the money that was stolen in that robbery where Schiffer's accountant was killed."

"Had any luck?" Byron pushed back in his chair and steepled his fingers.

"No."

Byron looked over to see his partner Gotthilf watching and listening from his desk.

"Who have you been talking to?"

Honister looked frustrated. "I have spoken to every merchant, every money changer, every burgher in the city who handles money. Everyone denies seeing any trace of large amounts of USE bills."

"Hmm." Byron glanced at Gotthilf out of the corner of his eye, and saw his partner making writing motions in the air. He nodded.

"You're talking to the wrong folks, Karl."

"What?" Honister looked surprised. "Wouldn't these be the very people who would most likely know about this?"

Byron's snort covered Gotthilf's muffled chuckle.

"They would—if someone bothered to tell them."

Honister was now confused, but spread his hands in a *please explain* gesture. Byron beckoned to Gotthilf, who stood and stepped over to stand beside his fellow sergeant.

"The people you want to talk to are the clerks," Gotthilf began, "not the merchants themselves. The clerks see everything, hear almost everything, and talk to each other in the course of business. They will bring something to their masters' attention if they think it warrants it, but they will see and hear things that the masters may never learn about."

Honister looked thoughtful, and gave a slow nod.

"So I need to go back and question the people who work for the masters, rather than the masters themselves."

"Yep," Byron said. "Let me give you another tip: don't question them in the offices."

"Ah, right," Honister replied after a moment's thought. "Catch them at their favorite taverns and buy them ale. Or watch for them at the end of the day and walk with them on the way home."

"You got it," Byron said. "Make it informal, make it casual and out from under the boss's eye, and they're much more likely to tell you things you want to hear."

"You might start with Johann Dauth at the Bünemann corn factor's office," Gotthilf added. "Tell him we sent you and ask him to help."

Trust Gotthilf to remember someone from a previous case who might be useful, Byron thought to himself.

Honister pulled his notepad out of its jacket pocket and made a note of the name. "Johann Dauth. Got it." He closed the notepad, tucked it away, and nodded first to Byron, then to Gotthilf. "Thanks for the help. Maybe I can pick up some information now."

Byron watched the sergeant leave the room, exchanged a grin with Gotthilf, and turned back to the report he was reading. He was going to recommend to Captain Reilly that he order mandatory spelling lessons for everyone who wrote reports. The "I'll spell it however I think it sounds" mindset of the down-timers was driving him nuts.

A few minutes later, another detective walked into the office and headed for his desk.

Byron looked up. "So, Kaspar, you still working on that murdered streetwalker case?"

"Yes, Lieutenant."

Although Magdeburg had a small red-light district—partly a holdover from the days of Catholic rule when such establishments were recognized by the city government of the time, and partly a result of someone just trying to make a few dollars—there were always a few women who drifted around the edges of Magdeburg's societies trying to just survive by practicing the world's second-oldest profession. The war and the rampaging armies had shattered so many families that the wonder was that there weren't more of them. They would hover around the edges of the various markets on market days and outside the taverns at night. Byron and Gotthilf had dealt with several of them off and on over the past year, including one case that still gave Gotthilf occasional nightmares.

"Making any headway on it?"

The detective pulled out his notebook. "Not sure where she came from. Called herself Annalise. Probably in her middle twenties, although like most of these women she's had a hard life so it's hard to tell. Long dark hair, brown eyes. According to some of the other girls she mostly kept to herself, but one of them said that she didn't talk like a Magdeburger. From what I can tell, that meant that she came from somewhere else recently, and that she may have had more education than these women usually get."

Gotthilf understood what Kaspar meant when he said the woman didn't talk like a Magdeburger. Given the scope of the massacre in 1631, there weren't all that many people left whom you could really call Magdeburg natives. But even in the short time since the city had been rebuilt and started expanding rapidly, a distinctive patois had emerged in the capital which made its residents easy to recognize. For one thing, almost all Magdeburgers spoke Amideutsch now rather than one of the older German dialects. For another, they spoke Amideutsch with a clipped, almost brusque, manner. Byron said it reminded him of the way people named "New Yorkers" had spoken in the up-time world he'd come from.

"Anything else?" he asked.

Kaspar glanced at his notes. "Only that she had a customer recently that had hired her several times. Well-to-do, from the sound of it, although that could have been just bragging."

"Anybody see this man?"

"No."

"Well, that doesn't help much," Byron said.

"Except that he sometimes paid her to sing."

"Sing?"

"Sing."

"Okay, Sergeant Peltzer," Byron said, "that's just weird enough that it might be a clue. Keep digging, and tell the girls that if their john asks for a song, they need to run the other way."

"Right, Lieutenant." The sergeant flipped his notebook closed.

Byron turned back to his reports.

Hermann crashed the last chord of the last aria of the last act, held it for a moment, then released the keys and let the piano action damp the sound. For a long moment no one breathed, then a collective sigh rose from the cast. Amber's mouth quirked for a moment. She waited for Frau Ballauf to take off her headset and lay it on the stage manager's desk, then they headed for center stage together.

"All right, gather round, everyone."

She waited for the cast and chorus to assemble.

"Okay, for the first complete run-through, blocking and all, that wasn't bad." She let everyone absorb the compliment for a moment, then continued with, "But it needs to get a whole lot better in the next couple of weeks." She pointed to Frau Ballauf standing nearby with a clipboard. The stage manager stepped forward, and started talking.

"Right. From the top. Make notes, people." She barely waited for everyone to pull paper and pencils out of pockets, then referred to her list and started rattling off observations. "Act One Scene One: Dieter, you've missed your mark every time in your first entrance. You have to hit your mark, or the lights won't pick you up and you'll be singing in the dark, which is not the effect Amber wants." The baritone ducked his head sheepishly, but dutifully wrote it down.

She turned to her next target. "Katherine, same scene, you need to be moving a couple of seconds earlier. Dieter is having to wait on you to present his line, and it's making the music and the scene drag."

✧　　✧　　✧

Schardius leaned back in his seat, listening to Frau Ballauf run down her list of observations and corrections. Even though she wasn't facing him, he was able to hear every word. The acoustics in the opera hall were really very good.

Although he didn't have much use for Frau Higham as a person—he never cared much for people who contradicted him— he had to admit she seemed to know what she was doing in producing the opera. What had been an amorphous assemblage of singers and words only a few weeks ago had been shaped by this woman into something to behold. The fact that it would continue to improve was also amazing.

Byron signed off on the last report and laid it in his *Out* box. He stood up, grabbed his jacket off its hook, and looked over at Gotthilf.

"Let's get out of here, before someone else brings something in for me to read."

Gotthilf grabbed his own jacket and was on his heels as he headed out the office door and down the hall to the closest outside door. Once out of the building, they stopped and took a deep breath.

"Now what?" Gotthilf asked.

"I think...Demetrious."

The two of them turned and plunged into the flow of people in the street.

"Thank you, Frau Frontilia. And lastly," Amber said, turning back to the cast, "I need more energy from everyone in the last half of the second act and the first part of the third act, through the battle scene. Marla and Andrea, you two especially. Don't give me more volume; give me more intensity. More edge, if you get what I mean."

Frau Higham was wrapping things up, Schardius decided. Time to go position himself.

He stepped out of the box and hurried down the hall into the foyer to exit the building. There was a bit of shadow cast by the late afternoon sun to the right of the door there on the colonnaded porch of the opera hall, and he settled himself to wait.

Schardius knew from observation the last few days that Frau

Linder was usually one of the last people to leave the rehearsal hall. He expected that same pattern today.

Gotthilf heard Byron grunt in annoyance. They'd just finished checking the last of their favorite informer's favorite haunts, and no luck. Wherever Demetrious was, he obviously didn't want to be found—at least, not by them.

Someone walking ahead of them caught his eye. He nudged Byron. "Isn't that Metzger's young friend Simon up there?"

Byron's gaze followed the tilt of his head. "Believe so."

"Is that other group of boys with him or following him?"

"Looks to me like they're following," Byron said after a moment.

Gotthilf picked up the pace a little, watching the boys as they drew closer.

"Yah, they're following, all right. And it doesn't look to me like Simon is very happy about it."

Byron nodded. "Yep."

"Shall we go talk to him?"

"Might's well. We don't seem to be finding anyone else to talk to today."

They sped up their pace until they were only a couple of steps behind the group of boys. One of them looked around. Gotthilf recognized him; Martin, one of the trio he had encountered the last time he had seen Ursula Metzgerin. That thought brought a frown to his face. He pointed a finger at the boy, and Martin's face paled at the sight. The big apprentice grabbed his friends by the arms and veered off in a different direction. Gotthilf snorted. Whatever the boy had been up to, he appeared to have had a sudden change of plans.

The two detectives dropped into step with Simon, one on each side of him.

"Hello, Simon," Gotthilf said.

The boy glanced at him. "Hello, Sergeant Hoch."

"Nice day, isn't it?"

Simon looked back over his shoulder, and relaxed a bit when he saw the other boys were gone.

"It is now."

"Not friends of yours?" Byron asked.

"No," Simon said in a low tone. "Not friends of mine. None of them wants to be friends with a cripple."

"Ah," Gotthilf said. "Bullying you, were they?"

"Nah," Simon shook his head. "Not yet. They just said some things, is all. But..."

"But they might have done something if we hadn't come along." Simon shrugged.

They walked a few more steps in silence, then Simon looked up at Gotthilf again.

"Can I ask you something?"

"Ask," Gotthilf replied.

"Why are you and Lieutenant Chi...Chieske bullying Hans?"

Gotthilf's eyes widened, and he heard Byron snort. Of all the questions that the boy could have asked, that had to rank as one of the most unexpected. He gathered his wits quickly.

"We are not bullying Herr Metzger," he said.

"Looks like it to me," Simon insisted. "You keep showing up where he is, or following him or me, and you keep asking questions and pushing."

Byron looked at Gotthilf over the boy's head with a sardonic expression and a shrug, as if admitting the boy had nailed them. Which, of course, he had.

"Well, yes, we do keep coming around," Gotthilf said. "But that's because we're pretty certain Herr Metzger knows some things about how some people got hurt." He carefully avoided the word *killed*. "Those are things that we really need to know so that we can bring the people responsible before a judge."

"Why?"

"Why what?"

"Why do you care who did it? They were all just poor folks like me, weren't they? Who cares about us?"

Several more steps passed in silence. "All I can tell you," Gotthilf finally said, "is why I do. A wise man I respect very much once told me something like this: 'They are victims, and no victim is ever going to be dismissed as just anything. Not on my watch.'"

Gotthilf laid a hand on Simon's shoulder, stopped, and turned the boy so he could look directly down into his eyes. "We may not be able to find out who has been doing these things, but we have to try. And we don't forget—not on my watch."

Simon stared up at him unblinking—not that he had to look up that far, Gotthilf conceded in a corner of his mind, given the not so great disparity in their height—for a long moment. At length, he nodded.

"All right. But why Hans?"

"Because we think he knows something that will help us," Gotthilf said. "And if he does not tell us, someone else might get hurt."

"Or killed," Simon said.

"Yah," Gotthilf agreed. "Or killed."

"I found one of the deaders in the river, you know," Simon looked away. "The last one."

"That's not in our reports," Byron spoke up.

"Yah, well, old Johann the fisher came along right after that and took over. But I saw him first."

The boy swallowed, hard.

"Wasn't pretty, was it?" The up-timer's voice was gentle. Byron could surprise Gotthilf, even after working with him now for almost a year.

"No."

"We want to stop that kind of thing. That's why we need to know what Metzger knows."

Simon looked up at Gotthilf one more time.

"Do you think that Hans did it?"

"No," Gotthilf replied. "But if he knows something, doesn't tell us, and someone else gets hurt, then it's just like he did it himself."

Simon looked down and muttered something low that Gotthilf couldn't hear.

Gotthilf waited. After a moment, the boy spoke louder. "I don't know anything, but Hans is real uneasy." He shrugged. "Can I go now? I have to deliver this package for the candler." He patted the front of his jacket.

"Sure, kid, take off," Byron said. "Just be careful."

Simon turned after a couple of steps and looked at them both. "Hans didn't do anything to those men."

"We know," Gotthilf said.

Simon nodded, turned, and trotted off.

Gotthilf turned back toward the police station, and his partner fell into step with him.

Byron looked at Gotthilf with a sidelong glance. "'Wise man,' huh? Well, at least you didn't call me a wise guy."

Gotthilf shrugged. "My pastor said you were 'a man of wisdom, integrity, and insight,' and suggested I listen to you."

"So do you memorize everything I say? If you tell me yes, I'm gonna have to be even more careful about talking."

Gotthilf snorted. "You barely talk now. If you restrain yourself even more, your tongue is going to dry up from lack of use." He turned sober. "I learn from you every day, Byron. But that statement, from our first day on patrol together, is engraved in my mind and heart. If I live long enough to slip into dotage, it will be the last thing I forget."

"Well..." The up-timer hesitated. "Thanks...I think."

Pietro carefully fitted the plug he'd just finished whittling into the hole in the end of the hollowed out log. Almost perfect. He pulled it out again.

"So, are you done yet?"

He looked up as Ciclope came in the door.

"Almost, *si*."

"Got the gunpowder?"

"Some."

"Already?" Ciclope was astounded.

"Brought it with me from Venice," Pietro said absently, flicking at one spot on the rim of the plug with his knife.

"You *what*?"

"Fellow never can tell when he might need to make a big boom."

Pietro put the plug back into the opening as Ciclope choked for a moment. It fitted perfectly this time. He turned the log upside down and shook the plug out.

"Seriously?" Ciclope finally got out.

"*Si*. In the bottom of my saddlebags. Not a lot of it, though. I need to find some more."

He nodded to where two other logs waited, hollows filled and plugs firmly in place. "Had enough for those, though."

Ciclope moved to stand over them. "So, how long to find enough powder to finish the other two?"

"Not long. I know where I can find some. The moon is dark for the next few nights."

"So we can move with this soon?"

"*Si*. Soon."

✧　　✧　　✧

At last, Frau Linder appeared in company with Frau Higham. Schardius watched and listened from his shadow.

"So what do you think, Amber?" the younger woman asked. "Are we good to go?"

"Oh, yeah," Frau Higham replied. "Every show I've ever directed was like this at this stage: full of rough edges. It's coming together well, though, and we'll be fine on opening night. Trust me."

"Okay," Marla replied. "If you say so. I do wish we didn't have the observer, though. He makes a lot of us nervous."

"Comes with the territory, kid. Producers and supporters always find a way to get these kind of perks."

"Mmm." Marla made a noncommittal noise.

"It's true. But as long as all they're doing is just watching the rehearsals, I'm okay with it. But when they start making passes at the girls—or the guys, for that matter—that's when I start kicking butt and naming names. Nothing like that's going to happen around one of my shows." Frau Higham's tone was quite firm.

"Good."

"Speaking of which, has Herr Schardius made a pass at you, or anyone else?"

"Not at me," Marla said in an icy tone. "And he'd better not. I honor my marriage vows and I honor my husband. I'm not for sale, and if he tries anything, you won't have to act."

"How so?" Frau Higham asked.

"Think about it," the younger woman said. She started counting on her fingers. "One—my brother-in-law is Lieutenant Chieske of the Magdeburg *Polizei*. Two—I am very good friends with Mary Simpson, who is very good friends with Representative Abrabanel. Three—I know Prince Ulrik." She concluded just as two large figures bounded up the steps of the opera house and came to a halt, looming on either side of her.

"And four," Frau Higham laughed, "you're a cheerleader for the Magdeburg Committees of Correspondence. Point taken. He'd be lucky to get out of town with his skin intact. You're probably safer than I am. Hi, Klaus; hi, Reuel." The two CoC guards returned her greeting.

"I don't know, you're a good-looking woman, Amber." They laughed together. Marla continued with, "But even if I was the sort who was open to that kind of proposition, Herr Schardius is no Johnny Depp."

"You had a crush on Depp? You and every other teenage girl in Grantville back then, I think."

"Oh, big-time crush; for about six months. *Edward Scissorhands* is still one of my favorite movies."

The two women chatted for a few more moments, then exchanged farewells, walked down the steps of the opera house and parted in different directions at the bottom.

Schardius was seething in his shadow, almost trembling; first, at Frau Higham's denigration of his morals and motives; and second, as he realized that the only major power in the city Frau Linder hadn't mentioned ties to was Otto Gericke, who was probably the last person Schardius could look to for assistance. Especially in something like this. The young woman was correct: against that rank of names, his ties to the Old Magdeburg *Rat* were nothing. He would have to be very careful.

It took a while, but Schardius contained his anger, forcing it into a corner of his mind, where it coiled and glowed like a forge in a smithy.

Foolish, oh so foolish Marla Linder would pay for her insulting him, he vowed. He would begin by taking care of her obvious object of *amor*. He wondered how long it would take to send someone to Grantville and get back a report. If she thought so highly of this Johnny Depp, then let him suffer for her.

Chapter 46

"Two days?" Otto Gericke asked.

Albrecht, his secretary, handed the radio message form to him so he could confirm what he had been told. It took only a moment for Otto to read it: Emperor Gustavus Adolphus planned to arrive at the docks in Magdeburg in two days.

He looked up from the form.

"Right. Get the word out, Albrecht: Princess Kristina and Prince Ulrik; all the members of Parliament in the city; the palace staff and the commander of the Marine palace guards; the naval base; and the newspapers. Send an unofficial notice to Spartacus and Gunther Achterhof."

Albrecht nodded. For a moment, Otto wondered why he was still standing there and not moving on getting the notices out. Then it occurred to him that the list was incomplete. He made a sour expression, and said, "And I suppose we should send a notice to the Old Magdeburg *Regierender Rat*. We would never hear the end of it if we left the old city council off the list."

Albrecht nodded again with a smile, and now headed for his desk to begin drafting messages.

Otto looked at the files on his desk and on the side table, and wondered if there was anything he could get done before he had to start dancing attendance on the emperor.

✧　　✧　　✧

"Really?" Kristina's face lit up with surprise and joy. "Papa will be here in two days?"

"Really," Caroline Platzer said with a smile.

Ulrik watched as the girl did a little dance of glee around her tutor/governess/friend. He had a smile of his own on his face, but inside he was far from overjoyed. Oh, it was good to know that Gustav would be here soon. The fact that the emperor was apparently back in his right mind was a matter for serious rejoicing, and the fact that he was well enough to travel was the subject of prayers of thanks. But "right mind" and "well enough" did not necessarily equate to "good health," and Ulrik, along with anyone with a firm grasp of the current political situation in the USE, had some serious concerns about the emperor's health and future prospects.

Very serious concerns.

A practical concern popped to his mind at that moment, and he walked over to where Captain David Beaton was standing with the Marines currently on bodyguard duty. Like most of his Marines, Beaton was a Scot; in his case, from Skye in the Western Isles. He wasn't the largest or most fearsome-looking man in his company, but not a one of his men would cross him, and given that he had several Highlanders and even an Irishman or two in his command, that said something about him. Ulrik had found him to be attentive to duty and competent at his work.

"In case no one else thinks of it," Ulrik said quietly, "it might be a good idea to get that car the princess and I rode in ready for the emperor."

"Yes, Your Highness."

Ulrik nodded, and turned back to the princess.

Schardius visited the opera house a few times every week, usually at dusk or later, when his appearances would be less noticeable.

By now he knew the inside of the place very well; even the basement, with its maze of storage rooms, equipment closets, stairs, and the under-stage area that was mostly open between the supporting pillars but contained provisions for trapdoors, elevators, and other strange theatrical equipment.

He always made a visit to the Women's Dressing Room. Sometimes it was the first place he visited backstage; sometimes it was the last. Tonight it was his last stop. He flashed his light around, and walked down the way to the table of his interest, where he poked around the various jars and bottles on the tabletop. He couldn't take any of them, of course, but he did lift the one bottle of scent and sniff at it. That smell—it sent fire through his head and to his groin. But he only allowed himself the one sniff.

Schardius started to turn away, but stopped as his light flicked across something lying on the floor under the table. Stooping, he picked it—or rather, them—up. He stared at them, and smiled. These—now these he could take. He sniffed of them. There was a hint of the scent, but it wasn't strong. He dared to open the scent bottle and pour a drop on each, then he closed it and returned it to its place.

Smiling a hot smile, Schardius turned to take his new trophies to safety.

Ciclope looked up as Pietro slipped through the door and closed it behind him.

"Did you get it?"

The Italian grinned and hefted his bag, which was much larger than it had been when he left, and judging from the effort he expended to lift it, weighed more as well.

Ciclope nodded toward the last hollowed out tree limb bomb case.

"Let's get it done, then."

"*Si.*"

Pietro set his bag on the table and pulled out a very finely woven cloth sack. It was the work of moments to fill up the bomb casing, pick up the waiting plug, rub a piece of wax around it, and press it into the hole, sealing the gunpowder inside the case. He rubbed the wax over the face of the bomb, then pressed a mixture of dirt and sawdust into the wax, hiding the circle where the plug met the wall of the bomb case.

The little thief picked up the completed bomb and set it with the other three of its mates, all masquerading as nothing more sinister than inert lengths of wood, suitable for someone's fireplace or furnace. He dusted his hands, and said with satisfaction, "That's that. We're ready to go now."

"Good," Ciclope said. "Sooner is better. Tomorrow? Day after?"

Pietro thought for a moment, then nodded. "*Si.* I've been watching the night watchman, and the early morning crew. I know the routines pretty well. Give me one more night to follow them, and we can go the next day."

"Good," Ciclope repeated. He pointed to where the not-so-empty sack of gunpowder sat on the table. "Why did you get so much more than we needed?"

Pietro flashed a triumphant grin. "Because I got these, too."

He reached into his carry sack and pulled out two pistols. And such pistols! Hockenjoss & Klott revolvers, they were. Five-shot beauties, Ciclope discovered when he took one in greedy hands.

"How..." he started, turning the pistol over and over in his hands.

"You visit a gun seller's shop, you'd be surprised if there weren't some guns there somewhere, wouldn't you? And I picked up bullets and these percussion cap things, too."

Pietro lifted more treasures from the carry sack.

Ciclope settled in for a long evening playing with his new toy.

Chapter 47

"Tell me again why we're doing this now, instead of in the middle of the night?" Ciclope muttered.

Pietro turned around in the early predawn light with an air of patience.

"Because I don't know how long it will take these to burn through and explode, so if we want to catch people, we need to load them in the fire about now. If we did it earlier, they might go off too early, which would wreck the machine but wouldn't hurt anyone. Now come on, and for God's sake, be quiet!"

The thief turned away and led Ciclope in a circuitous route through the darkest shadows, until they reached their destination: a wagon that had been jacked up to sit on columns of timber and brick, with its east end almost nosing the platform the steam crane was built on. It was the largest wagon either of them had ever seen, but then, considering what it carried when it rolled, it pretty well had to be.

The wagon bed had very high sides and a wooden roof. Uptimers who had seen it frequently remarked on how it resembled an old railroad car.

At the moment, a set of wooden steps led up to the door at the end of the wagon. Pietro handed his load to Ciclope, then paused, listening. After a moment, he slunk up the steps, then opened the door and whipped inside.

There were a couple of muted thumps, then Pietro appeared in the door and beckoned to Ciclope. He rushed up the steps as quickly as he could with the cumbersome loads.

There was barely room inside for the two of them, their loads, and the body on the floor. Ciclope unslung his load with a curse, but set it and the other one down with care nonetheless. Despite Pietro's assurance that bumping or dropping the packages would have no effect on them, Ciclope was still a bit nervous about being so cavalier with the bombs.

"Who's that?" he asked, pointing at the body.

"Nils," Pietro said, taking a knife from his pocket and cutting the cords that bound the bombs into two packages. "He's a Swede, one of the boiler tenders, usually works the early morning shift by himself getting the steam up to operating temperature."

"Dead?"

"Probably. If he's not, he soon will be."

"So this is the fabled steam engine," Ciclope drawled, looking at the equipment. "Looks like a big water tank to me."

"This is the boiler," Pietro said, opening the door to the brick firebox beneath the metal tank. "It looks like a water tank because it is a water tank. The engine itself is in the crane housing on that deck in front of the wagon."

"Oh."

The heat rolled out from the open firebox. Pietro bent down and peered through the open door.

"Okay, hand them to me."

Ciclope hefted one and passed it to Pietro, who shoved the log into the firebox with the fire iron that had been propped in the corner, then bent down some more to push it around inside the firebox. The process was repeated three more times, after which a few pieces of regular wood were added to the fire as camouflage. Pietro straightened with a smirk on his face.

"That's that." He closed the firebox door. "No one would think to look in there for anything. Now come on, let's get out of here."

Ciclope wholeheartedly agreed with that last sentiment. He was first out the door.

"Tell me again why we are here so early even the birds are still yawning?" Baldur groused, following suit with a gaping yawn of his own.

"Because," Ulrik said around the mouth of his coffee mug, "the emperor's latest message said he would be here just after first light. That being the case, someone should be here to meet him."

"And that would be you?" Another prodigious yawn from the Norwegian.

"That would be us and the princess," Ulrik said with a nod to the car. "Best foot forward, family unity, all that."

"Umph." Baldur was not a morning person.

"We wouldn't want to leave Gustav alone and at the tender mercies of the politicians, now would we?" Ulrik nodded to where the Magdeburg pack stood, headed by Senator Abrabanel and Mayor Gericke.

"Umph."

"Too much wine last night?"

"Umph."

Ulrik smiled, but he turned away from his companion and let him suffer the morning in his own way. He looked downriver, and was rewarded with a glimpse of a river barge in the distance, just having rounded the last curve on the other side of the Navy yard. He elbowed Baldur and beckoned to the car. The rear door closest to him flew open and Kristina bounced out. Caroline followed more sedately from the other side.

"Is he here? Is Papa here?"

Kristina clutched at his hand, a sensation that Ulrik noted that he enjoyed.

"Not yet," he said, "but soon. I think that may be his boat you see coming toward us."

"Yuck."

Gotthilf looked up at Byron's mutter. His partner was drinking a cup of the stationhouse coffee, and it obviously wasn't any better than it ever was. In fact, judging from Byron's expression, it might be worse than usual. He shuddered at the thought.

"Grade four," Byron announced as he set his empty mug on the tray set out for that purpose. "Definitely grade four."

"Enlighten me," Gotthilf said as they headed for the door.

"There's an old joke that says that coffee comes in four grades," Byron said. "Coffee, java, joe, and battery acid." He held up fingers to enumerate the list as he ran down it. "That stuff," he jerked a thumb over his shoulder, "would eat the enamel off your teeth."

"Ah," Gotthilf said. "Grade four. Got it."

"But it's still better than my mother's coffee."

Gotthilf shuddered again, and changed the subject as they headed down the hall. "There was an interesting theft report from a couple of days ago."

Byron looked at him and raised one eyebrow in a query.

"Someone stole two pistols and some caps and about five pounds of gunpowder from Farkas' gun shop."

"Whoa," Byron said. "That's scary. Make sure that gets out to all the patrolmen. We want to find those as soon as possible."

"I'll take care of it as soon as we get back."

"Right," the up-timer announced as they arrived at the bottom of the steps leading up to the station's front door. "Parade duty."

This time Byron shuddered.

As it turned out, the barge that Ulrik had seen was only the first of three, and it did not contain Emperor Gustav. What it did contain was a large contingent of his bodyguards, and they debarked first. They were Scots for the most part, and looked the type: hard-eyed, hard-bitten, no-nonsense men, each carrying an SRG rifle and with a short sword and at least one pistol hanging from a belt.

When the first one appeared on the gangplank from the deck of the boat, the Marines present got tense and fingered their own weapons. Captain Beaton moved to the front of the guards and stood with his hands behind his back. At least some of the bodyguards must have known him, as they stopped short of the Marines and waited.

Gustav appeared after the second boat docked. He wasn't the first man on that gangplank, either. That was another bodyguard.

Baldur grunted.

"What?" Ulrik said.

"That's got to be Ljungberg."

That was a reference to Erling Ljungberg, Gustav's new chief bodyguard, a man neither of them had met yet.

"How can you tell?"

"First man I've seen I'm not sure I could beat."

Ljungberg was a very large man, and even from a distance appeared as hard as seasoned oak. Ulrik didn't even want to contemplate a physical contest with the man.

The emperor finally appeared, striding across the gangplank in something approaching his normal manner. That was slightly belied by the fact that he was closely followed by Dr. James Nichols, and because Ljungberg waited at the end of the gangplank, one hand on his pistol and one not exactly outstretched, but definitely poised to make a grab.

The only concession that Gustav seemed to be making to his recent infirmities was that he moved with a bit of care on the flexing gangplank. But he stood tall and straight, and once off the wood moved in something like his normal manner. Not that he had much chance to walk around.

"Papa!"

Unable to restrain herself, Kristina burst from Caroline's grasp and hurled herself toward her father. Gustav's face sprouted a grin, and he opened his arms wide. She cannoned into him, wrapping her arms around his waist—or at least, around as much of it as she could reach. The emperor had lost some of his weight during his recent indisposition; but not much. His problem hadn't stopped him from eating, so he was still a very large man, and Kristina was still only nine.

He folded his arms around his daughter, and looked down into her upturned face. They stood thus for a long moment, drinking each other in. The silence was broken by Kristina.

"You look tired, Papa."

Gustav laughed. "I am, I'm afraid. But I'll get better now that I'm here in Magdeburg with you."

"You'd better," Kristina said with a determined jerk of her head.

Gustav laughed again, and released her from his hold. She in turn released him, but reached up and took his hand. Ignoring the other notables for the moment, he crossed to where Caroline and Ulrik stood.

The imperial hand was first offered to Caroline. "Thank you," was all Gustav said.

Then he turned to Ulrik and offered the same hand to him. Ulrik took advantage of the moment of the handclasp to study Gustav's face. There were lines there that he didn't remember from the last time they had met. And his eyes...they were different, somehow...not pain-filled, exactly, but they definitely showed that the emperor had not had an easy time of it.

Ulrik realized that neither of them had said anything; that Gustav had been studying him just as much as he had been studying the emperor. Now Gustav gave a firm nod, and clapped him on the shoulder. "We have much to talk about, I think, you and I."

"I agree," Ulrik replied, sticking his hand behind his back and wiggling the fingers where Gustav's grip had almost crushed them.

"At the palace, then," Gustav clapped him on the shoulder again, then turned toward Senator Abrabanel, Mayor Gericke, and those who waited with them.

There were two small hiccups before they could get the procession to the palace under way. The first was a matter of protocol—of sorts. The third barge had landed the remainder of the emperor's bodyguard company, so they now outnumbered the Marines that were present. Seriously outnumbered.

Despite that, on one side Captain Beaton was arguing quite forcefully that since they were in Magdeburg, it was his Marines' responsibility to guard the person of the emperor. On the other side Major Graham and Captains Stewart and Gordon of the bodyguard company were not having any such thing. And since they were all Scots, the language had moved from reasoned to impassioned in very short order; had sailed past vulgar a few moments later; and was now approaching a state of sulfurousness. Ulrik stepped closer to Kristina, aware that Baldur was now at his left and Caroline at his right.

"Enough," Gustav intervened. He looked down the street where most of the populace of Greater Magdeburg seemed to be standing cheek by jowl. "We are not going to move quickly through that. Army take the left, Marines take the right." And with that particular Gordian knot cut, the emperor turned to the horses that had been brought for the officers.

The second hiccup appeared in the form of Dr. Nichols and Erling Ljungberg standing side by side blocking his way. Ljungberg said nothing; merely crossed his arms and made an excellent representation of the Platonic ideal of an immovable object.

The good doctor, on the other hand, appeared to be an Aristotelian. He stepped up beside the emperor. Even though he pitched his voice low, Ulrik was still close enough to hear him.

"Don't even think about climbing up on a horse."

Gustav started to speak, and Nichols held up a peremptory hand.

"Don't be an idiot! You had a seizure yesterday on the boat. No way are you getting up on a horse today. Remember that conversation we had about being careful? This comes under that heading. Now get in the damn car and get to the palace, so I can finally get you to lie down and get some rest!"

One long brown finger reinforced the order by pointing to the car. Gustav looked from the doctor to the bodyguard, who might as well have been carved from granite for all the give there was in his face. He shrugged, and turned toward the car.

It took a moment to get everyone settled. Gustav, Kristina and Ulrik took the back seat, and Caroline rode in the front seat with the driver. Ljungberg and Baldur walked on opposite sides of the car beside the doors.

When the last door shut, Gustav looked over Kristina's head to Ulrik. "I must take more care. Help me remember that." At that moment, the emperor's face was very drawn. "It is hard."

Ulrik said nothing; merely nodded.

The car jerked into motion, and the people along the street began cheering and waving flags and banners as the procession got into motion.

Chapter 48

Water under pressure in a boiler has an interesting property. If the pressure is suddenly released, the water converts to steam as close to instantaneously as makes no difference, and almost as quickly expands to occupy a volume a thousand times as great. And the actual steam in the boiler, when the pressure is released, expands by a factor of thirteen.

If Ciclope and Pietro had understood any of this, it wouldn't have stopped them from setting the bombs—but they would have run a little faster and a lot farther before they stopped.

Steam plants are usually constructed along simple designs. That was definitely true with the design of this system. The boiler tank in the wagon was a wrought iron cylinder about one and one-half feet in diameter and a bit over eight feet long, with iron plates riveted on the ends to close the cylinder, and pressure pipes feeding from the end opposite the firebox to the actual steam engine in the crane assembly. It held about three hundred gallons of water, by up-time standards.

Feasible with the down-timer level of technology. And if operated with care, not inordinately dangerous.

But the placing of four gunpowder bombs in the firebox as the boiler was getting into operating pressure range had just turned the steam plant into a looming disaster.

The wax on the ends of the bombs melted immediately and flamed. The wax sealing the plugs in their holes didn't last much longer, but melted and leaked out very soon thereafter, increasing the flame for moments. It was inevitable that the flames would start trying to follow the path of the wax. After that, it was a race to see which bomb the fire would detonate first. All in all, Pietro had created an interesting fuse for his bombs, without even realizing what he was doing.

It took longer than one might have expected. And in the end, it wasn't the first bomb placed that detonated, but the third. But it didn't really matter, for its detonation caused two of the other three to detonate immediately.

In that instant, the metal door blew off the firebox and through the door at the end of the wagon. The bricks of the firebox shattered and blew out the sides. And the unfortunate Nils, whom Pietro had callously dismissed as dead one way or the other, had indeed expired before they left the wagon. But if he hadn't been, he definitely would have been dead now as his broken corpse followed the firebox door through the now gaping doorway.

That was bad enough. There was worse to come.

The bulk of the construction laborers were in the process of gathering to get their day's orders from the work gang bosses. The splinters from the door and the sides of the wagon scythed out through the area by the main gate to the site, downing several of them in screaming agony.

Most of the men the splinters didn't get were dropped by the shrapnel of the broken bricks. And the unfortunate boss of the masons caught the firebox door in the neck. It didn't decapitate him—quite—but he was the first person to die as a direct result of the explosion.

In the same instant that the firebox was shattered into debris, the force of the explosion blew the end of the boiler tank up, torquing the metal until something gave way. Surprisingly, it wasn't the pipe fittings at the other end of the tank. Instead, it was one of the rivets holding the end cap on the tank that failed. And with all that pressure in the tank, one was all it took.

The end cap started to bend under the pressure where the rivet failed, and a jet of steam forced its way out. The pressure began to drop. One hundred and eighty gallons of water flashed to steam, and the disaster now became a cataclysm. In the next moment, the end cap and a volley of broken rivets headed west at high velocities. Two of the rivets connected with workers standing on the outer fringe of the workers. One of them was Pietro.

The boiler tank itself, *sans* end cap, headed east in what later science historians would describe with gruesome glee as the launch of the first down-time-built steam rocket engine. It crashed out the east end of the wagon and into the steam engine housing on the crane deck, smashed the engine to junk, and carried it forward as it burst out the other end of the housing.

The tank was finally stopped when it ran into the bottom of the crane derrick assembly. This was also smashed, breaking the derrick itself free of the assembly and its various cables. All of the remaining impetus of the tank was transferred to the derrick, and it was launched like a missile. All accompanied by the sound of grinding, crushing, tearing, tortured metal.

The last bomb didn't explode. The gunpowder inside it had been a bit damp, so when the flame reached it, only the part nearest the wooden plug had exploded; just enough to blow the plug out. That in turn allowed the flames inside the firebox much better access to the gunpowder. This created the second rocket engine of the disaster.

The log shot out of the disintegrating firebox and through a hole blown in the wagon side by a firebox brick only a fragment of an instant before. Not being in the slightest bit aerodynamic, it looped crazily through the air until it hit the ground—not once but twice—hard enough to skip. Its flight ended as it jammed into the side of the existing hospital building, sputtering flames issuing from the hole in one end until the gunpowder at last was exhausted.

It might have been a subject of humor, if anyone had known about it, and if the collateral damage had not been so high.

But the steam—the steam was worst of all.

In the instant that the boiler end cap separated from the rest of the tank, one hundred eighty gallons of water under pressure expanded to almost two hundred thousand gallons of live steam at 327 degrees Fahrenheit and burst out into the construction site. The sudden release of the steam under pressure demolished the wagon, which sent more splinters and spears sailing.

The coals of fire from the firebox splashed out. Many of them sailed quite a distance, some as far as a quarter of a mile.

The walls and roof of the wagon survived long enough to channel most of the steam to the west. It instantly engulfed the screaming and moaning wounded, and those survivors who were trying to help them. They all experienced very short but very intense moments of additional pain, as their skin was scalded, as their eyes began to boil in their sockets, and as their lungs were seared from the inside when they uniformly took a gasp to scream in torment.

The few men standing dropped to the ground among their fellows, to writhe as every nerve under their exposed skin fired in excruciating pain. One very strong individual remained standing a few moments longer, raising his hands to clasp his throat as his vocal cords and trachea spasmed in shock and agony, blisters already forming in the delicate internal tissues. But within a very few heartbeats, he joined the rest of the victims in their fallen ranks.

From the perspective of the sufferers, the agony lasted forever. In reality, seared and blistered lungs quit functioning very quickly, and the injured men's hearts ceased laboring moments later. In just a matter of a couple of short minutes, they were dead. Motionless. All of them. Without exception.

The bodies lay there, under the cloud of deadly steam, as the first few dazed outlying survivors and neighbors began appearing in the nearby streets.

Chapter 49

Ciclope and Pietro had slunk around the side of the work site and slipped out the main gate just as most of the workmen began arriving. It was easy to then turn and stand on the outskirts at the rear of the crowd, for all the world as if they had just arrived.

So far things had gone well, Ciclope thought. He was awaiting the explosion with evil anticipation.

BOOOOOOOM-*BOOM!*

Gustav, Kristina and Ulrik had mounted to the top of the western steps of the palace when it happened.

BOOOOOOOM-*BOOM!*

The sound echoed from the shadow to the west. Every head in sight jerked that direction. Something long and dark rose and pinwheeled across the sky toward them, to fall with an audible crash.

The Marine guards jumped up the steps *en masse* to surround the emperor's party. Ljungberg and Captain Beaton were both urging the emperor to enter the palace, but he resisted them as he stared to the west to see a plume starting to rise over the city.

Moments later, pieces of wood, ash, and live coals started to fall among the crowd. The antiphonal "My God/*Mein Gott*" that had been sounding in the square was replaced with shrieks as the people were pelted by debris, and as live coals landed in hair, hats and scarves.

Byron took it all in for a stunned moment, cold wrapped around his heart, then snapped to and spun to Police Captain Bill Reilly, who was standing nearby.

"Bill, that's got to be from the construction site. Let me take our guys and run there. You get the fire team on the way. We'll meet you there, okay?"

"Go!" Bill waved his hand.

"Got your whistle?" Byron demanded of his partner.

Gotthilf pulled it out of his pocket.

"Blow *follow me*, and come on!"

Gotthilf put the whistle to his lips and pealed out the shrill rising and falling tones of that call. It pierced through the clamor of the crowd. Every watchman along the parade route and in the square headed toward them.

Byron didn't wait for them to gather, but took off at a dead run, heading for the nearest bridge over the Big Ditch. Gotthilf and the others followed.

Ciclope shook his head, trying to clear the fuzziness from his mind and the ringing from his ears. He suddenly became aware that he was propped up against the wall of the house across the road from the construction site, and he didn't remember walking that far back. He looked around; the scope of the destruction in front of him was shocking, for a moment at least. But since he had been expecting a bomb to blow up, it didn't occupy him for long.

Pietro. Where was Pietro?

There was a crumpled figure lying on the ground just outside the collapsed wall. Its clothing looked familiar. Ciclope stumbled forward, then bent to pull on an arm.

"Hey, Pietro, what are you doing?" he rasped. "Get up! We need to get out of here."

Ciclope's pulling on the arm turned the body on its back. It was Pietro, all right; Pietro with a hole in the middle of his forehead, oozing dark blood, vacant eyes staring up at Ciclope, a slack-jawed expression of surprise on his face. Ciclope recoiled for a moment.

"Damn."

After a moment, he looked around to see if anyone was watching, then ran his hands through the dead man's pockets. After all, they were partners, and Pietro wouldn't need anything anymore. He relocated a small purse and Pietro's revolver to his own pockets.

Ciclope rested a hand on the dead thief's shoulder. "Say hello to Satan for me, Pietro."

With that, he staggered to his feet and wobbled off, ears still ringing.

Reilly grabbed one of the trailing patrolmen.

"Phillip, right?"

The patrolman nodded.

"Get to the fire company; tell them to muster immediately by the hospital construction site, and to not only look at the ground, but also the roofs. Repeat that."

Phillip recited it verbatim.

"Good. Now get, and join the others at the hospital after that."

Phillip ran off, and Bill started up the steps.

"No, I am not moving. That was not an attack. It did not sound like a gunpowder explosion," Gustav was stating loudly as Bill arrived at the edge of the Marine cordon, "or not just a gunpowder explosion. What is over there?" He managed to remove the imperial hand from the clutch of his daughter and waved it in the direction of the growing plume.

"I do not know," Otto Gericke answered, "but he might," pointing at Bill.

"Let him through," Gustav ordered.

The Marines reluctantly opened their rank enough to let the police captain pass.

"Well?" The focus of Gustav's imperial eagle gaze shifted to the police captain.

"My guess at the moment is there's been an explosion of some kind, and the only thing that direction is the hospital construction site."

"What have they got that would explode like that?" Gericke frowned. "They don't have gunpowder or explosives."

Bill started to shake his head, then stopped as one horrible possibility occurred to him. "They've got that steam crane. If something went wrong and the boiler blew...it could be pretty bad." He pointed at the people below them slapping at coals in their hair and clothing, "And there's a lot of roofs between there and here."

Gericke paled. "Fire..."

"Fire company's been called. My guys have already headed that way; I've got to get over there."

Reilly dashed back down the steps and followed the route his men had taken.

Gericke's face was still pale, but there was no quaver in his voice as he turned to Captain Beaton. "Captain, your men had best take over security, since the *Polizei* have gone to see what happened."

Beaton looked to Gustav, who nodded without a word. The captain saluted, then headed down the steps, bellowing orders as he did so. His marines moved back down the steps and fanned out before them. The emperor's Scots started to move with them, but were called back by Major Graham after Beaton threw a couple of terse sentences his way.

Gericke turned back to Gustav.

"My apologies, Emperor. With your permission, I need to join Captain Reilly and his men."

"I will go with you," Gustav said, tugging at his belt. "I want to see this for myself."

"Oh, no you won't," Dr. Nichols said, appearing at the emperor's side. "Inside. Rest. Now. If anyone's going, I will. If the police captain is right, they're going to need another doctor a lot more than they're going to need you."

Gustav stared down at the doctor. Nichols didn't flinch, and his gaze bored back into the emperor's eyes. Gustav finally sighed. "As you will, Doctor. You are a far greater tyrant than I could ever be. I hope that history records that."

The imperial gaze swiveled to Ulrik.

"Go with them. Be my eyes and ears."

Ulrik nodded.

Gustav turned and entered the palace, Kristina at one side, Caroline Platzer at the other, and Erling Ljungberg looming at his back.

Byron pulled up, panting after the minute or so of flat-out sprinting. The back of his mind observed that his high school track coach would call him pathetic. But the front of his mind was occupied with looking at a scene that might have been found in Dante's *Inferno*. The fence around the western edge of the construction site was leveled, and debris and detritus was scattered everywhere. Various piles of building materials were tumbled in heaps. Several of the partially-laid brick walls had been toppled. The crane structures were demolished, which he had suspected he'd find after seeing the derrick from the crane lying broken on top of a crumbled stretch of wall around the old city on the other side of the canal. So it must have been the crane's boiler that blew.

Clouds of smoke and steam drifted in the air, seemingly idling above the windrows of bodies inside the worksite. That was perhaps the most horrific sight of all, and they hadn't even gotten up close and personal with the corpses yet. He knew that many of the men would be losing their last meal soon, as they began to recover the dead.

People were starting to gather, some of them coming out of the nearby houses and buildings. Byron could see a lot of broken windows from where he stood, and there were a few people in the street who seemed to be injured.

"Spread out," he yelled. "Nobody goes in without my say-so."

"I see smoke, and I see coals all over," Gotthilf huffed beside him, "but I don't see any fire."

"Yeah," Byron said. "And the coals seemed to be dimming, at least out there." He waved a hand at the disaster area.

"We need to get moving, try to help these people," one of the sergeants proclaimed.

"Wait, Milich," Byron said, lifting a hand. There was a thought niggling at the back of his mind, but it wouldn't step forward.

"We can't wait, they need us now!"

Just as the sergeant started to move forward, the thought came to Byron. It was a memory of his old granddad talking about his days in a factory in Pittsburgh, and about the disaster that caused him to leave the city and move back to Grantville.

"Yep," Grandpa Buck had said, rocking in his chair on the front porch as his knife flashed in whittling a stick, "that job was great, until the big boiler blew. Steam filled the plant, killed everyone in it. Then it killed a bunch of guys from another building who tried to go in and help the others. Takes steam a while to cool off, it does, and them boys got fried just like the others. And when the steam did cool off enough to let men in without scalding them, a few more went in and died before someone realized that the

steam had driven all the breathable air out from the building."
He'd paused in the rocking and whittling both, and pointed his
pocket knife at the young Byron, who was sitting on the porch,
arms wrapped around his knees. "You don't never have nothing
to do with steam, boy. It's a killer."

"Halt!" Byron yelled. He yanked Sergeant Milich back, faced
the patrolmen and placed his hand on his pistol. "Nobody goes
in until I say so, and I'll shoot the first man who tries."

The *Polizei* sergeants and patrolmen knew Byron for a no-
nonsense sort, who wouldn't say something if he didn't mean
it. Most of them had also seen him shoot. They froze in place.

At that moment, a pigeon launched off a roof across the street.
It swooped down, headed for something that had caught its eye
in the rubble. Three yards into the destruction zone, it flew
through a patch of steam fog, folded in mid-air and crumpled
to the ground.

"There!" Byron said in a loud voice. "See that? That sky rat
was killed by the steam from the exploded boiler. If you go in
now, you'll die, just like it did and just like they did." He waved
his free hand at the bodies.

"But we need to help them!" the sergeant said again.

"You can't help them," Byron said. "They're dead, all of them.
And if we rush in now, we'll just add more bodies to the pile."

"So what do we do?" Karl Honister asked, pushing through
the crowd.

"Spread out, keep well away from the site, and keep people
from going in. And find me some more birds, chickens, dogs,
mice, donkey, horse; something."

"Chickens?" Gotthilf asked as the patrolmen began fanning
out around the perimeter of the site.

"Need something to toss in to tell us when the heat is gone
and the air is good again."

"Ah."

"Go find me some rope, too. Lots of it."

Chapter 50

"So, steam boiler explosion, huh?"

Gotthilf looked around to see Dr. Nichols stop beside Captain Reilly. Reilly pointed at Byron. "He's the site commander."

Nichols looked at Byron. "Yeah," Byron said, waving his hand at the scene before them.

Gotthilf looked around to see Otto Gericke arriving with an appalled look on his face, Prince Ulrik at his side and a handful of Marine guards following the prince. He craned his head around, and was relieved to see that the emperor had apparently decided to remain at the palace. That was a very good idea, in his opinion.

"Hi, Doc," Byron said. "You know Dr. Schlegel? He's wearing his medical examiner's hat today." He pointed to a down-timer who turned from talking to Otto Gericke and came their direction.

"We've worked together some," Nichols said. "Hi, Paul."

The two men shook hands, then Nichols turned back to Byron. "How long since the explosion?"

Byron looked at his watch. "Not quite ten minutes."

"Hmm." Dr. Nichols looked around. He licked a finger and held it up. "I did part of my interning at a Chicago emergency room. You'd be surprised how many buildings still had steam boiler heating plants back in the '80s. I saw my fair share of scaldings, so I picked the brains of an old ER doc and his best friend, the retired fire chief." He dropped his hand. "You let anyone enter the scene yet?"

"No. Wasn't sure how long it would take to be safe."

"Good man." White teeth flashed in the dark face. "But the steam wasn't contained by walls and there's a bit of a breeze. My information says that if the steam fog is gone, it's cool enough to enter, and the breeze will have refreshed the oxygen in the area, so it should be okay."

Byron nodded and looked to Gotthilf. "Need that rope now."

Gotthilf pointed to a large coil of one-inch rope lying nearby.

"Right." Byron raised his voice. "Need a volunteer, front and center!"

Several of the patrolmen pushed forward. Byron pointed at Sergeant Milich. "You, Lorenz. Take a turn of that rope around your waist, then head into the worksite slowly. You're headed for where that wagon was, but walk all over the place without messing the scene up any more than you have to. Got that?"

"Got it," the sergeant said, hands busy at tying the rope around his middle. "What's the rope for?"

"So if the doc's wrong and you get hurt or drop, we can pull you out fast enough that we can maybe save your life. Still up for this?"

Milich gave a firm nod. Dr. Nichols grinned, not insulted by Byron's caution.

Byron clapped the sergeant on the shoulder. "Okay, get moving."

Milich moved forward gingerly, taking one slow step after another. As he approached the first clump of bodies, he slowed even more, placing his feet with care.

Gotthilf handed the rope to a couple of patrolmen with instructions to pay it out as Milich advanced.

"So, where did you learn enough about steam that you knew to keep people out of there?" Nichols asked Byron.

"Grandpa Buck was a factory hand in Pittsburgh when a big boiler blew," Byron said, without turning his head from following Milich's progress. "Told me to never have anything to do with steam."

"Smart man, your Grandpa Buck," Nichols observed.

"Yep."

Milich was about halfway through the worksite, nearing the largest group of bodies. He stopped suddenly, holding still, then stumbled a couple of steps away from the bodies and vomited.

The sound of his retching reached the crowd that was building up outside the perimeter of patrolmen. A few of the patrolmen chuckled. Gotthilf turned and faced them.

"Your turn is coming, boys. He's not the only one who's going to lose his breakfast today."

"What he said," Nichols said with a chuckle of his own, but he sobered quickly. "This is going to be ugly. Have any of you ever seen bad burns?"

"Yep. Worked a tanker truck fire as a policeman back before the Ring of Fire." Byron spat, as if to clear his mouth of a bad taste.

"I have treated several men who work around forges and foundries," Schlegel added.

"Okay, then, you know something of what to expect. It won't be crispy critters, but it will be pretty bad, just the same."

Milich had staggered on after expelling everything in his stomach. Now he was standing beside the remains of the boiler wagon, waving his hand in the air.

"Right," Byron said, beckoning Milich to return and turning to the waiting police photographer. "You're next."

They watched as the photographer and his assistant began taking pictures of the whole scene. After they had cleared the central area, Byron turned to the doctors and said, "Let's you and me and Sergeant Hoch go look the scene over before we let anyone else in." Gotthilf trailed in their wake as they stepped through the cordon of patrolmen.

It didn't take long for them to make their way through the scene. Nichols didn't spend long at any group of corpses, but Gotthilf watched as his eyes darted everywhere, missing nothing.

The final body, though—the one closest to the ruin of the wagon—apparently presented some sort of quandary to the doctor. He spent several minutes looking at the man, even going so far as to crouch beside the body and feel his arms and legs.

Finally he straightened, and looked to the patiently waiting examiner and detectives.

"Okay, here's my read of it all. If my count's correct, you've got forty-two dead guys here."

Gotthilf nodded. That matched his count. He pulled out his notepad, and started making notes.

"I know that a lot of them appear to have sustained injuries from the explosion, some of them pretty severe, but the cause of death for thirty-nine of the men is going to be exposure to the super-heated steam. Massive second-degree burns of the face, hands, and any other exposed skin, but the true killer is that they inhaled that steam, scalded their lungs, and ended up suffocating to death because of the blisters that formed internally. No questions, no mysteries there. And you can tell your men that death was certain after their first inhalation of the steam. Nothing anyone could have done about that, outside of a direct miracle from God."

Nichols nodded to Schlegel. "You might examine one of them, so you'll see what the damage looks like. In fact, take some pictures and write up an article on it. We'll get it published somehow. Steam power is going to be around for quite a while, and doctors and nurses need to know what accidents with steam can produce."

He waved a hand around. "Whether their other injuries would have been fatal is a moot point. That's a very painful way to die, I might add, although it wouldn't have lasted long, thank God."

Gotthilf found himself thanking God, indeed, that the torment of the workers had been brief.

Dr. Nichols continued with, "But that leaves three guys who aren't blistered, so that means they were dead before the steam got to them." He looked to Schlegel again. "You need to examine all three of them," he pointed back the way they came, "but I think the guy outside the gate just caught a golden BB of debris or something from the explosion. It looks just like he was shot in the head, but I'd bet you'll find a bolt or something lodged somewhere in the brain."

Next he pointed off to a group a little to one side of the site. "And the guy whose head was almost torn off, that's pretty self-explanatory."

Now he pointed down to the corpse at his feet. "But this guy, this guy I don't get. He's the closest one to where the boiler was, so he should have caught the brunt of the steam when the boiler blew. His jacket is wet, like the steam soaked into it, but there's not a blister on him, so that's not kosher. And he's got at least one broken arm, maybe a leg as well."

Gotthilf jotted all that down. Nichols' eyes were intent and he was now frowning. "Dr. Schlegel will need to go over this body with care," he said. "This guy was already dead when the steam hit him, and that's weird."

When he saw Gotthilf was frowning at his statement, the doctor elaborated. "Dead meat—and that's all this guy is now—doesn't blister. That's because when the heart stops pumping, blisters stop forming."

Gotthilf was still frowning. Nichols grinned. "Think about it,

Sergeant. Have you ever seen a piece of beef or pork blister on a grill or in the fire? Or a chicken breast?" Nichols shook his head, still grinning. "Never happen. Burn, yeah, but not blister."

His expression sobered and he turned back to the corpse. "So if he didn't blister, he was already dead when the boiler blew. I'm not going to go out on a limb and say there's something wrong here, but if I were you I wouldn't cross that idea off the list just yet."

Like Gotthilf, Dr. Schlegel was now writing notes in his own notebook. He looked up. "I think I understand your concerns. I will examine this man most carefully."

Gotthilf looked at Byron. His partner's eyes were narrowed, in that expression he knew from experience meant that the up-timer's thoughts were racing furiously.

After a moment, Byron straightened. "Okay, thanks, Doctor and Doctor. I think we can take it from here, but I'll want to see the results of those examinations as soon as they can get done."

Dr. Schlegel closed his notebook and slipped it back in a jacket pocket. Dr. Nichols nodded, then held out his hand. "Right. I've got to get back to the palace and see to the emperor. Good luck."

Otto Gericke looked around as someone stepped into place beside him on the side opposite of Prince Ulrik. He was faintly surprised to see his brother-in-law Georg Schmidt standing there also, face ashen, the latest in a sequence of the "important" people who had come to view the disaster.

"Georg," he said, turning back to watch the patrolmen starting to fan out across the disaster area.

"Otto," Georg responded. "I came as soon as I heard. This is horrible."

"Yes, it is," Otto responded tightly. "But what's even more horrible is the idea that Captain Reilly just shared with me."

"What was that?" Georg asked the obvious question.

"That this may not be just a terrible accident."

Georg furrowed his forehead. "What do you mean?"

"The up-timers have a saying that goes something like this: 'once is an accident, twice might be a coincidence, but three times is enemy action.'"

"What are you talking about?" Schmidt sounded bewildered now.

Otto started ticking items off on his fingers. "One: the fire that destroyed much of the stored timbers for this project. Two: the murder of the two employees and the theft of the payroll money. Three: the explosion here today." He crossed his arms and looked back to the disaster. "They may all be related. Someone may be trying to destroy this project."

If it was possible, Schmidt was even paler.

"How could that be? Who would do such a thing? What would they gain from doing it?"

"The who and the why of it are what the *Polizei* will be looking into shortly. If this is indeed some part of someone's evil plan, the detectives will find them. I know these men. They will not rest after this."

Otto brooded quietly for a few moments, watching the patrolmen gather the bodies one by one. "If this was indeed an act of what the up-timers call sabotage, I pity the fool who set it in motion. The Committees of Correspondence are not at all happy. This hospital addition was something they were supporting in full, and to not only see it almost destroyed, but to see so many men killed—many of them CoC union members and supporters—has them ready to strike out. Gunther Achterhof is livid. He had already arrived at the same conclusion, and he's convinced that there is an agency at work behind all of this. If Captain Reilly had not set them the task of checking all the roofs for coals and fire, they would be on a hue and cry through the streets of the city at this moment, searching for an instigator."

Schmidt said nothing more. After a few minutes, he turned and walked away without a farewell.

Gotthilf proved to be a prophet. When it came time to move the corpses of the dead workers, several of the patrolmen joined Sergeant Milich in depositing the remains of their breakfasts on the ground. Gotthilf had felt his own gorge start to rise a couple of times. He was able to firmly resist it enough that it settled down, but he didn't think he'd be eating much for dinner that night.

The heavy clothing worn due to the weather appeared to have provided some protection to the men. But the steam had ravaged any exposed skin. Faces, hands, necks—if it was uncovered, it was badly blistered. Fingers were so blistered they resembled sausages; hands were almost obscenely swollen.

But it was the damage done to the tender tissues of the face that seemed to trigger nausea the most. Eyelids were so blistered that the eye-sockets resembled some kind of horrible growth; ears were severely misshapen; noses couldn't be recognized; and lips were hideously swollen, like a travesty of a marionette.

"Halt!" Gotthilf barked, as a pair of patrolmen just dropped a corpse to the ground next to the forming line, leaving the limbs splayed any which way. They looked up in surprise as he stormed over. "You will treat these men with respect."

"They can't feel anything," one of the patrolmen protested.

Gotthilf reached up, grabbed the man's collar, and yanked his head down to his level. "Maybe these men can't, but they can." He motioned to where a crowd of mostly weeping women were gathering outside the cordon. "You will give these men respect, for their own sakes and the sakes of their families, or I will give you cause to regret the day you were born. Is that clear?"

"Yes, Sergeant!" the patrolman responded, echoed by his mate.

Gotthilf looked around at where the other patrolmen were watching what was going on. "Got that?"

"Yes, Sergeant." "Yes, Sergeant." "Yes, Sergeant." The answers came from all around.

"Good. Now, get after it."

Bill Reilly looked over at Byron. "Is he ready yet?"

Byron had a small smile on his face. "Almost."

"What did you say?" Andreas Schardius couldn't believe he'd heard what he thought he'd heard.

Johann Westvol flinched.

"I . . . I said that the steam crane at the construction site blew up, destroyed some supplies, and killed a bunch of the workmen."

Schardius could feel rage swelling within him. His teeth were gritting together so strongly he was surprised they didn't crumble. He surged to his feet and threw his chair across the room, to clatter against the wall and land on its back. He leaned forward, face dark, fists planted on his desk top.

"*What happened?*"

Georg Schmidt hurried back to his office, trying not to think of anything. He burst through the front door and hurried past Stephan's desk and into his own office, slamming the door behind him.

He didn't even take off his coat; just settled into his chair behind the desk and clasped his hands together tightly before him on the desktop.

After hearing the jumbled account from Westvol and Kühlewein, Schardius thought long and hard, waving the pair silent every time one of them tried to speak. At length, he stirred.

"This is disastrous. If we are going to have a chance of recovering from this, we've got to take steps."

A long forefinger pointed at Kühlewein. "You contact the insurance underwriter who wrote our accident policy. Make certain they know about this, and put them on notice that a claim will be filed. Make it very clear to them that they will not be allowed to fold up and disappear on us."

Now the finger pointed to Westvol. "You get in touch with our good friend Mayor Gericke, and tell him that if he wants his precious hospital project finished, he'd best find some ways to help us out of this hole. Tell him to get this Lieutenant Chieske on top of the matter, now, so we can sue someone!"

The finger dropped, but the eyes now bored into the two councilmen.

"I am convinced that someone is doing this to us. I can feel it, even if I can't prove it...yet. So both of you will start asking questions of your fellow members of the *Rat*, and start thinking of anyone who might be responsible for this. I want names, and I want them now."

The two councilmen hurried out of the room and Schardius rubbed his hand over his face.

Chieske again. He was really starting to dislike the man. First, right after he started with the *Polizei*, he shot Lubbold Vogler. Granted, Vogler was a fool and ordinarily would have been no great loss to Magdeburg in particular or the earth in general. His plan to teach children to pick pockets and become thieves had proven particularly idiotic. But the fool had also been Schardius' only contact with certain families in Hannover who used to facilitate the...exchange...of certain previously-owned assets from time to time—a contact he had not been able so far to replace.

Then there was the Bünemann affair.

And then Frau Linder revealed that he was her brother-in-law.

Now he was involved with investigating one of the biggest disasters to ever occur to one of Schardius' business ventures.

No, if it was all the same to God and the universe, he'd rather not have any more personal contact with the good lieutenant.

Georg Schmidt was still dazed.

He had never dreamed that what the two Italians had planned would be so deadly. He'd just thought the machine would be broken, maybe one or two men hurt or killed. He would never have allowed them to take it this far, if he had known what would happen.

And now the detectives were going to be looking for him. They didn't know about him yet; he'd hidden his tracks well and there were only a few of them, so hopefully they never would find him.

More problematic, his own enemies would start trying to identify him. He could handle Kühlewein and Westvol, but Schardius somewhat worried him. Still, he had plans for Schardius, so he wasn't afraid of him.

The Committees of Correspondence, however, were a different story. They were going to be looking as well, with hundreds of pairs of eyes and angry minds. If they managed to find anything— even one little hint—they would be on his trail, as implacable as the Erinyes. And once they found him, he would not face a magistrate, or even a senior judge. No, the court would be that of the streets, Judge Gunther Achterhof, presiding.

If the detectives or Schardius traced everything back to him, the scandal would ruin him. The death-price for over forty men, even common laborers, would simply complete the destruction.

But if Achterhof managed to identify him, it would be the end of everything.

Literally.

He twitched as a chill ran down his spine.

What was he going to do?

A long harrowing day was drawing to a close. Mayor Gericke and Prince Ulrik had finally returned to the palace to report to Emperor Gustav, taking their Marine guards with them.

The dead men had all been laid out in a row, and grieving family members had been allowed in a few at a time to claim them. Many of the bodies had been so badly blistered by the steam that they were only identified by the clothing they were wearing.

One by one, names had been given to the bodies. The police photographer took a picture of each body. Each name was written down, both by Sergeant Milich, who was tasked with collecting that information, and by one or more of the Lutheran pastors who had gathered—or in the case of two of the men, a rabbi. Bereft, sorrowing widows and children were going to need support for a time; especially those with no immediate family in Magdeburg.

Byron and Gotthilf were left with a half-dozen bodies that had apparently been single men with no families nearby, since no one had shown up to claim them. They had finally managed to locate a Schiffer work leader who hadn't been at the site when the explosion happened, one Gunther Bauer.

Bauer was lucky to be alive. If he hadn't been off dealing with a stubborn supplier, he'd have been in the middle of the bodies when the boiler blew.

Still in shock at the disaster and his preservation from it, Bauer had walked down the row of remaining corpses, giving names. He arrived at the last two bodies.

"That one is Nils Svenson," Bauer said, pointing to the body that Dr. Nichols had recommended be examined carefully.

"A Swede? Was he married?" Gotthilf asked as Milich wrote the name down and the picture was taken.

"Yah. Good guy. Not married. Lived in a rooming house over on Kristinstrasse."

"What was his job?" Gotthilf continued.

"I think he worked with the steam system. Yah, that's right—he was a boiler tender."

Gotthilf and Byron exchanged sharp glances. Now they really wanted that exam done.

"Okay," Gotthilf said. "What about this last one?"

"Peter something, I think," Bauer said with a tone of uncertainty. "No, maybe it was Pietro. Anyway, he wasn't from around here. Someone said he was from Italy. One of the northern cities, I think."

That caught not only Byron and Gotthilf's attention, but Karl Honister's as well. He turned around from the conversation he'd been having with another sergeant and stepped up beside Gotthilf.

"Could he have been from Venice?" Karl questioned.

"Mmm, maybe," Bauer said with a grimace.

"Any family or friends that you know of?" Karl asked sharply, beating Gotthilf to the question by a fraction of a second.

"No family, but he did seem to hang around with another workman. Guy with one eye. I don't remember his name."

332 Eric Flint & David Carrico

Both Gotthilf and Honister were busy scribbling in notebooks. Gotthilf looked up long enough to ask, "Is there anything else you can remember about him?"

"No, sorry."

"That's okay," Byron said as the two sergeants continued scribbling. "Thanks for all your help, Herr Bauer, and if you think of anything else, be sure and let us know."

All three of the officers shook hands with Bauer before he left.

"Maybe," Honister said fervently, "just maybe I have a bit of a lead on the robbery murder case."

"Go for it," Byron said. "Meanwhile, Gotthilf and I need to talk to the captain about this Nils fellow. It's starting to look like the captain's idea might have legs, as much as I hate to think about it."

A thought with which Gotthilf wholeheartedly agreed.

Schardius looked up, a snarl on his face, as his secretary opened the door.

"I am sorry to disturb you, Master Schardius," the man said, "but there is a merchant here from Hannover who insists on seeing you."

Schardius sat back. "Hannover, you say?" That piqued his interest. He wondered if it was one of the Praegorius family, the corn factors that had been rumored for over a year now to soon be establishing an office in Magdeburg.

"Send him in."

The secretary withdrew, and a moment later a stocky man in fine clothes entered.

"Good morning, Master Schardius. My name is Elting, Karl Elting. We had a mutual acquaintance in Herr Lubbold Vogler before his untimely death."

Schardius was stunned for a moment. He had been thinking earlier about the loss of the Hannover contact. Now it appeared the families from the other end were reaching out to him.

They shook hands, and the master merchant gestured to a chair. "Please, be seated."

After they took their seats, Schardius steepled his fingers. "What can I do for you, Herr Elting?"

The Hannoverian smiled. "It's more a case of what I can do for you, Herr Schardius. I bring you greetings from my employer, who wishes to resume the relationships you previously enjoyed through Herr Vogler. But before we discuss that, I have a proposition for you..."

Chapter 51

It took Dr. Schlegel another day to finish his examination of the three bodies that hadn't been blistered. Lieutenant Chieske and Sergeants Hoch and Honister were invited to the morgue to receive the results.

Gotthilf sniffed when he entered the corpse storage room. Even with the advantage of the outside cold, there was a certain aroma of decomposition in the room. He'd smelled worse before, though, and doubtless would again.

"What's up, Doc?"

From the smile on Byron's face, Gotthilf suspected that he'd just heard something that was funny in an up-time way. Sigh. Another question to ask his partner later.

Dr. Schlegel tilted his head at Byron's quip, then shook his head and moved to the wall with all the cabinet doors in it.

"First victim," the doctor began, opening one door and sliding out the tray with the body on it. "Male, Heinrich Kleist, thirty-five years old according to his wife. The injury to his neck, no surprise, was the cause of death. Instrument of death was the metal door found near the corpse." He pointed to the door, labeled, lying on a nearby table. "Confirmed by marks on the neck matching marks on the door."

"So, death from effects of the explosion. Nothing unusual about the corpse, Doc?"

"Correct." Dr. Schlegel didn't seem to be insulted by Byron's nickname for him, Gotthilf observed as he made notes. Of course, the doctor had been around up-timers for some time, both here and at Jena before.

"Any questions?" Dr. Schlegel asked.

Byron looked at the two sergeants, and when neither spoke, he replied, "Nope."

"The family has asked for the body to be released to them."

Byron looked around again. Honister shrugged. Gotthilf thought about it for a moment, then nodded. There was nothing more to be gained there.

The doctor pushed the tray back into the cabinet, closed that door, opened the one next to it and pulled out the next body.

"Second victim: male, tentatively identified as Peter or Pietro, approximately thirty years old, unclaimed by family, friends or church. As Dr. Nichols suspected, the cause of death was a piece of debris that penetrated the frontal bone of the skull, lodging approximately two inches behind it."

Dr. Schlegel reached over and picked up a small object off of the nearby table.

"From the looks of it, it might have been a broken rivet or bolt. It is iron, not lead, so it's not a bullet."

He passed it to Byron, who scrutinized it and passed it along to Honister, who passed it to Gotthilf, who looked at it, shrugged, and handed it back to the doctor.

"Death by explosion effects?" Byron asked.

Dr. Schlegel nodded. "Nothing particularly unusual about it."

"This was the guy that might have come from Italy," Honister spoke up. "Did you see anything to support that?"

"Nothing obvious in his belongings," Dr. Schlegel pointed to a paper envelope on the table. "I will say that his physical type—shape of the skull, for example—is more consistent with the Mediterranean peoples than it is with the Germanic folk. But that and a pfennig will get you a cup of coffee at Walcha's Coffee House.

"Any more questions?"

No one spoke. Gotthilf made more notes as that body was closed away and the third body was brought out.

"Third victim, identified as Nils Svenson, unclaimed by family or church, approximately forty years old. There is no question," the doctor said, "that this man was *not* killed by the explosion."

That statement grabbed Gotthilf's attention. "But he was found in the explosion scene," he said.

"Yes, and much of the damage to his body was caused by the explosion, no doubt," Dr. Schlegel responded. "But it was all postmortem. The actual cause of death was a stab wound in the back."

He rolled the body onto its side, gesturing for one of them to hold it there. Byron reached a hand out. Then the doctor pulled a light closer and picked a probe up off of the table.

"See here?" He pointed to the lower back. "Right above the left kidney. Penetrated the kidney, severed the main artery to the kidney. Fatal within moments due to internal hemorrhaging. Quite painful, as well, for the short time he had left to live."

"So if he was the boiler attendant on shift that morning..." Gotthilf started.

"He would have been in the wagon watching the gauges and tending the firebox," Byron finished.

"So when the boiler exploded, of course he would have caught more of the blast force than the men out in the yard," Honister said.

"Except that he was already dead." Gotthilf frowned. "Why?"

"Occam's Razor," Byron said. "The simplest explanation is mostly likely the correct one." He noticed the sergeants staring at him. "What? I went to school, too, you know."

Byron lifted a hand and ticked off fingers as he spoke.

"One: if he was on shift in the wagon, then someone either killed him for a personal reason, or he was killed because he was in the way. We can't figure out an unknown personal reason, but...

"Two: if he was killed because he was in the way, someone probably wanted access to something in the wagon.

"Three: there wasn't anything in that end of the wagon except gauges, the boiler tank, and the firebox.

"Four:..." Byron stopped ticking fingers and looked at Dr. Schlegel. "Doc, could you estimate time of death?"

"The saturation of his clothing by the superheated steam means I cannot estimate to within an hour," the doctor replied, "but my opinion is that he died not long before the explosion."

"Four:..." Byron resumed, "the boiler explosion occurred not long after he was killed." He looked at the sergeants. "Still think the captain's idea is crazy?"

Gotthilf wondered if he looked as stunned as Honister did.

At that moment, there was a knock on the door to the room, and a *Polizei* messenger stuck his head in.

"Lieutenant Chieske, Sergeants, the Schiffer people want to see you back at the hospital project site. They say they've found something you need to see."

"Right. Be right there." Byron turned to Dr. Schlegel. "Keep this one on ice as long as you can, Doc. We may not be done with him yet." He turned to Honister. "You coming with us?"

"No, I'm going to go through this and see if anything helps." He picked up the envelope of Peter/Pietro's belongings.

"Right. We're gone."

Gotthilf was on Byron's heels.

Honister headed back for his desk, by way of a bakery where he bought a roll for his lunch. Once inside the station, he bit off a large piece of the crusty bread, and chewed on that while he unsealed the envelope and dumped the contents on the desk.

Jacket—check.

Shirt—check.

Pants—check.

Shoes—check.

He looked them over carefully, but found nothing distinctive about them, other than a strong indication that Peter/Pietro hadn't bathed in quite some time.

Belt—check. Honister also examined this item with care. Alas, there was nothing significant here either; just a worn and stretched-out strip of leather, so grimy its original color couldn't be discerned.

So, what about the other contents? His finger pushed around the rest of the items from the envelope: a couple of small coins, a glass marble, a leaden amulet, and—hiding in the envelope with just the tip of the sheath poking out—a knife.

Honister unsheathed it and thumbed the edge; pretty sharp, it was. He stood so suddenly he almost over-turned his chair and hurried out, grabbing his hat off its wall peg as he rushed by.

A quarter-hour later he was talking to his consultant smith, Erhard Misch. "What can you tell me about this knife?" he asked, handing it over.

"This related to the same case?" The smith unsheathed the knife and walked over to the window to examine it in the best light.

"Yah."

"Much better made than those first knives you brought me. Made by a different smith, too. Nice work."

"Okay, so it's a more expensive knife," Honister said. "Is it from Italy? Venice? Genoa? Rome?"

Misch took the knife over to his work bench and bent over it with some small tools. A minute later he was back at the window examining the uncovered tang of the blade from which he had removed the hilt.

"Ah." There was a very satisfied tone in the smith's voice.

"What? What?" Honister demanded.

"Definitely made in Venice. I recognize the master's mark."

Honister felt his heart jump to a faster rhythm.

"That is what I wanted to hear!"

The smith peered closely at the blade and tsk'd. "Blood on the blade." He started to wipe it off.

"No! Wait, Erhard!" Honister jumped forward as a thought burst forth in his mind. "That may be evidence. Just put the knife back together for me. I've got to check something else out."

Moments later he was outside looking for a cab. And less than ten minutes later by his pocket watch he was jumping off in front of the morgue.

"Wait for me! I'll only be a few minutes."

Bursting through the doors, he looked around. "Is Dr. Schlegel here?" he demanded of the attendant on duty.

"No, but I can have him called in if you like."

"I don't have time for that. You'll do. Take me to the corpse storage room again and pull out the body of Nils Svenson."

In just a few moments, he was closely examining the stab wound in Swenson's back and comparing it to the knife. Same shape, no wider than the width of the blade. He felt the glow of conviction increasing.

"That's all I needed. Thanks."

Hurrying to the cab, he shouted, "Get me to the hospital project site, as fast as you can!"

Gotthilf was nonplussed. He and Byron arrived at the construction site not long after leaving the morgue. Gunther Bauer met them and said tersely, "Got something you guys need to see. Come on."

He led them across the site where the few workers Schiffer still had were trying to clean up the debris of the disaster, until they arrived at the side of the existing hospital. He pointed at something sticking out of the wall.

"That," he said, "was not there before the crane exploded." Then he crossed his arms and waited.

So now the two of them were staring at a limb of wood that at first glance was just growing out of the side of the building. They looked at each other. Gotthilf drew some consolation in the fact that Byron appeared to be just as bemused as he was.

"So, a tree limb," Gotthilf said.

"Yep."

"Sticking out of the hospital building."

"Yep."

"Hole in the middle of it."

"Yep."

Byron was being especially laconic this morning.

Gotthilf looked at the piece of limb, and realized that it was darker on the outside than bark would normally account for. He ran a finger across the top, and raised it to display a smudge. He sniffed his finger.

"Soot."

Byron's eyes snapped open wide.

"Oh, God, no."

The up-timer bent over and smelled the hole in the limb. Gotthilf was now very bemused.

Byron straightened with a look of mingled disgust and nausea.

"Send for the police photographer."

Gotthilf looked at Bauer, who nodded and took off to do that very thing.

Gotthilf looked back at his partner. "So, what is it?"

"Bad news."

"Will you stop with the excessive terseness?" Gotthilf demanded. "Just tell me what it is, and keep talking until I understand it."

"That," Byron leveled a forefinger at the obtrusive tree limb, "is a bomb. Or, I should say, it was supposed to be a bomb, but it misfired and became a rocket instead. Smell the hole."

Gotthilf bent and smelled an unmistakable scent.

"Burnt gunpowder."

"Yep." Byron whistled tunelessly for a few seconds. "Didn't you say something earlier about some gunpowder being stolen?"

"Yah," Gotthilf said with a grimace. "From Farkas' gun shop."

"Well, we may have just found it. Too bad we can't do the chemical analysis to prove it." Byron shook his head, then continued, "Now, if that thing was filled with gunpowder, and it ended up there," he pointed to the wall, "where is the most likely spot for it to have come from?" He pointed out.

Gotthilf followed the finger's line, and became nauseated himself. "You think the boiler's firebox..."

"That's what I think. I think we now have direct evidence of sabotage, and we now also know why Svenson was killed."

Gotthilf followed the line of reasoning. He couldn't disagree with it.

"Okay, I'll buy that much. But why was Svenson's body left behind?"

"Maybe they didn't care who found out," Byron replied, leaning against the wall with his hands in his pockets. "Or maybe they thought the explosion would destroy or cover up the evidence."

They were still discussing that topic when the police photographer showed up with his assistant. Sergeant Honister was on his heels.

"Lieutenant! Sergeant!"

Honister brandished a knife before them.

"Watch where you're pointing that thing," Byron said as he leaned back out of the way.

"Sorry."

Honister lowered the knife, but pointed at it with the other hand. "This was in the belongings of Peter-Pietro-whoever he was. Erhard Misch, the blacksmith I consulted, says it was also made in Venice—but by a different smith from the one who made the other knives. He said there was blood on the blade, so I took it back and compared it to the stab wound in Svenson's back. It's a good match."

"Good work," Byron said warmly. "Now, catch up to what we've found here."

A couple of minutes of intense conversation ensued, the end of which left the three of them staring at each other.

Gotthilf was the first to break silence.

"The captain was right."

"Yep," Byron agreed.

"The payroll theft and murders definitely seem to connect to this," Honister added. "So, where do we go from here?"

"We have two leads to trail," Gotthilf replied, pulling out his notebook and flipping pages to the one he remembered. "The money, and the friend that Gunther Bauer said was Pietro's—the man with one eye."

"Right," Byron said, straightening from the wall. He pointed to Honister. "You keep chasing the money; we'll search for the man with one eye. Hopefully there won't be very many of them in Magdeburg."

Gotthilf fervently agreed with that thought, but had a sinking feeling it would prove to be otherwise.

Chapter 52

The capital was shocked and horrified at what had happened. But life goes on, even in the midst of calamity, and Magdeburg was a city that had a history of clawing its way back from the brink of cataclysms. It had survived the great sack of 1631, after all.

After a week most of the city's populace was working like normal, with the explosion beginning to recede to the backs of their minds. The late breaking news from other parts of Europe began to crowd the stories about the explosion off the front pages of the newspapers. Only the immediate family and friends of the dead were still feeling the raw wounds of having their loved ones and friends ripped out of their midst so suddenly. And only the detectives searching for clues were still searching for meaning.

Simon found himself heading for the boxing ring one evening. The weather had warmed just a little that day, enough that there was slush in places in the streets. He splashed through a puddle and felt the water seep through the seams of his boots.

The sun had set, and the last of twilight was fading. He was glad to see the lights of the arena ahead of them.

He looked up at Hans. "Are you ready?"

A fist landed in a palm with a smack. "Yah. I don't know who it is at the other end tonight, but I'm ready. I've been ready for days."

"I know," Simon muttered. Hans had been edgy for some time. It had taken Simon a while to figure out that he wanted a fight.

They walked into the lighted area together. Men in the gathering crowd looked around and began making way when they saw who it was approaching. The murmurs of "*Stark* Hans" began moving through the crowd.

Hans had been looking around as he always did when he came here. When he spotted Tobias, he changed directions. Simon followed.

"Tobias," Hans said, wrapping a hand round the man's upper arm. Tobias winced when Hans squeezed. "Eighteen hundred dollars tonight, right?"

"Sure, Hans." Tobias nodded rapidly. "Eighteen hundred dollars for ten rounds."

"Good." Hans dropped his hand. "I'll see you after the fight." This time when they walked away it was Hans who muttered, "Ferret-face," and Simon who laughed.

"Hans," they heard another voice call out. Hans stopped still. It was a moment before he turned toward the speaker. Simon stepped behind his friend.

"Master Schardius," Hans replied, voice even. "I did not expect to find you here tonight."

"Oh, I have become quite the . . . what is the word the uptimers use? Fan, I believe. Yes, I have become quite the fan of these contests. To see men striking at each other, wanting to see who is the stronger, the better, but not knowing who will win is really quite exhilarating." The merchant brushed his mustache back with a finger. "I know you always win, Hans." There was stress on *always*. "It's almost boring watching your fights. But I keep watching, thinking that someday you might be surprised."

"Not yet," Hans said. Simon was surprised at the lack of anger in his friend's voice. He himself was ready to scream at the merchant.

"Not yet," Schardius agreed. "But all things come to an end, don't they? And true wisdom might lie in recognizing the end when it comes." He cocked his head to one side for a moment, then without a word turned back to his companions, who burst out laughing at something he said.

Simon moved back to Hans' side and looked up at his friend. "What was that all about?" He was pretty sure that the merchant had said something more than what the words alone would convey.

"I don't know." That was all Hans would say, but Simon thought his friend looked more concerned than usual.

They walked around to their usual bench and went through the ritual of stripping off shirt and jacket and the placing of the hat on Simon's head. Then they turned and watched the other end. That night's opponent came into view at that moment.

Hans grunted. Simon peered up at him from under the brim of the hat. "I know this one," Hans said, grinding a gloved fist in the opposite palm.

"Is he good?"

"Sometimes. Konrad is tough."

"Tougher than you?" Simon's stomach flip-flopped.

Hans grinned. "No. Especially not with you for my luck." He patted Simon on the shoulder.

"Hans! Konrad!"

They looked up to see Herr Pierpoint waving to them from the desk where the timekeeper usually sat.

"Come over here. There's been a change in plans."

They looked at each other. What could have changed? Hans shrugged and pulled his shirt and jacket back on. Simon tagged along behind Hans as he strode toward where Tobias and Herr Pierpoint were standing.

"What do you mean there's a change in plans? I'm supposed to fight Konrad, right?"

"Wrong. Your plans for the night are changed, Hans Metzger."

Simon knew he should know that cold voice, but he could not remember whose it was. He turned with Hans to see a face from the past.

"Karl..." Hans said. It was Barnabas' cousin Karl from Hannover. "Barnabas never said your surname."

"Elting."

"So. And what has brought you back from Hannover, Herr Elting?"

"Why, you have, Herr Metzger." Karl's voice seemed tinged with sarcasm. "We have unfinished business, you and I. I have brought a challenge for you. Face Hannover's champion fighter tonight for a purse of fifty thousand USE dollars."

Fifty thousand dollars! Simon's jaw dropped and his mind reeled. That sum was almost lordly. It made the eighteen hundred Hans would have won in the fight with Konrad almost seem like a beggar's wages. Fifty thousand dollars!

Simon's eye caught sight of someone standing behind Elting—Master Schardius, smiling. His mind snapped out of its shock and leapt to the conclusion that the merchant was involved. That meant... He turned to Hans and pulled on his sleeve with urgency. "Crows, Hans! Crows!" He hoped Hans remembered their conversation from a few weeks ago.

After a moment Hans dropped a hand on Simon's shoulder and squeezed.

"Very well, Herr Elting." Hans' voice was calm. When Simon looked, his face was still. It was the way he was around Master Schardius. He had taken Simon's warning. The boy almost sagged in relief. "Let me make sure I understand you. You want me to fight this 'champion' from Hannover—tonight—and you will pay fifty thousand dollars to the winner."

"Correct." Elting almost snarled.

"Winner take all?"

"Yes."

"Let's see it."

"What?" A bewildered expression crossed Elting's face.

"Show me—show all of us—the money." Hans pointed to Tobias and Todd Pierpoint. "Let them count the money."

Elting's face grew red. "You doubt me?"

Hans' face could have been carved from stone. "They count the money, or you've made a long trip for no reason."

Elting's face grew even redder, but he pulled a large purse from a coat pocket and handed it to Tobias. Simon watched with the others as the up-timer referee and the down-timer fight organizer pulled out five stacks of cash, put their heads together and counted the bills.

"Fifty thousand, just like he said," Herr Pierpoint announced after they restored the money to the purse and drew the strings closed. Tobias nodded in confirmation, ferret eyes wide. As the up-timer moved to hand the purse back to Elting, Hans held up a hand.

"Keep the purse, Herr Pierpoint." Hans turned to Elting. "Here are my terms."

"You can't set terms on a fight," Elting tried to bluster.

Hans' gaze was steady and cold. "You came to me with this challenge. Here are my terms.

"One—that man," he pointed to Herr Pierpoint, "is in charge of the fight. His rules apply. And his rulings are final.

"Two—no one in the ring except for me, Herr Pierpoint and your 'champion.'

"Three—Herr Pierpoint will deliver the purse to the winner of the fight at the end of the fight."

"Four," Elting spat out, "the fight continues until one of you is unable or unwilling to continue."

Hans considered that addition with a tilt of his head. "Or until Herr Pierpoint calls the fight over."

The two men exchanged nods, then Elting's face flashed a vicious smile. "Meet your opponent, 'Herr' Metzger. Meet Elias Recke, champion fighter of Hannover." He gave a shrill whistle. From the back of the crowd someone began pushing forward out of the shadows. A murmur grew in the crowd as the man came into the light.

Simon's first impression was "big." Recke was a good two inches taller than Hans, his shoulders were a good hand's span broader, and his head was like a block atop a neck like a tree trunk.

The more Recke moved into the light, the more Simon's heart sank. His face could have served as a model for Michelangelo's Judas. Every edge was hard; eyes were set close together and deep-set, with black hair drawn to a widow's peak over his forehead lending a demonic cast to his visage. The lights seemed to dim as he passed by them.

Recke's arms were long, his hands were huge, and his fingers were constantly flexing. The thought of those hands gripping him made Simon feel faint.

When Recke stepped through the last of the crowd, he said nothing; just smiled cruelly and pointed one long, hard, thick forefinger at Hans, who muttered, "Now I understand."

Ciclope sat at his usual table in the tavern, as far away from the bar and anyone else as he could manage. He nursed a mug of the noisome ale. That same kid with the weird arm had found him and delivered a message from Schmidt that they needed to meet. So here he was, waiting. He ought to be used to that by now, he thought to himself. After all, the man had always made them wait.

Them. Thinking that word was like hitting a bad bruise, only in his mind. He still had trouble dealing with Pietro's death. It wasn't that he particularly liked the scrawny thief, but they had been working together for months now, so he was used to him. Maybe kind of like an old married couple, who take each other for granted; not that that was an idea that gave him much comfort.

And Pietro was the only person in all of Magdeburg that he had trusted at his back—mostly—as much as he ever trusted anyone.

The ringing had finally left his ears a couple of days ago, and he was walking straight without a constant feeling that he was going to fall. Best of all, his appetite had returned, so he knew he was doing better. Except for the pitiful excuse for ale that was currently slopping in the bottom of his mug as he swirled it. The only thing that would make that enticing to him would be if he was literally about to die of thirst—and then he was sure he'd have to gag it down. He honestly thought that the tavern keeper had managed to liquefy compost and was serving it from his ale barrel.

Someone slid into the seat opposite him. He looked up into Herr Schmidt's eyes.

The man was still wearing the same ill-fitting clothes he'd worn at every one of their assignations, but he looked different somehow. His eyes were shadowed, and his face had a haggard look to it. He looked about as bad as Ciclope had felt right after the explosion, which was bad indeed.

"Where's your partner?" Schmidt said in a low voice.

"Dead," Ciclope muttered.

"The explosion?"

"Aye. We should have been clear of it, but something hit him in the head..." Ciclope shrugged.

"Too bad."

"Aye."

Ciclope tensed as Schmidt placed a hand inside his jacket, but he drew it out only far enough to show the top of a purse.

"I have some of the money I owe you," the merchant said.

"Keep it for now," Ciclope muttered in reply. "When we leave, I'll go first, then you can catch up to me and pass it to me then."

Schmidt relaxed a little and pushed the purse back under his jacket. "I'll have more for you later."

"Lieutenant."

The barely whispered word floated out from the mouth of the alley. It was evening, and dusk was closing in on the streets. The alley was already enshadowed in darkness. Gotthilf looked, and could barely make out a presence standing in the darkest part of the alleyway.

Byron didn't even hesitate. He turned smoothly and walked into the alley as if that had been part of his intent all along. Gotthilf followed on his heels, but his hand was inside his jacket on the butt of his .44 where it rode in the shoulder holster.

"Ah, Demetrious," Byron said in a low tone. "You've been a hard man to find lately."

A wry chuckle sounded from the darkness.

"There needed to be some distance between me and the likes of you. A few of the people in the streets had remarked on how often you seemed to come looking for me."

"Ah."

That was not a good thing, Gotthilf thought to himself. If the people of the city decided that old Demetrious was a stooge and informer, not only would his ability to find information for them end, someone might take it into their head to end Demetrious as well.

No, not good at all.

"So, you're here now. You have something for us?"

"I hear you look for someone new," Demetrious said, moving closer to them. "Someone perhaps not from Magdeburg, perhaps not even from this part of the world."

"You hear right," Byron said. "A one-eyed man, maybe came here from Venice, maybe with another man."

"Ah," Demetrious sighed. "Him."

"Him?" Gotthilf asked. "You know him?"

"I know *of* someone who may be the man you seek." Demetrious stepped up to them. "There is a man who wears a patch over his left eye who rode into Magdeburg from the south some time ago. This is a very hard man. No one likes him; most fear him, but do not know why. And he has a friend, a companion, who would go out at night from time to time, and always the next day someone in Magdeburg would discover they no longer possessed something that used to be theirs."

"A thief?"

Demetrious' shoulders shrugged in the gloom.

"Perhaps. It is but a word, after all, when there is no proof. But that friend has not been seen of late."

Gotthilf and Byron looked at each other, and shared a surmise.

"There is a man," Gotthilf said, "who on the day of the great explosion was standing not far from the steam boiler. A rivet or bolt from the boiler struck him in the head like a bullet. His body now occupies a drawer in the city morgue." It was funny, Gotthilf noticed, how his voice seemed to fall into the patterns and cadences of Demetrious' voice. There was something about the old man's voice that was just impelling.

"This man, it is the friend?" Demetrious asked in an off-handed manner.

"Had a knife made in Venice in his pocket," Byron replied, up-timer speech cutting across the rhythms.

"Ah." Demetrious rubbed his hands together. "So the one-eyed man is now alone." That wasn't a question, Gotthilf noted.

"Unless he's made friends here," Byron said.

"Not this one," Demetrious replied. "He does not reach out, not in friendship." He rubbed his hands together again. "But you want him?"

"Yah," Gotthilf replied. "We want him. He may not be the murderer we suspect he is, but either way we need to talk to him."

"Murderer," Demetrious said as if tasting the word. "That, he could be." The informant said nothing for a moment. "I will look for him, but there is risk. You will remember this."

"You find him and he turns out to be involved in what we suspect he's part of, and there will be a reward." Byron was very definite.

White teeth flashed in the dark alleyway.

"A man always appreciates being appreciated. I will find you before long."

Hans' shoulders started to sag. Simon started to panic. But then the big man's back stiffened, and he looked forward at Recke. He nodded. "I'm ready." The crowd started chaffering among its members. Simon could hear the bets being made.

Herr Pierpoint spoke up. "Well, I'm not. If I'm going to referee this fight," the up-timer pointed at Recke, "he needs to understand the rules. And since he's your man," Pierpoint pointed at Elting, "you'd better make sure he understands them and abides by them, because I will call this fight in a moment if he breaks them." The up-timer pulled the two Hannoverians together facing him and starting lecturing them, counting things off on his fingers.

"Come on," Hans said to Simon. For once the crowd ignored them as they pushed back toward their usual bench. Everyone was craning their necks trying to see the mystery fighter. They got to the front bench by the pit and Hans started taking off his jacket again.

"Hans!" Simon hissed. "What are you doing?"

"Going to fight," Hans replied.

"Why? You don't need to do this."

"Two reasons. First, fifty thousand is a lot of money. It would keep Ursula safe and provide for her for a long time."

"Okay," Simon replied. "I understand that. But is that enough of a reason to get yourself half-killed or worse when you could turn down the fight and do the providing yourself?"

"Reason two: Schardius ordered me to lose the fight."

"What?" Simon couldn't believe what he was hearing.

"He knew this was coming. Think about what he said tonight."

Simon thought back to earlier in the evening. What had the merchant said? *But all things come to an end, don't they? And true wisdom might lie in recognizing the end when it comes.* "Oh."

"I didn't understand it until the big man came out," Hans said. "Schardius wants me to lose. He's going to bet against me and rake in money."

"Are you going to lose?" Simon couldn't believe what he was hearing.

Hans gave a grim smile. "Not on purpose." His chest swelled, and he slammed a fist against it. "I fight for *me*. I don't take orders from anyone here. I won't lose for anyone, especially the *good master*," he snarled. "He's used me for the last time. I want that money, and I want to rub Schardius' face in the dirt. I've done too much for him. No more. No matter what happens, I will never work for him again." He spat on the ground. "*That* for the old carrion crow."

"What do you mean, he's used you for the last time?"

Hans bent over to whisper, "The man who went missing? Who was found floating in the river? His name was Delt. I found him and brought him to Schardius that night. He was angry with Delt for some reason." He swallowed. "I never saw Delt again."

"Master Schardius killed a man?" Simon pulled away to look at Hans' face. The boy was aghast.

"No, but I know he was there. I know what they did." Hans swallowed again. "I haven't slept well since then."

Hans straightened up. Simon was stunned. Hans, his friend, had been a part of that? They stood in silence for long moments.

The crowd began moving back toward them. Hans headed toward the ring. Simon followed, only to be pulled up by Hans' hand on his jacket collar.

"You go sit with Gus." He pointed to where the other fighter was standing, waving at them.

"What?" Simon couldn't believe what he was hearing. "I always go with you."

"Not this time."

"But I'm your luck!" Simon played his major card.

"And you can be my luck from there." Hans bent down and murmured, "You will be safer there. I want you out of the eye of Elting and Schardius."

Simon didn't have an argument for that. He watched as Hans picked up a scrap of towel and walked off to the edge of the ring. For the first time in a long time he felt alone, even abandoned. It was stupid, he knew, but it hurt to watch Hans climb up on the ring apron without him.

Gus came up beside Simon. They looked at each other, and nodded. Simon thought Gus was no exchange for Hans, but he was a face that Simon knew and was therefore a comfort. They didn't speak, and Gus didn't try to put his arm around Simon's shoulder or anything like that, but Simon was glad he was there anyway.

Herr Pierpoint had finished lecturing Elting and Recke, for the big man was following the up-timer to the other end of the ring. Recke took off his coat and shirt. He turned to lay them over the top rope, and gasps and mutters broke out in the crowd.

Simon felt his stomach churn. Recke's back was a mass of scars. "Oh, that's not good," he heard Gus mutter.

"Why?" Simon asked in alarm.

"That man's been flogged, not once but many times. That means he's been in someone's army. To be flogged that many times, he's either stupid, wicked, or vicious. And no matter which it is, it means he's dangerous."

Simon looked toward his friend.

"Hans!" When he looked up, Simon pointed to Recke and shouted with urgency, "Wolf, Hans! Wolf!" Hans glanced at Recke, then back to Simon with a nod. Simon leaned back. He'd done all he could do.

Herr Pierpoint moved to the center of the ring with his microphone. "Good evening on behalf of TNT Productions." His voice boomed out over the speakers. Simon had finally gotten used to them.

"There has been an unannounced change to our schedule. There will only be one fight tonight, for an unknown number of rounds." He pointed toward Recke. "Fighting out of the green corner, the challenger in tonight's main event comes from Hannover, where he is reputedly the toughest fighter in the city. Give it up for Elias Recke."

There was a smattering of applause, and a few boos, but most of the crowd was silent.

"Fighting out of the red corner," Herr Pierpoint began while Hans climbed through the ropes, "here is Magdeburg's resident champion, undefeated in his professional career, with a record of nineteen wins and no defeats. Give it up for Magdeburg's own Hans Metzger."

The crowd erupted in cheers. Simon saw Recke looking around with a sneer on his face. Hans, expressionless, simply stood in his corner, waiting. It was very unlike him, he thought.

The noise died away faster than usual. Simon must not have been the only one intimidated by the big man from Hannover. Herr Pierpoint continued. "You both know the rules. We won't go over them again." He pointed to Hans. "Are you ready?" Hans nodded. He pointed to Recke. "Are you ready?" Recke's big head creaked down and up. Herr Pierpoint tossed the microphone over the ropes to Tobias and pointed to the timekeeper. The bell rang. He stepped back and waved the fighters forward.

Herr Schmidt placed his hands on the table, letting them aimlessly clasp and reclasp.

"We need to change our attacks."

Ciclope could barely hear the man's voice. He bent closer to him.

"No more attacks on the project. The *Polizei*, the company, and the Committees of Correspondence will be watching things with very sharp eyes, right now."

Ciclope snorted. "I won't argue with that. Besides, with Pietro dead, I couldn't do another bomb or fire again anyway. That was his skill."

Schmidt nodded. "Well enough. Are you still willing to work for me?"

"I'm still here, aren't I?" Ciclope retorted.

"Well enough," Schmidt repeated. "There is a man...the man I've been trying to hurt with what you were doing. I believe it is time to start looking for more direct ways to hurt him."

"So what's the problem?" Ciclope sneered. "Kill him and be done with it."

"All right," Schmidt said, still in a near-whisper, "how much would you ask to do it?"

Ciclope's sneer grew. The fool wouldn't even say the word "kill"—he wasn't even honest enough with himself to admit he was asking for a murder.

"Ten thousand dollars; in good silver, mind you. I don't hold with paper money."

"All right."

Ciclope was surprised that Schmidt didn't try to bargain with him. He must be desperate.

Schmidt actually relaxed a little now.

"How will you do it?"

"Well, I'm not going to blow him up, with Pietro dead." Ciclope took his hat off his head with his right hand while pulling Pietro's pistol from his coat pocket with his left hand and sliding it under the hat on the table. He tilted the hat for a moment, so that only Schmidt could see the pistol. "But I can take care of him, have no doubt."

He slid the pistol out from under the hat and put it back in his coat pocket.

"Now, who is it you need removed?"

Schmidt's throat worked as he swallowed.

"Schardius. Andreas Schardius."

Chapter 53

From the beginning it was obvious this would be a fight like no other in Hans' career. The crowd knew it, and their yelling approached the level of a frenzy as the two men approached each other. Hans circled the bigger man slowly, hands up, arms tucked in. Recke just turned in place, flat-footed, fists at the level of his chin.

The action began when Hans stepped in and threw a punch at Recke's gut. The big man didn't bother to block the blow but threw a riposte at Hans. He ducked but not enough and the punch glanced off the top of his head. He stepped back and shook his head, testimony to Recke's power.

The first round consisted of the two fighters feeling each other out. The second started out the same way, but midway through it Recke went on the attack. He smashed a fist through Hans's guard and delivered a thundering body blow. It was followed up by a punch to the head and one to the chest. Hans was staggered and his defense wavered.

Recke was not lightning fast; nowhere near as quick as Hans. But he was faster than anyone in the Magdeburg crowd would have believed before the fight. The crowd noise faltered as they saw their favorite being stalked around the ring. Not every Recke punch connected, but enough did that Hans was definitely absorbing some punishment. A cut had opened on his left cheek and blood was beginning to trickle down.

Simon's stomach was churning so badly he thought he was going to be sick. He wished with all his heart that Hans had not accepted the fight, but he knew that Hans being who he was, that would never have happened.

The bell ending the second round rang. The two fighters retreated to their corners. Simon watched as Hans picked up the towel and wiped the blood from his face. He'd never seen Hans cut before. His skin crawled at the thought of it.

The third round began. Now Hans tried to take the fight to Recke. He would dance in and out, throwing mixtures of punches, trying to wear down his opponent. The problem was his punches seemed to be having no effect. Unfortunately, the same could not be said of the hits made by Recke. When the big man connected, everyone could see Hans absorbing the jolt.

Fourth round—more of the same.

It was early in the fifth round when Hans finally did some damage. After several attempts at body blows, he unleashed a straight right hand that landed full on the big man's nose. Everyone around the ring could hear the crunch of the broken cartilage. Blood began streaming from the now misshapen nostrils.

Recke wiped his hand across his mouth. When he saw the blood, he growled... or at least, that's what it sounded like to Simon. The big man hunched his shoulders and stepped up the pace, launching a flurry of punches that had Hans back-stepping and blocking and ducking. Punches landing on his arms and shoulders had Hans twisting. But then the worst one hit; a low blow caught Hans in the groin; he dropped to the canvas, clutching himself. The crowd screamed, Simon among them, and pointed to the Hannover fighter.

Herr Pierpoint jumped in between them and ordered Recke back to his corner. For a moment, it looked to Simon as if the big man was going to throw the referee aside and finish Hans off, but he finally backed away. Pierpoint didn't take his eyes off Recke, but backed up until he could kneel by Hans. He finally looked at Hans. "Can you continue?" Simon heard him ask.

The fighter put one fist to the ground and pushed himself up. The referee watched him stand, moving in slow motion.

Simon almost wished that Hans would give up. He couldn't stand to see him hurt anymore. But he knew that Hans would continue.

Hans stood straight, shrugged his shoulders and shook his arms. He took a deep breath and nodded to Pierpoint.

The referee faced Recke. "One more low blow, one more breach of the rules of any kind, and I give the fight to Metzger." His voice was loud and it carried well out into the crowd. He stared at Recke until the big man nodded. Just as Pierpoint was about to beckon the fighters to resume, the bell rang for the end of the round.

Simon was glad. That gave Hans more time to breathe and try to shake off the effects of the low blow. The boy's head was spinning. He was gulping great gasps of air himself, trying to keep from spewing or passing out. Gus laid an arm around his shoulders, and he didn't care.

The bell rang for the next round. Simon flinched in response.

Round followed round; Simon lost count. The evening became a blur. All he could see was Hans taking punch after punch, the new cuts that opened in his cheeks and forehead, the blood that ribboned down his face and dripped on his body.

Hans went down twice more. Each time it took longer to get back to his feet. And each time, as soon as he did get up Recke bored in; pitiless, relentless, ruthless. He was like a game hunter stalking a prize, taking aim with his fists, and watching as his prey weakened.

All Simon could do was watch numbly as his friend endured horrific punishment.

The end seemed near. The crowd was quiet. Simon hadn't been able to watch during the last round, but when the bell rang at the end of it, he looked to see Hans stagger back to his corner, where he leaned against it, gasping deep breaths. All too quickly the bell rang for whatever round it was. Hans gave a weary push to straighten to his feet and go out to meet his foe.

This time Recke unleashed a blow to the side of Hans' head. It snapped his head around and he dropped to one knee. Simon came to his feet, hand at his mouth. The crowd, which had grown quiet, burst out in fresh noise. The referee jumped between the two fighters and again sent Recke back to his corner. Once Recke moved, Pierpoint turned and began counting.

Simon looked at his friend, kneeling in the center of the ring. "*Stark* Hans," slipped from his lips. He took a deep breath and shouted, "*Stark* Hans." Heads turned near him. "*Stark* Hans," he shouted again, Gus chiming in.

The third time he shouted other voices joined him.

The fourth time it seemed that half the crowd was shouting.

"*Stark* Hans! *Stark* Hans! *Stark* Hans!"

Everyone was shouting now.

"*STARK* HANS! *STARK* HANS! *STARK* HANS!"

Simon watched even as he shouted at the top of his lungs. Before Herr Pierpoint reached ten Hans rose to his feet. In the glare of the lights he seemed somehow to swell, to be larger than life. When the referee got out of the way, he rushed in and delivered a thunderous blow to Recke's face, smack on top of his already smashed nose.

The fresh blast of pain must have staggered Recke, for he stopped still for a moment. That was all Hans needed. He became a rapid-fire automaton, throwing punch after punch after punch, all aimed at Recke's head.

The crowd continued to shout for *Stark* Hans, Simon included. He shook his fist up and down and jigged from foot to foot, all the while shouting and all the while with his gaze glued on his friend's magnificent return from the brink of defeat.

Blow after blow landed on Recke's blocky head, snapping it from side to side. Cuts opened, blood poured, his nose was smashed flatter and flatter and spread across his face.

The final blow was an uppercut that seemed to rise from the ground. It landed on Recke's chin. His head jerked back and he crumpled to the ground.

Hans stood over his foe, glaring at his battered form. It took Herr Pierpoint a moment to get him to move back, then the ten count began and this time there was nothing to stop it.

The crowd erupted in wild cheering. Hans lifted both arms in victory. The cheering resolved into thunderous chants of "*Stark* Hans. *Stark* Hans. *Stark* Hans."

Simon felt tears in his eyes as he chanted along with everyone else. He saw Hans turn to his side of the ring, look at him and grin. He waved back.

Behind the victor, the defeated Recke stirred. He pushed to his hands and knees, shaking his head, then clambered to his feet where he wobbled a bit. Recke passed a hand in front of his eyes. With each passing moment his vision and his mind obviously began to clear. He shook his head again and saw Hans.

Simon pointed to Recke, trying to shout to Hans to watch out. He couldn't be heard over the chants of the crowd. Others began to point as well. Hans saw that and began to turn.

Recke screamed and charged, arms spread wide. Simon watched in horror as Hans tried to evade. He spun far enough out of the way that Recke's hand scraped down his back, leaving bloody furrows.

The Hannoverian plowed into Hans' corner. Hans was on him before he could turn. The official fight was over and Herr Pierpoint was no longer in charge. What happened now was governed by street law.

Hans grabbed Recke's hair and slammed his head into the corner post over and over again. When he released Recke, Hans did so only to slam several blows onto his kidneys.

Recke was hurt. He tried to turn around and Hans let him stagger a few steps away from the corner before he kicked the back of the big man's leg. On one knee, Recke was almost helpless as Hans delivered fists to his face and head. Then Hans threw a kick to his belly and he doubled over.

Hans raised a fist. To Simon it seemed to reach up to the sky. For a split second, no one moved. Then the fist fell like a thunderbolt and hammered the back of Recke's head.

Recke dropped prone on the canvas. Hans stood over him, fists clenched, chest heaving.

The crowd had gone quiet watching Hans take Recke down. No one doubted that Recke deserved it after his attack, but Hans' violent response seemed to shock most of the crowd.

Hans toed the form of his foe with his boot. Simon was afraid he was going to give Recke another kick, but Hans spat on him and turned away instead. Tobias tossed Herr Pierpoint the microphone, and he stepped over to Hans and raised his arm.

"The winner," Pierpoint proclaimed loudly, "and *still* undefeated champion, *Staaark* Haaans Meeetz-geeerrrr!"

The crowd erupted in cheers and applause. Hans slowly climbed through the ropes and dropped to the ground, where he was immediately mobbed by what seemed like every male in Magdeburg over the age of ten, all shouting and congratulating and clapping him on the shoulder or back.

Simon had been ignoring certain signals from his own body for what seemed like hours. Now that the pressure of the fight was over and his adrenaline was dropping, he became aware that his bladder was about to burst. He turned to Gus. "I've got to pee. Watch this and tell Hans I'll be back in a minute."

He pushed Hans' shirt and coat into Gus' hands and headed for the darkness.

Chapter 54

"Schardius," Ciclope mused. "A merchant?"

Schmidt nodded.

"This is the man you've been trying to ruin all this time?"

Schmidt gave another jerk of his head.

"So what has changed that you want him dead instead of ruined?"

"All those dead men," Schmidt whispered after a moment. "The *Polizei* will be looking, the CoC will be looking, and Schardius himself will be looking. If the *Polizei* or Schardius find me, I am ruined. If the CoC finds me, I am dead. But I will take Schardius down with me, no matter what."

"Ah." Ciclope tilted his head to one side as he considered the man who had brought him and Pietro to Magdeburg; the man who was ultimately responsible for Pietro's death. "I believe I understand."

"So will you do it?" Schmidt looked at him with hard eyes.

Ciclope let the silence build, until Schmidt looked ready to explode.

"Yes, I will do it." He snorted as a look of relief passed over the other man's face. "Just stay out of his sight until I can deal with him."

"He has a lot of men around him all the time."

Ciclope patted the pocket Pietro's pistol was in.

"I can deal with that."

✧　✧　✧

Simon hoped there wasn't anyone from the CoC around, because he didn't have time to search for the outhouses they had insisted be built out by the arena. From the sounds he was hearing, he wasn't the only one who had the same problem.

A couple of minutes later, business done and feeling at least a gallon lighter, he tugged his clothes back into order and started back toward the lights. Just as he was about to step out of a pool of darkness behind one of the light poles, he heard something that made him freeze against the pole, praying that no one could see him.

"You idiot! Couldn't you have found at least one good fighter in all of the Germanies?" The voice was that of Andreas Schardius. That resonant sound couldn't be mistaken for anyone else. But the tone was so cold, and the words were so clipped. He didn't sound anything like he did in the midst of the crowd. Simon shivered. Their voices, which had been quiet at first, were growing louder, like they were walking toward him. He shrank to the bottom of the pole.

"I thought I had." That had to be Karl Elting, Simon thought. From the tone of his voice, he was angry, too. "That fool Recke was supposed to be the best. God knows I offered him enough to take Metzger out."

"A fool brought by a fool," Schardius snarled. Elting tried to object, but Schardius overrode him. "Shut up!"

They moved into Simon's view. He could see Elting being pushed back by Schardius' hand around his neck. Now he was afraid to stay, but also afraid to move. Staying won.

"Between the purse and the bets, you've cost me enough tonight as it is. Any more mistakes from you—well, after our talk the other day, you know what I would have done to that fool Vogler if the police hadn't shot him. You'll envy him if you say another word." The last was delivered with a snarl that made Simon shiver again. "We have to get back out there with the crowd. Smile. Be gracious. But don't think that this is over. You owe me."

Schardius stomped off, Elting following in his wake trying to explain.

Simon spared a moment for a big sigh, then headed back to Gus.

"Good job tonight," Amber announced at the end of the rehearsal. "Tomorrow night's dress rehearsal, the night after that we're on for real. Everyone go home and get some rest."

She watched as the cast and crew grabbed their coats and other things and headed for the door. A few of them still bounced with excitement, but most of them were dragging a little. Long days and nights of rehearsal were beginning to tell on all of them, she thought. It would be a relief to actually go to production.

"It feels like it's coming together," Marla said to her as she picked up her music folder.

"Yeah, I think so," Amber replied, "which is a good thing, considering we raise the curtain in forty-eight hours."

Amber looked at Marla for a moment, then looked around. Schardius hadn't come that evening, for which she was thankful. No one else was close. Frau Frontilia and the props manager were getting the props table organized for the next rehearsal, and were definitely out of earshot. No one else was around by now.

"So," Amber said, "has Herr Schardius come on to you yet?"

Marla shook her head, and said, "Nope. Not a whisper or a touch."

"Good," Amber said. "Sorry, I should have warned you even earlier that he might try that."

"You knew?" Marla's brows contracted.

"No, I didn't know for sure he would try anything," Amber replied. "But I was in community and professional theater for thirty years, girl. I've seen men like him before, many times. I even married one of them, God help me. So, no, I didn't know, but it still wouldn't surprise me if he tries something even now."

"If he does, I'll deal with it," Marla replied. "He won't get to first base with me, and if he tries anything he's liable to be singing soprano right along with Master Andrea."

Amber smiled. Andrea Abati had a magnificent singing voice with the power of a big man's lungs to drive it. But the voice itself was a soprano because Abati was a castrato.

"I'll be okay," Marla smiled in return. "Promise."

Amber placed her hands on Marla's shoulders.

"Okay, but if that changes, you tell me, right?"

Marla laughed. "I'm a big girl, Amber. I can take care of myself."

Hans won free from the crowd just as Simon got back to take the clothes from Gus. Seen up close, Hans looked even worse than he did from the ring level. There were several cuts on his face and his brows. Both eyes were blacked and one was almost swollen shut. He leaned a little to one side and winced when he touched a hand to his ribs.

The big man almost fell down on the bench. Simon and Gus helped remove his gore-sodden gloves, and both hands had swollen knuckles with blood oozing from split skin. Simon felt the return of his nausea and gulped to force it down.

Herr Pierpoint dropped through the ropes and handed the purse to Hans. "Great fight, Hans!" He clapped him on the shoulder. "Now go home and heal up and don't do this again."

Hans nodded without a word. He seemed to be having problems holding his head straight. Simon picked up the bloody towel scrap from the ground and tried to wipe the blood from his friend's face, but all it did was move it around. Hans picked at his shirt, so Simon handed it to him. Before Hans fumbled into it, he leaned forward and slid the purse inside Simon's jacket. "Hide that," he slurred.

"What do you mean?"

"Just hide it. Don't let anyone see it."

Gus helped Hans into his shirt and jacket. Hans plucked his hat off of Simon's head, rolled it into a bundle and stuffed it in the front of his own jacket. After a moment, Simon understood; Hans wanted people to think he still had the money. After another moment, the reasons why Hans might want that started to scare him.

Hans sat on the bench. Simon's worry increased. His friend was just staring at side of the ring; not moving, not speaking, just staring. He laid his hand on Hans' shoulder.

"Hans?"

The big man turned his head in slow motion and looked at Simon.

"What do I do now?"

The question confused Simon. Hans sounded serious, but how could he answer him?

"What do you mean?" he responded.

"You're my luck. What do I do now?"

Simon sat down beside Hans. How was he supposed to answer that question? He was just a boy. Then he remembered something.

"I talked to Pastor Gruber at St. Jacob's the other day," he said.

"That old man?" Hans asked. "I thought he was dead."

"No. He's still helping out there. Anyway, he told me something about consequences, about how the things we choose to do always have consequences, and we need to think about them."

"Consequences, huh?" Hans took the towel from Simon and rearranged the blood on his face. "Well, I can't go back to work for Master Schardius after tonight. That's one consequence."

"Truth," Gus muttered from behind them.

"You got hurt tonight," Simon said, remembering a long-ago conversation with Lieutenant Chieske. "Bad hurt. You may not be able to fight like that again."

"Umm," Hans said, without agreeing or disagreeing.

"And I think Master Schardius is going to be mad," Simon finished, remembering Ahithophel.

"Truth," Gus said in a very worried tone.

That got through to Hans. "He's likely to send someone to take the money back, either on the way back to...the...rooms...Ursula!"

Hans tried to shoot to his feet, but dropped back on the bench with a stifled groan, clutching his right side. He rose more slowly, and stayed on his feet this time.

"Gus, go ask Herr Pierpoint to come here right now, please."

Gus asked no questions, but took off looking for the fight manager. In less than a minute Simon could see him returning, Pierpoint in tow.

"What's up, Hans?"

"First, I took a lot of punishment tonight. I won't be fighting for a while."

Pierpoint looked a bit relieved. "Good. You need to rest and heal. Take as long as you want. After that fight, I'll have fighters coming from all over to step in the ring here. But if that's first, what's second?"

"How well do you know Lieutenant Chieske?"

Pierpoint looked mystified. "Byron? Pretty well. Why?"

"I need you—not someone else, just you—to take him a message without saying anything to anyone else about it. Right now. It's very important."

Pierpoint's mystification increased. "Can you tell me why?"

"No. Tell him he needs to come to my rooms in the city as soon as possible. I will meet him there. It is not a joke when I say it really is a matter of life or death."

"Okay," Pierpoint shrugged. "We're about done here. I'll head for his place now."

Hans seemed to slump a little. "Thank you."

"Thank me by getting well. We need you back."

With that, Pierpoint returned to where Tobias was standing by the time-keeper's table, then took off toward the road back to the main part of the city.

Hans looked at Gus. "Will you come with us? If something happens, someone needs to get Simon home safely."

Gus hesitated for a moment, then nodded.

"Let's go, then."

Ciclope sat staring at the table top, brooding. Schmidt had been gone for a while, but his mind was still occupied with thoughts of how to do what Schmidt wanted. And in the back of his mind, he was still—grieving wasn't the right word—he wasn't sure there was a word to describe what he was feeling about Pietro. He hadn't liked the scrawny thief all that well, but he had known him for years, and here in this foreign city he had been all that Ciclope had had from home. So, yes, he admitted to himself, he missed him. And yes, he acknowledged, he was angry about Pietro's death, and the manner of it. He just hadn't figured out what to do about it yet.

Someone slid onto the stool that Schmidt had occupied earlier. He looked up with irritation, but relaxed a little when he recognized the "associate" who had paid him and Pietro extra to make the bombs bigger.

"What do you want?" Ciclope snarled.

"First, to tell you that I'm sorry your friend was killed."

The expression on the other man's face was sober. For all Ciclope could tell, he was serious.

"We all die," Ciclope said. "But leave it to that fool to die from something like that." The stranger said nothing more. After a moment, Ciclope repeated, "What do you want?"

"Has Schmidt turned you loose on Schardius yet?" came the whispered reply.

The question was unexpected from one viewpoint, but given the history of Ciclope's short relationship with the man, he wasn't surprised.

"Yah."

The associate nodded. "I thought he might have." He leaned forward, and flicked something across the table so fast Ciclope couldn't tell what it was with his eyes. It landed in his lap, though, with a *chink* sound and the feeling of a reassuringly full purse of coin. "Another incentive payment," the man said. "Just to make sure that you, ah, bring the Schardius contract to a quick completion."

Ciclope dropped a hand to his lap to heft the purse. By weight and size, he guessed it was much as the first purse had been. So, fifty additional *Groschen* to do something he had already promised to do? Sure, he'd take the money. And he might try a bit harder, at that.

"When that's done," the associate said, preparing to stand up, "I'll meet you back here. I have another job for you, if Master Schmidt doesn't."

Ciclope just nodded. The associate left, and Ciclope's mind returned to its brooding.

Chapter 55

Karl Honister sat at his desk, going over his notes again. The lamp on his desk spilled golden light out in a circle from under the shade. It was the only light in the room. Everyone else had either gone home or was out investigating some new crime.

Even after talking to all the clerks, he still hadn't been able to put his finger on a link to the robbery cash. Someone in town had it, but they weren't spending it. Nor were any of the major business figures in town spending more than they usually did. There just didn't seem to be any tracks of it. It was like someone put it in a bag along with some big rocks and threw it in the river.

Okay, quit looking for the cash. Start looking for anything that was different. Anything at all.

He turned back to the beginning of the file and starting reading each report again, trying very hard not to skim them because they were familiar.

Page after page was turned over, one by one, with care to align them in a neat stack. That was mostly because he felt like wadding them into little balls or tearing them into shreds. Frustration did not do justice to his frame of mind.

It was in the report entitled "Second Interview with Johann Dauth" that Honister got his break. Halfway down the page, a phrase registered with him in a manner that had not occurred to him before. His finger tapped up and down on the page under that sentence while his thoughts raced down various different mental pathways.

It almost startled him when his hand slammed down on the page. "Idiot!"

Wasting no more time, he bolted from his chair, grabbed his coat and hat from their pegs on the wall as he strode by, and a bare moment later was outside, trying to find a vehicle.

"Why are we out here in the cold night again?" Gotthilf asked as he climbed into the police cart that Byron had brought the house.

"Todd Pierpoint came by, told me that Metzger apparently took a beating in a fight tonight, and says he wants to talk to us. Now. At his place."

Gotthilf mulled that over as the cart started moving and Byron gave directions to the driver.

"You think maybe he got some sense knocked into his head?"

Byron snorted. "As hard-headed as he is, I'm not sure that's possible. Would take a pretty hard tap to the noggin to do it. But I guess it could happen."

Gotthilf yawned, and the conversation lagged as the horse moved on down the street. After a minute or so he asked, "How is Jonni taking this?"

There was enough moonlight that Gotthilf could see Byron shrugging.

"She doesn't like it much. No wife does. Keep that in mind, if you ever get serious about a girl."

"Or if my mother does," Gotthilf muttered.

Byron chuckled, then continued, "But she knows what to expect. I was a policeman in Shinnston for a while, back in the old West Virginia before the Ring fell. And I was trying to get on with the sheriff out of Morgantown. We do this work, you and me, and we're right to do it, but we're not the only ones who pay the price for it. Jonni handles it okay, though, and I try to make it up to her in other ways."

"A good wife, then."

"One of the best."

Simon worried all the way back to the rooming house. Hans wasn't walking at his normal rate. He'd speed up, then he'd slow down, then he'd speed up again. A couple of times he stopped and held his hand against his right side. But every time Simon tried to help, Hans would wave him off and start walking again.

Gus didn't say anything. He just walked along, and kept looking around.

It didn't help any that Hans didn't walk the straightest route. Once they got closer to their own neighborhood, he started taking turns and twists seemingly at random. After the fourth such, Simon spoke up.

"This isn't the way home."

"Yah," Hans responded, his speech still sounding a little slurred. "Want to make sure no one is following us."

So Simon bit his tongue and trudged on after his friend.

After a few more jaunts, Hans seemed satisfied that they were alone, and set a straight course for their rooms. Just before they arrived, he pulled Simon under a stairway for a moment.

"Give me the purse," he said.

Simon handed it to him. Hans fumbled with it for several moments, then Simon heard the sound of paper crinkling. After another moment, Hans pushed it back to him.

"I took a little for me," he said. "Tell Uschi the rest is for her."

Simon stuffed the purse back in his jacket, and they walked the short remaining distance to their own stairway. A horse-drawn cart was coming down the street from the other direction, and they all melted into the shadows under the eaves of the house, out of the moonlight. The horse drew up in front of their stairs, and Simon felt that cold hand of fear make a fist in his belly again.

"Wait here," Simon heard a familiar voice say as two men got down out of the cart, one tall and one short. He sagged in relief as the moonlight confirmed that it was Lieutenant Chieske and Sergeant Hoch.

Hans apparently recognized them, too, as he lurched away from the wall. Both the *Polizei* men turned to face him, pistols appearing in their hands almost like magic, but their tension eased as soon as Hans walked into the moonlight.

"Herr Metzger," Lieutenant Chieske greeted him. "You're lucky we didn't shoot you."

"I have my luck," Hans mumbled, pulling Simon forward to stand by him.

"So I see," the up-timer said, putting his pistol back under his coat. "Todd's message was pretty urgent. Life-or-death, I believe you said."

"Yah. Mine."

Hans walked closer, and they got a good luck at his face. Chieske whistled, and Hoch exclaimed, "*Mein Gott*, man, you're beat half to death. How are you still walking?"

"You should see the other guy," Hans said with a rasp that might have been a dying chuckle.

"So, we're here," Lieutenant Chieske said. "Talk to us."

"First, you have to take Ursula someplace safe. Really safe. Take Simon, too."

"Hans!" Simon protested.

"You can't stay here," Hans said in a gruff tone. "They'll come here for the money, and anyone who's here will get hurt or killed. Nobody crosses Master Schardius and gets away with it. Remember the guy in the river."

Simon shivered.

"Money?" Sergeant Hoch asked.

"Big fight tonight," Hans rasped. "Brought in a man from Hannover. Schardius ordered me to lose. I won."

"How much?" Chieske asked.

"Fifty thousand dollars," Simon said after Hans didn't answer right away.

"*Fifty thousand!*" Incredulity overflowed from the sergeant's voice.

"Dollars," Simon responded.

A moment of silence reigned, broken finally by the up-timer. "So, you've broken with Schardius, then?"

Hans rasped again, then said, "Yah, I suppose you could say that."

"Give us what we want, and we'll see to their safety."

Hans seemed to soften a bit at that, as if up until this moment he had been holding himself rigid.

"Don't know as much as you think I do."

"Tell us what you do know," Sergeant Hoch encouraged as he pulled out his notebook and pencil.

"The guys found dead in the river, at least the ones I heard about, had all crossed Schardius in some way. You seem to already know that. I don't know anything about any of them except the last one, Delt."

Hans paused and took a slow deep breath, hand at his side again.

"He sent me out to find Delt that night. I brought him back to the warehouse, and Schardius sent me out again. But I listened at the back door."

Another slow breath.

"He talked to Delt for a minute. I couldn't hear exactly what he said, but his tone was angry. Then he went out the front door. I'm sure that they killed Delt after Schardius left, and threw him in the river."

Chieske pounced. "Who is 'they'?"

"I don't know if they all did it, or just one or two. It was the regular warehouse crew in the room. But the man you want is Ernst Mann, the warehouse foreman. If anyone knows Schardius' secrets, it's him. But he won't talk."

"We'll see," Chieske said. He looked over at the sergeant. "Got all that?"

He got a nod in response as Hoch put the notebook away.

Simon's head was spinning with all the revelations. He was slightly horrified that Hans had had anything to do with the body he had found in the river months ago. But he was also glad that his friend's involvement in the confirmed murder of the man had been very minor.

"Right," the up-timer said. "Go get your sister. I hope she travels light."

"Simon, tell her to get dressed, bring all her money, and leave everything else," Hans said. "Sergeant Hoch, would you go up with Simon and get her? The stairs..."

"Ah," Hoch responded. "Pain?"

"Broken rib, maybe," Hans muttered. "Cracked for sure."

Both the *Polizei* men winced.

"You need to see a doctor," Hoch said.

"In the morning," Hans rasped. "Now, my sister?"

"Right."

Sergeant Hoch beckoned Simon, and they started up the stairs together.

"Who is it?" a voice called from the other side of the door that Karl Honister had been pounding on.

"Detective Sergeant Karl Honister, Magdeburg *Polizei*. I need to speak to Johann Dauth."

"Who?"

"Johann. Dauth." Honister spoke slowly and distinctly, when what he wanted to do was ram his fist through the door and yank Dauth out to meet him.

There was a long moment of silence, but just as Honister was about to start pounding on the door again, it opened and young Dauth slipped out to face him, closing the door behind him. He had the look of someone who had just thrown on some clothes. His shoes not being fastened reinforced that idea.

Honister wouldn't have cared if he had appeared naked and painted scarlet to ape the demons of Hell. He wanted information, and he wanted it now.

"Sorry, my wife's in bed," Dauth muttered.

Honister brushed that aside. "This won't take long, Herr Dauth. I need you to remember something for me. It's very important."

"All right," Dauth said, his tone a bit uncertain.

"The last time we talked, you said something about one of the merchants in town buying up silver coin."

"Yah, that happens sometimes, usually when someone has to deal with a customer or a vendor outside the USE who won't take USE dollars."

"Was there anything unusual about this time?" Honister pressed.

Dauth's youthful face wrinkled in thought.

"Well, there were a couple of things."

"What?"

"There is usually a small discount charged in those kinds of transactions. The person asking for the exchange usually receives somewhat less than full value of what they're exchanging."

"Go on," Honister encouraged.

"Well, this time the merchant agreed to a steeper discount than usual."

"Much steeper?"

"More than I would have ever let my boss pay."

Aha!

"Anything else?"

Another moment of hesitation, then, "They even exchanged some gold coin for silver."

Honister started at that. Even in the current state of economic fluctuations, people with gold almost always held on to it. For someone to let go of gold coin indicated a serious need.

"Okay. Last question: who was this merchant?"

"I never saw him. I only dealt with an underling; but it was Master Georg Schmidt."

Master Georg Schmidt. Honister knew that name. Hardly anyone of the merchant or patrician class or of the political structure of Old Magdeburg didn't know it.

He nodded slowly. "That will be all for now, Herr Dauth. Thank you for your help. If I need anything more, I'll try to talk to you during the day."

Dauth slipped back inside his door, and Honister turned away, thinking furiously.

His father had had dealings with Master Schmidt, and didn't have much kind to say about him, so in and of itself he had no problems with making the merchant a suspect in his investigation. But Master Schmidt had connections, he did. To be precise, he was Mayor Otto Gericke's brother-in-law. And that may have just put Honister's investigation into a new light.

Hans drifted back to stand by Gus. He took one of the bills he had taken from the purse and jammed it into the other fighter's coat pocket.

"For you. Now get out of here. I don't think you want to be involved in what's coming."

"Truth," Gus muttered.

As the other man started to turn away, Hans said, "And Gus? Thanks. You didn't have to stand with me tonight. If I survive what's coming, I'll remember this."

Gus hesitated. "I hope you do survive," he said, and moved off.

Hans' answering thought was dark.

But that's not the way to wager, is it?

Chapter 56

Ursula was still awake when Simon walked in the door, followed by Sergeant Hoch. The candlelight was wavering on her face, her long hair brushed out and flowing over her shoulders.

"Simon...Sergeant Hoch!" One hand flew to grasp the closures of her robe, the other to grope for her cane where it rested against her table.

"Fraulein Metzgerin," the sergeant said, setting his back against the door and not moving.

"Where is Hans?" She asked, struggling to her feet with panic and worry plain to see on her face. "Is he hurt? Is he..."

Dead was the word Simon knew would have completed her sentence, if she could have brought herself to say it.

"He is downstairs waiting for us," Simon replied. "He said that you should get dressed, bring all your money and leave everything else."

Ursula stood up straight. "I will not take a single step until you explain what is going on!"

In the flickering candlelight, she looked positively regal. Simon's heart was drawn to her even more than it ever had been.

He ducked his head. She wasn't going to be happy. "Some bad things happened tonight."

"What?" Ursula's tone was sharp.

"Hans was offered fifty thousand if he fought a man from Hannover and beat him." He didn't want to say any more.

"So Hans took the offer." Ursula's voice was heavy. "I assume he won. What happened? Why isn't he here?"

Simon swallowed, still looking at his feet. "The other man was bigger than Hans, and meaner. It was a hard fight."

Ursula sighed. "How badly was he hurt?"

"Cuts, black eyes, sore ribs." Simon swallowed again. "He got hit in the head a lot."

Ursula put her hand to her mouth. Simon could see tears in her eyes. "Why did he do it?"

"For you," Simon squeezed out. "He wanted you to have the money."

He pulled the purse from inside his jacket and tried to hand it to her. She ignored it.

"I don't want the money," she almost wailed. "I want to see Hans."

"He is downstairs. He said for you..."

"To get dressed, bring my money, and leave everything else. I remember that. But why should I?"

Sergeant Hoch stirred, and said, "Because there are some very powerful men who want that money, Fraulein Metzgerin, and probably want your brother dead. They won't stop at hurting you to get to him. We're here to take you someplace safe, where they can't get to you."

"Dead? Hurt... me?"

Ursula seemed to have trouble taking that last in.

Simon stuffed the purse back in his jacket, and stepped forward to take Ursula by the arm. He turned her toward her room, nodding to the sergeant to bring the candle.

By the time they had shuffled their way to the door, Sergeant Hoch had lit another candle and brought the one on the table to them. Simon opened the door, took the candle and passed it to Ursula.

"Fraulein Ursula." He spoke to her calmly. "Get dressed. Get your money, all of it, and then come out so we can go to Hans."

She stepped forward into the bedroom.

Marla sat on her dressing stool. Franz was brushing her hair; long, slow strokes through the ebon tresses, stopping every minute or so to pass the fingers of his crippled left hand over the almost liquid fall of the hair.

This was almost a ritual for them. They didn't do it every night, but at least once or twice a week Franz would pick up her brush as they readied for bed. He didn't even have to say anything anymore. Marla would smile and sit with her back to him as he sat on the edge of the bed behind her.

He claimed it relaxed him. She knew it definitely relaxed her.

It was always a time of deep intimacy; a communing without words, a mutual submission and service that was both an offering of love and at the same time a celebration of it. And if such a moment at times led to deeper intimacy still, well, did not Solomon say in his Proverbs, "Rejoice in the wife of your youth... and be thou ravished always with her love"?

Normally Marla just sat there, still, eyes closed, simply enjoying the sensuality of the experience. Tonight, though, she stared at the mirror hanging over her small dressing table, watching Franz. His own eyes were half-closed, there was a small smile on his face, and he seemed to be moving with a languor.

It was funny, she thought to herself. He wasn't the handsomest man she'd ever met. She wasn't even sure he could be called attractive; pleasant might be about the best that could be said for his description. She remembered having schoolgirl passions over Johnny Depp and Leonardo DiCaprio, dreaming of being caught up by one of them. It had been years since she had thought of them, and she couldn't even remember what they really looked like. Every attempt to recall how they looked morphed into Franz's features.

She knew this man. She knew his heart, his goals, his passions. She knew his fire. She knew his love. And she knew that no one was his equal. No one was a better match for her than the violinist with a crooked tooth, a small mole high on his cheekbone, a hand with crippled fingers, and a smile that turned her insides to warm goo.

Her thoughts went back to Herr Schardius. She would be just as happy if she never saw the man again, but living in Magdeburg and moving in the circles around Mary Simpson, that was probably a futile hope.

Franz reached past her to lay the brush on the table, and lifted handfuls of the shining ribbons of night of Marla's hair to breathe deeply of it. She smiled a bit and banished the unpleasant thoughts; the frown line went away. She leaned back against his chest and he wrapped his arms around her. Intercepting his scarred left hand, she raised it to her lips and kissed the palm.

They stood together and she moved into his arms. Tonight was a time for celebration.

Schardius looked at Ernst. "You know what I want." It was a statement, not a question.

"Hans Metzger, alive or dead, here in the warehouse."

That was what Schardius had always liked about Ernst. He was so matter-of-fact about everything. Nothing seemed to stir him.

"Right. Now get after it."

The handful of men standing behind the overseer stirred, and they all went out the back door.

So, that was Metzger dealt with, Schardius thought to himself. And soon he would know who to blame for the destruction at the construction project. He didn't care that much about the people who'd been killed, but he deeply cared about the loss of money. That would be repaid by someone, one way or another.

But what to do about Marla Linder? That was the burning question on his mind at the moment.

Ciclope looked at the building that housed the Schardius grain factorage. Like most such operations, it had a small office space at the front of the large warehouse, which was close to the river for easy access to boats and barges bringing grain shipments. Seemed big enough.

He knew where it was, now. He'd come by tomorrow morning and see it in the daylight.

The door to the bedroom opened and Ursula came out, dressed and with her coat on. She had a bag in one hand that, from the way she was carrying it, had some weight to it.

She stopped after clearing the doorway and beckoned to Sergeant Hoch with the hand that held her cane.

"Take this, please."

Simon was pleased to see that Ursula had returned to her senses. Her face was alive, and her voice sounded normal to him, with a put-upon tone that was perfectly normal for the moment.

The sergeant stepped forward and took the bag from Ursula's hand. His eyes widened as he hefted it. All things considered,

Simon was glad the *Polizei* man had it rather than leaving it to him to carry.

Ursula looked around the sitting room, sighed, and moved toward the door at her slow pace.

"If Hans says go, we had best go."

"Wait," Simon said. He pulled the purse from his jacket. "Put this in the bag."

Sergeant Hoch looked to Ursula, who hesitated for a moment, then nodded. He placed the bag on the table and opened it up, whistling when he saw the coins filling the bottom of it. Simon handed him the purse, and a moment later it the bag was closed again around the addition to its load.

The sergeant picked the bag up again and looked at Ursula with a nod. She opened the outer door without a word and stepped out onto the landing. Simon hesitated for a moment, then grabbed Ursula's old Bible and her embroidery from the table and stuffed them inside his jacket before following her.

Hans watched as the door to their room finally opened and Ursula came out. She turned and locked the door after Simon and the sergeant joined her.

The eyes of Lieutenant Chieske and the cart driver were fixed on the crippled woman as she negotiated the stars. It made Hans almost sick to watch her lurching movements step by step.

He shook his head, hard, and moved back a step. After a moment, another step. After another moment, another step.

By the time Ursula reached the bottom of the steps, he had retreated totally into the shadows and was about to turn the corner of the nearest street.

Her plaintive "But where is Hans?" tore at his heart as he hurried away.

Hans had never been one for much more that rote lip service to the church, but for the first time in years, he truly prayed. *Go with God, Uschi. Maybe He can keep you safe now, for I can't. Please, God.*

Simon saw Lieutenant Chieske's head whip around after Ursula's cry. He joined both of the detectives in shooting glances in every direction. He even went so far as to run over to the nearby corner and look up and down the other street. Nothing caught his eye.

"Simon," Sergeant Hoch called out. "You've got to come with Fraulein Metzgerin. Come on."

With a heart full of dread for his friend, Simon turned his reluctant steps back to the cart, where Ursula waited with the detectives and their driver.

"No sign of him?" the lieutenant asked.

Simon shook his head.

"Right. He knows what he's doing, and he knows how to get ahold of us. Our job now is to get you two to safety."

"I'm not going anywhere without Hans," Ursula declared in strident tones.

"Sorry, Fraulein, but your brother has taken himself off on his own and of his own free will. I don't know where he went, or what he's planning on doing. But I do know that he asked us to take you to a safer place than this, and we promised to do it. Ask the boy."

Ursula looked to Simon, and he nodded. "I heard Hans ask it, Ursula, and I heard the lieutenant and sergeant promise to do it."

"But where is he?" Desperation now rang in the young woman's voice.

"Fraulein Metzgerin," Sergeant Hoch said, "the way he left tells us that he doesn't want us to know where he is. My guess is he thinks that by doing this he makes it safer for you. He may well be right."

The sergeant placed the bag in the cart, then turned back to Ursula. "Take Simon's word for it, if you won't take ours, but we need to get you out of here now, before those Hans is running from show up."

He held out a hand to her, a nonverbal plea.

For a long moment Ursula stood, rigid and unbending, in rejection. But then she sighed, her shoulders slumped, and she reached out a tentative hand to take his.

"Right. That's settled." Chieske looked over at Hoch. "Where do you think? The police station for now?"

Hoch shook his head. "My home. They would never think of looking for them there, and there are enough servants around the place to provide protection."

Chieske mulled that over, and nodded. "Works for me. We'll post a couple of patrolmen outside as well."

It took a bit of doing to get the young woman up into the

cart without violating her dignity. In the end, Sergeant Hoch scrambled into the cart and took her hands and Chieske placed his hands on her waist. Simon watched with envy as they lifted her into the cart with seeming lack of effort.

The next moment the lieutenant almost threw Simon up into the cart, then he vaulted up to sit beside the driver. He pointed a finger at the driver, the sergeant rapped out some directions, and with a lurch they were off.

Simon looked back. Those rooms were the closest thing to a home he had known for a long time. It hurt to leave them this way, especially since he didn't know if or when he'd see them again.

Or if or when he'd see Hans again, for that matter.

Chapter 57

Hans leaned against the side of the hovel by the riverside. He had made his way step by careful step, keeping to the shadows, through the exurb and into and through the Neustadt, until he had arrived at the part of the riverbank claimed by the poorest of the fishers. Now he was watching to see if anyone had followed.

A veil seemed to pass in front of his vision. He thought for a moment it was blood seeping into his eyes again from the cut on his forehead, but it cleared before he could run his sleeve across his face. He looked up; just a wisp of cloud passing across the moon.

Right. Enough waiting. He slid around the corner of the shack and knocked on the door. No answer; no sound of anyone stirring. He waited a moment, and knocked again.

"Who comes knocking on my door in the middle of the night?" a woman's voice demanded.

Hans put his mouth against the crack around the door and spoke just loudly enough to be heard by the person on the other side of the door.

"Hans Metzger."

There was a moment of silence, then, "Bide a moment."

He heard a bar being drawn, then the door opened into a darkness blacker than the night outside.

"In."

Hans stepped through the door, then moved to the side so the woman could close it and put the bar back in place. Then a couple of shuffling steps, followed by the scratching of a match, brought a flicker of light, which was transferred to a stub of a candle on a chipped and cracked dish.

The light revealed the face of old Anna the clothes seller. She lifted the dish and held it closer to Hans' face. He winced as the brightness neared his eyes.

"Frau Anna."

"Heaven above, lad, what have you been doing to yourself?"

"Won a fight," he said with a tired smirk.

"Well, if you look like that, I'd hate to see the loser. That have any bearing on why you're here disturbing my sleep?"

Hans nodded, suddenly weary.

"Yah. Some men will be looking for me. Need different clothes."

"Ah. That kind of fight, was it?"

"Yah."

"Fraulein Ursula know about this?" She gave him a sharp look.

"Yah, and she's in a safe place by now."

"Well, sit down there on the edge of the bed and I'll see what I can find. Sorry that I don't have a proper chair, and all."

He lurched over to the bed and sat as she began rummaging through bags lined up against a wall.

The cart pulled up in front of a large house off of Gustavstrasse in the Altstadt of Old Magdeburg.

"Excuse me a moment," Gotthilf murmured from where he sat by Ursula Metzgerin. He was rather reluctant to remove her hand from where it had been holding his arm; for stability as the cart moved, he was sure. But it had provided a pleasant sensation, nonetheless.

He hopped to the ground and looked up at his partner. "Give me a moment to make sure someone is up and can get rooms ready."

Byron looked back at their passengers.

"Right, but you'd better make it quick, because Simon's already asleep and I doubt she'll be able to stay awake much longer."

Gotthilf pulled his key from his pocket as he stepped up to the front door. A moment later he had the lock open and entered the house. An oil lamp provided light in the short entryway.

"Gotthilf, is that you?"

His mother's voice sounded from the salon to the right, and she appeared in that doorway a moment later holding a candlestick.

"Yes, honored mother."

She smacked him on his arm. "Funny boy. Did you solve whatever the problem was that your lieutenant called you out for?"

"Almost. Mother, I have two guests that I need you to provide rooms to sleep in tonight."

She frowned at him.

"Guests? Why didn't you tell me about this earlier? You know I don't like these kinds of surprises."

"I didn't tell you about it earlier because I didn't know I needed to guest them until just a few minutes ago. They were part of the problem I was called out for, you see."

The frown deepened.

"Gotthilf, I don't think I can have any kind of person associated with the city watch or your *Polizei* affairs in my house."

"I think I agree with your mother, Gotthilf."

His father's deep voice resonated in the entryway, and he looked up to see him standing in the doorway to his office, his sister Margarethe hovering behind him.

Gotthilf took a grip on his temper and tried to sound reasonable.

"It is a young woman not much older than Margarethe, a Fraulein Ursula Metzgerin. In fact, Margarethe knows her. She is in danger, and may well lose the last of her near kin very soon. With her is a boy, who is a sort of ward of her family. They have done no wrong, but they need safety and protection."

He saw his mother wavering. Her maternal instinct was quite strong, and the thought of a young one being in distress was sure to evoke her sympathies.

"Well..."

Gotthilf played his last card. "She and the boy are both crippled."

His mother caved in. "All right. At least for tonight."

As his mother bustled away to see about getting a room ready, Gotthilf looked to his father, who had an amused look on his face.

"Skillfully done, my son. I foresee a career in politics for you."

Gotthilf shuddered. "Do not curse me so, please."

He looked up and stared his father in the eyes. "I was serious, you know, when I used the word guest. I want them treated as my guests. It is important to me."

His father sobered, and nodded after a moment. "I will see to it."

"Let me bring them in, before they freeze solid out there."

Gotthilf hurried out the door and back to the cart. He reached up to Fraulein Ursula.

"Come, let me help you down."

He lifted her from the cart, settled her on her feet, and waited for her to place her cane and stand. Byron had lifted the sleepy Simon to the ground on the other side, and picked up Ursula's bag.

"This way," Gotthilf said. He kept pace with Ursula's slow steps to and through the door. Once the door closed behind them, he turned to where his parents were standing together.

"Father, Mother, this is Fraulein Ursula Metzgerin, a young woman of good character who is known to Margarethe from catechism class several years ago. And this is her young friend Simon Bayer.

"Fraulein Metzgerin, this is my father Johann Möritz Hoch and my mother Frau Marie Rebecca Ficklerin. This is our home. Be welcome in it."

Ursula had a panicked wide-eyed look. His father nodded with his usual reserve, and his mother swept forward to take the young woman under her wing.

"You poor dear, you look half-frozen. Come with me, and we'll get you settled someplace warm."

She took Ursula's free arm, and led the bewildered young woman to the stairs to the upper rooms. Margarethe moved in on the other side, already chattering.

Gotthilf winced at the thought of Ursula dealing with stairs, but there was no help for it. The only rooms available were upstairs, and it definitely wouldn't be proper for him or Byron to pick her up and carry her.

Byron nudged Gotthilf, and he looked around.

"You'd better take this," the up-timer muttered as he passed the bag to Gotthilf. "I'll see you in the morning. Good evening, Herr Hoch." The elder Hoch waved a hand in response and dismissal.

As the door closed behind Byron, Gotthilf's father looked down to Simon, who was visibly wavering on his feet.

"And what do we do with this one?"

"Put him in my room for tonight. We'll do something better tomorrow."

"Right." The elder Hoch waved a hand at the stairs. "He's your guest. See to him."

"Yes, sir. Come on, Simon."

The boy somnolently followed him up the stairs. They turned in to Gotthilf's room. Gotthilf placed the bag on his dressing table.

"We'll give this back to Fraulein Metzgerin in the morning. Let me find another blanket or two."

When Gotthilf came back to the room a few moments later, Simon was sprawled in the chair, head sagging, chin dropped, mouth open. He chuckled, picked the boy up, laid him on his bed, and covered him with a blanket.

Wrapping himself in the other blanket, Gotthilf sat in the chair and propped his feet up on a stool. Yawning, he wondered where Hans Metzger had taken himself.

"Herr Hans."

Hans heard the voice, but couldn't move.

"Herr Hans, wake up."

A hand poked at his shoulder, which stirred fleeting pains in several different locations in his body. Hans opened gummy eyes. It took him a moment to remember where he was, and to realize that he must have gone to sleep in old Anna's bed. He started to sit up, only to drop back when pain knifed through him.

"Aaah!"

"That sounded not so good," Anna remarked from where she stood holding the candle dish. "Ribs?"

"Yah." Hans grunted as he slowly levered himself up to a sitting position.

"You get that jacket and shirt off," the old woman said.

It took him a while, as almost every movement of lifting his arms and twisting his torso also twisted the phantom knife in his side. After some doing, however, his dirty, bloody clothing was lying in the floor.

Anna held the candle close to his side.

"Yah, you have some bad bruises there. Broken?"

"Probably."

The one word response was about all Hans could manage at that moment.

"Bide here and I'll wrap them." The old woman shuffled over to another bag, and pulled out some lengthy pieces of cloth. "I knew there was a reason I hadn't taken these to the paper makers yet." She turned back to Hans. "Put your hands on top of your head."

An eternity later, a sweating Hans, light-headed, nauseated and holding his gorge down with some small difficulty, nonetheless felt somewhat better as Frau Anna tied off the last of the cloth bindings that wrapped his torso tightly.

"That has it," she said as she trimmed off the surplus with a pair of scissors. "Take your hands down now."

Hans lowered his arms, and essayed a deep breath with caution. "Better," he admitted. "My thanks. Where did you learn to do that?"

She gave a surprisingly girlish chuckle. "Ah, lad, when you're married to a fisherman, you pick little tricks like this up along the way. I had to wrap my husband Nikolaus' ribs more than once before the ague took him off."

A shirt landed in Hans' lap.

"Put that on, and then we'll find you a coat."

He struggled into the shirt. It hurt, but not as much as taking the old one off had.

It took a few more moments, but they finally found a worn baggy coat that would fit over his shoulders and his wrapped torso.

That done, a thought occurred to Hans and he turned back to where his jacket lay. He kicked it over to where he could bend over to pick it up while keeping a hand on the wall to steady himself and help lever himself up again.

From one pocket, he removed the small fold of bills he had taken from the prize purse. He peeled one off and gave it to Frau Anna. She smiled at the sight of multiple zeros in the bill denomination, and it disappeared into one of her own pockets.

From another pocket, he pulled his fighting gloves. They were clammy and stiff with clotted blood, but he still pulled them on over his abused hands, wincing as he did so. He looked up at old Anna.

"Any chance you have some old gloves that might cover these?"

She thought for a moment, then shuffled over to a box in the corner. She dug around in it and finally surfaced with an old pair of leather fishermen's gloves.

"These belonged to Nikolaus. Might be they will work."

Nicholas must have had huge hands, as the gloves did cover his hands in the fighting gloves. Extra coverage, extra cushion, and extra disguise, all together.

From another corner, Frau Anna produced a knobby walking

stick. "Here, lad. Good oak it is, for all it looks like a piece of rotten driftwood. Lean on that and walk bent over, and the devil himself would overlook you."

The walking stick had a satisfying heft to it, Hans decided. He gave old Anna a knowing smile, and received one in response.

"My thanks again," he said, laying a hand on the door. "But you'd best forget you ever knew me, and I was not here tonight."

"All I saw tonight were bad dreams, lad."

They shared another grin, then she blew the candle out. A moment later, the bar drew back and the door opened.

Hans slipped out. He headed back into the Neustadt. There was a place or two there he might be able to stay out of the chill until morning.

He had no illusions about his long-term survival prospects. There were enough hard men in the exurb that if Master Schardius wanted to pay a high enough price, he would be eventually be worn down and swarmed under. But—his hand clenched the walking stick and his lips peeled back in a silent snarl—before that happened he would make sure he had plenty of company when he stood at the gates of Heaven.

Plenty of company.

Chapter 58

Miklos Farkas opened the door to his shop not long after the sun appeared above the horizon. He glanced out to make sure that the doorstep was clean and clear, glanced up to see that the sign shaped like a pistol was hanging straight, then closed the door to keep the heat from escaping the shop. It might be spring by the calendar, but winter didn't seem to have received that message yet.

A Hungarian in the capital city of the USE, Miklos made no secret of his origin. He couldn't—his accent would betray it every time he opened his mouth. He could speak the local dialect, and his command of Amideutsch was good enough to chaffer with the up-timers at need, but even they would remark on his accent at times, so, best to make a virtue out of necessity, as it were. He did bow to convenience somewhat, though, and often called himself Michael. That was a name the Germans could say without tying their tongue into knots.

No customers yet. Not surprising; a gun shop, after all, would not be swarmed with customers. He'd made allowance for that in his plans. It would take some time for his clientele to build to the point where his shop would be sustained. The question was whether his money would last until that point. He shrugged. That was up to Jesus, Mary, and the saints. With maybe a little help from a certain scrawny Hungarian.

He was in the back savoring his morning cup of coffee when the bell on the front door rang. "Just a moment," he called out. Not wanting to appear too eager, he finished the cup in one slow draft, then turned and went back into the sales room.

Ah. A merchant.

Farkas made a lightning assessment of the man. Middling height, somewhat blocky, florid face. Clothes pushed the edge of the old sumptuary laws, but were not flashy. Well trimmed beard. Large gold ring on his right hand. All in all, the most affluent customer Miklos had seen for weeks.

"And what kind of pistol are you looking for today, master? I carry only the best, the finest of pistols, all made by the masters of Hockenjoss and Klott in Suhl."

The merchant said nothing. Farkas affected not to notice his silence. The man might just be curious, or someone who moved on impulse. It happened, even in the gun trade. He prattled on as he pulled a light wooden case out and set it on top of the counter.

"Take this one, now. This is a Model Forty-Four revolver." Miklos picked it up and showed it to the merchant from various angles. It was a sizable gun, and it seemed to intrigue the man. He stepped closer.

"Six shot, cap and ball. A guaranteed man-stopper, master. Six-shot cylinder, as I said..."

Miklos let his spiel flow on, but he could tell from a slight crease in the forehead that the merchant had been repulsed by the "man-stopper" comment. After a moment, Miklos set the pistol back in its case.

"But perhaps that is too obtrusive for the master. Something smaller, yes, that might be best." He brought another case from under the counter, dark walnut this time, set it beside the first, and folded the lid back to reveal a smaller, neater pistol.

"Behold the Model Thirty-Two."

Again Miklos picked the pistol up and held it in the light, making his pitch. This one seemed to look a little better to the merchant—the forehead crease was gone—but he still wasn't caught, looking around the store and obviously thinking about leaving.

Miklos let his mouth carry the routine speech about the gun, while he continued to measure the customer. He was concerned about something or someone. Look at the way his shoulders were tightened, almost hunched. Miklos was sure of it. So why wasn't the man jumping at the protection the pistol could offer?

Ah, of course. Still too big.

"*But*," Miklos said with emphasis as he laid the second pistol back in its case, "perhaps the master wants something that is not obtrusive at all, something that is, shall we say, discreet."

The two cases were pushed to either side, and a third case was pulled out and set between them. It was covered in black leather, and opened to reveal something that this time caught the merchant's eye. His hand reached out and picked up the pistol almost without his thinking of it.

Got you!

Miklos suppressed his smile with the skill of a trained merchant, without even thinking about it.

"See how light it is, master, and how it nestles in your hand? It is the most unobtrusive of weapons, yet it uses the same thirty-two-caliber ball as its larger brother here."

He rested a hand on the other .32 for a moment.

"Very discreet, no one would ever realize one was carrying it, yet the perfect thing to have in one's pocket if one were accosted."

Miklos paused for just a moment. It really was a pretty design, very striking in its lines. The customer couldn't take his eyes off it.

"May I?"

Miklos took the pistol back from the man only long enough to show him how to hold it, then handed it back to him.

"Pull the trigger, master. Slowly, don't jerk it."

Click.

Miklos almost laughed at the way the man's eyes lit up.

"How...how much?"

Miklos shifted into closing mode, and the ensuring bargaining was lively; to be expected, when dealing with a merchant. But it didn't take long for him to bring about the sale, and at a tidy profit.

Then, of course, he had to spend a few minutes showing the new owner how to load and care for his weapon.

"Good day to you, master," he called out when the man left. And as the bell on the door jangled, he realized he had never gotten the man's name. How had he managed to forget that? Or was the merchant really a very sly man, to keep that information hidden?

Miklos shrugged as he put the paper money away and closed and stored the pistol cases. A man dressed that well wouldn't be unknown in the city. He'd find him if he ever needed to. Besides, he'd be back when he needed more bullets and caps.

"...so I checked with some of the other merchants' clerks, and most of them supported Herr Dauth's account. It appears that Master Schmidt was paying a steep premium to acquire quite a bit of silver coinage."

Otto Gericke watched as Detective Sergeant Karl Honister spread his hands above the folder sitting before him at the table. The sergeant had been ordered to give this update to Captain Reilly and himself by Lieutenant Chieske. Knowing the lieutenant, there was a reason why.

"You think there's a connection?"

That was from the captain. Honister lowered his hands to the table and interlaced his fingers.

"I can't prove it yet, but there almost has to be a connection between a large amount of USE dollars going missing, and at or near the same time a merchant doing everything he can to scrape together silver coinage, even to the extent of paying ruinous fees or converting even more valuable assets, such as gold. There is something not right there; I just can't put my finger on it. And I don't have a motive for it, either."

Ah, now it became apparent. Gericke stirred.

"My brother-in-law was not a happy man when his consortium did not receive the award of the contract for the expansion of the hospital. He blamed me for it."

He shrugged. "If he is involved, one reason might be to buy the money from whoever stole it originally. Even paying those fees, if he got a good enough discount in buying the dollars from the murderers, then he could still make a tidy profit. And he has sufficient business connections that the money might never be seen here in Magdeburg. For all we know, it may already be split up and on its way to Hamburg, Frankfurt, Amsterdam, or Venice."

"But that's still more 'what' or 'how.' The question is still *why* would he be involved in this?" Honister asked.

Gericke finally put into words the suspicion that had begun to form in his mind the day of the explosion.

"Georg Schmidt is ordinarily a very sharp man who stays within the limit of the law, but he is also what the up-timers would sometimes call petty. He will nurse a grudge until it dies, then take the bones of it and hang it on the wall as a relic. Perhaps— just perhaps—he may have crossed the line into vindictiveness." He pinched the bridge of his nose for a moment, eyes closed. "He was very angry."

Gericke lowered his hand and looked at the two police officers.

"Your thought that the fire, the murders and robbery, and the explosion might have a common thread? Look to Georg Schmidt. And if you find evidence, pursue it. The fire, I might have over-looked." Gericke shook his head. "Although, with the Committees of Correspondence involved, I probably couldn't have even done that. But the murders, and the deaths from the explosion added to it all? No, those cannot be overlooked, or we will have anarchy in the streets. He must be either cleared or indicted, and soon."

With that, Gericke stood up.

"I will be in my office if you need me."

Andreas Schardius opened the envelope from Grantville. He had commissioned a researcher in Grantville to identify this Johnny Depp that Marla Linder had indicated she valued so highly and provide all the information available on him. The report had arrived today. Unfolding the pages, he skimmed the cover letter with its polite language. He tossed that page aside, and moved on to the report.

"What?"

That exclamation after reading the first few lines was the only sound he made until he reached the end of the report. But the paper began to curl and crumple as his fingers tried to draw into a fist.

When he finished the report, he sat there, every muscle in his body locked, breath ripping into and out of his nose, head lowered, and tremors of rage coursing through his body.

An actor? Marla Linder had dared to compare him to an *actor?* And one who hadn't even come back through the Ring of Fire with Grantville at that?

His planned revenge crumbled to dust.

Schardius shot to his feet, grabbed his chair, raised it, and almost smashed it against the wall behind his desk. After strug-gling for a few seconds, he managed to restrain himself and set the chair back down on the floor.

He felt a little better, then. His mind wasn't in the total grip of rage, at any rate. Grabbing his hat and coat, he flung open the door, startling the office workers gathered outside his office. A moment later, he was on the street.

He wasn't aware that he was being followed.

Franz watched as Marla paced, eyes shining.

"Dress rehearsal today. One more day, and we do it for real."

He rejoiced to see her like that. So far she had come, so much she had endured after the stillbirth of their daughter Alison. The thought that Marla was back to her old self almost made him want to throw a party. And he just might do that, after the opera.

The fire was there in her eyes for everyone to see. And she was ready—past ready, as was he—to show the world—or at least Magdeburg—that Marla Linder was back.

Reilly looked at Honister after the mayor left.

"Sounds to me like the mayor knows something we don't."

"Yah."

"Also sounds to me like you have your orders."

Honister closed his folder. "Indeed."

Schardius stood, slightly hunched over, staring through the slight crack in the lath and plaster wall that gave him a view of the Women's Dressing Room from inside a storage closet on the other side of the wall, a closet that opened from another hallway.

His attention was so riveted on what he was seeing in the other room, he wasn't aware of the door into the closet opening slightly.

He also wasn't aware that he wasn't the only person who had a copy of the custodian's key.

"Metzger."

Hans heard his name growled as a heavy hand fell on his shoulder. He turned in the direction of the pull, throwing who-ever was behind him off balance, and brought the walking stick around and jammed the knobby head of it into the other man's solar plexus.

"You always were a fool, Hermann," he said to the now-almost-paralyzed warehouseman. He looked over Hermann's shoulder. "Möritz, Fritz."

They said nothing, just spread their arms and tried to rush him.

Hans shoved Hermann toward Möritz's feet and turned to face Fritz as the other two men went to the ground. He swung the walking stick at the other man's head. Fritz raised his arm to block the stick, and as he did so, Hans kicked him in the groin.

Fritz shrieked and bent forward to clutch at his abused manhood, only to meet Hans' fist as it crashed into his jaw.

Crack. The jaw was broken, and Fritz collapsed unconscious. Hans took a two-handed grip on the walking stick and turned to face the other two men. Möritz had almost regained his feet when the walking stick slammed into the side of his head. The knob on the end of it shattered the skull in the left temple, right behind the eye. Möritz's eyes rolled up in his head and he fell onto his back.

Hermann had managed to roll onto his knees. He held his hands up, pleading, as Hans turned on him.

"Don't...don't...do..."

Hans was sorely tempted to crush his skull also. But Hermann suffered more from stupidity than outright malice. It would be enough to cripple him for a few weeks.

Or maybe permanently—a club was not exactly a precision instrument—but Hans didn't care much. He swung the walking stick down and smashed Hermann's left elbow. The man shrieked and then passed out.

Turning to leave, Hans paused for a moment to stomp on Möritz's throat to cut off the wounded man's stertorous breathing.

He'd never liked Möritz. He was a sneak as well as a bully, a man who wouldn't be above stabbing someone in the back just to do it. He was a good match for Master Schardius, and Hans would shed no tears over the death Möritz had brought upon himself.

Chapter 59

Gotthilf awoke suddenly, aware that someone was in the room with him. He opened his eyes the merest slit, and relaxed when he realized that it was Simon's sitting up in bed that had awakened him. Then he became aware of being stiff and sore; and no wonder, since he had spent what was left of the previous night sleeping in a wooden chair with his feet propped up on a stool.

"Mmm," he grunted, dropping his feet to the floor and standing. Muscles in his back complained about the change in position for a moment, then subsided. He took the blanket that had been wrapped around him, folded it twice and draped it over the chair.

Simon was looking around with a frown on his face. It wasn't hard to deduce what was on his mind. Gotthilf walked over to the odd-looking piece of furniture in the corner and flipped up the lid to reveal the chamber pot.

"You go first," he said. He turned to his wardrobe to give the boy a bit of privacy, and soon the sounds and smells of a healthy boy relieving his system filled the room.

Gotthilf tossed his jacket on the bed, took off his shoulder holster, and stripped off his shirt. Then he reached into his wardrobe and picked up a fresh shirt. Hearing Simon stirring around again, he turned as he pulled the shirt on over his head.

Simon looked up from where he had just managed to buckle his belt one-handed. His head tilted as he contemplated the wardrobe.

393

"You have a cabinet just for your clothes? How many shirts do you have?"

Gotthilf looked in the wardrobe. "Here and in the laundry, seven or eight."

Simon's eyes widened at the thought of that much wealth. "You could wear a different shirt every day of the week."

Gotthilf chuckled as he reached for his holster rig and shrugged into it. "There have been times when my mother forced me to do just that."

Simon stared at the rig. "You carry a gun all the time?"

Gotthilf shrugged. "I deal with dangerous people, sometimes. So, yes, I carry a gun all the time. Two, actually. Big pistol here"—he placed his right hand on the .44 in his left armpit—"extra loaded cylinders for it here"—he touched the cylinders on the right side strap—"and smaller back-up pistol here." He turned to show Simon the .32 holstered in the small of his back, grip upward. He picked up his jacket and put it on.

Simon had a disconcerted look on his face.

"Have you ever shot anyone?"

Gotthilf abandoned a flippant answer before it was fully formed in his mind.

"Yah, but only to keep them from hurting someone else."

Simon considered that, tilting his head again as he thought. When he reached his conclusion, he nodded firmly and looked up at Gotthilf.

"So," Gotthilf said. "Ready for something to eat?"

That got an enthusiastic nod from the boy.

"Well, get Fraulein Metzgerin's bag and let's get to the table while there is still food on it."

Simon grabbed the bag off the table with his one hand and lugged it out the door. Gotthilf followed him, chuckling. "This way," he said as he headed for the stairs.

They clomped on down the stairs together, and Gotthilf led the boy to the eating room at the back of the house. They arrived to find Frau Fickler at one end of the table, flanked by Margarethe on the left and Fraulein Metzgerin on the right. That encouraged Gotthilf. His mother took Scripture seriously in many ways, one of which was that anyone she seated to her right was someone for whom she had some sort of favor.

Gotthilf nodded to the women.

"Mother, Fraulein Metzgerin, Margarethe."

He guided Simon to a chair, and sat next to him. The kitchen girl brought small bowls of broth to them, along with fresh rolls. Simon sat as if paralyzed, as if he had been struck by a gorgon's gaze.

Gotthilf chuckled at that thought. His mother might be a bit of a scold at times, but this was the first time he'd seen evidence that she might be a medusa. He nudged Simon and whispered, "Watch me."

Amber looked around from the edge of the stage under the proscenium. Not for the first time she wished the stage had an apron area in front of the proscenium. But it didn't, so she mentally shrugged and moved on in her mental checklist.

Franz Sylwester stood with baton in hand in the orchestra pit, watching her as the musicians in the pit watched him. The chorus and soloists were standing in the wings in full makeup and costume, ready to make their entrances. Frau Frontilia was standing at the stage manager's desk wearing the headset, ready to start giving cues. Backstage hands were poised by the scenery flats and furniture that would have to be moved on and off stage. Even the props manager was focused on her, hands on the first props that would have to be passed out.

"All right, folks," Amber called out. "One time through, no stops, just like it's for real; because tomorrow it is for real."

Amber left the stage and walked past the stage manager's desk, collecting a high five from Frau Frontilia with a grin. She walked through another door into a hallway that paralleled the auditorium. It didn't take long to circle around to the main doors. Walking through them, she walked down about halfway to the stage, then moved to a seat in the center.

Taking her seat, she said one word.

"Begin."

The maid ushered Byron Chieske into the eating room. Gotthilf set his half-eaten roll down. This was only the second time that Byron had called on him at home in their entire partnership. Of course, the first time had been last night, and look what had come of that.

"Time to go?" Gotthilf asked.

"Something interesting has come up," Byron said. "We need to get on it right now."

"Is it about Hans?" Simon asked eagerly, starting to get up from his chair.

Byron pressed down on the boy's shoulder, but Gotthilf noticed he didn't answer the boy directly.

"No, you can't come with us. We'll let you know when we find out where Hans went."

As he got to his feet, Gotthilf saw Fraulein Ursula sit back with the same disappointed look that Simon had.

"Promise?" Simon asked.

"Promise," Gotthilf replied.

Outside there was a police department cart waiting for them.

"Is this about Metzger?" Gotthilf asked as he climbed into the cart.

"Probably," Byron said. "But he's not at the scene now, even if he was earlier."

Hans ducked into The Chain. It was early in the day, and hardly anyone was there besides Veit behind the bar, a girl sweeping the floor, and a couple of addled-seeming women who had to be the worst sort of prostitutes. He went over to where Veit was tending to the ale barrels, and dropped a pfennig on the board that served as a counter.

"Genever," he rasped. "Short cup."

Veit grabbed a squat brown bottle from the shelf behind him. It wasn't the good gin that Hans usually got, but since he was only buying a cup, he didn't expect the good stuff.

Veit put the cup of gin on the counter, and counted out three quartered pfennig pieces as change.

Hans picked up the cup and threw his head back as he drained it in three swallows. When he put the cup down, he saw Veit was staring at him.

"Hans?" the barman whispered. "What are you doing here?"

Hans leaned forward.

"Buying a drink. Why?"

"There were men in here earlier looking for you. Hard men. Very hard men."

Hans shrugged. "Yah. Some of them found me a little while ago. I'm here, they're not."

Veit's gaze moved past Hans.

"They're back."

Erling Ljungberg opened the door and glared at Ulrik. It wasn't a personal glare, Ulrik decided after a moment; not something directed at Ulrik for cause. Rather, it was more of a *general notice to the world* glare, delivering a warning that today was not a day to cross the emperor's bodyguard.

After a moment, Ljungberg stepped aside, and Ulrik entered the room to discover the emperor seated in one of two chairs, waiting.

"Come, Ulrik," Gustav beckoned. "Join me and take in some of this excellent coffee." The emperor slurped at his cup with gusto.

Ulrik took the other chair and accepted a cup from the servant. He stared at Gustav over the rim of the cup. Whatever he had expected when the emperor had summoned him for their first private conversation, it wasn't to be seated in comfortable chairs and drinking coffee as if they were two merchants sitting at a table in Walcha's.

Gustav seemed oblivious to that stare as he finished his cup of coffee. He set the empty cup on the small table between the two chairs, but when the servant moved to refill it, Gustav pointed to the door instead. "Leave us," he said.

The servant bowed and left without a word.

Gustav looked around. "You, too, Erling."

The bodyguard said nothing, but to Ulrik's eye seemed to solidify into one of those standing stones that could be seen in some of the forest glades; stones that were rumored to be part of pagan sites. Looking at Ljungberg's face at that moment, Ulrik could believe that. A more fitting image for old Wotan's face he couldn't imagine.

"Erling, I am as safe with this man as I am with you," Gustav said. "Stand outside the door, if you must."

Now Ulrik was on the receiving end of a personal glare from the bodyguard. It was much more...*pointed*...than the previous glare had been. He had no doubt that it promised all manner of mayhem and hurt to him if Gustav suffered even a stubbed toe while they were alone. But after a moment, Ljungberg turned and left the room, closing the door behind him with a certain amount of firmness.

Gustav chuckled.

"A good man, that, who takes his responsibilities seriously."

"Don't tell me that he wouldn't harm a flea," Ulrik responded, "for I won't believe that."

Gustav chuckled again, then said, "Oh, he is a hard man, there is no doubt. But he is *my* hard man, which is what's important."

Ulrik had to nod at that.

"So," the emperor continued, "you have been here—on the ground, so to speak—for some time. You must have observations of the politicians, the CoC, and what has been going on. Talk to me."

At the end of the discussion, Ulrik was exhausted. Gustav had drained him of almost every thought. Gustav, on the other hand, was still sitting erect, eyes shining, rubbing his hands together.

"So," the emperor proclaimed. "All is good. All has gone well here in Magdeburg, not least because of you having the wisdom to bring Kristina here."

"Your daughter..." Ulrik began.

Gustav held up a hand. "Please, I can see what is before my eyes. She is young, but she has an instinct now as to who she can trust. In the Grantvillers' future, she lost that instinct." He shrugged. "But here and now, she has it. And she trusts you. And you have not betrayed that trust, unlike some others."

The emperor's face darkened as he referred to the late Chancellor Oxenstierna. Ulrik tensed a little. Like all those who had close contact with Gustav, he had been lectured by Dr. Nichols as to what to expect if the emperor suffered a seizure. He also knew that strong anger had been known to trigger a seizure. Ulrik really didn't want to have to put Dr. Nichols' teachings into practice. Gustav took a deep breath and let it out, and Ulrik relaxed as the emperor's color lightened.

"So," Gustav repeated. "What do we need to talk about that I haven't asked?"

That gave Ulrik the opening he had been wanting.

"The people, Gustav."

"The people? What do you mean?"

For response, Ulrik pulled out the broadsheet with Frau Linder's song on it, unfolded it, and passed it to the emperor.

Gustav scanned it, then read through it again slowly. He looked up and tapped the broadsheet with his finger. "Much better poetry that you usually see in these," he observed. "But what is so important about this?"

"That is a song," Ulrik explained. "It's an up-time song, translated by a Silesian writer named Logau. But it was sung by Frau Marla Linder, in a public setting."

Gustav thought back. "I have heard this Frau Linder sing, in the great *Messiah* performance last winter. She is good, but..." He pointed to the broadsheet. "What does she have to do with this?"

Ulrik almost shook his head. He wasn't sure he could explain it to someone who hadn't heard it sung in person.

"When Frau Linder sings this song, the music sinks hooks into you, and you never forget it." Ulrik remembered the expressions on the faces of the servants in the palace on the day of their arrival. "Never."

He pulled out a clipping of Logau's column about the January 19th performance in the Green Horse, and handed it to Gustav. This time when the emperor looked up, his face was serious. Before he could speak, Ulrik forestalled him with, "I found that broadsheet in Luebeck, over one hundred fifty miles from Magdeburg, before we flew down in the airplane. And," he held up a forefinger, "Frau Linder's performance was recorded by an up-timer, played on the radio at least once, and Trommler Records is selling records with that song on it," he pointed to the broadsheet, "from that performance." He ended up pointing at the column clipping.

Gustav was not slow on the uptake. "How many records?"

Ulrik shook his head. "I don't know. But the rumors Baldur has been hearing indicate a lot."

Gustav frowned.

"Has this harmed us?"

By "us," Ulrik figured he meant the Vasa dynasty.

"No. On the contrary, it helped us against the chancellor." Ulrik gave a mental shrug. Despite his birth, he was committed to the Vasas. He was part of the "us" now.

"So what is your thought, Ulrik? What is your concern?"

Ulrik gave a physical shrug this time. "Your real foundation needs to be the people. And that woman," he pointed back to the clipping again, "at this moment is the voice of the people. Not of the CoC. Not of the Fourth of July Party. The people."

✧   ✧   ✧

Simon slipped from his chair and carried Ursula's things over to where she was sitting. He set her Bible and the embroidery in front of her, followed by the bag with the money.

"What is that?" Frau Marie nodded toward the bag with raised eyebrows.

"Her money," Simon said with a tilt of his head toward Ursula.

"Money?"

Frau Marie's gaze sharpened and swiveled to bear on Ursula, as did Margarethe's.

Simon took advantage of their distraction to slip out of the room. He grinned as he passed through the door, but it faded after a moment and he ran to the front door, just in time to see the police cart rolling away at a rate he couldn't hope to catch.

Well.

If the *Polizei* didn't want him to be with them, he'd go look for Hans on his own. So he started walking down the street in the same direction the police cart had gone.

Gotthilf stared at the three men; one dead, two moaning in pain. Byron was whistling tunelessly beside him, rocking on his feet.

The police photographer finished his work, and Dr. Schlegel did a quick preliminary examination of the body.

"This one died within the last hour or so," the doctor said. "I won't know more until I get a look at him in the morgue." He jerked his thumb over his shoulder to where his assistants were tending to the man with the broken jaw and the other man with the smashed elbow. "Evidence is that they were beaten by someone who knew just what he was doing. One crushed throat and two incapacitating injuries. Remind me not to meet this man."

Gotthilf made notes.

"Thanks, Doc," Byron said.

The doctor began directing his assistants to pick up the bodies. Byron turned to the waiting patrolman. "What do you have, Friedrich?"

The patrolman pointed across the street. "The two shopkeepers there say they saw everything. These three men tried to attack an old guy with a cane, but somehow the guy with the cane hammered them instead. They said it didn't last very long."

Gotthilf saw something on the corpse as it was carried by. He stopped the medical examiner's assistants and reached over to turn the head of the corpse so he could see the temple area better.

Dr. Schlegel moved up on the other side of the litter, and Gotthilf felt Byron step up beside him. The doctor reached down and touched the indentation of the skull that had caught Gotthilf's attention.

"Blunt force trauma, I believe your up-time doctors would call it, Lieutenant," the doctor said. "I'll determine if it is pre- or post-mortem in my examination."

The assistants moved on.

"Metzger?" Gotthilf asked.

"Almost got to be," Byron responded. "Like the doc said, this was done by someone who knew what he was doing, and if there is anyone in town who knows how to deal out punishment, it's Hans Metzger. I've got a bad feeling about this."

The up-timer turned to the police photographer, who had just finished packing up his gear. "Nathaniel, as soon as you can, get some prints of those men done. I want someone to take them to the warehouse of Andreas Schardius and see if anyone recognizes them."

"Right, Lieutenant. I'll see to it."

Byron resumed rocking on his feet, whistling softly. After a little bit of that, Gotthilf said, "So what are you thinking?"

His partner looked around. "I'm thinking that now we know why Hans Metzger left."

Gotthilf raised his eyebrows.

"He's bait."

Chapter 60

Hans turned his head to see two of the Schardius warehouse crew ducking under the doorway. He set the walking stick on top of Veit's counter and straightened to his full height. One of the warehousemen spotted him and nudged the other. They circled around him.

"Hans?" Veit's voice held a strong note of concern in it. "What is going on?"

"You'll find out in a minute," Hans murmured as he turned to track the movements of the warehousemen. "I suggest you duck right now, though."

The two warehousemen were standing about ten feet apart. They had said nothing since they walked in. That was all right with Hans; he really had nothing to say to them anyway.

One looked at the other, then back at Hans. He waited, and predictably the two men tried to rush him at the same time. He heard Veit hit the floor behind the counter. At the last split-second Hans stepped to one side. One of the men blundered by him into the board on trestles that Veit used as a counter, knocking it over. Veit yelped as the board landed on him, then yelled in earnest as the assailant landed on top of the board.

Hans cursed as his walking stick went flying, even as he kicked the other warehouseman in the side of his knee. There was a *snap*, and the man fell to the floor screaming with his left leg

402

bent in a direction it wasn't supposed to bend. He immediately forgot Hans and clutched his knee, curses pouring from his lips alternately with moans.

Hans pivoted to find the other assailant trying to get to his feet. This effort was impeded more than a little because Veit was squirming for all he was worth, yelling at the top of his lungs as he tried to get out from under the counter.

Wasting no time and no breath, Hans grabbed the assailant by the collar and back of his jacket. With one step and a twist of his powerful body, ignoring the sudden sharp pain in his ribs, Hans swung the man in a semi-circle and launched him into the nearest wall. Then he picked up a nearby chair by its back and slammed it across the head and upper shoulders of the assailant, who dropped instantly to sprawl across a nearby tabletop. From the looks of his head and neck, if he wasn't dead at that moment, he would be soon.

The hard oak of the chair was still intact when Hans dropped it and turned back to the other man, who had struggled to sit up and was rocking back and forth holding his knee, tears trickling down his cheeks as he moaned.

"Wh...why?" the wounded man stammered. "We're just supposed to take you to the boss."

"Sorry, Max," Hans said in a matter-of-fact tone. "I don't work for the boss anymore." He considered the man for a moment, and decided there was no need to inflict any further damage on him. From the looks of that leg, Max wouldn't be walking for weeks—and would probably walk with a limp thereafter.

Hans looked around and spotted his walking stick over by the wall. He went over to pick it up, not moving quickly because he was starting to limp a bit himself. Between the fight with the Hannoverian in the ring and the brawls that had followed, he was starting to get worn down. When he turned back to the counter, Veit had managed to get to his feet and was staring at the two downed men with wide eyes. The Chain was not a peaceful place most days, but having one dead man and one half-crippled one on the floor before noon was unusual even for that den.

Hans tapped Veit on the shoulder, and when he turned, handed him a hundred dollar bill.

"That's for the damages. Send for the *Polizei*, and tell the truth. Tell them that these men attacked me, and I fought back in self-defense."

"Will...will they believe that?"

"Ask for Lieutenant Chieske. He'll believe you."

Andreas Schardius slipped into a seat in the back of the auditorium. The rehearsal was well under way; toward the end of Act One, from the look of it. Yes. Here came the castrato playing the role of Nimue, dressed in a blue flowing robe; the orchestra began the flowing ripples and subtle rhythms of Nimue's duet with Merlin. Schardius tried to focus on the music, but his mind kept straying to other topics, not the least of which was someone who would be onstage soon, Marla Linder.

And indeed, the final scene of the act opened with Frau Linder stalking onstage in a costume of red and gold, singing a bravura aria against the background of the chorus and orchestra.

What a magnificent creature she was! He took something from his pocket and sniffed at it. It left him in a curious state of tension and excitement. Heat was building in his loins, and his hands twitched at the thought of holding that long white neck.

All the while he was aware of the weight in his other pocket.

Ciclope lounged outside the fancy building. Schardius was inside, doing something masterly, Ciclope was sure. He had been watching him since he arrived at his factorage this morning. The man had come in early, had received visitors, then had left his office and strode across the Altstadt to the nearest bridge into the Neustadt, where he then proceeded to the big building, the "opera hall," he heard someone call it.

Schardius was a big man, and Ciclope had seen people step out of his way and flinch before him. But Ciclope also had a sense that while Schardius might be callous, mean, and cruel, he wasn't hard. So while he hadn't decided how to approach the man yet, Ciclope was pretty certain there wouldn't be any problems when he did approach him.

Before Ursula could react, Frau Fickler had pulled the bag over and opened it up. The older woman's eyes opened wide. She looked at Ursula, and said, "Child, how much is here?"

"With what Hans brought to me last night," Ursula said, voice trembling slightly, "I think somewhere near sixty-five thousand dollars."

Now Margarethe's eyes widened in surprise, but her mother's narrowed. Frau Fickler's lips pursed as she thought. "Margarethe," she said, "go find paper and a pencil. Quickly."

As the girl darted out the door, Frau Fickler started pulling smaller purses out of the bag and setting them to one side.

"Yes, I know them," Ernst Mann, warehouse manager at the Schardius factorage, growled as the pictures were displayed by the *Polizei* officer. He pointed in turn to the two pictures: "Möritz Flanns and Jochum Wessell. They worked for Master Schardius. What happened?"

"Well, we're still investigating that," the *Polizei* officer said, "but they both got into fights with another man."

"Just one?" Mann asked. He knew what had to have happened, but he also knew he had to act ignorant of the facts.

"That's what the witnesses are saying. Do you know what they might have been doing out so early this morning?"

Ernst steadfastly denied any knowledge of the dead men's affairs. After a while the officer left, brushing past some more warehousemen coming in.

"What is he doing here?" Otto Rusche asked.

"He came to tell us that Möritz and Jochum were killed."

"Metzger?"

Ernst muttered a curse, then spat and said, "Had to be. The stupid fools must have thought they could take him themselves."

"Well, we won't be seeing Hermann, Fritz, or Max around for a while, either," Otto said. "They must have been in the same fights, because they are all in the hospital."

At that, curses volleyed through the air for some time before Ernst broke it off. "Will they be back soon?"

"No." Otto ticked off finger as he spoke. "Hermann's elbow is broken. The doctors aren't sure his arm will heal right. Fritz has a broken jaw. They were able to do something with wire to hold it still, but it's soup and gruel for him for months. And poor Max's knee was shattered. He'll never walk right again."

Once again curse volleys echoed from the warehouse walls. It was some time before Ernst finally ran out of breath and paused to think.

The master had left Metzger up to him. Fortunately, the master wasn't here at the moment. That gave him a little time to salvage the situation.

Another warehousemen came in. "Jurgen," he said to him, "do your cousins still want to work for Master Schardius?"

"Yah."

"Are they hard enough to do what has to be done?"

Jurgen gave a gap-toothed smile and nodded with vigor.

"Good. Go get them." He looked around the room at his remaining men. "We will take care of Metzger. The master said alive or dead. Dead is easier."

Low voices cursed in agreement.

"So this Schardius is the main guy you've been investigating all along?" Captain Reilly asked, looking across the table at his top two detectives.

"Yes," Gotthilf answered, seconded by Byron's nod. "We've been quietly trying to investigate rumors since December, but until we found this Metzger person, we weren't having any luck finding anyone who would admit to knowing anything."

"And last night he decided to talk to you?" The captain sounded skeptical.

"Yah," Gotthilf said. "Metzger had one of his fights out at the new arena last night, and something happened there that caused him to break with Schardius."

"We might be able to get more details about that from Todd Pierpoint, or this kid Simon that hangs around Metzger a lot," Byron interjected.

The captain nodded, and looked back at Gotthilf, making a "get on with it" motion with his hand.

"Metzger asked us for protection for his sister and the boy Simon, told us enough that we can justify questioning Schardius and his associates, then disappeared."

"Disappeared." Captain Reilly sat up straight at that word. "He's not going to show up in the river, is he?" The captain's frown made an appearance.

Byron shrugged. "Maybe. Schardius might want that to happen, but Metzger is one tough dude. Of all these 'hard men' in Magdeburg, he is without a doubt the hardest. They might take him down, but I promise you there will be more bodies in the street than his if they do."

"For all that he's apparently the best around at professional fighting, Metzger seems to be a relatively nice guy," Gotthilf offered. "But the one thing we hear from all our sources is that he's fanatical about protecting and providing for his sister, Fraulein Ursula Metzgerin. Our guess is that he's gone out to try and draw the attentions of those men who might otherwise be asking her where the money is."

"Fifty thousand dollars, you said?" the captain asked.

"That's what we were told," Gotthilf replied.

"That's a lot of money."

"And that's why we think Schardius is sending guys after it. That's enough even for him to notice the loss."

"That, and the loss of face," Byron added. "Sounds like some of those stories out of Pittsburgh, boss."

Captain Reilly nodded slowly, tapping his fingertips on the table while he thought. The fingers stilled, and he looked directly at them.

"Right. Don't go after Schardius yet. You're going to have to brief Mayor Gericke about this. We'll need his approval as mayor and magistrate before you go after one of the leading lights of the city."

The captain stood. "Leave word of your whereabouts at the central desk at all times. I'll call you in as soon as I have confirmed an appointment with the mayor."

Frau Fickler finished adding the numbers up, and looked at the stacks of coins and bills on the table in front of them.

"That makes sixty-three thousand nine hundred fifty dollars, plus another forty-nine *Groschen* and one hundred ninety-seven pfennigs."

The three women, older and younger alike, sat and stared at what amounted to a small fortune. Frau Fickler had teased the story out of Ursula about Hans' pugilistic career, so there was no question about where it came from or who it belonged to. What to do with it, however, placed them in a definite quandary.

"Does Gotthilf know about this?" Frau Fickler asked.

"I do not think so," Ursula replied in a low voice. "Or at least, not how much is there."

Frau Fickler pondered for a moment. She was beginning to like the soft-spoken Metzgerin girl. She had a pleasant manner about her. The older woman had also wormed out of the girl the fact that she did fine embroidery, which meant that the girl wasn't afraid to work. That also spoke well of her.

The fact that the Fraulein had such wealth also elevated her in Frau Fickler's eyes. She pondered that wealth for a moment, then stirred.

"Margarethe, go bring your father here."

Simon was starting to get worried. He'd been almost every place he could think of looking for Hans, and there was no sign of him.

He had to be here somewhere.

Had to be.

Gotthilf turned around when he heard the report. "Two more?" he asked.

"Yep," Byron replied as he scanned the patrolman's notes.

"Metzger?"

"Definitely," Byron said. "According to Veit, the owner and barman of The Chain, that is."

"Let me guess: self-defense."

Byron pointed a finger at him. "You got it. According to Veit, they attacked Metzger first without a warning or an argument or anything."

Gotthilf nodded. "So if he's chosen to be bait, it sounds like he's doing a good job of it."

"Yep. Score: Bait, five; hunters, zero."

"Of course," Gotthilf finished, "the hunters only need to score once to win."

"Point," Byron said with a wry twist to his mouth. "So let's go see if we can find the bait ourselves before that happens."

"And we'd best send word to Schardius and his men that it might be prudent to stay out of sight," Gotthilf observed.

"Point," Byron said after a moment. "Send Peltzer to pass them the word."

Chapter 61

Demetrious the seeker, as he thought of himself, faded back against the city wall buttress. From there he could see the front of the new opera hall. He could also see where the one-eyed man was standing near the front of the Royal Academy of Music.

The one-eyed man was watching the opera hall, which meant he had to be watching someone in the opera hall. That was something Lieutenant Chieske would like to know. But the lieutenant would be even more pleased to know just who it was that the one-eyed man was watching.

Demetrious settled in for a wait.

Margarethe returned to the eating room in just a few moments, followed by her father.

Herr Hoch was a solid bulk of a man. He gave an impression of being almost square from shoulders to waist. That, combined with dark hair containing only wings of silver at the temple and a dark spade-shaped beard, made him a man that everyone took seriously, even at first acquaintance.

Ursula sat up straight, pressing herself against the back of her chair. Herr Hoch smiled at her, but spoke to his wife.

"Yes, my dear?"

Frau Fickler waved her hand at the table top. "Johann, before you is the wealth of our young guest, Fraulein Metzgerin."

His eyes passed over the stacks of bills and coins. He didn't say anything at first, but his eyes did widen just a bit. After a moment of consideration, he gave a nod—almost a bow—of respect to Ursula, who found herself nodding back.

Herr Hoch returned his gaze to his wife.

"I am certain you would not call me from my own accounts just to impress me with Fraulein Metzgerin's worth. Is there some other reason I am here?"

His smile lightened what could otherwise have been a very snide remark.

Frau Fickler returned his smile, and said, "Our young guest cannot carry all this around with her all the time. Nor would it be safe for her to just leave it in the room we have given to her. Would you be willing to stand as fiduciary to her and take her wealth into your custody? At least, until she understands better what choices she can make?"

"Ah."

Herr Hoch's eyes now turned to Ursula again.

"Is that agreeable with you, Fraulein Metzgerin?"

"Please, what is fid... fidu..."

"Fiduciary?"

"Yes. What does that mean?" Ursula asked, hoping she didn't sound as nervous and panic-stricken as she felt.

"It means that I would take your money into my charge with the responsibility of preserving and protecting it for you. I would not invest it or spend it without your approval."

Ursula considered that. It would be a comfort to her to know that all that money was being properly taken care of. On the other hand, could she trust Herr Hoch? All she really knew about him was that he was Sergeant Hoch's father.

As if he could read her mind, Herr Hoch smiled. "We will write up a simple contract where I shall be fiduciary for, let us say, three months. I shall do nothing to or with your money without your approval. And at the end of three months, I will return the money to you, or you can decide to have me continue as fiduciary, or have someone else assume that role."

Ursula considered some more. She could see Margarethe nodding vigorously from where she stood behind her parents. That affirmation, and what she knew about Sergeant Hoch, finally convinced her.

"I...I think I would like that, please."

Herr Hoch smiled again. "Good. I will bring you a contract in less than an hour. After you sign it, then I will remove the money for safekeeping. Meanwhile, you should take a little of that to keep with you for immediate needs."

"I will see to that, dear," Frau Fickler said.

"Very good," Herr Hoch said, standing. "I will bring the contract back shortly."

The older woman began gathering the money and placing it back in the bag. She set a very small stack of USE bills, some pfennigs, and an empty purse in front of Ursula.

"This will be your daily money, my dear."

Ursula spent some few moments tucking the money into the purse. Finally she looked up, to see the other two women looking at her with smiles.

"Thank you for your help, Frau Fickler." Ursula looked down at the purse clutched in her two hands, and fought back tears.

"What's wrong, my dear?" Frau Marie's face now showed concern. Margarethe came and sat on the other side of Ursula.

"My brother fought to get that money, to provide for me. But I would give it all just to know he is safe."

A single tear trickled down Ursula's cheek as her two new friends moved in to comfort her.

The final climactic chords crashed to an end. Franz brought his baton down in the final cutoff, and the music stopped. The dress rehearsal performance of *Arthur Rex* was completed.

There was a moment of silence, Amber stood up and walked up the aisle, clapping as she did so.

"Bravo!" Amber called out. "Bravo!"

The chorus on stage began to clap and stomp and whistle. Amber let them blow off some steam, but after a minute or so, she stuck her fingers between her teeth and blew a sharp shrill whistle of her own. In a few seconds, there was perfect quiet.

"Great job today, kids. Absolutely great. You, too, gentlemen," she said, looking over at Franz and the orchestra. Franz nodded in return.

Amber turned back to the stage.

"Okay, one last reminder. Here's tomorrow's drill: backstage and technical team here at 3:00 o'clock tomorrow afternoon.

Soloists here at 3:30 for makeup. Chorus here at 4:30 for makeup. Musicians here at 5:00. Everyone in costume by 5:30, everyone in place by 5:45, overture starts at 6:00. That right, Frau Ballauf?"

"Yes, Frau Higham," the stage manager responded from the side. "And use the back door, everyone."

"Got that?" Amber looked at the assemblage.

"Yes, Frau Amber," came the chorused response.

"Great. Now go hang the costumes up, and show up tomorrow sober and not hungover."

The performers began to disperse, chattering loudly.

Amber wrapped her arms around herself and watched them go. This was really going to happen, she thought to herself. They had pulled it off.

Now, if only Herr Schardius would go away. She could feel his eyes on her back, and it made her itch.

It had been a long day for Simon Bayer. He had trudged over all of the Altstadt and most of the Neustadt and a lot of the exurb looking for Hans, with no luck in finding him.

Simon's feet hurt; he was tired, thirsty, and hungry. He was also sick at heart. He didn't know what Hans was up to, but ever since the fight last night he was worried for his friend.

As the sun started to approach the western horizon, Simon went to Frau Zenzi's to sweep, as he did every day. The good frau tried to talk to him a couple of times, but he didn't say much in response. She finally gave up and gave him a roll and a hug around the shoulders when he finished.

Simon sat down on the building steps and nibbled on his roll. Even though his stomach was empty, the bread tasted like ashes to him. When Schatzi made an appearance, he gave her the whole roll.

He smiled briefly as she gulped the bread down, then looked at him with her head tilted and her tail wagging a little.

"Sorry, girl," he said, showing an open hand, "no more."

Tonight, very unusually, the dog didn't trot off, but continued to stare at him. Simon looked at her, and whispered, "Where is Hans, Schatzi? Do you know?"

At that exact moment, Schatzi shook all over, sneezed, and moved on down the street.

"I guess that means 'No.'"

Simon stood, dusted off the seat of his pants with his left hand, made sure his right was firmly in its pocket, and started walking down the street.

"Hey, Simon!"

His head whipped around at the shout in momentary expectation of Hans. The next moment those expectations crashed, as he saw it was Lieutenant Chieske and Sergeant Hoch in a police cart.

"C'mon, kid, climb aboard."

Lieutenant Chieske held down a hand. Simon grabbed it and was pulled up into the cart.

"Did you find Hans?" Simon asked.

Sergeant Hoch shook his head.

Simon looked out at the passing buildings.

"Where are you, Hans?"

Hans looked out from the alleyway as Simon passed by in the cart. It was good to know that the boy was still safe and in good health. If Simon was, then Uschi was as well.

He had been watching for some time; watching, but not moving into view, not speaking. It wasn't safe to do so; not for the boy, and not for himself.

"God go with you, Simon," a rare prayer passed through his lips. He remembered almost the last thing Simon had said to him. *Consequences.*

"We have been looking for your brother," Gotthilf said with patience for the third time. "But it is hard to find someone who doesn't want to be found in less than a day."

"But what is he doing?" Ursula demanded. "Do you know?"

Ursula stood as straight as she could, rigid with fear and anger, facing him and demanding answers. Margarethe and Frau Marie stood behind her, saying nothing. It amused Gotthilf in one corner of his mind to see that his sister had the same identical frown as his mother.

"No, we do not know what Hans is doing," he replied.

Ursula must have seen something in his face.

"What do you think he is doing, then? Surely you have a guess!"

Ursula's tone was savage and her face was hard. It was obvious she would have an answer from him.

"You will have no peace from this," he warned her.

"I don't want peace! I want the truth! I want to know what is happening with my brother!"

Ursula's face was pale, almost as if carved out of ice. It drew Gotthilf; drew him in a way no other woman had ever drawn him.

"Very well," he capitulated. "We think—and it is only a guess, mind you—we think that he has set himself up as a stalking horse to trap those who would hunt him and you."

At that, Ursula wavered on her feet, and Gotthilf sprang forward to ease her onto a chair. His mother and sister clustered around her, and he stepped back.

After a moment, the young woman raised her head and motioned Frau Marie and Margarethe back.

"Is he still alive? My brother?"

"We think so. No body has been found."

The word *yet* hung in the air between them, for all it had not been spoken aloud.

Ursula leaned back and placed both hands atop her cane before she spoke again.

"*His* body has not been found, you mean. But what of others? What of those you say would be hunting him?"

Gotthilf shrugged. "There are two corpses in the city morgue, apparently dead at your brother's hands, and three men in the city hospital with serious injuries. Two of them may be crippled for life. The witnesses we have are all clear that they attacked him."

Ursula's hand flew to her mouth at the mention of the dead men, and if possible she grew even paler.

"So, if we are correct in our guess," Gotthilf finished, "your brother's plan to hunt the hunters has succeeded to this point." He looked away from Ursula to see Simon crouched in misery in a corner of the room. "It remains to be seen how successful it will prove to be in the end."

Chapter 62

Hans had very little warning.

There was a sound of running feet behind him. He looked around to see half a dozen or more men swarming toward him in the moonlight.

Hans had been heading toward that same nook in the Neustadt where he thought he would be safe for the night. Now, all he could do was tuck himself into an angle in the freestanding wall of an old building that had burned in the great fire of 1625 and had never been rebuilt. At least there no one could get behind him, and they were forced to come to him almost head-on.

He settled his back against the stones of the walls, holding the walking stick in both hands. He was glad that Frau Anna had given him the stick. It would be put to use one more time tonight.

The pack slowed their pace, and came to a stop just beyond his reach, settling into a semi-circle. They were silent.

"Devil got your tongues, lads?" Hans mocked.

"You are a dead man, Metzger," a cold voice said.

"Ah, is that you, Ernst?" Hans laughed. "I wondered how long it would be before you found me. Of course, I've been leaving a trail behind me all over town."

He laughed again. "Got some new boys, have you, Ernst? Did you tell them the reason you need them is because I hammered five of your men into the mud yesterday, left two of them for dead and the others probably crippled for life?"

"You are a dead man, Metzger," Ernst Mann repeated.

"Maybe I am. But I'll tell you this: if I am, I'm not the only one. Hope you've all made your peace with God, boys, because I'm not going to meet Him alone."

Several of the men drew knives at that. Hans blessed Frau Anna yet again for the heavy coat, the gloves, and even the wrappings around his ribs. He didn't expect them to keep him alive to see the dawn, but they would keep him alive longer; long enough to put paid to this pack, perhaps. He trusted Chieske and Hoch to take down Schardius, but he was going to make sure that the devil's tools before him didn't return to their master.

He had no fear, he realized. None. He knew he was going to die here. But every one of these men that he took with him was one less that could threaten his sister. And at that thought, a white heat filled him.

"Come on, boys," he taunted them. "Either come take me now, or crawl home to your holes as craven curs!"

The fight didn't last long. Fights with those kinds of odds seldom do. And to an outside observer, it would have seemed just an extended flurry of grabs and hits. But to Hans, time seemed to slow down as he prepared to sell himself dearly.

The first man to die didn't see the walking stick in Hans' hand until right before it rammed through his eye and into his brain. He dropped with a choked scream, fouling the footing for those who followed him. Unfortunately, the walking stick wedged in the eye socket. Hans cursed as he had to release it.

The second man came from the left. His knife snagged in Hans' coat. Hans reached out and grabbed the man's shoulder, then delivered two rapid hammer blows to the attacker; one of them smashed out several teeth and the other might have broken his jaw. Hans pushed him back to fall over the body of the dead man.

The third attacker had tripped over the dead body. His knife lunge missed Hans entirely. But his body didn't. Off-balance, he tripped again and fell into Hans' right side, with his shoulder landing squarely atop the broken rib.

"Ungh!"

White fire sheeted through Hans' mind as pain blazed throughout his body. He fell back against the wall behind him, and for a moment that support was the only thing keeping him on his feet.

But even as Hans grappled with the pain, his hands seemed to move of their own accord as they grabbed the man's head and twisted.

The third attacker dropped at his feet, head looking back over his shoulder.

There was a brief pause as the others drew back a step or two. Hans breathed heavily, air rasping in and out of his throat. Hunched over the pain, he stepped his left foot forward a bit and turned his right side away from the attackers. He knew he couldn't take another hit like that last one.

They stared at each other in the moonlight; Hans on one side and Ernst Mann and his remaining cohort facing him across a puddle of moonlight.

"So, it is down to you, Ernst," Hans rasped. "You and Otto and Jurgen and Wilhelm. Are you enough? Are you enough to do what that devil Schardius has ordered?"

"We are," Ernst replied in his cold voice.

The warehouse manager beckoned the others close.

While they whispered, Hans breathed deeply, sucking in as much of the cold air as he could. He could feel the sweat beading up on his back, chilling in the cold. He had lost his hat, and could feel the night breeze off the river stirring his hair. He glanced up for the barest of moments to see the moon sailing above him.

A good night to die, he decided.

Hans drew himself up as the others separated, spreading out as much as the angle of the walls allowed. He beckoned to them.

"Come and get me."

The last of the fight was short and savage. Otto launched himself from the far left, making cuts and lunges with his knife that at first were blunted by the heavy coat. Jurgen stood to the front and swung fists at Hans' face and head. Wilhelm came from the far right and somehow managed to snake his arm around Hans' throat, attempting to choke him.

Hans had no choice. He kept his left hand and arm raised somewhat to shield the knife. The fists he just had to duck or ignore, because the arm around his throat had to go. He reached up and began breaking fingers. Wilhelm grunted as the first one snapped, hissed with pain when the second followed. When the third followed, he bellowed and tried to push away.

Hans reached back and grabbed Wilhelm by the hair, hauling him around in front of him to take a couple of hits from Jurgen's hard fists while he gathered himself. Then he threw Wilhelm to the ground and kicked him in the head—possibly hard enough to kill him; certainly hard enough to take him out of the fight. Then Hans threw fists at Jurgen and Otto. Some landed, some did not. He felt some stinging places where Otto's knife had penetrated the coat or the rib wrappings. He could feel blood trickling down his face from where Jurgen had reopened some of the cuts he had sustained in the fight with Recke. But he was still on his feet, still taking and dealing damage. The night was not over.

Hans surged forward, grabbed Jurgen's shoulders and smashed his forehead into his foe's face, shattering his nose and spraying blood over both of them. He pushed the dazed Jurgen away and rounded on Otto, who was moving in to stab him again. Before he could block it, Otto's knife had sheathed itself in his left side, low down below the rib wrappings.

A cold pain shot through Hans. He knew that now his minutes were limited. He could feel blood beginning to flow out.

Hans' left hand dropped down to pinion Otto's hand on the hilt of the knife. His right hand flew out to grasp the front of the other man's throat. With a grunt and a heaving twist, Hans crushed and tore his foe's larynx.

Dropping the convulsing Otto to die where he lay, Hans turned back to Jurgen, who was standing still and clutching his bleeding nose. Still holding the knife in place in his wounded side, hissing at the fresh pain felt with every movement of his body, Hans delivered a kick to demolish Jurgen's right knee. Then he aimed a boot at the other man's throat. But before he could deliver it, he felt a blow on his back, and a fresh stinging. He turned his head slowly, to see Ernst backing away, staring first at his knife and then at Hans. Obviously the coat and wrappings had played their part one more time.

Hans followed through with the kick to Jurgen's throat. The *crunch* was a pleasing validation that there was another foe down. All the while he stared at Ernst, standing wide-eyed in the moonlight.

"Come take me now, Ernst," Hans husked. He could feel his legs starting to tremble, his arms droop from the blood loss. He didn't have long.

Ernst obviously hesitated. Hans had taken out a half-dozen of his men before his eyes. Four of them were dead and another might well be.

On the other hand, it had to be obvious that Hans was hurt.

Hans waited. He had no hope of chasing Ernst if he ran. He hunched over a little more, not altogether feigning hurt.

Ernst stepped closer, then with a rush he stabbed at Hans. The knife didn't penetrate the rib wrappings. Just as Hans gripped his shoulder, Ernst drew the knife back and thrust again.

"Die, damn you!"

This time the knife went in low, between the hips and below the wrappings. It was sharp, and penetrated the trousers, skin, and abdomen with ease.

Hans hissed at another wave of cold pain. This one would kill him, he knew. The blood was flowing faster. He so much wanted to rant and rail at Ernst, tell him what he thought of him and his master the devil Schardius. But there was no time.

He wrenched Otto's knife out of his body with his left hand, turned it, and thrust it into Ernst's belly. Hans watched as the other man's eyes opened wide in shock and his mouth dropped open. He gave a heave with his shoulder, and ripped Ernst open from navel to sternum. Ernst's eyes rolled up in his head and he collapsed, sliding off of the blade of the knife.

Hans dropped Otto's knife and stumbled a step or two away before he dropped to his knees, then sagged to one side and rolled onto his back.

"Thank you, God," he murmured, "for allowing me to defend my sister. If my hands are too bloody to enter heaven, then I will enter hell knowing that she is safe."

The darkness closed around his vision, narrowing until only the whiteness of the moon could be seen. As that grayed out and the darkness continued to close in, one last thought passed through his mind.

Consequences.

Chapter 63

Franz awoke to a feeling of weight on his chest and something tickling his nose. He opened his eyes to see Marla's face just inches from his own, a tress of her own long hair in her fingers teasing his upper lip and nostrils.

When she saw his eyes open, she swooped in for a languorous and lingering kiss, then bounced up to sit beside him in the bed.

"It's opera day, Franz. Get up! We have so much to do!"

She jumped to her feet and began getting ready for the day. Franz rolled over on his side, and watched her gathering clothing and washing her face, all the while humming a melody that he finally recognized as "I Feel Pretty," from *West Side Story*. One of these days he hoped that Andrea Abati would follow through with his oft-stated plan to stage that musical. He would really like to see how the *Adel* and the patricians and the bürgermeisters would react to it. Probably not going to happen soon, though, given how dissonant the music was. One day, though.

"Franz!" Marla pounced on him again, dragging on his hand. "Get up!"

No help for it, he decided. And in truth, today was going to be a busy day. So he sat up and swung his feet over the side of the bed.

It didn't take long to prepare. Franz donned his normal conductor's suit: black velvet long trousers in the up-time style, and a short-waisted royal blue velvet jacket over a white shirt. He ran a comb through his hair, and he was ready to go.

Normally it would have taken Marla somewhat longer than that, but since she would be putting on stage makeup at the opera house and arranging her hair to match her costumes in the performance, she had just thrown on a shirt and her jeans.

"Ready to go?" Franz asked.

"Ready," Marla replied, pulling a pair of brown leather gloves out of her coat pockets.

"What happened to your other gloves?" Franz asked, opening the door for her.

"I guess I've lost them. I thought I left them at the opera house, but when I went back to look for them the next day, they weren't there."

"Too bad. I was just getting used to pink, purple, and green all in the same knit."

Franz ducked as Marla swung at him.

Gotthilf was already gone the next morning when Simon came down to the eating room. Ursula and Margarethe were there; Ursula sitting quietly picking at a roll, Margarethe chattering about something.

"I'm going to go look for Hans," he announced baldly. "I'll be home when I find him." He turned to leave. His last sight was of Ursula sitting with a forlorn look on her face.

Byron and Gotthilf were back in the captain's conference room. The mayor had come to them, rather than making them do the walking.

"So," Gericke said when they finished their recital. "Four dead men, and you suspect Master Schardius on the basis of the word of a dock worker?"

When put that way, it did sound weak, Gotthilf had to acknowledge to himself.

"That, and some very strong instinct," Byron said. His voice was firm.

"Instinct," Gericke said flatly.

Neither Byron nor Gotthilf responded to that.

Gericke sat back in his chair. Nothing was said for a long moment, then he sighed.

"Your 'instinct' has proven right before," the mayor acknowledged. "I cannot ignore that. But if you are wrong...if Master Schardius is indeed blameless, as he will protest, then your careers will be ended, and likely mine as well, and he will crush us all in court for slander. How certain are you of this?"

"Very," Byron said. Gotthilf backed him with a firm nod.

Gericke sighed again.

"All right, continue, but God help us all if you're wrong. What more do you need?"

Gotthilf pulled a couple of forms from his folder. "Search warrants, Mayor, for his residence and place of business. In duplicate."

"Ah," Gericke said. "I must change hats, as you up-timers would say, and be Magistrate Gericke for the next few moments."

Captain Reilly passed a ball-point pen to the mayor, and a minute later Gotthilf had one set of the forms in his folder and was folding the other set to go in his jacket.

"You'd better be right," the captain said as he followed the mayor out of the conference room.

Ciclope staggered out of his rooming house. He cursed himself for drinking so much ale the night before.

Today was the day, he decided. Today he would take down the target of Herr Schmidt's fear, earn his fee, and leave this forsaken city. He hungered for Venice, and it was time to leave.

Andreas Schardius frowned. The doors to the warehouse portion of the factorage were closed. He stormed through the doors of the office. "Why is the warehouse not open?" he demanded of his secretary.

That worthy shrugged, and said, "Herr Mann has not arrived, nor have any of the other warehouse workers. We felt it was best to leave it closed up until someone arrived to take charge."

"Hummph," Schardius snorted. "Did Ernst not say something about being late? Do you know anything about why he might be late?"

"Herr Mann said nothing to us, and he was still here last night when we left. But it might have something to do with the deaths."

"Deaths?" That word stopped Schardius in mid-tirade.

"Yah. The *Polizei* came yesterday, and told him that some of our warehouse workers were dead, killed in a fight. He and the others left right after that."

Schardius' mind churned at that revelation. A couple of things became clear: Ernst was seeking Metzger, and Metzger was not going to come easily. And that was probably why he and his men were still not here this morning; they were still looking for Metzger. So; mystery solved.

"Carry on," Schardius ordered. "Notify our customers that there won't be any deliveries today. Check the arrival schedule; I don't believe we have a barge coming in today, but make sure. Tell Ernst to notify me immediately when he appears. He'll know where I am."

Gotthilf looked around at the bodies. "It's almost like a slaughter house," he muttered.

"Not enough blood for that," Byron responded. "There's only two with stab wounds. The rest of them he just beat to death."

They were waiting for the police photographer to finish taking pictures of the crime scene and the bodies.

"We screwed up," the up-timer muttered. "We should have found him." He stepped out of the way of the photographer. "We should have found him," he repeated, looking over at his partner.

"It's hard to find someone who doesn't want to be found," Gotthilf replied.

Neither one of them drew any comfort from that thought.

Simon walked out the front door of the grand townhouse, hoping that he hadn't just lied to Ursula. The problem was, he had no idea where Hans could be.

For lack of anything else, Simon started back the way he and Hans usually went to the fight arena; down the Gustavstrasse, across the bridge over the Big Ditch into the Neustadt, heading for the gate at the northwest corner of the city.

He wasn't far from the gate when he glanced down a side street as he crossed it and saw a gathering of people. A cold hand gripped his heart and his feet took him that direction before his conscious mind realized it.

He pushed through the crowd. When he got to the front of it, he was up against a piece of rope that was rigged as a barrier between the shells of two burned buildings left from the sack of the city that hadn't yet been torn down. There were several men standing or walking around, and he could see what appeared to be several bodies lying on the ground. The cold hand around his heart got colder.

"So what do we do now?" Gotthilf asked.

"I don't know," Byron muttered.

Dr. Schlegel came over to them, tugging gray leather gloves back on after looking at each corpse. "You can probably tell cause of death as well as I can," he announced. "Time of death was obviously last night some time, but because of the cold I can't be more certain than that until I do the medical exams."

"Yeah," Byron sighed, "it's pretty obvious what happened. I'm not too sure that pinning down when it happened will be very useful in this case, but you never can tell. Let me know what you find out."

The doctor nodded, then turned and began issuing instructions to his attendants as they waited for the photographer to finish his work.

"Sergeant! Sergeant Hoch!"

They both looked around at the call.

"Oh, great. It's the kid," Byron said. "How do we break the news to him?"

Friedrich von Logau looked up from his notepad as a burgher with a stern face jostled him going by. He looked across the table to his friends.

"Who was that?"

Johann Gronow leaned forward and murmured, "That was Master Andreas Schardius, the leading corn factor in Magdeburg. A very wealthy man, is Master Schardius, with connections to the *Regierender Rat* in Old Magdeburg."

"Rumor has it," Plavius joined in, "that he paid for all the cost of staging the opera."

"No," Gronow said. "Only a third. I heard it from Frau Higham herself."

"He is also rude," Friedrich said, adjusting his chair.

"Imagine that," Seelbach laughed.

✧   ✧   ✧

Schardius checked his pocket watch as he left the coffee house. Hours to go yet before the opera began. He still steered his steps in the direction of the opera house.

Simon grasped the rope tightly as Sergeant Hoch approached. "Hello, Simon."

"Yes, Sergeant. Please, is it Hans?"

The sergeant looked solemn. "You shouldn't be here, Simon."

The cold hand turned his heart to ice. "Please, Sergeant. Is it Hans?"

Sergeant Hoch hesitated, looked over his shoulder, then nodded. Simon closed his eyes. He felt the sergeant pat his shoulder.

Simon opened his eyes. "Please. I have to see."

"I don't know," Sergeant Hoch said.

Just then Lieutenant Chieske walked over. "What's going on here?"

The sergeant explained that Simon wanted to see. Simon poured his yearning into his eyes. It must have worked, for the lieutenant looked at him and nodded. Sergeant Hoch lifted the rope and Simon bent under it.

"Stay with me and don't go wandering around," the sergeant cautioned. Simon nodded.

It was only a few steps. One of the other men moved aside at a word from the lieutenant, and Simon could see everything. There were several bodies lying on the ground. All dead. And yes, much as he didn't want to admit it, one of them was Hans. He lay on his back with a knife hilt sticking out of his abdomen.

"It must have been some fight," Lieutenant Chieske mused. The lieutenant continued talking, but Simon didn't hear him. His eyes were fixed on his friend. Hans would never again whistle tunelessly, never again laugh when Simon called Tobias "Ferret-face," never again put his hat on Simon's head and grin when it dropped down to his ears. Hans was gone, and there was a hole in his heart now.

"'All men die, Simon.'" The memory of Pastor Gruber's voice came to him. "'What matters is how you die.'" *Samson indeed,* Simon thought. "'So the dead which he slew at his death were more than they which he slew in his life,'" he murmured.

"What did you say?" Lieutenant Chieske asked.

"Nothing." Simon gave one final glance to his friend. "Fraulein Ursula will want his body."

"It will be released from the morgue after the investigation is complete."

Simon took a deep breath and looked around. No one was close by. "It was Master Schardius, wasn't it?" he asked quietly, almost in a whisper. The two policemen said nothing else, simply drew him farther away from the crowd and the other policemen and waited.

In a whisper, Simon told them about the conversation he overheard after Hans' last fight. It didn't take long. The two policemen looked more and more intent as he spoke.

"You're sure he said Vogler?" Lieutenant Chieske asked, keeping an eye on the crowd.

"Yes."

The lieutenant looked at the sergeant. "Schardius, and tied to Vogler," Sergeant Hoch breathed. "Delt we were looking for . . . but a link to Vogler. That answers so many questions."

"I can't tell you how much I wish we could have learned this another way," Lieutenant Chieske said in a low voice. "What Hans finally told us and what you've just told us is important, and will help us continue our investigation. I just wish it hadn't come to us at so high a price."

Simon blinked back tears. "Hans was a hard man," he said. "He had trouble trusting watchmen, even you new policemen. But in the end, he told you."

Before he left the scene of Hans' death, Simon looked back at his friend one more time. After a moment, he heard a whine and looked up. There was a dog looking at him from another ruined wall. "Schatzi? Is that you?" The dog whined again with a slight wag of the tail, standing over something dark lying on the ground. Simon walked over and picked it up. The dog whined again, then disappeared behind a mound of rubble.

Simon looked down. He was holding Hans' hat. There was no mistaking it. Simon knew every spot and wrinkle and crease and nick on it. That brought the loss home to him even stronger. He stood there with his eyes burning for a long moment, trying to hold his feelings in, but they burst forth and he began to sob, tears running down his cheeks. He turned his back on the *Polizei* and the crowds as the cold hand around his heart expanded to fill his entire being.

Hans was dead. Simon's world was now a very dark place indeed.

✧   ✧   ✧

Friedrich von Logau was seated at a table in Walcha's Coffee House with his friends. This was not unusual. Friedrich was not doodling with a new epigram, however, and that was a bit unusual. Instead, he was listening to Karl Seelbach read from his latest essay on the natural order of government.

He was also thinking about getting out his notepad and beginning an epigram. Karl was not the greatest reader in the world, and his approach to the topic was...arid, to say the least.

Friedrich's attention was distracted by a movement. For a moment, he felt as if he had been transported back two months, for approaching their table were Marla Linder and Franz Sylwester. He raised a hand to interrupt Seelbach's drone.

"We have guests, my friends."

They all turned to see who it was. When they saw Frau Linder, chairs began to scrape on the floor as each man stood. They had all seen Frau Linder's great performance at the Green Horse, and to a man they revered her for it.

"What have we here?" Frau Linder asked with a grin as she drew near. "A gathering of gentlemen of leisure?"

"Nay," Johann Gronow replied. "We are all workmen here, toiling under the lash for a pittance."

"I know better than that." Marla laughed. "You're all writers, every man of you."

"Alas, she knows us well," Johannes Plavius said with drama, throwing the back of a hand to his brow.

"All is revealed," Friedrich said in despair. "She will tell the world, and we shall be reviled."

Frau Linder broke into laughter, and clapped her hands.

"You guys are as crazy as musicians."

They all bowed to her, deeply and with flourishes.

"Thank you," Friedrich said with some sincerity. "From you, we will accept that as a compliment."

Frau Linder's deep curtsey was marred only by the gamine's grin on her face.

She then turned to Gronow.

"Herr Gronow, I have not had an opportunity to thank you for your libretto for *Arthur Rex*. It is superb." Behind Frau Marla, her husband Franz Sylwester nodded in agreement. Gronow stood there with an idiot grin on his face, saying nothing.

"Since I knew where you could be found, Frau Amber Higham,

director of the production and wife of Heinrich Schütz, the composer, asked me to drop these by."

Marla held up her hand, and Herr Sylwester placed several cards in it. She handed two to Gronow and two to Friedrich.

"There you go, boys, your own personal invitations to the premiere performance of the opera *Arthur Rex*, music by Heinrich Schütz, libretto by Johann Gronow. Don't be late."

She waved and smiled, Franz nodded, and they turned and headed for the door.

The four men looked at each other. Silently Gronow passed one of the invitations to Seelbach, and Friedrich did the same with Plavius. They all four read the richly engraved invitations, verifying that they were indeed entitled to attend the performance that evening.

Their mutual silence was broken by Plavius.

"Friedrich, lend me two pfennigs, please."

"Whatever for?"

"I must go redeem my best coat from the loan agent. I cannot go to the opera wearing this."

Plavius waved a hand at the threadbare, worn, and stained garment he was wearing at that moment.

Friedrich sighed, and dug into a pocket.

"Simon?"

Sergeant Hoch's hand was on his shoulder. Simon dragged his sleeve across his face and looked up at him.

"We need to go tell Fraulein Metzgerin. Do you have a pastor?"

Simon started to shake his head, but found himself nodding instead. "Pastor Gruber, at St. Jacob's."

Simon didn't speak during their walk to the church. His mind was occupied with *Why did Hans take the fight? Why? If he hadn't taken the fight, he wouldn't have crossed Master Schardius.* Those grieving thoughts ran over and over through Simon's mind as one step followed another. *Hans could have turned down the fight, couldn't he?* Heart numb, heart cold, he took aimless steps in a shell of silence amid the bustling of the streets.

Simon's next conscious perception was of the sun shining on the front of St. Jacob's church as he neared it. He stopped for a moment, looking at the gray stone of the building. Again he heard Pastor Gruber's voice from their talk about Samson. "But he was a very proud man, filled with what the Greeks call *hubris*, so he did what he wanted."

It dawned on him that, as much as he liked his friend, Hans and Samson had been alike in something besides their physical strength. In the end, Hans' pride and anger brought him down. But Simon also took some consolation that, just like Samson, Hans had company in his death.

"Simon?"

Pastor Gruber approached them from the small side door of the church, clutching his coat and holding his hat on his head against the fitful breezes.

"Pastor Gruber?" the sergeant asked.

"Yah, that is me."

"I am Sergeant Gotthilf Hoch, of the Magdeburg *Polizei*. Would you come with us, please?"

The pastor said, "Certainly, but why?" He fell into place beside Simon as they turned.

Simon looked up at him. "My friend Hans is dead. We need to tell his sister."

"Ah." The old pastor had a very sad expression on his face. "Of course I will come with you. Has this Hans a surname?"

"Metzger," Sergeant Hoch replied.

"Hans Metzger." The old pastor's eyebrows climbed. "The fighter?"

"You've heard of him," the sergeant asked in amusement.

Pastor Gruber coughed a bit, then said, "Sergeant, one hears many unusual things serving in a church like St. Jacob's."

"I can imagine." The sergeant's amusement grew.

The old pastor looked down to Simon again. "Samson?"

Simon nodded, biting his lip as tears trickled again. "Yah."

"I see."

The old pastor laid an arm around Simon's shoulder. Simon shuddered, then leaned against the old man, finding solace in an embrace that he had experienced so very seldom in his life.

There were no more words spoken, but from time to time as he trudged along, Simon would look up to see Pastor Gruber's lips moving silently. Maybe he was praying; maybe he was reciting scriptures. Either way, Simon drew some small amount of comfort from that.

They came to a stop in front of the Hoch family townhouse.

Pastor Gruber's eyebrows raised again, and he looked over at the sergeant.

"My family's home," Sergeant Hoch explained. "Fraulein Metzgerin has been staying here, for her protection."

"I . . . see." The pastor's voice was neutral.

The two older men looked down at Simon. A long moment passed before he realized they were waiting on him to move. With a heavy sigh, he walked up the steps and opened the front door, followed by the two men.

Ursula looked up from a bench in the front hall where she was reading her Bible. Her eyes glanced over Simon and she stood, searching behind him, looking for that familiar face; looking for her brother. Finding only Sergeant Hoch and the elderly pastor, slowly her eyes returned to Simon. He steeled himself to face her, and he grieved when she saw the hat clutched in his hands and the light in her eyes began to die.

"Hans?"

"Won't be coming home, Ursula. Ever."

Her face crumbled. Tears began to flow. She stood there, bereft, unable to move. Simon went to her and for all that she was years older than he was drew her into an embrace with his one arm. She began to sob brokenly as her tears drenched his shirt.

"Shh, shh," Simon said. He didn't know how to comfort her. "I'm here."

Over Ursula's bowed head Simon looked out the door and made two vows.

He knew he could never replace Hans, but he would be a brother to Ursula. That vow he made in his heart to her.

The second vow was made to Hans. *I'm not a hero, not a Samson. I can't do what you did. But maybe like the lad in the Bible story I can help you bring down a temple. If I pick at the walls and take the mortar I find to Lieutenant Chieske, sooner or later the walls will crumble. I can't be a Samson, but maybe I can be an Ehud, a left-handed sneak. For you, Hans, I will try.*

Chapter 64

Demetrious stirred when the one-eyed man began to move again. There was no doubt in his mind. The man was following the big merchant. That would be of interest to the lieutenant, he thought. Why he was following the merchant was a question Demetrious could not answer.

He shrugged. That would be for the lieutenant to discover.

Demetrious started following his target.

Marla strode into the backstage area, followed by Franz.

Amber looked up from a conversation with Frau Frontilia at the stage manager's desk. "You're early," she remarked.

"Yep," Marla threw back over her shoulder. "Couldn't stand the waiting."

Amber chuckled, and turned back to Frau Frontilia.

Marla headed for the dressing area. "Hey, Sophie," she called out as she walked through the door. "We ready?"

Her dresser looked up from where she was hanging costumes on the wall. "Yes, Frau Marla," she said with a smile. "The costumes have been cleaned and pressed and are now hung up in the order you will need them."

"Great."

Marla hung her coat on a nearby peg, then pulled her Zippo lighter out and lit the wicks of the two oil lamps that sat on her makeup table flanking the small mirror. The overhead lights were electric, but she wanted a little more light on her face while she was applying her makeup. Then she turned to Franz and put her arms around his neck.

"You, my good sir, may be good to go in your formal duds, but I've got over an hour's work to do to get ready." She gave him a hard kiss, then released him. "So be off with you to your orchestra pit."

Franz cupped her cheek, and she leaned into the caress.

"Sing well," he said.

"Always."

After Franz left, Marla stripped off her shirt and jeans. She was wearing her old black dancer's tights and leotard, which showed off her figure very well indeed to Sophie, whose eyes widened a bit.

Marla chuckled. "I know," she said, "it's probably a bit revealing. But after all the rehearsals, I've decided that if I'm going to be skinning in and out of costumes all night I can't have bulky underclothes on. These will help me preserve at least an illusion of modesty, and a little bit of warmth as well."

She pulled out a stool from under the table, and sat down. Sophie draped a towel around Marla's shoulders. She opened the makeup case, leaned forward into the light, and began applying her makeup.

Friedrich von Logau looked up from his notepad and pulled out his pocket watch. He and his friends had reconvened at Walcha's after freshening their attire. He looked across the table to his friends.

"Well, if we desire to stand around outside the opera house so that we can be seen by all to be in the best company, we had best leave. Drink up."

They all drained their cups in unison, set them down, and got to their feet.

Simon didn't say anything when Gotthilf left. He looked around to see Pastor Gruber, Frau Marie and Fraulein Margarethe all sitting with Ursula, trying to comfort her. They could do more for her than he could. But his comfort would come from knowing that Schardius was being dealt with, so he slipped out of the room and out of the house and followed Gotthilf down the street.

✧   ✧   ✧

"Here you go, boys," Byron said as Gotthilf handed one of the signed warrants to Karl Honister and Kaspar Peltzer. "Sorry to pull you off your other cases, but we need Schardius' house and office searched today. You guys take his house, Gotthilf and I will take his office. Take a couple of patrolmen with you, and send word immediately if you find anything."

The pair of sergeants nodded and headed off.

Byron looked at Gotthilf. "Let's go."

"Lieutenant."

Just like the last time they heard that low-pitched voice, Byron smoothly shifted direction to the mouth of the alley as if that had been his destination all along. Gotthilf motioned to the patrolmen behind them to stop, then hurried to catch up to his partner.

Once in the alley, Demetrious faced them from under a stairway.

"It's been a while, Demetrious," Byron said. "What do you have for us?"

"The one-eyed man you asked about, he was not easy to find," Demetrious replied, folding his arms and pressing his fingertips together. "But find him I did, and followed him, too. The man, he is chasing someone, I think."

"Chasing?" Gotthilf asked. "What do you mean, chasing?"

"He follows someone at least part of every day."

"Who?" Gotthilf and Byron spoke in unison.

"Merchant fellow, name of Schardius."

"Schardius!" Byron said with the intonation of a curse.

"Are you sure?" Gotthilf demanded.

"Aye, I am sure."

The two detectives looked at each other. Neither one knew what to make of that.

"Thanks, Demetrious. We will owe you one for this."

Demetrious touched his forehead, and moved back down the alley without another word.

Simon looked down the alley when he passed it after the two detectives came out. He didn't see anything or anyone. He shrugged his shoulders, and hurried to keep the *Polizei* men in sight.

✧   ✧   ✧

Marla set the makeup brush down, and looked at herself in the mirror, turning her face from side to side and tilting it up and down. She gave a firm nod, and turned away from her table.

"How do I look, Sophie?"

Her dresser pushed through the gathering actresses and stared at her with furrowed brow.

"It still looks too heavy to me," she said, "but it looks as good as what you did yesterday for the dress rehearsal."

"Like I said last time," Marla responded, "it has to be heavy and exaggerated somewhat to be visible past the fifth row." She stood and put her hands on the small of her back, bending backwards to stretch stiffened muscles.

Schardius licked his lips, eyes almost bulging from his head from attempting to see more of Marla through the crack in the wall. To see her in such form-fitting clothing! If only he could have had a camera, to capture the scene of her bending and stretching in what was almost black painted nudity.

His breaths came shorter and faster, and he tugged at his culottes.

"Tell me again what this opera is," Gustav said as a servant helped him into his coat.

"Well, you remember when we went to see *Messiah* last winter?" Kristina replied.

"Yes." Gustav shrugged his shoulders to settle the coat, and the servant started fastening buttons.

"It's supposed to be like that," Kristina said, "only louder, longer, and with costumes."

"Hmm." Gustav checked the hang of the coat in the mirror, and waved the servant away. "And what is this about?"

Kristina looked to Ulrik. "King Arthur of Britain battles Saxons and Jutes for the safety of his people," the prince said, abbreviating the story to its barest essence.

"Hah!" Gustav snorted. "The Saxons will lose." The emperor's grudge against John Georg of Saxony was apparently still alive and well, even though the Saxon elector had been well and soundly trounced already and was now dead himself.

Gotthilf wiped his sleeve across his forehead. "What time is it, Byron?"

The up-timer looked at his wristwatch. "Bit after five o'clock."

"I'm not finding much."

"Me neither."

At that moment, Gotthilf opened a desk drawer. Nothing much in the drawer: pens, pins, a pair of scissors; the typical type of stuff that you'd expect to find in a desk drawer. He reached into the back of the drawer to see if there was anything else to be seen. His fingers ran into the back panel of the drawer a lot sooner than he'd expected.

Gotthilf pulled the drawer all the way out and set it on top of the desk. It was much shorter than he expected it to be, given the dimensions of the desk itself.

"Byron."

"Hmm?" His partner was poking through a storage closet.

"Come look at this."

Byron stepped over to the desk. "Odd. Where did it come from?"

"Top drawer, right side of the desk."

Byron looked at it for a minute, then walked around and pulled out the top drawer on the left side. It proved to be over twice as long as the right side drawer.

They looked at each other with raised eyebrows. Byron pulled a small flashlight out of his pocket, and knelt at the right side, shining the beam into the drawer space.

"My last set of batteries. I'm really gonna be bummed when they run down, because no one's got anything as small as an AA going yet. Hmm."

"Hmm, what?" Gotthilf responded.

"Solid wood back there. No lines, grooves, buttons, locks; nothing."

Byron flicked the light off and thought for a moment. Then he pushed the chair out of the way, lay down on his back and pushed into the leg well of the desk. Gotthilf heard the light flick on again.

"Aha!" came the muffled voice from under the desk.

"What did you find?" Gotthilf bent over and tried to see.

"Another drawer, only it opens out here. Now, if I can only figure out how to..." There was a *click*. "Gotcha! Come to papa." Gotthilf heard the sound of a drawer sliding out, then Byron held it out to him. "Take it."

Gotthilf took the other drawer and laid it on the desktop as well. Byron slid his body out from under the desk, then flipped up onto his feet and turned to examine his prize.

"Oh . . . my . . . God."

Something—some slight change in the light falling on the wall before him, or perhaps a slight noise—caught Schardius' attention. His head started to turn. There was a sudden rush of footsteps behind him, and a hard shoulder rammed into his shoulder blades, sending him into and through the laths of the wall.

For one very short sharp instant Schardius bewailed in his mind the loss of his splendid viewing point.

Then he was through the wall and falling.

The two detectives spread the papers out on the desk. Gotthilf couldn't believe his eyes. Every piece of paper from the hidden drawer connected to Marla Linder in some way. There were copies of newspaper articles that mentioned her or her performances that went back to when she first appeared in Magdeburg in late 1633. There were copies of broadsheets with her song lyrics, including the latest one, the one that had made the CoC run their printing presses almost nonstop for a couple of weeks.

The last two items were in Byron's hands, and had been the cause of his exclamation. One was a picture of Marla, from a sketch that had been printed in one of the newspaper articles. The other was the article that announced the performance schedule for the new opera, with today's date circled in red ink.

The papers were trembling a bit in Byron's hands. Gotthilf looked at his partner's face. His jaw muscles were bunched, and the muscle tic in his left cheek was twitching, which sent Gotthilf's sense of alarm soaring.

"What is it, Byron?"

"We need to find this scumbag, and now."

Simon had been waiting outside the Schardius factorage for what seemed like forever. It had been at least two hours, judging by the movement of the sun in the sky. If they didn't come out pretty soon, he was going to have to run to Frau Zenzi's to sweep. He didn't want to do that until he knew what was going on. Obviously something was, or they wouldn't have spent all this time inside the building when Schardius wasn't even there, according to one of the clerks.

He finally started walking back and forth across the front of the building, counting steps. "...thirty-seven, thirty-eight, thirty-nine, forty." Turn about and walk the other direction. "One, two, three, four..."

It was in his third circuit that he saw something. It was lying in a low spot right beside the steps up to the front door of the building. He stopped counting and walked over to pick it up.

A glove. Pink, with purple and green bands across the back of it. Made for a right hand, so it wouldn't fit him. No luck there.

Simon was still standing there turning the glove this way and that when the door burst open and he was almost run down by the two detectives.

Byron had barely let Gotthilf stuff the papers into an envelope and put them in his jacket before he hurtled out of the office.

"Hermann," Gotthilf ordered the patrolman as they ran by, "no one in the office until we say differently."

"Yes, Sergeant," followed them out the door.

Gotthilf barely avoided running over the person standing outside the building, then he did run into Byron who had stopped short.

"Simon!" Byron barked as he grabbed something out of the boy's hand. "Where did you get that?"

The boy pointed to a spot beside the steps leading to the building entrance. "Right there."

"Great find, kid. I'll tell you how great later." Byron twisted and whistled shrilly, then yelled, "Cab!"

A one-horse light cart pulled up. The two detectives bounded up into it. "The new opera house, now, and *schnell!*"

Simon stared after the rapidly moving cart, jaw agape. What had that all been about, and what did the glove mean? Did it have anything to do with Hans?

Well, if they were in such a hurry to get to the opera house, maybe that's where the answers were.

Simon started trotting down the street, headed for the nearest bridge into the Neustadt.

✧　　✧　　✧

"Can't this thing move any faster?" Byron demanded of the driver. He began cursing in a stream, seemingly without breathing.

"You going to tell me what is going on that has you so worked up?" Gotthilf asked.

Byron broke off the curses long enough to say, "That bastard Schardius has been stalking Marla. That's what all those papers are about. They're his collection on her. And this," he held up the glove, "this is her glove. I recognize it. No one else in Magdeburg has anything like this, and there's no way she would have been anywhere near his office to drop it. So he had it, a trophy, which is also part of a stalker's pattern. Somehow he lost it outside his office, and we're just lucky that Simon found it for us."

"So why are we going to the opera hall?"

"Because Schardius bankrolled the opera production, according to Marla. He won't miss the premiere performance. And if he's stalking her, he for sure will be there tonight."

"Point," Gotthilf replied. "He will want to see what his money bought."

"In more ways than one," and Byron resumed cursing.

A horrible thought occurred to Gotthilf. "Peltzer's dead street-walker..."

The same thoughts ran through both their minds. Long dark hair...was asked to sing....

Now the curses were being uttered antiphonally from both sides of the cart.

"Can't your horse move any faster?" Gotthilf demanded of the driver.

Chapter 65

Friedrich and the others stood outside the Royal and Imperial Opera Hall for some time, making themselves visible to the incoming select premiere night crowd, posturing and engaging in what could only be called witty repartee. Their breath frosted as they spoke, and they laughed at that, accusing each other of being filled with nothing but hot air.

Before long the sun began to dip below the horizon, and the air definitely began to chill. The four friends looked at each other, and with nods they moved as one up the steps and through the central door of the opera hall.

The foyer area, what Friedrich had heard an up-timer call a lobby, ran the full width of the building. Foyer was not a grand enough word to him to describe the room. It seemed more of a gallery, with doors all along the west side into the various seating areas of the auditorium, high ceilings, and three large crystal chandeliers.

The four of them milled around a bit, until Franz Sylwester literally stumbled over Friedrich's walking stick with an "Oof!"

"Steady, there," Friedrich said as he grabbed Franz's elbow to keep him from sprawling on the floor.

A moment later, Franz was stable again, brushing his hands down the front of his royal blue short-waisted jacket. "My thanks," he said.

"Aren't you supposed to be in there?" Friedrich motioned to the auditorium with his head.

"In a few minutes, perhaps, but Frau Amber has me out here greeting all the big name guests," he leaned over and lowered his voice, "especially those who gave money for the hall or the production."

"Ah," Friedrich said, as they all exchanged knowing smiles. The power of gold, indeed.

"But listen," Franz said, "would you like to see behind the curtains for just a moment or two?"

Friedrich didn't need to look at his friends. "Of course!"

Franz shared a conspiratorial grin. "Then come with me."

Gotthilf threw a couple of bills to the driver and tumbled off the cart in Byron's wake. He was surprised to see Honister walking toward them across the opera house plaza.

"Hey, Karl," Byron said.

"Lieutenant," Karl responded with a nod. "I was on my way to find you when I saw you pull up here. What's to do?"

"According to our informant," Byron said, walking fast, "our one-eyed dude is around here somewhere. Seems he's been tailing Schardius, who we think is inside." He jerked his head at the opera hall.

"Schardius? Why?" Honister seemed mystified by that revelation.

"We were hoping you could tell us," Gotthilf replied, trotting to keep up with his long-legged partner.

"I have no idea," Honister said, "unless..."

The detective fell silent for about three steps, mind obviously racing.

Honister finally looked up again. "Only one thing makes sense," he began. "The fire, the murder and robbery, and the explosion were all aimed at the hospital expansion project. We could never come up with a motive for trying to destroy the project itself. It is popular, and it is needed; destroying it just didn't make any sense. But what if they weren't aiming at the project? What if they were aiming at the backers of the project?"

Gotthilf turned that thought around and over and around in his mind, examining it from every angle. The more he thought about it, the more he became convinced that Honister was right.

"And Schardius is involved with the group that got the contract for the hospital expansion?" Byron asked.

"His name is not on any of the proposals or contracts, no," Honister admitted, who was starting to sound winded keeping the pace. "But it appears to be common knowledge that he provided much of the initial financing for it. I heard that from more than one source, including Mayor Gericke himself."

"If he is the 'money man,' as up-timers might put it," Gotthilf said, "then taking him down would probably destroy the consortium that has the contract for the expansion." Byron gave him a questioning look. "If Schardius dies, his money gets tied up in his estate. The committee that oversees execution of wills will allow expenses to be paid to keep his household solvent and for day-to-day expenses in his business. Whether a project like this would be included in that day-to-day category would depend on the decisions of the committee. And the committee monitors the estate until the heirship is determined and validated, which could take anywhere from weeks to months."

"Even if he's contractually bound to provide it?"

"That depends on how the contract is written and on how the committee would interpret the contract. But even if it was ruled that the money had to be provided under the terms of a contract," Gotthilf finished, "just a significant delay in receiving it could be enough to take the project down."

"Lawyers." Byron said the word like it was a curse. Gotthilf decided that now was not the time to tell Byron that his older brother was studying at Jena to become a lawyer.

Byron turned back to Honister.

"Makes sense to me. Keep an eye out for One-Eye, and arrest him if you see him." Honister stopped at the bottom of the steps to the opera house portico. "And arrest Schardius if you see him, too." That was thrown over Byron's shoulder as he started up the steps two at a time. Gotthilf huffed and puffed as he trailed behind.

Franz unlocked a single door set off to one side of the foyer, motioned Friedrich and the others through, and closed it behind them.

"This way," Franz said.

Friedrich fell into line behind the others as they went down some stairs and then along a dimly lit hallway with doors appearing along either side. "Where are we?" he heard one of his friends ask.

"This runs along below the lower bank of the box seats," Franz replied from the front of the line. "It will take us to the service area under the stage, and from there we can climb up to the backstage area without being seen by the audience."

And so it proved. The hallway opened into a very open space, with pillars interspersed across it that supported the massive beams that underlay the stage. Various pieces of equipment could be seen around the perimeter of the space, most shrouded in canvas. Stairways could be seen in various locations.

"This way," Franz repeated. He led them to a stairway at the side of the space. The door at the top opened to the backstage.

The four of them just stopped in amazement to watch. Several people in bright costumes stood in front of them, chattering away in low tones. Young men and women dressed in muted brown bustled around, adjusting scenery and furniture, or carrying items from one side of the stage to the other while the curtain remained down.

One very large fellow in a resplendent costume and holding what appeared to be a very large sword stood near a small podium-style desk, laughing with Frau Amber and a short down-timer woman wearing some kind of contraption that covered one ear and had a short arm that curved around in front of her face.

"That's the stage manager's headset," Franz muttered in his ear, obviously having noticed his interest. "It connects to the auditorium intercom—kind of like radio, only with wires. She gives instructions through the microphone to the people running the lights and curtains."

Interesting. First electric lights, and now this. Friedrich wondered what other innovations were coming to theaters because of Grantville. *Electric trap-doors, maybe?*

Crash!

All the actresses jumped and several screamed when one of the side walls seemed to explode and a man landed on one of the makeup tables. Everyone moved back as the man struggled to get to his feet.

Marla stepped forward. "Herr Schardius! What are you doing?"

"Isn't it obvious, ladies?" a mocking voice said from inside the space Schardius had been in. Then came a shrill, high-pitched laugh. "He was peeping through the wall at you!"

Chapter 66

Angry voices began to rise. Schardius was very shaken. For just a moment after he gained his feet, he stared around at the angry women who were starting to shout at him. He gave his head a sharp shake, and, knowing he was exposed now, pulled his pistol from his jacket pocket.

"Shut up!" he barked, gratified to see faces go pale and voices go silent. "Nobody moves, nobody says anything!"

Despite his orders, one person did move. Marla Linder stepped forward until she was at the front of the crowd, shielding those behind her.

"What do you want, Schardius?" she demanded fiercely.

His thinking crystalized, snapped into sharp focus.

"You."

Her eyes widened with surprise, possibly shock. But if anything, her expression grew fiercer still. "I don't think so!"

"You will come with me, or I start shooting," Schardius snarled. He grabbed one nearby young woman, barely more than a girl, pulled her in front of his body and stuck the pistol in her ear. "Shall I start with this one?"

"Wait!" Marla said. Schardius exulted to hear a note of uncertainty in her voice. He said nothing, only cocked the hammer of the pistol.

The young woman was trembling, and a smell of urine suddenly filled the air.

"All right," Marla conceded. "Just don't hurt Sophie, and let them go."

Byron and Gotthilf pushed their way through the crowd on the portico and made their way through the doors into the foyer of the opera hall. They stopped inside the doorway, craning their heads as they tried to look over the crowd. Being taller, Byron was more successful at that than his partner. After a minute or so, he said, "There!" and pointed toward a group of people near one of the main doors into the auditorium.

They both held their badges up and began making their way toward the spot where Amber was. "Clear the way! Make a hole, people!" Byron shouted.

"Official *Polizei* business!" Gotthilf called out.

Between them, the crowd in front of them thinned out and they made their way to Amber, who was starting to move to one side with everyone else. Byron grabbed her by the elbow.

"It's you we need to see, Amber. We've got a security issue we need your help with. Where can we talk?"

Byron's urgency clearly registered on Amber. "This way," she said, and led them through a door guarded by ushers. "This is one of the hallways leading to the lowest level of boxes."

They walked down the hall until they were past the last of the box entrances. At the very end of the hall, Amber turned in front of a door and faced them. "This is as private as we can get at the moment. What is this all about?"

"Has Andreas Schardius made advances to Marla or any of the other women in the production?" Byron asked harshly.

There was a sudden explosion of shrieking women from the Women's Dressing Room. "He came through the wall." "He's got a gun!" As the others tried to get them to calm down, Friedrich caught a glimpse of what looked like Frau Marla, dressed very oddly, going through the door through which he and the others had entered the backstage area from the basement. She was followed by someone in a dark cloak which swirled just enough to show something glinting in the hand directly behind her back. The cloak swirled back, but Friedrich saw the cloaked figure's shoulder make a sharp movement which was followed by Frau Marla jerking almost as if she were reacting to a jab.

Friedrich's thoughts raced for just a moment, then he turned from his friends and moved with stealth to another door to the basement. The door was in a shadowed nook, so he could open it without a betraying blaze of light warning whoever was below. He had to wait for a lull in the conversations and other noise, but after a moment or two one happened and he slipped through the door.

Closing the door with care, Friedrich eased down the stairs, listening to steps receding across the floor of the basement area. When he got to the bottom of the stairs he stepped to the shadows and followed, moving on his toes for speed and quietness.

"Stop here," Schardius said as the entered a pool of light under a single fixture. "Turn around." He studied Marla's face; the heightened color, the widened pupils, her deep breaths.

"Why are you doing this?" he heard her ask. He said nothing, simply caressed her cheek, and let his fingers trail down her neck and across the skin revealed by the scoop neck of her garment—her oh-so-revealing garment.

Marla flinched at the first touch, then stood ramrod stiff as he poked the gun barrel into her stomach.

"Why?" Schardius finally replied. "Because I have wanted you for twenty years, my dear."

"What are you talking about?" Marla demanded. "Twenty years ago I was three years old, and I for sure wasn't anywhere you were!"

"*La Cecchina*," the man said. "The songbird of Florence. That was you twenty years ago. I was never able to have her, but now you are here, and you I shall have."

Friedrich slunk to a pillar and peered around its edge carefully. Frau Marla and her abductor stood in a pool of light. He could see clearly now that the man was holding a pistol in his right hand while his left was touching her face. And enough of the abductor's face was in view that Friedrich could identify the man: Andreas Schardius. That rocked him back a bit.

"You're crazy!" Marla exclaimed.

Friedrich pursed his lips and shook his head. That was perhaps not the wisest thing that Frau Marla could have said. Truthful, without a doubt, but definitely imprudent in this situation. He pondered what to do. Running back upstairs to get help would leave Frau Marla with no immediate succor, and who knew what the madman would do?

But what could he do down here alone, against a madman with a pistol? He pressed himself against the pillar, and thought rapidly. Meanwhile, the conversation continued on the other side of the pillar.

"I suggest you keep a civil and contrite tongue in your head, woman." That was said in a level and calm tone that nonetheless caused the hair on Friedrich's neck to stand on end. He didn't know about Frau Marla, but Schardius was definitely putting some fear into him.

"I'm a married woman," Marla said. "I'm not beautiful. I'm big and clumsy. Why do you want me? I'll never be an ornament for your house, or your arm, or a court. Why are you doing this?"

"Your voice," Schardius said, finally exhibiting some passion. "I want your voice."

Friedrich looked around the pillar again in time to see Schardius first stroke Marla's neck and throat, then wrap her hair in his fist and pull her head to his for a brutal kiss.

Marla placed her hands against Schardius' chest and pushed with all her might. After a moment, she broke free, leaving more than a little of her hair in the madman's grasp. She raised the back of her hand to her mouth. It came away bloody, from where the "kiss" had broken the skin of her lips against her own teeth.

"You're a madman," Marla hissed. "You're not a man; you're an animal, a crazy insane thing!"

Schardius backhanded her with his left hand. Marla staggered a step, and Friedrich winced. At least Schardius hadn't used the pistol to hit her.

"Another word and you are dead," Schardius said as he straightened his arm with the pistol aimed directly at Frau Marla's head.

Amber blinked. "I've been worried about that, but Marla says he hasn't approached her."

"Byron thinks Herr Schardius is stalking Frau Linder," Gotthilf said.

"He had a stalker's file in a hidden drawer in his office desk," Byron explained. "And we found this outside his office building." He held up the glove.

Now it was Amber who turned pale. She obviously recognized the glove as well as Byron had. It was distinctive, Gotthilf admitted. Amber was made of strong stuff, though, and carried on by asking, "What do we do?"

"Is Schardius here yet?" Byron's tone shifted from harsh to gunmetal hard.

"I haven't seen him, but I wouldn't necessarily see him tonight. He's supposed to be in the audience, not backstage."

"Is Marla here?"

"Yes, she came in early. She's already backstage."

"We need to be there *now*!" Byron's head started swiveling, looking for doors.

Amber turned, pulled a key-ring from her pocket and opened the door she was standing in front of. "Come on."

They passed through the door, and she locked it behind them. Gotthilf looked around. All he could see were wires and cables, curtains and panels, and people scurrying around.

"This way," Amber motioned to them. "She was in the dressing room when I left her about half an hour ago over on stage right." She snorted at their confusion. "The other side of the stage. Now come on."

Amber led them across the stage behind the main curtain, into a loud crowd of actors and stage hands. It took some time to get everyone to settle down and get a coherent story out of the shaken women who had been in the dressing room.

"You're sure it was Herr Schardius?" Byron at length demanded.

Universal agreement from all the women, loud, and in some cases obscene.

"Where's Marla?" was his next question.

It didn't take long to determine that she wasn't in the crowd. Someone ran back to the dressing room. Gotthilf could see both Byron and Amber becoming more and more unhappy that Marla was not to be found.

"Now what?" Byron demanded. "Where else do we look?"

"I don't..." Amber began.

Desperate, Friedrich grasped the only idea that had come to him. He took a firm grip on his walking stick and twisted a metal collar that circled the shaft of the stick just below the handle, then thrust a hand into a pocket, pulled out a big USE fifty cent piece, and tossed it off to his right. It struck a wall and fell to the floor, where it clattered around for a bit.

Schardius reacted to the noise by swinging the pistol that direction. Friedrich drew the narrow-bladed sword from the stick that was its sheath and flowed around the pillar with it raised. He slashed the sword down on Schardius' wrist.

Schardius cried out and the pistol fired. Friedrich interposed between himself between Schardius and Marla, sword raised and ready to slash or stab as needed.

They all heard the muffled sound. Most looked around curiously, but Byron and Gotthilf both jerked.

"That was a shot!" Byron hissed to Amber. "From below us. Basement?"

Amber didn't say anything, but hurried over to a door near the back of the wall and flung it open. Byron and Gotthilf drew their weapons and started down the stairs into the dimly lit basement. Byron wasted no time, but hurried down as quickly as he could. Gotthilf followed at a slower pace.

"You . . . you . . ." Spittle was running from Schardius' mouth, as he wrapped his left hand around his right wrist and started to lift the pistol again. Friedrich prepared himself to lunge.

At that moment, the door to the stairs banged open, and feet thundered on the stairs.

"Marla!" a man called out urgently. "Marla!"

"Down here, Byron!" Marla called back from behind Friedrich. He didn't take his eyes from Schardius, whose own eyes where shifting right and left. As the feet hit the basement floor, Schardius darted into the hallway opening through which Friedrich and the others had come not many minutes before.

Friedrich lowered his sword and spared a quick glance for Frau Marla.

"Are you all right?"

"I am now," she said, standing up straight and relaxing her hands from the claws they had formed.

"Marla!" Byron called out. "Marla!"

"Down here, Byron!" they heard the answer.

At that, Gotthilf hurried down to follow his partner to the

pool of light where Marla was standing, alongside a man with a sword.

"You, drop the sword," Byron barked, zeroing his automatic at the bridge of the man's nose.

"Byron, don't!" Marla said. "He's a friend—he was protecting me!"

It took a moment, then Byron lowered the pistol.

"Okay. It was Schardius, then?"

"Yes." Marla sounded a bit shaken, and Gotthilf didn't blame her. "He went that way." She pointed to an opening.

"It's a hall that will bring you out in the foyer again," the man added.

"Great. You stay here. We'll be back."

Amber shut the door behind the two policemen, and turned to face the crowd of actors and stage hands. "All of you, just shut up and get back to your places. Now!"

Such was the force of her personality and the habit of obedience that most of them did so.

Amber beckoned to Frau Frontilia. "Is Franz Sylwester backstage?"

"I think so," the stage manager replied.

"Send him here."

Schardius made his way down the hall. He still had his little flashlight, but he didn't think he could crank it up and hold his gun with his wrist cut, so he trusted to his memory. From his recent excursions in the basement, he knew the hallway had no obstacles before he reached the stairs. Once he made it to the foyer, he was well on his way to freedom.

"Franz!" Marla shouted. She flew to her husband's arms, and he enfolded her in a hug so tight and strong that Friedrich almost expected to see them merge into a single body.

Frau Amber Higham appeared at Friedrich's side. She was cursing bitterly and with great fury, a mixture of American, German, and it sounded like Spanish. She wasn't repeating herself, which impressed him. She also rattled off some curses he had never heard before, which also impressed him. Those he made mental note of.

She finally had to stop and draw a breath. She panted for a few seconds, then took a deep sigh and seemed to settle down. She turned to Marla and held out her hands.

"Marla, I have to apologize. I thought Schardius was just a typical producer looking for some thrills. It almost killed me when Byron said he was a stalker type, and he was fixated on you."

"No one knew, Amber," Marla replied, detaching herself from her husband and taking the other woman's hands. "No one could have guessed. I thought he was just a creep; just a watcher."

"Instead he abducts you," Frau Amber said, enfolding the younger woman in another embrace.

"I will bear witness to that," Friedrich spoke up, "assuming they capture him. Plus assault, battery, and threats to kill Frau Marla. The man," he concluded in a very dry tone of voice as he handed his coat to Frau Marla to hide her oh-so-worse-than-nude attire, "is not sane."

Byron pulled out his flashlight. "We don't have time to look for the light switches. Come on."

The two of them followed the dim yellow spot as it tracked across the floor. After a few steps, Gotthilf said, "Blood spots."

"Yep," Byron replied in a satisfied tone. "If nothing else, we can trail the bastard with that."

Neither of them spoke more, intent on the task at hand.

Schardius heard the murmur of voices behind him, looked over his shoulder, and saw the dim little spot of light bobbing toward him down the hallway. His foot struck the first step in the stairs, and he almost fell over. He turned, held his pistol in both hands, and pulled the trigger once.

Bam!

He turned and hurried up the stairs as quickly as he could.

Amber released the hug and returned Marla to her husband.

"Now to go upstairs and break the news that we have to cancel tonight's performance."

Marla broke out of Franz's embrace and faced them all with her hands on her hips.

"Amber Higham, I don't care if you are the director, if you think that I've come this far and worked this hard on this part to shut down because of something stupid like this, think again! I'm not hurt, and if I don't do something to lightning rod the mad out of me, I'll explode. On with the show!"

Behind Marla, Franz had worry in his eyes, but he was smiling. He spotted Friedrich looking at him, and he shrugged and spread his hands in an unmistakable "What are you going to do?" signal.

Amber took a long hard look at Marla. "Well, okay, if you're sure..."

"I've never been more sure of anything in my life, except marrying Franz," Marla replied. "Trust me."

"Okay," Amber said after another hard look at Marla. "If you're that certain, then let's get upstairs and get this show on the road!"

The sound of a shot from the hallway spurred them on.

The two detectives ducked to each side of the hall at the flash from the other end of the hall. Byron turned off the flashlight.

"Black powder gun," Byron said quietly.

"Probably H and K six-shooter," Gotthilf replied. "Sounded like a forty-four caliber, like mine."

They listened, and only heard the sound of steps receding.

"Slow and careful," Byron said. He took the flashlight, turned it on and flashed it down the hall for a moment, then shut it down again. "No obstacles, looks like he's gone up the stairs."

"Right."

They made their way down the hall, hugging the walls on each side.

Schardius made his way to the top of the stairs. He stopped for the barest moment to try to catch his breath, then turned the door handle. It moved, and he peered around the edge of the door. No one was near, and he slipped out of the door and across the foyer as quickly as he could.

Freedom! was his thought as he burst through the door into the portico and started down the steps.

Chapter 67

Karl Honister looked over at the local patrolman who had shown up on his rounds perhaps a quarter hour earlier, and was hanging around the plaza watching the latecomers hurrying for the door, mostly members of the *Hoch-adel*. It was growing darker, and the moon wasn't very high in the sky yet.

"So, Phillip," Karl said, "have you seen the emperor yet?"

"Today?" the patrolman replied. "No, Sergeant Honister. Not yet, at any rate."

Honister pulled out his pocket watch and held it up so the setting sun shone on it.

"It's 6:15, so the opera is going to start late. It wouldn't be prudent to start without Gustav in his seat."

Phillip laughed, just as the big outside lights mounted on the front of the opera house turned on with a loud *click*.

Amber led the charge back up the stairs to the backstage. As soon as they were all through the door at the head of the stairs, she slammed it.

"I want that door bolted, barred, and blocked up," she announced to all and sundry. "Pile stuff in front of it until no one can get it open from the other side." She pointed to the backstage crew dressed in brown. "Now! Move it, people."

Brown-shirted stage crew coalesced from all of the backstage area, and within a couple of minutes they had moved some heavy furniture not being used in this production in front of the door.

While this was going on, Amber turned to Marla and looked at her in the better light. She lightly touched the singer's left cheek. "Okay, your makeup is smudged, and you've got a small scratch that's bled some there. You'd best get back to the dressing area and repair that, then get dressed for the first scene."

Marla handed Friedrich's coat back to him, and turned and moved with speed in that direction. Amber turned to the stage manager and they had a low-voiced conversation.

Friedrich looked around, all of a sudden realizing that he hadn't seen Gronow, Seelbach, and Plavius. He looked to Franz and opened his mouth, but Franz beat him to it.

"I had your friends led to their seats before I came downstairs. Now I must get back to the orchestra, so I'll take you with me. People will start getting restless if we don't have something going."

Franz's eyes got very serious, and he placed his hands on Friedrich's shoulders. "My friend, I have no words. What you did down there..." Franz's voice wavered a bit, "...that means more to me than you will ever know or I will ever be able to express. Thank you."

Friedrich didn't try to downplay what Franz was saying. He just gave a solemn nod and placed his right hand on top of Franz's.

They stood that way for a long moment; then Franz dropped his hands, turned, and linked arms with Friedrich. "And now, let me escort you to your seat."

They both saw the flare of light as the door at the top of the stairs was opened.

"Come on!" Byron flicked on his flashlight, heedless of the risk, and they rushed down the hall and hurtled up the stairs.

They burst through the door in time to see one of the outer doors just settling in its door frame.

Schardius froze for a moment on the steps when the lights came on. There was so much light! He'd been counting on the darkness to hide him.

He gave his head a hard shake, and continued down the steps.

It had all gone so wrong! All his desires, all his plans, all lying in the plaster dust on the dressing room floor.

He would never survive this, he knew. Not in Magdeburg, at

any rate. His name and reputation would not just be smeared, they would be burnt in the fires of gossip and ridicule, until they were nothing but a memory.

But Magdeburg was just one of many cities in Europe. If he could just get to the warehouse, he had money there, and Ernst could get him away. He had money, he had connections. He could start over. Maybe in Vienna.

He hit the bottom of the steps and started running. One part of his mind cursed Marla Linder as his feet pounded the plaza pavement; one part of it mourned her.

Honister looked around at the sound of cursing and yelling people. A man broke free from the flow of opera-goers going up the steps. It looked like—it was—Schardius. He headed that direction, holding up his hand.

"Halt! Master Andreas Schardius, I arrest you—*gun!*"

The sudden sight of the pistol in the merchant's hands being aimed in his direction tightened every muscle in Honister's lower abdomen and groin, and raised his voice at least two octaves. His shout echoed off the surrounding buildings, and was probably heard clearly on the other side of the Big Ditch and its walls.

Schardius fired one shot, but Honister was already ducking and twisting to pull out his own pistol. And now he bitterly repented that he had not followed Sergeant Hoch's lead and moved up from a .32 to a .44 with more shots. Five just wasn't enough in a situation like this.

Franz released Friedrich's arm at the end of his row. Friedrich stepped across feet to the empty seat between Gronow and Plavius.

"Where have you been?" Plavius demanded, not bothering to hold down his voice amid the other conversations going on around them.

Friedrich didn't answer right away, settling his walking stick between his knees and punching Gronow on the leg.

"Johann, pass me your flask of schnapps, and don't try to tell me you don't have it."

With a sigh, Gronow pulled a silver flask from an inside jacket pocket and handed it to Friedrich. Friedrich took off the cap and drank two big swallows before he turned back to Plavius.

"Where have I been? That's a tale for later tonight."

❖   ❖   ❖

Byron and Gotthilf burst out the door onto the portico and went down the steps at a reckless rate of speed, risking falling or worse in the desire to catch up with the fleeing Schardius.

"Come on, Karl!" Gotthilf yelled as they rushed by him.

"Schardius, drop your gun and put up your hands!" Byron yelled from in front of them, his long legs shortening the distance with every stride.

Schardius responded by twisting his body and squeezing off another shot as he ran. No one saw where it went, but it slowed everyone down for a step or two.

Ciclope's ears perked up. From all the yells, that was Schardius running toward him being chased by all those men. He burst from the shadows by the Royal Academy of Music building, then simply had to stand and watch as Schardius ran by him, with four policemen hot on his heels.

Ciclope cursed bitterly. A lost opportunity, but if he had shot at Schardius, it would have been impossible to explain to the *Polizei* later, especially since he would have been shooting in their general direction as well. He doubted that they would have been restrained about shooting back at him.

He calmed himself, and began running through his options. If the *Polizei* captured Schardius, there wasn't much he could do about that. But if Schardius managed to elude them, where would he go? Easy answer, Ciclope thought to himself—the warehouse. The place was stout enough to be a fortress, and who knows what all he had stashed there.

Ciclope pushed his own pistol back into his pocket, and headed for the western bridge across the ditch into the *Altstadt*.

"Halt!"

Captain David Beatty held up his hand, and the Marine detail around the emperor's car stopped. This perforce caused the car to stop.

Erling Ljungberg and Baldur Norddahl stopped their horses alongside his.

"What's toward?" Baldur asked, trying to find a comfortable position on the saddle.

"Gunfire," Beatty said. "That way," motioning to the north and a bit east; almost the direction in which they were traveling.

There came a few more shots, and this time they all heard it.

"Sergeant MacDonald," Beatty snapped, "front and center!"

A large red-haired man stepped out of the Marine detail and saluted. "Aye, sir!"

"Take Private MacDougal with you, go find out what's what up there, and bring the word back to us."

"Aye, sir!"

The sergeant saluted again, beckoned to another Marine, then led off down the boulevard, unslinging his rifle as he did so.

"Trouble?" Ljungberg asked.

"I doubt it." Beatty's broadly accented tones were calm, almost serene. "But I'll not risk the emperor or the princess. Or the prince, for that matter."

Baldur grunted in agreement with that last.

"We will bide right here until we know what's happening," the captain finished. "And if I don't hear word, or if I don't like what I hear, then we fall back on the palace."

Ljungberg looked back at the car. "How easy is it to turn that thing around?"

"No need." The captain laughed. "Harold can drive it in reverse almost as fast as a horse will run."

Ljungberg pursed his lips as more shots sounded from ahead of them.

Not for the first time in his life, Gotthilf cursed his lack of height. Schardius was running like a frightened prey animal, with long-legged Byron following like a sight hound with quarry in his gaze, even though Schardius shot back at them at least twice more. They swept east at a rapid pace, and it didn't matter how fast Gotthilf moved his legs, he lost ground with every step.

"I didn't ask to be short," he panted. "It's not fair."

"All right, people!" Amber called out after Marla returned with makeup freshened and costume straightened. "Get in your places, and get set. We're waiting on the emperor. I don't know why he's late, but it doesn't matter. Our job is to be ready. As soon as he's here, we begin. Break a leg!"

Amber went out the door that led to the stage right lower box seats hallway. It only took her a couple of minutes to make her way around to the front foyer, then through the main doors and down to the railing surrounding the orchestra.

"Franz!" she hissed. He turned slightly and leaned toward her from where he stood at the front of the orchestra.

"The emperor should be here soon. Keep an eye on the imperial box. When the imperial butt hits the imperial seat cushion, you start the overture. Got it?"

Franz flashed a smile, then turned back to the orchestra.

Amber straightened and looked around the house. It was filling nicely. Most of the box seats were occupied. The imperial box was the only one that was totally empty. The wine was starting to flow in some of those boxes, which worried her for a moment. But then she decided that Marla and Dieter could overpower anyone in the auditorium—could probably overpower all of them combined. A small smile appeared at the thought of someone trying to outshout Marla's voice. Let 'em try.

Simon heard the gunshots as he stood on the east bridge from the Altstadt to the Neustadt. He had been staring at the water in the Big Ditch as it rolled under the bridge for some time. Now he looked up at the sound of the shots. It sounded like they were coming toward him. He moved off of the crest of the bridge toward the north shore, craning his neck to try and see what was going on.

Schardius fired back at them one last time as he ran. It was a shot fired half-wildly, but by a stroke of bad luck the bullet struck the leg of Phillip the patrolman. He fell with a shout of pain in front of Gotthilf.

Gotthilf slowed, but Karl Honister knelt beside the patrolman and waved Gotthilf on. "I'll take care of him, you catch up to your partner."

Finding new reserves of strength, Gotthilf stepped up his pace.

Simon heard running steps coming toward him. He looked to the west, and could see a man running for the bridge, with another man apparently chasing him.

Simon moved to one side to clear the way, but the first man reached out and grabbed the corner of the bridge railing and swung himself around in a tight arc, which brought him into a collision with Simon.

"Oof!"

They both went down. The man was panting hard, and he swung and scrabbled at Simon, trying to win back to his feet. Something hard connected with Simon's head, and he saw stars.

The chasing man stopped at the foot of the bridge.

"Stop running, Schardius! Throw down the gun. It's over."

Simon recognized that cold voice. It was Lieutenant Chieske. He looked up, and through the fading stars he recognized the man who crashed into him as Andreas Schardius. But not the smooth, urbane, in-control Master Schardius. This wild-eyed man had disheveled hair, disarrayed, ripped, and stained clothes. His hands trembled.

"No," Schardius panted as he scrambled to his feet. "No," and the pistol in his hand began to rise as he started to back away.

Gotthilf was panting as he drew even with Byron. They were spread out, facing the wild-eyed Schardius, whose pistol was wavering between them. Gotthilf's gun was rock steady in his hands, for all that his chest was moving like a bellows.

"Give it up, Schardius," Byron said, edging forward a half-step. As Schardius' pistol aimed toward his partner, Gotthilf eased forward himself.

"It's over, Herr Schardius," Gotthilf said. "Give us the gun."

"No!"

Simon reached out and grabbed Schardius' leg, wrapping his one arm around the man's ankle and pulling his own body on top of the foot.

Schardius shouted as he tried to move, and discovered he was tied to that spot. Simon could see the pistol begin to waver towards him. He scrunched his eyes closed, and hunched his shoulders.

Bam! Bam! Bam!

Several shots went off in almost the same instant. Simon flinched, and Schardius yanked his foot out from the boy's hold. Flat on his back, Simon saw the merchant stagger back to the opposite side wall of the bridge and raise his pistol one more time.

Bam! Bam!

Simon heard two final shots from behind him. Schardius jerked backwards, overbalanced as the side wall caught him behind the thighs, and fell into the Big Ditch without a sound.

Lieutenant Chieske cursed and the detectives rushed to the railing, guns leading the way. Simon shakily pushed his way to his feet and moved to stand beside them. He looked over the side wall to see Schardius floating in the Big Ditch, face down, arms spread out like wings. After watching the body for long moments, with no movement other than the ripples of the water, it finally came to Simon that Schardius was dead.

At that thought, the cold hand that had wrapped Simon's heart since he had seen Hans' body that morning began to loosen and thaw. Quiet tears tickled down his cheeks, but there was a smile of sorts on his face. Justice had been done, in his mind, and he had played some small part in it. It was enough.

"Simon?" Sergeant Hoch said as he put his pistol away under his jacket. "What are you doing here?"

"I was following you to the opera house," Simon replied. "I wanted to see you arrest Herr Schardius."

"Well, that's twice you've been in the right place at the right time," Lieutenant Chieske said, resting a hand on Simon's shoulder. "But let that be enough. You almost got shot this time."

"It was worth it," Simon murmured. "For Hans."

Baldur came back from the side of the car, where he had been answering questions from the occupants inside.

"They want to know how much longer we're going to be sitting here," he reported.

"Well, I would say 'As long as it takes,'" Captain Beatty said, "but since I can see Sergeant MacDonald and Private MacDougal returning, I think not much longer."

The two Marines walked up to the captain's horse. The fact that they had their rifles slung from their shoulders was an indication of how peaceful they felt the situation really was. They came to a halt, and saluted.

"Well?" The captain's voice was dry.

"Och, 'twas not so much of a much," Sergeant MacDonald reported. "Ain domned fool, a murderer and a rapist to boot, decided to play at guns with Lieutenant Chieske and Sergeant Hoch." The sergeant's wide grin exposed two missing teeth. Some of the Marines had personal experience with those two members of the *Polizei*, and had a healthy respect for them as a result.

"Ah," the captain replied. "I assume the fool is no longer a problem?"

"Nae problem a'tall," MacDonald chuckled, "seeing as how he is full of large holes and floating in the Big Ditch."

"Take your places, then," the captain ordered. He looked back at the car, then raised his hand and pointed ahead.

"Forward."

There was a stir in the auditorium as Emperor Gustav, Princess Kristina, and Prince Ulrik filed into the imperial box. Franz raised his baton. All the orchestra members' eyes were instantly on him, and instruments were raised to play.

"Tell me again why I'm coming to this," Gustav muttered.

"Because Frau Marla is singing in it," Kristina replied. "I like her."

Gustav looked over her head at Ulrik.

The prince shrugged. "What she said."

They took their seats in the box's front row.

Chapter 68

The overture began with a slow passage by the clarinets in their lowest register. Mournful, plaintive, almost haunting, the melody ebbed and flowed. Friedrich was reminded of walks in forests where everything was shadowed.

At the end of the passage, the low part was taken over by the horns, and the clarinets began playing up an octave. Somehow, the effect was not just a doubling of the notes and more volume; there was an eeriness to the music that made Friedrich's neck hair prickle.

Halfway through this second iteration of the passage, Friedrich noticed drums playing a beat pattern. They were so soft, he wasn't sure when they had actually started, but as the pattern recurred over and over again, they grew a little louder with each repeat.

At the end of the second passage, Franz the conductor cut the woodwinds off, and led the drums to grow louder, and louder, and louder, culminating in a massive roll on every instrument that had a skin head, from the raspy snare drum to two of the big thundering kettle-drums.

Just as it seemed the thunder would deafen Friedrich, there was a crash of the cymbals, and the entire orchestra, led by the trumpets, entered with a majestic march.

Friedrich sat back, marveling at what *Kappellmeister* Heinrich Schütz had wrought. That was his last conscious analysis of the opera until the end of the first scene, as the music just subsumed him.

Amber, seated next to her husband Heinrich Schütz, leaned over and spoke in his ear.

"Superb, darling. Simply superb."

His hand tightened its grasp on hers, and he flashed her a smile.

Byron slid his pistol back into its holster.

Gotthilf leaned over the edge again to watch the body slowly floating down the canal toward the river in the sluggish current. Byron walked over to stand by Gotthilf as Honister arrived.

"Phillip's okay. Bullet creased his thigh. He was bleeding pretty good, but I wrapped his shirt around it, so he'll keep until someone can get him to the hospital. Where's Schardius?"

Gotthilf pointed over the railing. Honister took a look, and shrugged.

"We going to let him float out to sea?" Gotthilf asked.

"That's a thought," Byron said with a morbid chuckle, "except that the CoC might gig us for water pollution. So Sergeant Honister, here"—he grinned at Karl—"needs to go roust out some fishermen to grab the body and bring it to shore."

Honister had a bit of a *why me?* look on his face, but he headed toward the riverbank.

Gotthilf looked over to where Simon was standing on the other side of the bridge, leaning back against one of the end pillars.

"Simon okay?"

"Yah. Been a long day for him, though."

"That it has."

As the overture drew to a close, the curtain opened to the first scene, where Arthur, played by the baritone Dieter Fischer, was trying to have a council of war with his captains and knights, only they kept making ribald jokes at his expense because of his upcoming marriage. The music was fast and light, and the musical repartee was witty and flew back and forth at a fast pace. The refrain was particularly infectious.

> *The king is getting married,*
> *Call the bishop out.*

The king is getting married,
And not to some old trout.
The princess is a beauty,
A thing of grace is she.
Oh, the king is getting married
Under the dragon tree!

Friedrich laughed right away, and as the song progressed there was more and more laughter sounding around him. The audience gave generous applause when it ended.

Marla entered from stage left as the applause died down. Amber sat up straight. There was a difference now, an air about Marla that she had never seen before. She stalked onto the set like a predator. There was an edge, a precision about her movements that was almost lupine. The audience saw it; felt it. The susurrus of conversation died away, even from the box seats. Everyone was fixated on the young woman in the red and gold costume, ignoring even the men who followed her as her captains.

Whatever it was, even the other singers and actors felt it. Amber saw Dieter stand straighter and taller as he stood forward as Arthur to welcome Marla/Guinevere. He sang an extended aria welcoming her to his court. She sang an extended aria thanking him for receiving her. The other actors sang a rousing chorus praising the wisdom of the two rulers, and urging them to get on with the marriage. That got a few chuckles from the audience.

Arthur and Guinevere moved downstage toward the audience and the lights dimmed behind them, giving an illusion that they were secluded. Their duet that followed had a formal title in the libretto and score, but Amber thought of it as "The Pre-Nuptial Agreement Song." Arthur and Guinevere circled around each other musically and physically, testing each other's commitment, and striving to retain their rights as independent rulers.

It was interesting, Amber thought, that even during the dress rehearsal Dieter had always come off as slightly less than Marla in every scene they shared, even though he was physically larger. It would be hard not to, of course; good singer though he was, Marla's pipes were just that much better than his. But tonight, standing there in his costume of tin armor and imperial purple cape, Dieter was holding his own. Or, just maybe, tonight Marla had moved to a higher plane and dragged Dieter along with her.

Either way, as they moved closer physically, musically, and relationally in the plot, Dieter tonight had a *dignitas* that was serving him well.

The duet ended with them enfolding each other's hands, admitting their love and pledging to each other.

More applause. Amber beat her hands together like everyone else, although she did draw the line at cheering. There were those around her, though, who felt no such compunction.

On stage, Arthur and Guinevere joined hands and walked toward the figure of a bishop who progressed from the rear to join them. The opera chorus joined the characters in celebrating the marriage of Arthur and Guinevere in high style. The music sounded very liturgical, but was richer and more resplendent. Everything climaxed in an awesome display of harmony and counterpoint as the chorus divided into an eight-part choir and sang a short fugue on *Alleluia* as Arthur and Guinevere both knelt before the bishop and he placed crowns on their heads.

The chorus ended in a resounding *Amen* as the two rulers stood and faced the audience and Arthur drew and raised his sword.

Friedrich wasn't a musician, but he could recognize great art when he heard it. He clapped until his hands hurt. He wasn't the only one.

The lights blacked out for the scene change.

Gotthilf looked around as Karl Honister and Dr. Schlegel joined him and Byron to watch the fishers they'd rousted out to retrieve the body of Schardius before it vanished downstream.

"Yes," Dr. Schlegel said, "my assistants will have it on the way to the morgue just as soon as it gets on land and they get back from taking your patrolman to the hospital. Nasty wound in the thigh he's got, but nothing life-threatening." He looked over the bridge railing. "And as far as this one is concerned... But based on your evidence, I doubt I'll need to do much of an examination of him. It's pretty obvious what he died from, and you were there when he died."

The fishers managed to drag the corpse into the boat with them without capsizing. They worked their oars to turn the boat, then headed for the pier where they were standing.

"So, Lieutenant, your sister-in-law is singing in this opera thing?" Honister asked.

"Yep."

"Why aren't you at the opera house watching it, then?"

"She offered tickets. Not my cup of tea," Byron snorted. "I'm not partial to plays or musicals, and especially not opera. My tastes run to Alan Jackson and Martina McBride, and fat chance of ever hearing them again."

Honister turned a confused expression to him. Gotthilf slapped him on the shoulder and said, "Never mind. I'll explain later."

The lights rose on the second scene. There was a chorus that revolved around a council to plan a battle with the invading Saxons. Arthur, Guinevere, and their captains were there, as was the bishop, who was revealed to be Merlin Ambrosius. The sound of the music was martial and stirring, with echoes of the grand march from the overture. It ended with a mass shouted "Death to the Saxons!" That got a roar of approval from one of the inhabitants of the imperial box. The emperor still remembered, it seemed, just who had betrayed him a couple of years ago.

After the applause, Merlin and Arthur moved downstage into a pool of light. The duet that followed would have been considered great, except that Amber knew what was coming next. Even so, Merlin (the tenor) and Arthur (the baritone) had a lengthy discussion about honor, sacrifice, and wisdom, and why they were all necessary characteristics of a good ruler. For all that the words sounded stuffy on paper, Amber thought to herself, Heinrich's music made them sing. She squeezed his hand as the duet came to an end and Arthur left the stage, then settled down into her seat. She knew what was coming next, and that thought thrilled her.

Friedrich's eyes were fixed on Merlin, who had remained at center front in a spotlight. The singer raised his eyes, and opened his mouth.

"*Our Father, Who art in heaven . . .*"

It was a beautiful melody that Schütz had crafted. But it was interrupted. Another voice was heard.

"*Merlinus . . .*"

It was a soprano, with a striking timbre and an intonation that projected cool as contrasted to the warmth of Marla's voice earlier.

"*Who's there?*" Merlin sang, looking around.

There was only silence, and he resumed his meditation, this time with the orchestra supporting him.

"*Our Father, Who art in heaven...*"

Again the second voice was heard:

"*Merlinus...*"

And again Merlin replied, "*Who's there?*"

This time there was a response. A different spotlight picked up a figure that approached from stage right; tall, slender, flowing blonde hair, dressed in robes of teal and silver.

"*One who brings a gift, Merlinus...*"

And thus began the duet "*Die Magie Der Nacht*"—"The Magic of the Night."

The sylph Nimue circled Merlin, offering him access to great magic; greater than any he had ever known; the magic of Solomon himself.

Merlin countered the temptations by continuing to sing the *Pater Noster.*

To Friedrich, the contrast between the texts and the contrast between the soaring melodies of the sylph and the quiet contemplative voice of the bishop almost wrenched at one's heart. Almost, almost one could hear echoes of the temptations of Christ in the wilderness in it.

The temptations were varied, and subtle. The duet was obviously a trial to the heart of the bishop, yet he remained steadfast. It finally came to a conclusion.

Nimue sang one last time, "*Will you take it?*"

Friedrich rejoiced in his heart when Merlin sang, "*No.*" Then his heart sank, for as the sylph turned and exited the way it had come, Merlin's head turned and followed it.

That did not bode well for the character, he thought, even as the lights blacked out for the scene change and applause erupted around him.

The body of Schardius landed on the pier with a *thump.* Gotthilf looked down at it in the moonlight. The open eyes staring sightlessly off into the night; water rivulets running from face and hair; soggy clothes bunched and twisted.

"Not very impressive now, is he?" Byron said, as Dr. Schlegel bent to examine the body.

"No," Gotthilf agreed. "And for all that he was, or tried to be, in the end he is nothing more than cold clay, waiting to be put back in the earth."

The third scene of Act One presented a series of arias and choruses that evoked the strains of battle, as the imminent battle was realized. Swords were heard clashing; horses were heard to neigh; hoof beats were heard thundering in the distance as Arthur led his knights in the final charge. Friedrich felt his pulse quickening through it all. He sat on the edge of his seat, almost visualizing in his head the ranks of the Saxon foe breaking under the charge of the British horsemen.

Guinevere stood on a hill and sang encouragement to Arthur and to her captains.

It was loud, it was brash, it was glorious to Friedrich, especially when Arthur strode onto the stage in full armor, splashed with blood. He sang one entire aria to explain that none of it was his.

The final victory chorus was built on a full statement of the march from the overture, with trumpets sounding calls over it all and drums rumbling beneath. It ended with Arthur and his knights lifting their swords in triumph.

The curtain dropped on the end of the first act to loud sustained applause.

The emperor accepted a glass of wine from Baldur, and looked over at Ulrik. "An interesting story so far. And I begin to see what you mean about the woman's voice. Almost I would like to hear this song she sang."

During the *Entr'acte*, there was a bustle backstage as certain set elements were changed out by the crew and as the leading characters changed costumes. Marla made a fast change with Sophie's help, and headed back to the wing she would enter from in Act Two.

Marla took her spot, and stood, eyes closed. Despite the crush of the activity, everyone gave her room. No one moved so close as to even brush her with the hem of a wide sleeve. Her face was still, but her hands made small movements.

Dieter walked up to the castrato Andrea Abati, who was resettling the blond wig he wore as Nimue. He nodded in Marla's direction. "What is she doing?"

Abati glanced at his some-time pupil, and replied, "I think she's doing what the up-timers would call 'getting her game face on.' She's flowing through all her lines and songs in her mind, gestures and all."

Dieter gave his head a little approving shake. "She is pure diamond tonight."

"That she is," Abati replied as he finished adjust the wig. He turned full-face to Dieter. "How do I look?"

"Very eerie, Your Nimueship," Dieter said with a smile.

Abati bent down a bit to let one of the dressers touch up his pale makeup. Dieter began reviewing his own songs.

They were both looking at Marla when the orchestra began the *entr'acte* music. Even across the width of the stage, her eyes seemed to glitter.

Abati nudged Dieter. "Tighten your sword belt, lace up your boots, and stay on your toes. I'd say she's ready for the fray."

The second act began with a chorus that indicated that some time had passed since the end of the first act events. Things were not totally peaceful, but farmers could work the land and craftsmen build their tools without horrific danger. That was attributed to Good King Arthur, and the people sang his praises.

After that song, the upstage lights dimmed, and the figure of Nimue was seen to glide downstage in a spotlight out of the stage left wing. Friedrich sat up straight, as he had already decided that everything in this story was going to hinge on the sylph. He knew that the part was being played by the Italian castrato, Abati, but he could see and hear nothing manly in Nimue; and that made him chill just a bit.

Nimue paused at the front of the stage and lifted her hands together, freezing for a moment as the orchestra held a dissonant chord, then opening them in a broadening gesture as the chord resolved into a motif that sounded ominous.

"*Morrigan,*" Nimue sang.

The orchestra paused for the barest moment, then repeated the ominous motif.

"*Morrigan,*" Nimue called again.

This time there was a response:

"Who calls the Morrigan?" sounded a strong contralto. Another spotlight picked up a striking figure who strode onto the stage from the stage right wing to confront Nimue. Dressed in dull red with a black cape that was flourished like wings, this figure was undeniably a woman; one with cruel lines on her face.

Friedrich hissed between his teeth. He knew that face was the product of skillful makeup, but at the distance he was removed from the characters, in the light that was there, this breathing image of the goddess of battle and discord looked like nothing less than a monster. So he could imagine Medea looking when she slew her children before Jason's eyes.

He shivered as their duet began.

Amber watched the duet with a clinical eye. Margaret, the woman singing the Morrigan role, was perhaps the weakest singer of the major roles. Her voice was acceptable—indeed, she had an awesome lower register—but her pitch control was sometimes a bit erratic, and she had taken forever to learn her words. So if there was one song in the whole production where Amber crossed her fingers and prayed for a good outcome, it was this one.

Tonight, thankfully, it worked well. The Diabolical Duet, as Amber thought of it, soared and roared, Nimue at times leading the Morrigan, and at times the reverse being the case. The lines were all sung cleanly and clearly, and the plot of the opera advanced by means of the plot between the characters.

She sat back in satisfaction as the final notes were sounded by the orchestra.

Friedrich shook his head as the duet ended. It was now clear how at least part of the story was going to unfold. Poor Merlin.

And so it proved. In the following arias, plots were made with Medraut, who turned out to be Arthur's illegitimate half-brother, to plot to overthrow Arthur and assume the throne. Even the Saxons were brought into this, which received a few catcalls from the imperial box.

The lights blacked out for the end of scene one to medium applause.

Friedrich turned to Gronow. "You wrote the libretto. This is not going to turn out well, is it?"

Gronow just smiled and said nothing.

"Pig," Friedrich muttered. "Then at least give me another drink of your schnapps to bolster my courage."

Gronow passed the flask over just as the lights came up for scene two. Friedrich took a hurried swig and passed it back, eyes on the solitary figure advancing from upstage.

Merlin, dressed in the finest of bishop's garb and carrying a crozier, stood in the spotlight, and began again the beautiful melody Schütz had written for the *Pater Noster*.

"Our Father, Who art in Heaven..."

This time when Nimue advanced from the wings, the Morrigan came with her, shadowing her every step, halting at the edge of Merlin's pool of light as Nimue glided to within a hand's reach of the beleaguered bishop. Nimue's spotlight was blue in this scene, and the Morrigan's was red, as contrasted to the white light in which Merlin stood. The visual effect was quite striking.

Every word that Nimue sang, every note that she uttered, was supported, harmonized, and enhanced by the voice of the Morrigan. The effect was almost spellbinding, musically speaking, and Friedrich had to wrench himself from that enchantment repeatedly to pay attention to the story.

Merlin tried. He would battle back with the *Pater Noster*, force Nimue back a step, to circle a little wider. But the power shown by the sylph as bolstered by the goddess ultimately was more than he could resist, or endure, or defeat. The end came when Merlin dropped his crozier and fell to his knees, grasping at the hem of Nimue's robe.

The music swirled into an air of triumph, as Nimue picked up the crozier and seemingly broke it and cast it aside, then grasped Merlin by the arm and chivvied him to the Dragon Tree at the rear of the set upstage. The Morrigan had already seemingly ascended to the branches of the tree, and the black cloak was spread out like wyvern's wings. Nimue waved a hand, part of the tree's trunk opened, and she thrust Merlin inside. The trunk closed with the sound of a thunder clap from the orchestra.

"This does not bode well," Friedrich muttered. Gronow chuckled beside him, and he thumped Gronow's thigh with his leg.

Amber smiled and nodded as Nimue began her victory aria. Abati's silver voice was just superb for the role. This aria in particular demanded musical athletics that very few musicians she had known in the up-time could have done full justice to. Abati could, and his exultation—it still felt funny to think "his" when the sound she was hearing was high soprano—sounded eldritch, fey, beautiful, enticing; all of that. And to Abati's credit in playing the role, Amber admitted, it also sounded evil.

The applause after the aria was quite loud, although not perhaps as extended as it could have been, Amber decided. Credit it to the fact that it was sung by one of the bad guys, she supposed.

The scene progressed after that aria. Nimue enlisted the aid of Arthur's aunt Morgause, who in this story was only a few years older than Arthur himself. Then, bolstered by the Morrigan's magic and music, and drawing on the magic of Merlin himself, the three women wove a web around Arthur. Without Merlin's influence, counsel, and magic to help bolster and protect him, Arthur succumbed to the temptation, and the lights blacked out on the second scene as Morgause drew him through the curtains of her bed.

Friedrich looked over at Gronow during the few moments the curtain was down. "It does get better than this, doesn't it? If all I wanted was tragedy, I could have stayed in my room and read Poe and Goethe."

Gronow just chuckled.

The third scene of Act Two was short; only three songs in it. The scene opened the next morning after Arthur's seduction with Arthur stumbling from stage left into the court before the Dragon Tree. He was disheveled, bleary-eyed, and unsure of what had happened. Nimue was waiting and musically pounced on him, delighting in informing him of what had occurred the previous night—the fact that not only had he committed adultery but he had also committed incest—and gleefully predicting his doom and the destruction of his kingdom. The Morrigan was standing in the branches of the Dragon Tree again, and her harmonies reinforced Nimue's music.

The second song segued directly from the first, as Guinevere entered the court from stage right, asking one and all what was occurring. That was Nimue's cue to sing yet another aria, exulting, telling Guinevere in no uncertain terms exactly what Arthur had done the night before. The sylph exited, up stage left, still exulting.

Friedrich decided that he could really come to hate Nimue, woman or no. But his eyes now fixed on Guinevere, standing alone, betrayed and scorned.

And thus began the third song of the scene, what was called "The Betrayal of Passion Duet" in the score.

Arthur began the duet by trying to apologize, but Guinevere rounded on him. The resulting duet was tempestuous and wracking, as Guinevere castigated him—no other term could express the depth of hurt and anger and even rancor that poured from her lips. Arthur had trouble singing a single sentence against the chastisement and reproach thrown at him like storm-waves from the sea.

He finally broke through long enough to sing one declamatory line, *"But I love you, I need you!"*

The music paused for a brief moment when the chord sustaining the last word finally ended. Friedrich noted in the corner of his mind that Schütz's use of these breaks was inspired, but his attention still hung on Marla, waiting to see what she would do next.

What resumed was an echo of the ominous motif from Nimue and the Morrigan's duet. It sounded, and sounded, and sounded, until Friedrich was ready to scream "Get on with it!"

The kettle drums started a muted roll, rumbling underneath the building of a dissonant chord by the horns and the clarinets. Guinevere finally entered on yet another dissonant note, softly, sadly.

"You...

"You never loved me."

The voice paused while the chord and the drums sustained their tones. Then it resumed, like a scalpel of ice.

"I was never more to you

"Than a prop for your throne!"

As soon as Guinevere bit off the final syllable, the strings entered, and the orchestra played a swirl of sound that cascaded upwards and ended like a shriek. There was a moment of pure silence. No one breathed, in the audience, the orchestra, or the stage. Then without another word, she turned and exited stage right, steps sounding loud in the silence.

Arthur stood alone in the spotlight after that excoriation. He dropped his outstretched arms; his head bowed. Slowly the spotlight narrowed, narrowed, narrowed, until it only lit his face. Then it cut to black, and the applause began.

Chapter 69

After Dr. Schlegel hauled Schardius' corpse off, Gotthilf stared at Byron. Byron stared back at him. They both turned to look at Simon, sitting against a wall with his knees drawn up and his arm wrapped around them.

"We need to get back to the opera hall, but someone needs to get him back to your house," Byron said.

"What time is it?" Gotthilf asked.

Byron looked at his watch by the light of the moon. "Not quite eight p.m."

"You're sure Honister said the performance had begun?"

"Yep. He backtracked to make sure that Schardius didn't drop or throw anything away, and he said he could hear the orchestra from outside."

"Well, then based on the program, the opera won't be over for a while yet," Gotthilf said. "I'll run Simon home in the duty carriage, then meet you back at the opera house."

"Right."

Gotthilf walked over to the boy, bent down and held out his hand. "Come on, Simon, up with you. You need to tell Ursula what's happened."

Simon stirred, grasped the offered hand, and let Gotthilf pull him up. He followed Gotthilf to where the police department carriage waited for them. Once inside, he leaned against the side. He said nothing.

"So," Gotthilf said after a few minutes of slow progress, "does it help any knowing that Schardius is gone?"

Simon stirred. "Some," he said.

Gotthilf didn't push the issue. He suspected, though, that Pastor Gruber might be talking to the boy about this soon.

Amber felt Heinrich squeeze her hand again. He leaned closer. "This shall be your triumph, tonight."

Amber shook her head.

"No, this is your work, yours and Johann Gronow's."

"My dear," Heinrich murmured as the applause and cheers continued to sound from all around them, "what we did was nothing more than preparing the canvas and mixing the paint. You have painted the masterpiece, you and your singers."

Friedrich sat back in his chair, half-exhausted. God above, there was still one more act to go!

He looked over at Gronow, and muttered, "You are not going to give me a hint as to how this ends, are you?"

Gronow grinned. "Did you give us advance warning of what you had crafted for Frau Linder two months ago? No. As Saint Matthew recorded in his gospel, 'Whatsoever ye would that men should do to you, do ye even so to them.' And you, being a good Lutheran, would desire to be obedient to the Holy Writ. I am merely observing that because of your prior actions, you want to be treated in the same way. *Ipso facto*, and *quod erat demonstrandum* for good measure."

"Never trust an editor," Friedrich muttered with a scowl, settling back and crossing his arms.

Princess Kristina's face split in a huge yawn. She sank down in her chair. Ulrik wasn't sure she would last out the evening, as much as she professed to enjoy the show. Even now her eyes were drifting shut.

Ulrik looked over to Gustav. The emperor was holding his chin, and tapping his foot. He apparently caught Ulrik's gaze out of the corner of his eye, for he turned his head and winked at the prince.

"What do you think of it?" Ulrik asked. He was a bit surprised to discover a moment later that he really wanted to know the emperor's opinion on what they were hearing.

"A bit heathenish, perhaps," Gustav conceded, "but compared to the tales my Finns tell around the campfires at night, this is actually somewhat mild." He chuckled. "The music is quite good, I think. I'm rather glad I plucked *Kappellmeister* Schütz from your brother's court." That was said with a wicked grin.

"And the singing?"

"Oh, very fine, I would say. The baritone is as good as any I have ever heard, and he has the stature to play a proper king." Gustav patted his ample midriff as if to exemplify the concept. "And the castrato—Abati, is that his name?—he is excellent. Although I still shiver at the thought of what was done to him."

Gustav twitched his shoulders as he said that last. Ulrik nodded in complete agreement.

"And Frau Linder," he prompted after a few seconds.

"Yes...Frau Linder," Gustav responded. "We have heard even in Stockholm of *La Cecchina*, the ornament of the court in Florence. Perhaps in Frau Linder we have her equal."

Or even her superior, Ulrik thought to himself as Gustav held his wine cup out for a refill.

Franz pushed his hair back and looked around the orchestra. There were smiles everywhere. They all knew they were doing well; the opera as a whole was going well. And despite all the murmurs about egotistical and arrogant singers, they all knew that the soloists were nothing short of superb tonight. Excitement was in the air in the orchestra so thick you could almost drink it.

The applause finally started to die down. Franz looked to the stage curtain, knowing that it would rise shortly. When the performance began he had been concerned about Marla. The things that had happened tonight would have been enough to put almost anyone in a funk. But she'd said she was mad, and apparently that gave her extra spirit, for tonight she *was* Guinevere, more so than she had ever been.

One more act, he thought as the lights blinked in the signal to begin. One more act.

He raised his baton.

Despite his determination to remember everything that happened in the last act, Friedrich was really only able to remember bits and pieces of it from that first performance, except for three great songs. By some odd coincidence, they all involved Marla Linder.

The first was the duet in the first scene where Guinevere sat alone under the Dragon Tree and poured out her heart to it; her anger, her pain, her dejection, her wounded pride, and finally her bereftness. That was a wonderful poignant moment, which was answered brilliantly when the voice of Merlin responded to her from the tree.

Merlin revealed what had truly happened to Arthur. Guinevere was slow to understand, but once she did grasp the events, and the parts played by all involved, she burned with wrath against Nimue.

Merlin cautioned her:

> *Beware the sylph's strength!*
> *Take warning from my fallen state.*
> *No man may confound the creature's might.*

To which Guinevere responded:

> *No man, you say?*
> *But I am not a man, nor have I ever been.*
> *With Saint George and Saint Michael to*
> *   strengthen my hand,*
> *I will be this creature's bane.*

Merlin made no reply as the music echoed motifs from the overture march, and the drums rumbled beneath.

The second bright remembrance for Friedrich was in the second scene of the third act, where Guinevere tracked down Nimue and made good on her promise. The duet was strenuous and musically challenging, as one would expect between two sopranos of such power and skill. But the presentation was also strenuous as Guinevere appeared in armor, sword in hand, and proceeded to lay into the sylph, who managed to produce a sword just in the nick of time to avoid being skewered by the queen's first thrust.

Back and forth they went, declaiming lines of the duet as they did. Friedrich had to chuckle. Neither of the singers would have lasted long as bravos on the streets or as soldiers on the battlefields. But for stage fencing, it wasn't bad, and it was certainly exciting.

As the duet began moving toward its conclusion, Nimue was obviously getting the worst of it. At that point, she sang:

> Morrigan!
> I, your ally, abettor, and adjunct
> Do pray your aid
> Against this fell foe!

The Morrigan, once again in the branches of the Dragon Tree, raised her wings and sang:

> No friend of thine am I!
> I live for strife,
> And your foe brings strife home to you.

At that point, Nimue seemed to lose heart, and it was not long before Guinevere thrust her blade home to the sylph's heart.

The loudest applause of the evening so far broke out, and the final cadences of the accompaniment went unheard by most. It was several minutes before it died down enough that the opera could continue. From the way that Guinevere's chest was heaving, Friedrich suspected that was a benefit to her.

The final pearl of the evening was the final scene of Act Three. The planned-for rebellion had broken out, and there was no help for it but Arthur and his knights had to meet the forces of Medraut in battle. Most of it occurred off-stage, of course, but the sound effects of the battle were loud and alarming. On-stage, Arthur bitterly regretted that Guinevere and her captains had not followed him to the battle. His men were holding, but at a high price. And then the fateful breakthrough happened—Arthur's front line broke, and Medraut and his champions came through.

It was almost a dance, Friedrich thought. The scene of Arthur battling one warrior after another, singing his rage against his half-brother, while Medraut waited, spilling his hate verbally, was powerful. Friedrich forgot to even criticize the fencing as the force of the scene gripped him.

The inevitable end came: the audience groaned and cried out when Arthur's sword was trapped in the body of his last opponent, and Medraut seized his opportunity to lunge in and transfix the king. Arthur fell to his knees, bent over the sword thrust through him.

Medraut turned away from the stricken king, and launched into a victory aria, but seemingly halfway through it, the orchestra trumpets began to sound fanfare figures. Medraut looked around, but continued singing. A few measures later, the fanfares sounded again, and this time a flood of actors entered the stage, Guinevere at their head. She had brought her troops at last. As they put paid to the bedraggled remnants of Medraut's army, she took in the scene before her, and even from his seat in the audience Friedrich could sense her drawing up, swelling, beginning to loom over the battlefield and the hapless Medraut.

> *Too late,*
> *Alas, too late to save!*
> *Then I will avenge!*

And true to her word, Guinevere soon battered Medraut to defeat. He fell to his hands and knees facing upstage. Her sword rose, held in both hands, then fell swiftly. There was a *chunk* sound. The queen bent over, and when she straightened she was holding the head of Medraut.

> *Thus the traitor*
> *Is paid his due!*

Many in the audience flinched at the head, men and women alike. It was rather lifelike, complete with glassy eyes and ragged skin at the neck. But after a moment to feel properly horrified, they broke out in wild cheers and applause, including at least one roar of approval from the imperial box.

When the applause died down, Merlin appeared, singing an explanation that the defeat of Nimue had opened the Dragon Tree and released him, but that he had not been able to catch up with Guinevere and her captains.

And Merlin, singing to the melody that had been the *Pater Noster* in earlier scenes, drew the sword from Arthur, placed him in the barge that floated out from stage left, and in a final duet with Guinevere promised that Arthur was going to the Isles of the Blessed where he would be healed of his deadly wound and lie sleeping for the time of the people's need.

Arthur raised up to sing a short farewell, promising to return when he was needed most, then floated off to stage right.

The final grand chorus began with a mass shout of *Ave Arthur, Rex Quondam Rexque Futurus!*, then reprised the great Alleluia fugue from the wedding scene, with Guinevere standing in front, sword lifted high, voice skirling over them all.

And with that, the final curtain dropped.

Ciclope had made his way across the western bridge into the oldest part of the city. After almost running into the procession of Marine guards and the emperor's car on the Gustavstrasse boulevard, he stuck to the side streets, moving always in the direction of the Schardius warehouse.

He was still muttering about the loss of his kill. If the *Polizei* cost him his ten thousand dollars . . .

A noise intruded on his consciousness as he was walking by one of Old Magdeburg's many churches, and he turned his head to look over his shoulder.

"You? What are you—"

Chapter 70

Friedrich found himself on his feet, beating his hands together as hard as he could, stomping his feet, and shouting nonsense at the top of his lungs. After a minute or two of that, he grabbed Gronow around the shoulder and gave him a fierce hug. "You genius!" he shouted in his friend's ear. "I forgive you!" And he went back to clapping and shouting.

Gustav pursed his lips and nodded. "If this is what an opera is, maybe I will come to more of them. The final music was a little harsh, though."

"The up-time influence, I'm afraid," Ulrik replied. "They tell me we will become accustomed to it."

"I thought it was good," Caroline Platzer replied from the row behind them. "Not that I'm a connoisseur of operas, you understand. They didn't stage them in Grantville very often." Her grin was sly enough that Ulrik knew she meant that the Grantvillers had never had one.

"Frau Linder," Gustav mused, "she is like steel on the stage. Is she like that away from the stage, from the music?"

Ulrik pointed to Baldur to answer.

"From all accounts she is a very pleasant woman, but one with a very strong view of the world," the Norwegian responded.

"Frau Caroline, do you know Frau Linder?" Gustav asked.

"Not well," she replied. "I was an out-of-towner, not one of the Grantville natives. But I am acquainted with her, and certainly know of her. I would say that she's not a tough broad—not a hard person—but she is a passionate person who will stand up for what she believes in."

Gustav folded his hands together and tapped his lips with his forefingers several times. "We shall officially ignore the song on the radio and the records," he said finally. "This is a woman who it is better to have as a friend than a foe. She could not have played that queen as she did if she is not capable of hardness. Let us not make her discover just how hard she can become."

The emperor stood, stretched, and yawned. "Now, I believe I would like to return to the palace and rest. You," he pointed to one of the Marine guards standing in the rear of the box, "go tell the driver to warm up the car." As that worthy almost leapt out the door, Gustav turned back to the family group. "But tomorrow—do we have a Trommler record player in the palace?"

Caroline looked up from where she was trying to get Kristina to wake up enough to walk. "I believe so, in the great room with the piano."

"Good. I believe that I would like to hear Frau Marla's infamous song for myself. Do any of you own the record?"

No one spoke for a moment, then Baldur cleared his throat. Ulrik looked at him in surprise. "I wouldn't have thought that of you, Baldur."

Baldur shrugged. "I've heard her sing before. I like her voice." He grinned. "Besides, it's a first pressing copy of the record. In a few years, it will be worth a small fortune."

They gathered their coats and other paraphernalia. Baldur finished off a couple of near-empty wine bottles.

"Frau Caroline?" Gustav said.

"Yes, sir?"

"Please arrange with the palace staff to have the major figures in this opera invited to the palace."

"Can do, sir."

Gotthilf dismounted from the police department carriage, joining Byron and Karl Honister at the bottom of the front steps of the opera building.

"Kid delivered safe and sound?"

"Yah. Turned him over to my mother and Pastor Gruber. Between them, they'll take care of him."

Gotthilf looked at the other two men. "Well, what are we waiting for? I don't know about you, but I'd like to get some sleep sometime tonight."

Byron shrugged. "Let's do it."

They started up the steps together.

Franz stepped backstage into a scene of almost riotous celebration. Three different less-than-delicate drinking songs were being sung by different groups of the cast. Dieter had donned Nimue's blond wig, and was singing part of Nimue's victory song in a falsetto that was so high it was almost painful. It didn't help any that he was intentionally missing pitches and slurring words.

Marla was laughing, but she was wincing as well. She saw Franz standing and grinning at her, and she flew to him, producing an "Oof!" when she made contact and threw her arms around him. She was still wearing her final costume with the tin armor, and it was not very forgiving.

Franz returned the embrace, and they stood there like that for a long while, oblivious to all the pandemonium occurring around them. Finally, he broke the hold and held her shoulders, reaching up to tuck an errant strand of hair behind her ear.

"Mad all gone?" he asked with a small smile.

"Yep." She grinned back. "Not that I wouldn't mind a little time to kick Herr Schardius where it would hurt the most a time or three." She looked around. "Speaking of that snake, I wonder what happened to him."

Franz lifted his eyes above her head. "I think we're about to find out." He pointed to Byron and Gotthilf coming through the side door. They descended first on Amber. After a brief conversation, she looked to Franz and Marla and beckoned. They followed her and the detectives to the Men's Dressing Room, on the opposite side of the stage.

Amber closed the door behind them, and the din outside dropped to a dull roar. "Okay, guys, what's up?"

Byron heaved a big sigh, and began, "You don't have to worry about Schardius anymore. He's dead."

Amber's eyes widened, and Marla grabbed Franz's arm in an exceedingly tight grip.

"He ran for the east bridge to the Altstadt, and kept shooting at us. We had no choice but to return fire. He made it to the bridge, but took a hit there and fell over the wall into the canal. By the time we fished him out, he was dead. So," Byron shook his head, "he won't be bothering you or anyone else anymore."

Marla shivered for a moment. "I detested the man, yeah, but I don't think I wanted him dead."

"If it is any help to you," Gotthilf put in, "we were tracking him anyway because we suspected him of being involved in several murders. Not a nice man, Herr Schardius."

"I wish we'd known all this up front," Amber said bitterly. "Mary wouldn't have taken a lead pfennig from the man if we'd had any idea that he had that kind of baggage. We were all a little uncomfortable around him, but we couldn't nail anything down, and we needed the money."

"If there is a next time," Gotthilf replied, "which I pray God there isn't, listen to your instincts."

"Oh, you betcha," Amber said.

"Anyway," Byron concluded, "we're going to need to take statements from you two ladies, and from the guy with the sword, whoever he is and wherever he went..."

"Friedrich von Logau," Franz interjected.

"Thanks," Byron replied as Gotthilf pulled his notebook out, "but that can wait until tomorrow. No pressing need for it now, the way things worked out."

"But we do need that room sealed off," Gotthilf said. "It's a crime scene now. We at least need to get the photographer in there first thing tomorrow."

Amber shifted uncomfortably. "I knew you would want that, so I had it closed down, and the room behind it—after we got the costumes out."

The two detectives both started to frown.

"Sorry, guys," Marla chimed in. "But only two or three people went in, people who were already in there, and as much as possible they walked around the footprints and stuff. But we had to have those costumes."

Byron looked at Gotthilf, and after a moment they both shrugged.

"It's not what I would want," Byron said, "but in *this* case, I don't think it's going to matter. But keep everyone out of there until after we're done tomorrow morning."

"We won't be here until after two in the afternoon," Amber said. "That's our regular schedule. We have a few more performances to give before we pack this show away."

"That's all for now," Byron concluded. "We'll be in touch." He shook hands with Amber and Franz, and gave Marla a big hug. "Glad we got here in time tonight." He separated with a big grin. "Jonni would have killed me if I'd let anything happen to her baby sister."

"Get out of here," Marla said, grinning also.

When they came out of the room, they found Mary Simpson and Rebecca Abrabanel standing by the stage manager's desk, talking with Frau Frontilia and Heinrich Schütz.

Heinrich held out his hands, and Amber took them. "A triumph," the older musician said. "A veritable triumph, thanks to all of you."

"Indeed," Mary said. "The first modern opera in Germany, written by a German, sung in German, performed by—mostly—Germans. And the emperor stayed awake through the whole thing. All in all, a cause for celebration."

"I think an even greater cause for celebration," Rebecca said, "is that our own monarch returned to us. He is not the King Arthur of legend, of course. No real kings are. Still, things would probably be much worse now if he hadn't."

"Amen to that," Amber said.

Dieter had apparently been listening in on the conversation. Still wearing the blond wig, he turned to the celebrating cast and crew.

"Hey, everyone, be quiet! Quiet!"

Dieter had a big voice, so it wasn't long until a condition of sort-of quiet existed. He held up the wine bottle he'd been drinking from. "Everyone fill your hands. I'm going to propose a toast."

It took some hunting and scurrying, but before too many moments had passed everyone had some kind of container with either ale or wine in their hand.

"Everyone got one?" Dieter asked, looking around. "Good. Here's my toast: *To Gustav Adolf, the Once and Future King!*"

A roar went up in response, glasses/bottles/cups/etc. were clinked together, contents were drunk, and a rousing cheer echoed in the rafters.

The ensuing party, although not the earliest to celebrate the emperor's restoration, was certainly one of the rowdiest. But what could you expect from a bunch of musicians and actors—and one very rowdy Italian singer?

"Do you carry that sword stick with you all the time?" Gotthilf Hoch asked Friedrich von Logau when they caught up with him at Walcha's Coffee House for their interview.

"Oh, no," Friedrich replied. "That is my evening walking stick. My morning walking stick," he lifted the tool in question, "is merely solid oak. At night, you see, one sometimes needs a bit more than to thump someone to discourage them."

Byron snorted. "So do you know how to really use that blade, or were you just lucky?"

Friedrich smiled. "I am rather good with it, in fact. Years with Viennese and Italian fencing masters. Boring, really, but it has come in handy on occasion."

"Such as a certain night in a certain opera hall basement," Gotthilf said.

"Indeed."

Chapter 71

Karl Honister and Mayor Gericke entered the building that housed Georg Schmidt's offices, to be confronted with what appeared to be a miniature mob. A number of men were gathered around the door leading to Schmidt's office, all of them talking excitedly.

Honister tried to shout over them, but quickly had to give that up as an exercise in futility. It took a blast on his patrolman's whistle to bring silence.

"What's going on?" he demanded, as soon as he removed the whistle from his lips. A babel of voices responded, and he blew the whistle again.

In the resulting silence Karl held up his badge wallet, flipped open to display the snarling lion mask. "Sergeant Karl Honister, Magdeburg *Polizei*." He stowed the badge in a pocket and pointed to one man.

"You—what's your name and why are you here?"

"Samuel Heilbronner. I work at the ledgers for Master Schmidt."

"Right. Now what's going on?"

A couple of the other men tried to speak, but Karl held up his hand. Samuel said, "Someone said the master has killed himself, and we all came to see if it was true."

"*What?*" Karl and the mayor spoke in unison, in identical tones of mingled disbelief and astonishment.

"And it is true," Samuel averred, with nodding heads all around to back him up.

"All right," Karl said, snapping into detective mode. "You, Samuel, did you see it happen?" Negative headshake. "Right; then you run and find a patrolman, tell him I'm here, and I want a police photographer and a crime scene team here yesterday. Got that?"

Samuel nodded his head quickly.

"Good. Run."

Samuel did as he was commanded.

Karl looked around.

"The rest of you, back up. Get out of the way. Line up against the hallway wall."

Once the crush of bodies was untangled, it proved to be seven more men.

"Did any of you see what happened?"

Headshakes all around.

"Right. You stay right here, then. Don't leave, but don't come in the room, either."

Karl turned toward the office doorway. He said over his shoulder, "I assume you're coming with me, Mayor?"

"You assumed right," was the response.

"He did what?"

Byron sounded stunned. Gotthilf didn't blame him. He was shocked himself.

"According to the report, Schmidt blew his brains out with a pistol right before the mayor and Honister arrived for their meeting."

"You're kidding!"

"No, I wish I were. Karl sent for the photographer and for some help."

Byron picked up his hat.

"Come on. We'll go chip in."

Karl Honister watched from the door as the photographer took pictures of everything in the office.

"I want close-ups of the head and body," he called out. The photographer waved a hand in acknowledgment and murmured something to his assistant.

There was no question that Master Schmidt was dead. Bullet holes in the temple were usually a good indication that life was gone. Schmidt's head had lolled back against the back of his chair, so that his vacant eyes stared toward the ceiling. His right arm hung over the side of the chair, with what looked to be a .32 revolver, similar to the one that Karl carried, lying on the floor below his fingers.

He looked around to see Lieutenant Chieske and Sergeant Hoch push through the crowd in the hallway and pass by the patrolman guarding the door. In a moment, they were standing by him looking into the inner office.

"Messy," Chieske said.

"Yah," Karl responded.

"So what happened?"

Karl beckoned to a man sitting in the corner of the outer office.

"Who is he?" Hoch asked.

"This," Karl said as the man approached, "is Stephan Burckardt, personal secretary to Master Schmidt. He was here when it happened. Tell it again, Herr Burckardt."

"I was working at my desk," Burckardt said, pointing to a small desk to one side of the room. "The master had dictated several letters earlier, and I was writing them out for his signature. I heard the noise. I knocked on his door..."

"The door into his office was closed?" Hoch interrupted.

"Yah."

"Was that unusual in any way?"

"No." Burckardt shook his head. "The master often closed his door when he wanted to concentrate on something. I didn't think anything of it."

"Okay, you knocked on his door. Did you get an answer?"

"Uh, no."

"What then?"

"I, uh, I knocked again."

"Did you say anything?" Chieske asked.

"I think I said, 'Master Schmidt, are you all right?'"

"Then what happened?" Hoch again.

"I opened the door, and saw..." Burckardt swallowed hard, and waved a hand at the doorway.

"Did you go in? Did you touch anything?"

This time from Chieske. Karl saw that his two fellow detectives were alternating questions, not giving the secretary much time to think.

"Yah." Burckardt swallowed again. "I, uh, I touched his neck, I think."

"And after that?"

"I, uh, I was still in there when the mayor and he," he pointed to Honister, "arrived."

"The blood drops were still fresh when we walked in," Karl added. "It had to have happened just a few minutes before we got here. I'm surprised we didn't hear the shot."

"But you didn't hear it?" Gotthilf asked.

"No."

"And neither did I," Otto Gericke spoke from behind them. They turned toward him.

"I was just upstairs tending to my sister. She's now a widow, and she is not taking this well. But her pastor, Dr. de Spaignart, has arrived, so I have left her in his care."

Karl noticed a certain air about the mayor, what you might call a *he's welcome to her* attitude, which for a moment seemed odd. But then, thinking of his own sister, perhaps he could understand.

"So this happened before you could talk to Herr Schmidt?" Byron asked.

"Yah." Karl knew he sounded bitter. He had reason to. His whole case had just been shut down.

"Get lots of pictures, get the body to Doc Schlegel, and grab all the papers you can find." Byron again. "Maybe you can still figure something out."

"Right."

The other two detectives left. So did the mayor. Karl was left to watch the photographers and wait for the medical examiner. He ignored the men in the hallway who were still looking in and talking not-so-quietly.

He pulled a search warrant from his pocket, looked over at the secretary.

"You have boxes here?"

"I think so."

"Go find them. All the files and papers in this office are going to the *Polizei* station."

Standing in the shadow of the *Heilige-Geist* Church, Gotthilf stared at where Dr. Schlegel was doing a preliminary examination of yet another corpse. Beside him, Byron was muttering one curse after another under his breath.

Gotthilf elbowed his partner. "Stop it. We don't even know that that's our guy."

Byron snorted. "A one-eyed guy turns up shot to death in a back street of the old city. After everything that's been going on, I somehow doubt that this is just some random guy who lost an eye somewhere somewhen. There can't be that many one-eyed men around Magdeburg right this minute."

After a moment of consideration, Gotthilf gave a reluctant nod of agreement.

"Nathaniel," Byron called over to the police photographer who had finished packing up his equipment, "I need copies as soon as you can get them."

The photographer touched the brim of his hat, and headed off, followed by his assistant.

Dr. Schlegel stood and wiped his hands on a towel. "Dead since before midnight," he said, forestalling the detectives' first question. "Probable cause of death, bullet wound to the head. I'll examine the body in detail as soon as we get it back to the morgue, but the blood evidence indicates the bullet wound was not post-mortem, so I doubt I'll find anything else. Assuming I don't, you'll have a report later today."

"Okay, thanks, Doc," Byron said.

The two detectives stood and watched the medical examiner's assistants load the corpse on a stretcher and place it in a wagon. Even after the wagon had been gone for some time, Byron continued to stand, staring at the blood that had pooled on the paving stones.

"We're missing something," the up-timer finally said. "With all that has happened, there's something we haven't picked up."

The two detectives arrived back at the police station just as Karl Honister lugged the last box of files from Schmidt's office to his desk. He set it down with a sigh.

"That's all Schmidt's stuff?" Byron asked.

"Yah."

"Well, drag it all into the conference room. We'll bring our files.

There's at least one piece of the puzzle missing, maybe more, and the three of us are going to go over all this stuff until we find it."

Karl gave a long-suffering sigh, picked up the box he had just set down, and headed for the conference room.

The three detectives spent over thirty-six hours in that conference room. They reviewed every piece of paper they had. They compared notes. They talked. They argued. They shouted. They drew charts and circles and arrows on big pieces of paper. They drank—reluctantly—gallons of horrible station house coffee. They sent Peltzer out with a photo of the one-eyed man to have Demetrious confirm that he was the man the informer had been tailing.

Bill Reilly peered in on them every hour or so during the day, shook his head, and withdrew without saying anything.

They were dazed, not even sure what day it was, when it happened.

Gotthilf stared at the cold dregs of coffee in his cup. He sniffed it and shuddered, his acid-stoked stomach rebelling at the thought of pouring more of that noxious stuff into it.

"This stuff is even worse than Grade Four," he muttered. He walked over to a window, popped it open, and tossed the dregs out right into a sudden gust of breeze, which carried the dark droplets back into the room. Many of the droplets landed on the hand holding the cup.

Gotthilf stood there, blinking, staring at his spotted hand. A thought wormed its way to the front of his mind, slowly, effortfully. When it arrived, he dropped the cup and turned back to the conference table, where he pawed through the piles of papers and files until he found what he wanted. He looked at the photograph, then at his hand, then back at the photograph, then back at his hand.

This cycle went on until Byron asked, "What are you thinking, partner?"

Gotthilf focused on the photograph. "Schmidt didn't kill himself."

It took a moment for that to register, then Byron straightened from his slouched position, and Honister raised his head from where it had been pillowed on his arms.

"What?" Byron again.

"Schmidt didn't kill himself."

"How do you know that?" Honister husked, trying to clear his throat.

Gotthilf looked at the other sergeant. "Was Schmidt right-handed?"

Honister looked in his notebook. "Yah."

Gotthilf turned the photograph around.

"There's no blood spatter on his hand."

"There was blood spatter on the gun," Byron said, looking for and holding up the report about that.

Gotthilf pointed to the photograph of the hand dangling just above the gun at the crime scene. "No blood on the hand. Blood on the gun but not on the hand means..."

"He wasn't holding the gun!" the three of them chorused.

"So he was murdered," Honister said. "How do we find the killer?"

"Who benefits from it?" Byron said. "And to find that..."

"Follow the money," they chorused again, and dug into the papers before them with a new will.

Chapter 72

Gotthilf looked around the room. It looked like everyone was there. The last few days had been hectic; frenetic, even. But today's meeting would provide closure to the events of the last few months, he thought.

He looked around at the room itself. They were in a lecture room at the hospital; appropriate enough, since the hospital expansion project seemed to have been the trigger for much of what had occurred since January. It amounted to neutral territory: not the mayor's office, or the police station.

It was a bit sterile, though. Four bare walls, hardwood floors, big windows admitting light from the south. No decorations. Given that the room had to be able to be scrubbed down to uptime hospital standards, its utilitarian décor was understandable.

Facing him were several people—the interested parties, one might say.

Mayor Gericke was at one end of the arc of chairs. Beside him was a woman he had introduced as Frau Sophie Gericke verw. Schmidt. By the name everyone knew that she was his sister, the new widow of Georg Schmidt.

Gotthilf had heard that Frau Sophie had two young daughters at home. He was saddened at the thought that they no longer had a father; but the thought of the kind of man Herr Schmidt had proven himself to be tempered the sadness.

On the widow's other side was Stephan Burckardt, Schmidt's secretary.

The next group in the arc was Marla Linder and her husband, Franz Sylwester.

Next to Franz sat Gunther Bauer, the new project manager of the hospital expansion project, and beside him was Herr Schiffer himself.

There was no one alive in Magdeburg who had a legitimate connection to Herr Schardius who could represent his interests. He, of course, was dead, his wife had died before the sack, and he had no children. More distant relatives were too far from Magdeburg to attend this meeting, so Mayor Gericke had appointed Jacob Lentke to stand in for Schardius' estate. He had his gouty foot propped up on a stool and his cane resting over his lap.

Facing that arc was a trio of *Polizei* behind a short table: Gotthilf on the left, Byron in the middle, and Karl Honister on the right.

Albrecht, Mayor Gericke's secretary, entered the room from the door behind the interested parties, stepped around to whisper in Byron's ear, then took a seat behind the mayor and picked up a notebook. He had been deputed by the mayor to take notes to document the meeting.

Byron looked to Mayor Gericke, and nodded. The mayor nodded back, and Byron looked first to Honister, then to Gotthilf.

Gotthilf felt his stomach muscles tighten, and he leaned forward just a bit. This was the end of the hunt, and he was ready.

"Thank you for coming today," Byron began. "For those of you who don't know me, I am Lieutenant Byron Chieske of the Magdeburg *Polizei*. This is my partner, Sergeant Gotthilf Hoch." He gestured toward Gotthilf. Gotthilf nodded, and Byron concluded the introductions with, "And this is our associate, Sergeant Karl Honister." Another gesture, this time toward Karl, who also nodded in response.

"You are all here, because you have all been touched in some way by events that occurred here in Magdeburg in the last few months; events which are connected in some way with either the late Herr Georg Schmidt, or the late Herr Andreas Schardius, or both." Byron stopped at that point and looked to his partner.

Gotthilf let the pause extend a moment longer, making sure that everyone facing him felt a bit of tension as they waited for him to begin. "It all began," he at length began, "when the contract for the hospital expansion project was awarded back in January to a consortium headed by Herr Georg Kühlewein and Herr Johann Westvol. There was another consortium competing for the project, of which Herr Georg Schmidt was a member. And it appears that Herr Schmidt did not take losing the contract with good grace. We don't know—yet—how he made contact with them, but the information we have been able to develop leads us to believe that he hired two Italian criminals to come to Magdeburg to disrupt the hospital project with a view toward driving the consortium into either abandoning the project or into bankruptcy."

Otto Gericke's lips thinned, but he said nothing. Frau Gericke looked down at the clasped hands in her lap, but said nothing.

Herr Schiffer harrumphed. "Can I look to Herr Schmidt's estate, then, to recover damages?"

"That will be a matter for the courts, for the *Schöffenstuhl*," Mayor Gericke stated. "Have your lawyers prepare their briefs and submit them."

Herr Schiffer sat back in his chair with obvious dissatisfaction.

"Thanks to information from Herr Bauer," Karl Honister picked up the thread, "we know that these two men"—he held up photographs—"were both hired by the Schiffer work bosses at the project as laborers. Not long after they started, the project began experiencing a rash of minor accidents. We suspect they were the cause, but we don't know that for a fact. We do know, however, that they were centrally involved in the three big attacks on the project: the fire that destroyed the wood stockpile; the theft of the payroll and the murder of the accountant and his guard escort; and the placing of the bombs that caused the steam crane boiler explosion. Once we had them identified, with a lot of legwork by our patrolmen, we were able to find their rooms, where we discovered evidence that linked them to all three crimes."

Karl went on to describe some of the evidence they had, and how it all tied to the two men from Venice. He didn't spend much time on it, but he made it clear that that case was very solid. One of the things he did mention was the money from the robbery, and how Schmidt had been exchanging it for silver for the robbers.

Byron took over. "That would be bad enough. But we also have some evidence..." Gotthilf noted that he was careful not to describe it as strong, "...that Herr Schmidt's passion had become aroused not just against the project, but against one particular member involved with the consortium who won the bid: Herr Andreas Schardius."

Marla's eyes opened wide, and she stiffened upright. She had probably been wondering why she was here, Gotthilf thought to himself in amusement, and the mention of the hated Schardius name would have been like a dash of cold water in the face.

"Herr Schardius was not involved in these alleged offenses," Byron took over. "In fact, we were investigating him for other crimes, but his only involvement in Herr Schmidt's activities was apparently as a victim. But he is not present today because in an apparent fit of madness he kidnapped Frau Linder," he nodded to Marla, "and attempted an assault on her. She was rescued without harm..."

"Thank God," Marla and Franz uttered in unison. Gotthilf almost smiled at that, but he resumed watching the rest of the group waiting for his cue.

"...but in the resulting turmoil Herr Schardius was shot resisting arrest."

There was a murmur in the room for a moment. Byron looked at a file open in front of him, then held up a picture of One-Eye, as they had started calling him. "We have evidence, though, that this man—one of the two Italian thieves and murderers— was trailing Herr Schardius. We also have evidence that he was being urged by Herr Schmidt to assault Herr Schardius, perhaps to kill him. He was shot and killed by some unknown assailant the same night that Herr Schardius died, the night before Herr Schmidt died."

Byron closed a file sitting in front of him as a sign of finality, then looked to Gotthilf.

"But that still leaves us with the question of how Herr Schmidt died." He opened a folder. "The obvious assumption was that he committed suicide, based on the circumstances of how his body was found." Frau Gericke sniffled, and everyone glanced quickly that direction, then away. "And there is no question that his death was caused by the gunshot to his head. But..." Gotthilf paused for a long moment, "we no longer believe that the gunshot was self-inflicted."

The mayor's eyes widened, and the widow choked on a breath. Everyone else in the room looked surprised.

"But," Stephan Burckardt ventured, "the gun was on the floor under his hand."

Marla looked over at Burckardt for a moment, then looked away.

"Yes, it was," Gotthilf said. "And that fact misled us for quite some time. But we discovered some evidence that proved Herr Schmidt was not holding the gun when it was fired. So then we had to look for someone who would benefit from Herr Schmidt's death."

Gotthilf closed the file in front of him, and began staring at one individual in the group as Byron picked up the narrative.

"We have a few suspects in mind, but we don't think it will take us long to find the killer."

"How?" Jacob Lentke asked from his seat at the end of the line.

"Herr Schmidt's murderer didn't understand that when you shoot someone from close range," Byron replied, "especially a head shot like that one was, there will be a very fine mist of blood splashed out from the wound by the bullet, and part of that mist will land on the shooter's hand and arm. Also, what you might think of as burnt gunpowder soot will also be deposited on the shooter's hand and arm. And both the blood and the gunpowder is very hard to wipe off."

Gotthilf continued to stare at one person.

"We have tests now that we can use to find traces of blood and traces of gunpowder on people's hands and clothing." Byron shrugged. "We'll do the tests on the hands and clothes of our suspects. It won't take long to find him."

Burckardt frowned. "How is that possible?" His tone was excited and he waved his hands in front of him. "It sounds like magic!"

"No, that's science," Byron replied.

Burckhardt laughed abruptly. The sound was nervous and high-pitched; quite distinctive, in fact. "It's utter nonsense!"

Marla stood up so quickly that her chair tipped over behind her as she backed away from Burckardt. "You!" she said. "You're the one who pushed Schardius through the wall. I recognize that laugh." She pointed a finger at him, and shouted, "I recognize that laugh!"

"What?" Burckardt said. "I don't know what you're talking about."

"Byron," Marla turned to her brother-in-law. "I'm sure he's the one."

"Ridiculous!" Burckardt said, standing up himself. Franz stood and stepped up beside his wife, facing the secretary.

Byron stood up also. As tall as he was, he was a threatening figure even though his hands were still at his sides. "Herr Burckardt," he said sternly, "even if Marla's testimony and the testimony of the other women in the room wouldn't stand in court, the tests for blood and gunpowder will. It's science," he repeated. "What will we find when we test your hands and your clothes, Herr Burckardt?"

Burckardt looked around in a panic. Then he bolted through the door behind them.

Byron made no attempt to pursuit him. He just chuckled. "And now he has in effect confessed. You two had best go collect him before he gets hurt."

"Right," Gotthilf said with a grin. He headed for the door, followed by Honister.

The two sergeants stepped out the front door of the hospital, to behold Burckardt surrounded by scowling members of the Committees of Correspondence. Gunther Achterhof was standing in front of him with a slight smile, hard and cold, gently tapping a smith's hammer against the palm of his left hand.

Chapter 73

"We were very sure it was him," Byron explained to Mayor Gericke and Captain Reilly as Burckardt was being hauled away in handcuffs. "There were indications that he skimmed some of the money off of the currency exchanges he did for Schmidt, and we found some of the payroll money in his pocket. Stupid," he said, shaking his head. "But smart enough to come with us rather than the CoC. We'll see what else we can shake out of him."

"Jacob, are you still muttering about the destruction of the *Schöffenstuhl* files?" Otto Gericke asked Jacob Lentke as he handed him a glass of wine at the end of their weekly conference.

Jacob took the glass with a frown. "Of course I am. Six hundred years of jurisprudence wiped out by that supreme vandal Pappenheim. Lawyers will curse him for generations to come."

Otto smiled into his glass as he took a sip. He was going to enjoy this, he thought to himself.

"Jacob, how many cities are there in the *Magdeburger Recht* association?"

"Twenty-eight, twenty-nine, thirty," Jacob replied. "I never can keep the list straight."

"And how many of them received copies of judgments in the cases they referred to you?"

Jacob frowned. "The ones who submitted cases would receive

copies of the decisions in those cases, yes. That doesn't mean that copies went to all the cities, though, although a few would sometimes request copies of other judgments to provide precedents for issues they were facing." His eyes began to widen as a thought apparently struck him.

"So," Otto grinned, "hire some of the starving law students at Jena to go to those cities..."

"And make copies of their copies of the decisions," Jacob said with excitement. "Otto, you are brilliant!"

"I know," Otto replied smugly.

Gotthilf found himself alongside Byron confronting Gunther Achterhof. The CoC leader had stepped in front of them while they were walking to the police station several days after the conclusion of what was becoming known as the Burckardt Affair. He wasn't sure just what Achterhof had in mind, but he wasn't about to step back from him, hard reputation or no.

"Chieske, Hoch." Achterhof nodded to them.

"Herr Achterhof," Gotthilf replied as Byron returned the nod.

"It took you a while, but you found the truth in all of it." Achterhof shrugged. "And I think you found more than we would have." He nodded again. "Good job."

The CoC man's tone had sounded a bit on the begrudging side; but then, he wasn't exactly known for being effusive. He nodded again, and turned and walked off, several of the known CoC strong men gathering behind him.

"I think that may have been the lamest 'Thank you' I've ever received," Byron chuckled. "But coming from that man, I think we can take it."

"Yah," Gotthilf said. "We ought to write it up in a report and put it in the files."

Byron laughed.

"Your Majesty," Marla said as she sank into a graceful curtsey. She was wearing her favorite concert dress, the empire waisted royal blue velvet, and the curtsey did it justice. Franz made a bow, thankful in the back of his mind that he could wear trousers and didn't have to follow his wife's suit.

They were part of the people associated with the opera who had been invited to the palace. As royal receptions went, this one appeared to be pretty low-key; more of a salon than a presentation. Gustav was mingling with his guests, trailed by Princess Kristina and Prince Ulrik.

"Ah, the famous Frau Marla Linder, with the most beautiful voice." Gustav sounded almost avuncular. "My daughter tells me that you also play the piano very well."

"I try," Marla responded.

"One day we will have you come and play for us. Oh, not now," Gustav raised a hand as Marla turned toward the piano. "Another time, where we can give the attention such an event would deserve. But at the moment, I want to thank you for your labor in performing *Arthur Rex*. It was," the emperor seemed to be searching for the right word, "compelling."

Gustav started to move on to another guest, but paused for a moment, raising a hand again. He leveled a serious gaze at them both. "And thank you for your love of music during this difficult time."

Neither of them knew what to say to that. Gustav nodded and turned away.

"What was that all about?" Marla whispered.

"I think you may have just received a thank you for 'Do You Hear the People Sing?'" Franz murmured.

Simon opened the door to their rooms. He and Ursula had returned there a few days after Hans' funeral. Neither of them was comfortable in the big house on Gustavstrasse, for all that they had been made truly welcome. They had talked about it, and they both felt happier here, in this place that Hans had made his and theirs.

Simon was surprised to discover Gotthilf standing on the outside landing holding a book in his hands.

"Hi, Sergeant Hoch. Did you need something?"

"Is Fraulein Metzgerin up? I mean, is she dressed...er, available..."

Simon was fascinated to see just how dark a shade of red the detective could turn.

"May I speak with Fraulein Metzgerin, please?" Gotthilf finally got out.

"Sure. Let me get her."

Simon left the detective standing on the landing, and went and knocked on Ursula's door.

"Ursula?"

"What?" came the muffled reply.

"Sergeant Hoch is here, and he would like to speak with you."

The door flung open so quickly it startled Simon. Ursula peeked out. "He's here? To see me?"

Simon rolled his eyes. "Yes, to see you."

Ursula fussed with her hair and her cap, tugged at her bodice, brushed off the front of her skirt. "Do I look all right?"

Simon rolled his whole head this time. "Yes. Now come on."

Ursula followed him to the door.

"Here she is," Simon said to Gotthilf. He stood in the doorway until Ursula pushed on him, then he stepped to one side.

"Good afternoon, Fraulein Metzgerin," Gotthilf said very formally.

"Good afternoon to you as well, Sergeant Hoch," Ursula replied, resting both her hands on the head of her cane.

"I, uh..." Gotthilf stammered, "Simon told me that you read the Bible a lot. I thought that you might like to have something else to read. I, uh...here."

He thrust the book at Ursula. She received it, then turned it around so she could read the title.

"*The City of God*, by Saint Augustine."

"It is a great book," Gotthilf said, rather stiffly, "very enlightening and uplifting."

Simon snickered. Ursula's head swiveled until her eyes bore down on him, twin gun barrels. "Don't you have someplace else to be?" she asked crossly.

"Yes," he said after a moment.

"Go there. Now."

"Yes, Ursula."

Simon squeezed out the door and around Gotthilf to clatter down the steps. At the bottom, though, instead of continuing on his way to the street, he ducked around and tiptoed under the landing. He thought he could hear them from there.

Sure enough, he could. Quite well, in fact.

"—fine gift," Ursula was saying. "I am sure I will enjoy reading it."

"It was given to me years ago by my grandmother."

"Oh, I cannot take it, then," Ursula said. "It must be important to you."

"It is," Gotthilf replied, "but I want you to have it."

There was a moment of silence, then Ursula said, "All right. But why?"

There was a longer moment of silence. "It is a courting gift," Gotthilf finally said.

"A courting gift? For me? You must be joking."

"No, I am not." That was said in a rather firm tone.

"But why me? I'm not pretty, I'm not well-educated...I am broken..." Ursula's voice trailed off.

Simon heard Gotthilf take a step closer to Ursula. He wished he could see.

"Our Savior was broken, Fraulein Metzgerin," Gotthilf said in a low tone, "and He is called beautiful."

"But I am not the Savior," she laughed, in a gulpy sort of way.

"But you are still beautiful."

There was a very long silence after that. Simon tried to peek up through the boards of the landing, but he couldn't see anything other than Gotthilf's boots.

"Then I suppose," Ursula finally said, "you had best call me Ursula...Gotthilf."

Simon dropped into step with Sergeant Hoch as soon he stepped off the bottom step. "So, are you going to marry Ursula?" he asked.

"You heard," Gotthilf said with a sidelong glance.

"I heard. Well, are you?"

Gotthilf stopped and looked down at him. "If she will have me."

"Good."

They resumed walking, and after a while, Simon spoke up. "Ursula is special."

"I know she is."

"And she's been hurt a lot, so you'd better take really good care of her."

They stopped again, and Simon stared up at the detective with all the fire he could muster. Gotthilf didn't laugh; he just considered Simon, soberly and carefully. After a moment, he nodded.

"Understood."

"All right then."

Ursula leaned back against the closed door. The book was clasped in her arms and held to her bosom. She bent her head and smelled the rich leather of the binding.

A courting gift. From Gotthilf Hoch.

If only Hans could have seen it.

The tears welled up, but she managed a tremulous smile at how her brother would have ranted.

Marla's eyes got wide when Franz announced the arrival of the first royalty check from Trommler Records for "Do You Hear the People Sing?"

"How many zeros?"

Her eyes got wider when she grabbed the check from his hands and read it for herself.

"I quite despaired of you, you know, for some time," Johann Möritz Hoch said to his son Gotthilf as they walked home from church on a Sunday after services. He was taller than his son, but otherwise they looked very much alike, walking side by side with their hands clasped behind their backs.

"How so?" Gotthilf asked. "I mean, you had made it clear that you thought I lacked initiative, that I was lazy. But what occasioned despair?"

"I thought that you had no will, no spine, no inner fire to excel," the elder Hoch said matter-of-factly.

"I didn't."

"Mmm, no," Johann disagreed. "I was wrong then, and so are you now. I would say now that you did not lack the fire, but rather that you had not found the matter that would awaken it."

Gotthilf considered that. "Point," he responded.

They walked some distance before the elder Hoch spoke again. "I was not happy to see you join the city watch," he said. "I did not consider it a service that would add to your reputation. And this new *Polizei* which took its place seemed at first like more of the same." Gotthilf looked over at his father, who held up a hand. "I have spoken with Otto Gericke—or, I should say, he has spoken with me. He made it clearer to me the nature of the work that you do. He is quite your champion, the mayor is."

Gotthilf felt some inner warmth at that thought. Before he could respond, his father spoke one last thought.

"It is not the work I would have chosen for you, Gotthilf. But you are a man, and you have chosen for yourself. And in the end, considering all, it is a worthy work. It occurs to me that I have reason to be proud of you. And so I am."

That thought was one that Gotthilf stored away in his heart, for it had been long indeed since he had last heard those words from the elder Hoch.

"Thank you, Father," he managed to reply.

Herr Hoch seemed to hear what Gotthilf was trying to say. He nodded gravely, and they continued to pace side by side, enjoying the sun, the afternoon, and the new aspect of their relationship in companionable silence.

Gustav looked at one of the Marine guards in his fancy dress uniform.

"Hmm. It has a certain style, I think. I wonder what it would look like in purple velvet."

Caroline Platzer rolled her eyes.

"I want one too," Kristine insisted, bouncing.

Ulrik rolled his eyes.

"Once we promised to keep him away from Achterhof and the CoC, Burckardt started singing like a canary," Byron said.

"Spilling his guts, huh?" Bill Reilly asked.

"Yah," Honister responded. "He seems to be proud of what he had done, pitting Schmidt and Schardius against each other, and maneuvering the two Italians to eventually take both of them down."

"Although he thought One-Eye was going to shoot Schardius for him," Byron said. "He was surprised that Gotthilf and I got him instead. It was apparently his idea to kill One-Eye all along."

"He had some grandiose idea of taking over both men's businesses," Gotthilf added, "both the licit and the illicit. He had picked up a pretty good understanding of what Schardius was trying to become: one of those crime bosses you described way back when. If he hadn't gotten nervous about how we were closing in fast, he might have gotten away with a lot of money, and maybe even a foothold in the crime boss racket."

"He does know he's going to hang for this, doesn't he?" Reilly asked.

"Yah," Gotthilf responded. "He just wants to stay out of Achterhof's hands. He has no desire to experience the Old Testament, ah..."

"Up close and personal," Byron concluded.

"So, good job there at the end of it all," the captain acknowledged.

That was the end of the meeting about the Schmidt/Schardius/ Burckardt mess. Honister left, but Reilly motioned for Byron and Gotthilf to stay.

"We never did nail anyone for the Delt murder, did we?"

"No," Byron said. "We have three potential witnesses..."

"That would be the men in the hospital?" Reilly asked.

"Right," Gotthilf responded. "And we have talked to them, but they tell conflicting stories, and with all the other potential witnesses and suspects dead, well..."

"We may never be able to take the Delt case to a magistrate," Byron finished. "But these three do agree enough with what Metzger told us that it's pretty certain that Schardius and his warehouse manager were the ones who orchestrated the murders, even if they were perhaps carried out by underlings."

The police captain stared at the table for a long moment, then sighed. "Right. Put the Delt file and the other cases in inactive status. We won't pursue them any further, but we won't close them either. Maybe something else will come up someday."

He closed the folder in front of him.

"And now for one last piece of business. Sergeant Hoch?"

Gotthilf looked at him. The captain sounded awfully formal, and there was a very serious expression on his face.

"Yes, Captain?"

"Turn in your badge."

Gotthilf was stunned. He shot a glance at Byron, but his face was like stone.

"Captain, I..."

Reilly held out his hand. "Give me your badge."

Mind whirling, wondering what he had done, Gotthilf pulled his badge wallet out of his pocket and handed it to the captain.

Reilly took it in his left hand, then slid something across the table to Gotthilf with his right. Gotthilf looked down at another wallet, then looked back up at the captain.

"Go on, take it," Reilly said.

Gotthilf picked up the wallet and opened it. Inside was another badge; a snarling lion's face cast in brass staring at him, with Magdeburg *Polizei* engraved above and the word *Inspector* and a number engraved below. He looked up to see both up-timers grinning at him.

Reilly stood up and leaned across the table to offer his hand.

"Congratulations on your promotion, Inspector Hoch. And congratulations on becoming the first detective inspector of the Magdeburg *Polizei*."

Gotthilf shook his hand, mind still whirling, but this time in a daze.

Byron held out his hand as well, saying "Good going, partner."

"Thank you," Gotthilf stammered. "I didn't expect...thank you both."

"You earned it," Reilly said, "especially during the last few weeks. But the reward for a job well done, of course, is..."

"More work," Byron said, rising. "Come on, partner. Let's go encourage the good citizens of Magdeburg to keep on being good citizens. And the first round's on you tonight."

Gotthilf followed his partner out of the conference room, smiling down at his new badge.

"That will be all, then," Gustav said, concluding the meeting. Otto Gericke began gathering his papers and stuffing them back into their folders.

The emperor had wanted an update on the status of the rebuilding of Old Magdeburg. They had spent over an hour poring over plans and drawings. Gustav had seemed almost like a child in his glee at how many of the projects were either completed or nearly so. The one sour note had been the state of the hospital expansion, but even that was recovering after the explosion.

Gustav turned at the door and looked back at Gericke with a mischievous grin.

"And by the way, Otto; you can now start styling yourself Otto von Gericke. The Holy Writ says to not bind the mouths of the kine that tread the grain. You're not an ox, but you get the point.

"Go home and tell your wife. We'll save the formal announcement for later."

With another flash of that grin, the emperor left a dumbfounded Otto.

Gotthilf looked up from his desk when Byron walked in, and whistled. "You are looking rather well-dressed today," he commented. Indeed, Byron was wearing an up-time suit, complete with white shirt and up-time style long tie. "What is the occasion?"

"Jonni got tickets to the opera from Marla, and we're going

this evening." Byron's face displayed an expression that could only be described as long-suffering.

"But I thought you said you didn't like the opera, that you didn't want to go see it," Karl Honister observed from his desk.

"You remember what I told you about sometimes doing things to make Jonni happy because of what she has to put up with because I'm a cop?" Byron asked.

"Yah," Gotthilf nodded.

"Well, this comes under that heading."

Byron sat down in his chair and leaned back. "And let me introduce you boys to a piece of gen-u-ine hillbilly wisdom: if Momma ain't happy, ain't nobody happy."

Gotthilf considered his family; particularly his own mother.

"Point."

Simon left Frau Zenzi's with his usual roll. He didn't need the rolls now like he used to. Between his improving earnings as a messenger and the money that Ursula had, neither of them went hungry anymore. But Frau Zenzi insisted, and to make her happy he did it. Besides, he thought as he took another bite of the roll, it was still some of the best bread around.

Schatzi appeared from around the corner of a building, and stopped close to him, tail wagging slightly. Simon took one last big bite, then tossed the rest to her. She caught it out of the air, and wolfed it down before he could even chew his piece twice. He laughed around the bite. She looked at him with her head tilted for a moment, then turned and headed back the way she came.

Simon was still chuckling when he started back down the street. He wasn't quite ready to go back to the rooms yet, so he just wandered for a while.

In the days since Hans' death, he had passed through what Pastor Gruber assured him was a cycle of emotion that almost everyone encountered. He had gone from being numb, to angry, to questioning, and he was finally arriving at acceptance. Oh, he still had days where he was angry with Magdeburg, with the *Polizei*, with himself. But he had come to see that Hans had made the choices that took him to that end. And like it or not, at that end, Hans had willingly paid that price.

Consequences.

That word had been rolling around in his mind ever since

that night. But now, instead of thinking about Hans and his consequences, he had started thinking about his own.

He could see that he had choices to make. And he wanted to be wise in making those choices. He had no desire to come to the same end as Hans. At the same time, he had no desire to remain a crippled orphan. For the first time in his life, he had developed an ambition to do more than just stay alive another day.

There were four men who had recently made a difference in his life. Four men representing four choices. He had been considering them for days now, and he was still considering them.

Before long he found himself standing outside St. Jacob's church. The evening light made the front of the church almost seem to have a golden glow. Small and old and shabby it might be, but at that moment it was a beautiful building.

At that moment, Simon made a decision; one that he had been weighing for some time. He went to the small side door and knocked. There was the sound of movement behind the door, then it was opened. Pastor Gruber stood in the opening.

"Yes, who is . . . Oh, it's you, Simon. Come in, my boy."

The old pastor ushered him back into the same crowded little room they had last used.

"Well, what can I do for you, Simon? Do you have an interesting question today?"

The pastor's gnarled hand reached into the breast of his coat and pulled out his old worn Bible, in expectation.

Simon leaned forward on his stool.

"I need to make a choice, Pastor, about what I want to do with my life, now that Hans is gone."

"I see," Gruber stroked his beard. "And what are you considering?"

"You know what I have lived through, what I have felt, over the last few months. You know the men who I have been around." Simon waved his hand in an all-encompassing gesture. "You know what has happened."

The pastor nodded. "Go on, lad,"

"Hans was my first friend," Simon whispered. "And for long, he was my only friend. I learned how to be a friend from him. And I miss him."

Simon swallowed. "But I don't want to be hard like him. I can't fight. I can't work like he could. I don't want to be a Samson. I want to be something other, something more."

"I understand," Pastor Gruber murmured.

"Andreas Schardius." Simon's eyes narrowed to slits as he hissed that name, feeling the anger flare in his soul. "From him I learned what an enemy truly was. I learned how to despise people, and look on them as prey. From him I learned the kind of person I definitely do not want to be."

"Commendable."

"Gotthilf Hoch." Simon sat back and held his hand palm up before him. "A good man, a just man, a fair man. I like him, and I'm glad he's going to marry Ursula. From him I learned that every person is worth something. Even me. And if it wasn't for this," he shrugged his right shoulder, "I might want to be one of the *Polizei* like he is. But they would never take me with only one arm. And I'm not sure I would want to be in a job where I might have to shoot someone."

The pastor pursed his lips and nodded.

Simon took a deep breath, and said, "And finally, there is you."

Pastor Gruber's eyebrows flew up and his eyes opened wide.

"Me?"

"Our talks here, beginning when I was scared to even come in the building, to when you talked to Ursula and me after Hans was killed...that meant a lot to me."

"Just doing what I could to help," the pastor said.

"I know. But I learned from you, as well. I had to ask Ursula for the word; I never heard it before. From you I learned compassion."

Pastor Gruber cleared his throat, and said softly, "Thank you, Simon. That means a lot to this old pastor."

They sat in companionable silence for several moments. At length, Pastor Gruber spoke.

"You know, lad, I've heard trained men two or three times your age who couldn't have laid out your situation and your learnings that clearly or simply. But you said you had a decision to make?"

"Yes," Simon said. "And I have made it."

He stood from his stool, crossed the room, and knelt before the pastor. He held his hand out to him.

"Pastor Gruber, I want to be a man of compassion. How can I become a pastor? Like you?"

Cast of Characters

Abati, Andrea	Musician, renowned *castrato* from Rome.
Abend, Veit	Tavern keeper for The Chain.
Anhalt-Cöthen, Ludwig von	*Fürst* (head of principality) and manager of the *Stift*, the properties formerly owned by the Archbishopric of Magdeburg and now owned by Gustav Adolf.
Ableidinger, Constantin	Member of USE Parliament; leader of the Ram movement.
Abrabanel, Rebecca	Member of Parliament from Magdeburg Province; leader of the Fourth of July Party; wife of Michael Stearns.
Achterhof, Gunther	Leader of the Committees of Correspondence.
Bäcker, Gus	Boxer; friend of Hans Metzger.
Ballauf, Frontilia	Assistant to Amber Higham.
Bauer, Gunther	Work leader for Schiffer Construction; later project manager for hospital construction site.
Bayer, Simon	Orphan; friend of Hans Metzger and his sister Ursula.
Beaton, David	Marine captain.
Burckardt, Stephan	Secretary for Georg Schmidt.

Chieske, Byron   Up-timer; Lieutenant, Magdeburg police force.

Ciclope ("One-Eye")   Venetian gangster.

Cochran, Atwood   Up-timer music teacher and radio personality.

Dauth, Johann   Employee at Bünemann corn factor's office.

Delt, Joseph   Murder victim.

Demetrious   Police informant.

Dreher, Tobias   Partner of boxing promoter Todd Pierpoint.

Elting, Karl   Representative of certain families in Hamburg who have ties to Andreas Schardius.

Farkas, Miklos   Hungarian gun shop owner.

Ficklerin, Marie Rebecca Mother of Gotthilf Hoch.

Flanns, Moritz   Warehouseman employed by Schardius.

Frost, Dan   Up-timer; former Grantville police chief; now independent consultant on police investigation.

Gronow, Johann   Writer, librettist, editor of *Black Tomcat Magazine*.

Gruber, Moritz   Lutheran pastor.

Haygood, Lady Beth   Up-timer, head of Duchess Elisabeth Sofie Secondary School for Girls; chief lieutenant of Mary Simpson.

Heilbronner, Samuel   Employed as a ledger poster by Georg Schmidt.

Higham, Amber   Up-timer; drama teacher; wife of Heinrich Schütz.

Hoch, Gotthilf   Detective sergeant, Magdeburg police force.

Hoch, Johann Möritz   Father of Gotthilf Hoch.

Hoch, Margarethe   Sister of Gotthilf Hoch.

Honister, Karl   Detective sergeant, Magdeburg police force.

Katzberg, Hermann   Musician; associate of Marla Linder and Franz Sylwester.

Kolman, Leonhart   Crew boss for Schiffer Construction.

Kühlewein, Georg   Bürgermeister, merchant, current year's mayor of Old Magdeburg's *Regierender Rat*, partner of Andreas Schardius and Johann Westvol.

Lentke, Jacob   Bürgermeister, lawyer, member of *Regierender Rat*, close friend of Otto Gericke.

Linder, Marla   Up-timer, gifted musician in voice and two instruments, married to Franz Sylwester, prominent in the music and arts scene of Magdeburg.

Logau, Friedrich von   Poet; associate of Marla Linder.

Mann, Ernst   Warehouse manager at the Schardius factorage.

Meissner, Klaus   CoC activist; bodyguard for Marla Linder.

Metzger, Hans   Warehouseman; professional boxer.

Metzgerin, Ursula   Sister of Hans Metzger.

Milich, Lorenz   Police sergeant.

Nichols, James   Up-time physician.

Oxenstierna. Axel   Chancellor of Sweden.

Piazza, Edward   Up-timer; President of the State of Thuringia-Franconia.

Pierpoint, Todd   Up-timer, partner with Tobias Dreher in boxing promotions.

Platzer, Caroline   Up-timer; companion for Princess Kristina.

Plavius, Johannes   Writer, part of Logau and Gronow's literary circle.

Pietro   Venetian gangster.

Reilly, Bill   Up-timer; Captain, Magdeburg police force.

Saxe-Weimar, Wilhelm IV, duke of   See: Wilhelm Wettin.

Schardius, Andreas   Merchant; partner of Georg Kühlewein and Johann Westvol; patron of music and the arts.

Schlegel, Paul	Down-time physician; informally, Magdeburg's chief medical examiner.
Schmidt, Georg	Bürgermeister, merchant, married to Otto Gericke's older half-sister.
Schultze, Christoff	Lawyer, former resident of Magdeburg, chief assistant to *Fürst* Ludwig von Anhalt-Cöthen, step-father to Otto Gericke, friend of Jacob Lentke.
Schütz, Heinrich	Composer; husband of Amber Higham.
Schwartzberg, Thomas	Musician, part of Franz and Marla's inner circle of friends and performers.
Seelbach, Karl	Writer, part of Logau and Gronow's literary circle.
Simpson, John Chandler	Up-timer; USE Navy admiral, husband of Mary Simpson.
Simpson Mary	Up-timer; Magdeburg socialite; wife of Admiral Simpson.
Stearns, Michael	Former prime Minister of the United States of Europe; now major general in command of the 3rd Division, USE Army; husband of Rebecca Abrabanel.
Sylwester, Franz	Musician married to Marla Linder, prominent in the music and arts scene of Magdeburg.
Traeger, Rueul	CoC activist; bodyguard for Marla Linder.
Vasa, Gustav II Adolf	King of Sweden; Emperor of the United States of Europe; also known as Gustavus Adolphus.
Vasa, Kristina	Daughter and heir of Gustav II Adolf.
Wessell, Jochum	Warehouseman employed by Schardius.
Westvol, Johann	Bürgermeister, merchant, partner of Andreas Schardius and Georg Kühlewein.
Wettin, Wilhelm	Prime Minister of the USE; formerly Duke of Saxe-Weimar.